VENGEANCE THWARTED

PRUE PHILLIPSON

KNOX ROBINSON
PUBLISHING

London • New York

To Alan

*who found most of the books I needed for my
research in his vast library*

KNOX ROBINSON
PUBLISHING

1205 London Road
London SW16 4UY
&
244 5th Avenue, Suite 1861
New York, NY 10001

Knox Robinson Publishing is a specialist, independent publisher of
historical fiction, historical romance and fantasy

A CIP catalogue record for this book
is available from the British Library.

ISBN 978-0-9567-9013-2

Manufactured in the United States of America
and the United Kingdom

Visit our website to download free historical fiction,
historical romance and fantasy short stories by your favorite authors.
While there, purchase our titles direct and earn loyalty points. Sign up for
our newsletter and our free titles giveaway. Join our community to discuss
history, romance and fantasy with fans of each genre. We also
encourage you to submit your stories anonymously
and let your peers review your writing.

www.knoxrobinsonpublishing.com

Printed and bound in Great Britain by
Marston Book Services Limited, Didcot

CHAPTER 1

September 1640

WHEN Sam's mother called him in, Bel Horden determined she would stay out longer. The day was too important to end now. Thirteen years old, squat and ugly as she knew she was, she was in love with Sam Turner. This was momentous.

She would climb into the forked beech tree and nestle in that smooth hollow between the three branches to enjoy the sensation. The tree had lured her every time she had watched Sam from behind its broad trunk, but her cursed petticoats had made climbing impossible. Now they were tucked into Sam's breeches so she must seize her chance. He had actually unpegged his spare pair from the clothes line and held them out to her when she hesitated to get down in the mud by the ditch he had dug to separate the English and Scottish armies. He had forgotten about his breeches when his mother called.

"She'll come seeking me if I don't go at once and she mustn't know you're here." He had flung the last stick soldiers into the ditch, tossed earth on the bonfire and run.

Bel grinned now as she launched herself into the tree, nails scrabbling at the bark as her fingertips reached for the dip in the fork. The trunk splayed out at just enough of a slope for her shoes to heave her up, fat and ridiculous though she felt in Sam's breeches. For a second she thought she would slide back again but will-power held her flattened to the tree as she reached for the stump of a twig with one hand and clawed the other over into the hollow so that she could get her elbow in and scrabble up the rest of the way. Her pinafore ripped but she didn't care. The dress was unharmed. She stood upright and hauled Sam's breeches higher, tucking her skirts further down. Sam was two years older and taller of course. That had made it all the more wonderful that he had let her be the Scottish general who had so lately beaten the English at Newburn on the Tyne. Perhaps he was deferring to her because she was the young lady from the Hall, but that was of no account. She never would be a young lady.

She sat down cross-legged, scrunching among the dead leaves and twigs in the hollow and hugged herself with delight. She wasn't worried that it was getting dark. She had long since marked certain trees with the sharpest carving knife from the kitchen to create her own secret path through the woods from the Hall to the farm. And now she had a secret friend too. Sam had asked if she would come again. He had no idea how often she had watched him from the wood. It was only because he was playing at being two armies that she had dared to approach this time.

"May I play?"

He had been astonished but quickly agreed the game would be better with two. Now she was a little anxious that he would be in trouble for the filthy state of his breeches tomorrow. He could pretend they blew off the line perhaps. She looked up at the leaves above her. The early September evening was beginning to stir with wind.

I'll leave them on the ground under the line when I go, she decided.

But she was in no hurry to take them off. He had looked away when she scrambled into them, just like a gentleman. She stroked their coarse surface. She had always wanted to be a boy and wear breeches but that must change now if she was in love. When she had gazed at him in Nether Horden church in his Sunday best, she had wanted to be his brother. When she had watched him from her wood as he went quietly about his chores on the farm she had thought what a contrast he was to her own brother, Robert, a grown man but mean and indolent.

Now Sam Turner was no longer at a distance. He had spoken with her, laughed with her, their imaginations had twined together as they agreed the battle should be a stalemate, so many casualties lost on both sides and the stream, as he put it gleefully, "absolutely running with blood." Her stomach had curled with excitement that he was actually talking to her, and finally he had asked her to come again.

Home held no attractions for her. Henrietta was worse than Robert. She never lost an opportunity of putting her down or telling tales on her. Her mother seldom talked to her but when she did she became so voluble that she ended up lapsing into her native French.

"Oh, Arabella, you are so rough and wild! You have no grace, no delicacy, no refinement. Why can you not copy Henrietta? See how she moves. How did I bear such a hoyden?" And so on into French. Her father would look at her and shake his head and tell Nurse to scold the obstinacy out of her.

Bel put them all from her mind and peered eagerly about her from her new elevation as the last glow of the sunset began to fade. The Turners' farmhouse was a little distance away to her left. There were no lights showing there yet as it was not dark enough for them to waste candles. To the right of her vantage point was the plank bridge that carried the track to the Hall over the Horden Burn. It was from a tiny tributary of the burn that Sam had dug his ditch and near it on the dirt floor by the trickle of water he had lit his bonfire. He knew better than to light a fire far from water when the hay was in and everything was tinder dry.

Opposite her, on the other side of the track was the haystack and to the left of it the hen-house. The chickens that had been scrabbling all over the farm were coming to roost there. Many spent the day in the field behind the barn that sloped down to the bank of the Horden Burn. Below the plank bridge the burn flowed through a gorge and she could hear it splashing down its shallow waterfalls. Farmer Turner would come out soon to fasten the henhouse door against foxes. Perhaps she should think of making her escape. She watched a few minutes more as the red crests popped up beside the barn and the last hens pecked their way among the straw to their resting place.

Reluctantly she eased herself out of the fork and slithered down the trunk. As she landed on the ground her eyes were drawn to the corner of the haystack. Someone was staring straight at her. Her spine tingled. It was a stranger – a man with flaxen hair lit by the last light in the western sky. He seemed to be hesitating whether to run or not but a hen came right by his legs and all in a second he had shot out a hand and grabbed it by the neck and turned to plunge down the field behind.

Bel gaped in astonishment at the brazen act and then there came a shout from the track up to the Hall.

"Hold! Put that down or I shoot." And without a pause a pistol shot rang out, there was a squeal and the sound of feet plunging away into the darkness. With squawks of protest the hen flapped to the ground and came scuttling back to join the others in a scrambling run to the hen-house.

Bel shrank petrified behind the beech. She knew too well who had fired the shot. Her brother Robert. People had now come running from the farmhouse.

She heard Robert say, "I winged him. I'll wager it was a looter from the Scots army. He dropped the bird. She'll live. We can leave him be. He'll not be back."

"I thank you, Master Robert." Farmer Turner's voice sounded out of the dusk. "A blessing you were passing."

"I was sent to find Arabella. Have you seen her come by this way?" The track by the farm led to the village of Nether Horden.

"Nay, but we'll help you look, won't we, Ma? There's villains about."

Bel remained still as a stone while they went down the track, then she peeped out. Seeing that the wind had raised a red glow in the bonfire again she drew a glowing stick from the heart of it to light her way through the wood. Kicking on more dirt she was just going to set off when she heard a noise from below the bridge, a scrabbling sound and a grunt of pain. Terrified that the robber was after her she threw the stick away and plunged into the wood.

Once hidden she crouched down and unbuttoned and wrenched off Sam's breeches, kissed them, rolled them into a ball and threw them back towards the clothes' line. For one more second she looked towards the stream-bed expecting to see a ghastly face peer above the bank. There was a glow from somewhere. Oh it was her stick. Some dried grass where it fell had caught fire.

She dare not venture onto the track again. The fire would burn itself out. She turned and ran, making her way from one cut to another in the trees. She was thrilled to find that she could still discern them though there was scarcely any light left in the wood. It was flattering, she thought, that Robert had consented to search for her, but she was in for punishment unless she could get home unseen and pretend she had been up in one of the attics all the time. Sam, she was sure, would not betray to his family or to Robert that she had ever been near the farm.

In four minutes' fast running she had reached the back of Horden Hall. No servants were about. They must all be looking for her. Three minutes later she was lying in bed, the curtains drawn round her, feigning sleep.

Daniel Wilson felt his shoulder and realised he was not mortally wounded after all. No one was pursuing him and when he dragged himself up the bank and looked back towards that beech where he had seen the fat boy climb down there was no sign of him. He was cross that he had dropped the chicken. Nat had told him to get one because they had had nothing to eat for twenty-four hours. It was so easy. It had just run by his hand. He saw that some of the scattered straw on the dirt track was ablaze. That would bring the farm people out again, so he would do best to run back to Nat as long as he could remember where he had left him.

It wasn't difficult to pick his way, bent double, along the top of the bank. Keeping the streambed to his right he should find the anglers' hut where – if his last picture was a true one – Nat lay curled on the floor, his head throbbing with a fever.

The pictures in his mind of the last few weeks since he and Nat had left home were all jumbled together and it was an effort to sort them into any sequence. As soon as Nat was better it would be all right. Nat was clever. Nat would take charge again.

When the thicker dark of a timber wall materialised among the trees he grinned with relief. At least he had fresh water in his leather bottle from the waterfall but the loss of the chicken shamed him. Nat needed food to give him strength and he himself was ravenously hungry.

He felt round the wall to the door and pushed it open. As it hung lopsidedly from one hinge it scraped the floor and Nat stirred and groaned out, "Dan?"

Daniel knelt beside him and raised his head and held the water bottle to his lips. Nat gulped eagerly.

"I dropped the bird. Forgive me. There was a bang. My shoulder. It's bloody but it's nothing much. A scratch."

Nat reared up in the darkness. "You were shot at?"

Daniel nodded vigorously.

"Did no one follow you?"

Daniel shook his head.

"The fat boy saw me but he went away after the bang. There was some fire. The wind was blowing it along."

"Do you mean gunfire? The wind carried the sound?"

"Fire on the ground. I got the water to bring you. Have some more. Are you well now?"

But Daniel knew his brother was not well. He could feel his body shaking with the fever. He himself was never ill. Their mother often said, "You, Daniel, are my strong boy. There is often a little runt with twins. Nat is the little runt." It was hard to understand that because Nat had grown to within an inch or two of Daniel's height now that they were both nineteen and though Nat's shoulders weren't as broad, he was usually hale and hearty. More than that, his body was as quick and agile as his brain. He would not have lost the chicken, Dan thought sadly. What can I do for him now?

He lay down close to him and wrapped his arms round him to make him warm again. In a few moments he was asleep.

Nurse carrying a candle put her head round the bed curtain. "Oh my lady, here she is asleep in bed as ever was."

Bel could picture the head of her mother peering above stubby Nurse's square face – the long slender nose, oval chin, the smooth black hair twined with one of her silvery drapes, the hard dark eyes.

"She hides deliberately out of mischief. She shall be locked in her room tomorrow. See to it."

Bel heard the door close and the key turn in the lock. She had had worse punishments. At least she could get up now and undress, all in the dark and carefully pour some water from her brass ewer into her basin so that her face and hands would look clean in the morning. She laid her clothes neatly over the back of the box chair in the window, except for her torn pinafore which she pushed to the bottom of the linen chest in the corner. Finally, she found a clean shift and slipped into it and sat on the bed for a while brushing her hair and thinking of Sam and how she could get back to see him when her imprisonment was over. She was sorry now that she had hacked off her dark curls lately. Sam had looked hard at her but said nothing.

Outside her room there seemed to be some running about and excited talk but she couldn't make out the words. Maybe the robber had been caught. She hoped he had. She slipped into bed again.

A few minutes later her door was unlocked and Nurse crept to the bed, pulled back the curtain and gently shook her.

"Now, Bella, you tell me where you were all that time. I looked in all the places you hide and told her ladyship you must have been under one of the servants' beds because I'm too stiff to get down to look, but I did look and you weren't there at all. Did you sneak outside like you've done before?"

Bel thought quickly. If the robber had been caught and they knew she had been wandering in the woods when marauding Scots looters were about she could be locked up all the time. She would have to confess the one really secret place which she knew she would never dare to enter. She grinned up at Nurse. "Don't tell anyone, Nan, but I was in the *priest's hole*."

Nurse started back, her candle lighting up her fear-filled eyes. "You know about that! How could you?"

"I heard them talk when they moved me here from the room next to Henrietta. They said it was to make a little chapel, but I knew there was more going on. They said workmen were repairing the wall in the dining-room below and they kept the door locked till it was finished but it wasn't that. They made a hole in the floor where my bed head had been and some steps down and a false wall below and that's where their priest goes when he stays here. I knew the dining-room was smaller but they put a screen there and pretended it wasn't."

Nurse put her finger to her lips. "Nobody's to know that. There's people out in the wicked world would come in and tear the place to pieces till they found him and then they'd kill him."

Bel couldn't help another grin though the place had fearful associations. "*I* won't tell."

"No, don't you dare and don't you ever go down there again. I can't think how you got in and out without anyone seeing you, you naughty girl."

"Oh I have rabbit's ears. You've told me often. I can hear the rustle of a skirt from far away. I know when the coast's clear and when it's not."

"Well, don't you ever pull a trick like that again and I won't tell her ladyship. You're not supposed to be in the chapel at all since you made such a rumpus there the first time they let you go to Mass." Her voice changed and Bel heard a surprising note of sympathy as she added, "Mind, I hold no truck with Popish things myself but I keep my mouth shut in her Ladyship's hearing. And you'll have to grow up, my girl, and learn a bit of wisdom yourself one of these days." The habitual tone of hectoring was back. "And you're to be locked in tomorrow and I'm not to talk to you. Eh, ay, you'll wear me out in my old age if you go on like this." And out she went, locking the door, with not a word of goodnight.

Bel was used to being in disgrace with everyone and now that she was in love with Sam Turner she didn't care. She lay awake thinking how being in love had changed many things. Perhaps even the priest in his hole was no longer frightening.

It was a day three years before when she had found her former bedroom unlocked for once. She had seen Mary the maid taking candlesticks downstairs to polish and wondered if she might not have locked the little chapel up again. So she had tried the door and peeped round and looked straight at a hooded head emerging through the floor. It had vanished at once and the trapdoor with its rug draped over it had shut with a bang. But even while she stared it had been cautiously raised again and the whole man had emerged with his finger to his lips. She had never seen him close to because he always slunk about with his hood up but now he threw it back and stood tall over her cowering figure. He was as fierce and beautiful as an avenging angel and his voice was stern.

"Miss Arabella, why are you never at Mass with your mother and sister?"

"I go to Church with Father," she had breathed back.

"But that is not the true church. Do you want to be a lost soul?"

His voice had softened as if he'd just realised she was only a child so she had straightened up and barked back at him, "Oh I'm a lost soul anyway. Everyone says I'm wicked."

He had reached out a hand to her then and there was something more devilish than angelic about his smiling eyes and she had run, slamming the door behind her. Ever since then she had avoided the chapel and if she knew the priest was in the house she kept to her room. Sometimes she heard Henrietta ask her mother, in an odd wheedling voice, "When is Father Patrick's next visit?" If her father was by, Bel sensed his heavy disapproval in the air.

The thing between men and women was a sinister mystery to her then but especially – she was sure – if it involved a Popish priest.

Now that she was thirteen and had spent the afternoon with Sam she realised for the first time what it meant to feel an attraction. Sam was open and as innocent as the day. He wasn't beautiful like Father Patrick – a Satanic beauty she decided - but he had strong, honest features and she wanted to be with him again soon so she must be in love.

Just before she fell asleep she had a moment of faint but real sympathy for Henrietta.

CHAPTER 2

DANIEL woke to a bright day shimmering at every crack in the ramshackle hut. His shoulder was sore and stiff with encrusted blood. That was nothing. He looked at Nat who was at last sleeping like a baby, his breathing steady. How hungry he would be when he woke up!

I must get him food, he thought to himself. I mustn't fail again.

He went out, dazzled by the dappled light on the stream. Mustn't go east this time. There would be other farms. He set off westward but the stream course forced him south. Somewhere that way was the big town called Newcastle where he and Nat had been with the English army for a while. But when they started marching again, Nat had got the camp fever and they were left behind. Dan had a picture in his head of throwing their pikes and uniforms into a ditch. There was another picture of him rowing Nat across a river in a very small boat. They had wandered in woods. It was frightening being away from home in Darrowswick where he knew all the footpaths, but Nat was with him – even if he had to half carry him. Now he was alone. That was bad, but he could find Nat again if he kept to this stream. There must be food somewhere and he was now dressed as a peasant not a soldier. He had liked marching but he could never stick his pike in a horse's belly or in a man below his breastplate.

Watching the stream he saw big flat stones in it leading across. That was tempting. He liked the idea of jumping from one to the other. And there was a chimney ahead as well, among the trees. He could see the smoke and smell something cooking which made all the juices in his mouth rise up and shout, "Hunger!"

I will ask politely, he thought. If they are Christians they will feed the starving.

Slithering down the bank he hopped across on the stones. Another time he would have gone back again for the fun of it but hunger made him follow the path to where it joined a lane. There was a whole village ahead he could see now, low houses clustered round a green with a church tower peeping over the top. He knocked at the door of the first cottage which stood on its own.

A woman peeped round the door, gave one look and slammed it in his face. He could hear her yell to someone inside. Two men appeared, one from each side of the house armed with pitchforks. They were shouting, "Here's the villain," and more people, men, women and children began emerging from their cottages.

The figures dotted the green like a festival day but they were not happy, they were not dancing. They were running towards him and brandishing sticks and stones.

"A crust of bread," he began to say as the pitchfork men grabbed him, one each side. He looked hopefully towards the women and children for signs of charity in their faces. A tiny boy snatched up a stone from the road and threw it with astonishing aim. Daniel was so surprised to see it coming that he didn't dodge it and it hit him above the left eye.

"Belay that," shouted one of the pitchfork men to the child. "We've got him safe. You could have hit us."

Daniel heard the voice but for a moment he was stunned and saw nothing till he felt his arms being pinioned to his sides.

Many more voices were yelling round his head.

"We should string him up now."

"Put him in the stocks."

"Take him to Sir John."

"Someone run and tell Turner we've got the man fired his stack."

"Are we sure? He's not dressed as a Scots soldier."

"Look at his flaxen hair and the wound on his shoulder where Mr Robert winged him."

"Has he got anything to say for himself?"

Daniel felt his cheek slapped. He blinked and saw red fierce faces crowding close.

"Speak up then. You went looting from the Scots army. You stole a chicken."

"Ay and when Master Robert shot at you, you hid and came back in a fury and fired the stack. That's a hanging offence that is."

"Can Sir John deal with him?"

"Why not?"

"The Scots' Commander is the law now. He'll not punish his own for firing one of our stacks."

Daniel heard the maze of words but the pictures in his head were confused. The words didn't fit them. There had been fire – that was true enough. He could see the picture where flaring straw was running along the ground. A gust of wind had brushed his cheek at the same time. But that picture had stopped, perhaps when he turned to run away. There was also quite clearly – though it had been half dark at the time – the shape of the fat boy slithering down the tree trunk. He liked children and in the pale blob of the boy's face he had felt the eyes looking at him, but he didn't know if it was a kindly look or a hostile one. What had happened then? The boy had vanished. Was that before or after the fire picture?

A woman's voice said, "Why don't you answer, you Scots villain?"

That at least was not right. They were angry because they thought he was from Scotland. He tried to find the face that had spoken so he could beam at it and reassure the woman. He wanted to tap his chest but his arms were fastened to his sides with a piece of rope. He nodded his head at the many faces around him.

"English," he said with confidence. "English army."

The reaction of the faces made him wonder if he had said the wrong thing. He had been dressed like a soldier. He had marched like a soldier once and carried a pike. But when Nat had told him to leave his pike and put his own clothes on from his knapsack, had not some words been said about not being a soldier any more? Words were hard to remember but there was the picture to it. He could see Nat sliding their pikes down a bank to some water and they had sunk out of sight completely.

"By the Lord, he's a deserter. He must go before Viscount Conway."

"The army has retreated to Durham. Lord knows how far south they will go now."

"Take him to Sir John."

"String him up now."

"Let's hear what he has to say." His face was slapped again. "You fired the stack. Ah, here comes Turner and his boy. Turner, this is the man fired your stack. Speak up, villain!"

Daniel struggled with his pictures. "There was a fat boy –"

"Hah! That's a lie. What would our boys get fat on?"

The little lad who had thrown the stone was pushed forward. A man plucked up his ragged sleeve to show his arm. "There, that's what our children are like. Skin and bone. A fat boy indeed! *You* set the fire."

Daniel began to wonder if he'd ever seen a fat boy. The fire must be true though because they were all talking about a fire. He had a tinder box in his knapsack but he wasn't wearing his knapsack. He was good at making a fire in the hearth at home or a bonfire in autumn for the leaves from the parsonage trees. Was the fat boy a dream? He did have dream pictures. Nat told him when they were dreams but he was far from Nat and he didn't know how he could get back to him.

He was frightened and closed his eyes against the grim faces. Now he could hear horses' hooves and felt a change come over the crowd.

"Heaven be praised! Here's Sir John – and Master Robert!"

Daniel thought he might now be happy too till he heard the voice that went with the bang, the pain and dropping the hen. He had run from the voice, slithering down the stream bank and crouching till all the other voices that clamoured afterwards had gone away.

"That's the man," the voice said now with the same sharpness as "Hold! Put that down or I shoot."

Daniel kept his eyes shut so as not to see the lips that made cruel sounds.

Another voice spoke, mild but with authority.

"Ay, Robert, but did you see him fire the stack?"

"Indeed not, sir. I would have raised the alarm at once and it could have been saved. We only saw the flames rising into the air when we had given up the wild goose chase for Bella. But there was no one else around. He came back and did it deliberately out of revenge. He's a robber and a fire-raiser and should hang at once."

"Ay, we all say that, Sir John. We got to make an example of him. He's confessed to being an English soldier who ran away from the battle."

"Has he indeed?"

Daniel opened his eyes and saw the man who spoke in an educated voice. He wore a fine large curled hat such as gentlemen wore and his eyes under grey eyebrows were staring straight at him.

"You are an English soldier?"

Daniel looked up into the eyes. They were straight honest eyes in a face that had no other distinct features but a small grey beard. An old man's face, about the age of his own father who was nearly fifty.

I must answer honestly. Nat said I was not a soldier when I put on my own clothes.

"No, sir."

"He said he was just now," several voices cried. "He's a liar and deceiver. He made up a story about a fat boy firing the stack. String him up at once, Sir John."

"We are not savages. He must have a proper trial."

"What about the Scots army, Sir John?" cried one of the pitchfork men. "Folks say they've took Newcastle and are sending troops to seize all the land round here. If we hanged him quick the deed 'ud be done and they could do nowt about it."

"They'll fire the village if we hang a Scots spy," a woman's frightened voice cried out.

"String him up, Father. He's English. He doesn't talk like a Scot." The cruel voice spoke again. Daniel looked this time, a quick glance and saw a young man on horseback with a nose and beardless chin as sharp as his voice. This man pulled his restless beast next to Sir John and muttered, "Why dilly-dally, sir? He's plain guilty. The people want action. Get the man hanged and they can all get back to work."

Daniel knew he had better hearing than most men, better than Nat's even, and he felt that most of the shuffling crowd had not heard this. He looked back at the man called Sir John. I have hope in him, he was saying to himself. But good men can be persuaded against themselves. Nat had said that to him about their own father. "Father didn't want us to fight. Mother persuaded him because you wanted to dress up as a soldier. But you don't want to hurt people and now we're away from Mother I'm thinking like Father." He'd said it many times before the picture of the pikes sliding into the ditch. Daniel didn't have many thoughts, but now he could feel that the Sir John man might be persuaded by the son with the sharp voice.

He saw Sir John look about him as Father sometimes looked when he wanted to escape from Mother's voice. He spotted a woman in a shawl and bonnet at the back of the crowd. "Dame Leary," he called out, "are you not holding school today?"

She bobbed to him. "It's harvest holiday, Sir John, but I can call them in if you think best, Sir John."

"No, leave them. We will hold court in your schoolroom. Take the accused inside. You that apprehended him and Farmer Turner and young Sam and my son are all witnesses. I will pick twelve men from the rest of you that I know to be honest souls to act as jury. Let us go in."

The man they had called Farmer Turner came forward plucking the brim of his hat. "Nay, Sam and I cannot be witnesses, Sir John. We saw nothing but the stack burning. We went to help look for young Mistress Arabella. I did ask Sam about his bonfire but it was well out and way beyond the wee burn. And this man snatched Sam's breeches off the clothes' line for his own are ragged as you can see. But when he found they were only a boy's he threw them down in the dirt. So I'd like to be on the jury. The man's guilty as hell and he's nigh ruined me. I'll have to slaughter my beasts if they've nowt to eat this coming winter."

Daniel looked at Sir John's face for an answer to all this. It had been a lot of words and again they didn't fit any of his pictures.

Sir John was shaking his head at the man called Turner. "A juryman must not be sure of guilt or innocence before he listens to the evidence."

He pointed out twelve other men. Daniel counted them. He could count up to twenty if he had to but after that the numbers muddled him.

He was propelled forward then across the green to a low stone building with more windows than an ordinary house. Inside were six rows of worn desks and a platform with a bigger desk and a chair at the end of an aisle between the rows like a church. Sir John sat there and Daniel was placed in front of him while the twelve men were ordered to sit in the front row.

It seemed as if the whole of the village crowded in behind when he peered round at the clumping noise of all the clogs on the wooden floor. The people called witnesses stood in a line by the nearest window but Daniel kept his eyes from the face of the cruel young man.

Sir John asked for a clerk to record the proceedings but no one offered their writing skills except Farmer Turner and his own son, Robert.

"You are both too concerned in the matter. Dame Leary, it is most irregular to call a woman but it is your schoolroom and I trust you can find paper and ink."

"Pencil, Sir John."

"Why are you wasting time on so plain a case, sir," the sharp cruel voice called out.

"Be silent, everyone in the court," Sir John said. "Pencil will have to do. It can be written over in ink afterwards." He opened the desk and took out a Bible. "Let us proceed."

Daniel looked up with hope at the Bible. Soon he might be allowed to go and find Nat and all this strange bewilderment would be over. Nat would be in charge.

Bel stretched in bed and remembered she was a prisoner for the day. It was a pity because she could see sunshine outside. Someone had been in already and opened the shutters. She put her toes out of bed and wiggled them into the thick Turkish rug. When she stood upright she looked towards the door and saw a tray on the floor with an egg and a toasted muffin and a mug of mild ale. She fetched it and sat on the bed with it on her knee and ate and drank, stuffing the food in as she never could when she was under scrutiny. There was some luxury in this.

She wondered if her egg had been laid by Farmer Turner's hen who had escaped strangulation. Had they caught the man with flaxen hair? She didn't like to remember that she had for a moment been frightened by him. She hoped he was locked up. At any rate she was locked in, so he couldn't escape to get at her.

It was better to think of Sam. He would be taking the scraps from the farmhouse kitchen to scatter for the hens. Did they troop thoughtlessly out over the farm with no memories of the scare the night before? Were they all in love with the cock who strutted about as if he surely thought they were. Would Sam Turner strut if he knew that Arabella from the Hall was in love with him?

"He doesn't need to strut," she said aloud. "He's as good as me, in fact better by far. But I know I could be a better person if I spent more time with him."

She clasped her knees and thought over the whole of that afternoon with him. He had called her Young Mistress Arabella at first, till she had told him she never answered to that. She would to Bella but what she called *herself* was Bel.

"Just B-E-L," she had said. "One L. Why waste letters? Your name is three letters. That's good. I like things to be very simple. Have food when you're hungry. Go to sleep when you're tired. Wear something thin and cool in summer and warm in winter. People try to make everything difficult – rules about eating and drinking at set times. Get into bed and blow out your candle even if you're still wide awake. Wear the most dreadful clothes with a thousand buttons –"

He had laughed and remarked that some people couldn't eat when they were hungry because there was no food and they had only rags to put on summer or winter and no candle to light or bed to sleep in. He had sat back on his heels to say it in the middle of their game but so calmly and smilingly that she hadn't felt humiliated as she often did at home. Of course he was right and it was good for her to think about poor people and try in the midst of all her rebelliousness to be thankful.

I think, she reflected, that was when I really began to be in love with him, only he never managed to call me Bel to my face. But that's what makes me angry. Grown-up people make true love impossible. I would never be allowed to marry a farmer's son. Yet Sam is honest, heroic, kind. Father is honest but he is not wise to let Mother pander to Robert, and he doesn't know at all how to manage Henrietta. Robert is not honest. He's a hypocrite. He sometimes takes Mass with Mother but reviles Popery behind her back. And he's a coward too. He rode with Father's troop to Newburn to fight the Scots, but after the battle he rode back again and said, "Our men had no heart for it. Some of them were more vicious against their own officers. One wretched captain was beaten to death on the way north because they suspected he was Catholic. I wasn't going to risk them finding out I have a Catholic mother."

Bel had grown up knowing that her proud, beautiful and confident mother was nevertheless a sort of liability to the family. She didn't care that Father Patrick went about in peril of his life but she hated having this secret Popery thing within the walls of Horden Hall and she was very afraid that though her father didn't like it either he might one day succumb to it. Her mother was the power in the home.

"King Charles is in thrall to a Catholic wife," Robert would say, looking at Father with eyes like black diamonds so Father had no doubt what he was thinking.

But Sam, she thought, is at the Parish Church with his family Sunday by Sunday. They are not complicated people like us. They live in their modest farmhouse and milk their cows and toil in the fields and have no time to rebel or to spite or bully each other. That's how I want my life to be, just straight and simple and true. Sam and Bel. What a good sound that has!

And then she put down her tray at the door and her chamber pot beside it and crept back into bed. She wouldn't be able to see him again till tomorrow.

CHAPTER 3

DANIEL looked at the boy they called Samuel Turner who had been summoned as the first witness. He had removed his hat to reveal curls the colour of ripe conkers and a fresh, sun-bronzed face with brown eyes.

He looks an honest boy, Daniel told himself, but I have never seen him before. Did he see me sometime and I didn't know it? He tried to listen carefully to everything the boy said.

First he swore on the Bible to tell the truth. Then Sir John asked him, "Have you ever seen this man before?"

"No, Sir."

"What were you doing yesterday afternoon?"

"I mended the stone wall next to the bridge, so my father gave me two hours to myself. I acted out the battle of Newburn with sticks for soldiers. It was a game, sir. Then I heard my mother call me in so I covered up the bonfire with earth and went inside. About a quarter of an hour later we heard a shot and all ran out. Master Robert came up and said he'd fired at a man who'd grabbed one of our hens."

"Did you see anyone?"

"No sir. Master Robert said he'd dropped the hen and run away. Then we all went to look for your young daughter but we didn't find her at the village."

"Why did you stop looking?"

"Someone shouted that they could see fire and we knew it must be at the farm so we all ran back."

"Did you see anyone then?"

"No sir."

"Are you certain your bonfire was out?"

"Oh yes, sir. Dead and cold. But it was a long way from the stack. I would never make a bonfire near the stack."

"And all afternoon you never saw a stranger lurking about."

"No, sir."

"I understand you found a pair of your own breeches on the ground?"

"My mother saw them first, sir, and asked me why I'd made them dirty again when she'd cleaned them the day before."

There was a ripple of laughter at that, quickly dying away. Daniel understood about dirty clothes. Jenny, the maidservant at the parsonage, was always grumbling at him for making his clothes dirty.

"What did you tell your mother?" Sir John asked.

"*I* didn't make them dirty, sir."

"Thank you, young man. I think you have said all you know."

The boy bowed his head and was stepping away when Sir John exclaimed, "Ah, one moment. Did you see a fat boy anywhere about?"

The boy looked startled but said quickly, "Why, no, sir."

"Right, you may return to your place."

Sir John now called his own son. Daniel's heart quailed when the thin cruel voice swore on the Bible.

"Have you seen this man before?"

"Yes, sir. Yesterday at Turner's Farm."

"Recount what happened, exactly."

The cruel eyes burnt into him so Daniel looked down at his breeches. They were ripped at the knee, perhaps on a tree stump when he slithered down the bank.

"As I walked from the Hall to the Turner's Farm," the cruel young man said, "I saw a fair head in the field behind the haystack. It caught the last light of the sunset and I thought, what's he up to? He's a stranger, so I stepped off the track onto the grassy edge and trod softly. I saw him eying the hens running up the field. He peeped round the haystack to see if anyone was about and then suddenly grabbed a hen as it ran past him. I gave him a warning shout and then fired. Thanks to my good French pistol I hit his shoulder and he squealed out. You can see the blood on his shirt this minute. He disappeared from sight behind the trees on the bank and I thought he had run away but it seems he hid down there –"

"Now you are guessing. You didn't look."

"Turner and his folk came out. The rest you know from young Sam. But it's plain enough the man was hiding till we'd all gone the other way. No one else was about. He went for the breeches – see his own rags – and when they didn't fit and his wound was paining him he went wild and fired the stack. Get the man hung." There were murmurs of approval from the crowd behind Daniel.

"By what means could he have set fire to the stack?"

"Soldiers carry tinder boxes."

One of the pitchfork men shouted out from the witnesses' line, "He had nothing with him when we took him, Sir John, but he'd throw it away. He's a deserter."

"You will have your say in a moment," Sir John said. "Robert, if you have nothing more to say you may stand aside."

Daniel was shocked to see the young man raise his black brows and curl his thin lips to frame the word, "Fool!" Honour thy father and mother, he had been taught. It was one of the Ten Commandments.

The woman who had opened the door to him was pushed forward now and sworn in. "Oh, Sir John," she cried, "I'd been told the robber was very fair and here he was stood at my own door, his clothes all bloody and torn. I slammed the door and shouted to my lads and they grabbed their pitchforks and ran round the house and seized him. I gave them my clothesline to tie him up when they had him safe. That's it there and I'll be wanting it back.

It's good rope, that."

Now there was a sudden commotion among the crowd gathered in the doorway. Daniel looked round. Perhaps it was Nat come to rescue him. No, it was a man leaping from a horse. Daniel saw its big head shaking up and down behind the people.

"Is Sir John Horden there?" The man was pushing his way in. "The Scots are on the march here. They've orders to turn us out of our houses."

Amid the shouts and cries of dismay Sir John called to the messenger, "How long till they are here?"

"Half an hour at the most."

"We will conclude this properly. Pray do not run away any of you. The Scots will ask to billet here, that's all. They will not turn you out. Prisoner, what is your name?"

"Daniel Wilson, my lord."

"Answer me at once. You've heard what's been said – that you tried to steal a hen, you set a fire, you were going to steal the breeches but they were too small, you saw a fat boy whom you are blaming for these things. Are you guilty?"

Daniel stared at him. How could he answer so many words? Nat always said, "Line the pictures in your head and use them when words come hard to you."

Sometimes he could count his pictures on his fingers. That was what he must do now. He spread the fingers of his right hand that was trapped against his side and looked down at it. The hen picture first. He curled back his forefinger and said, "The hen, yes, my Lord, but I dropped it with the bang and the pain." The fire picture. He curled back his second finger. "The fire, yes my Lord, there was fire and a wind. It blew the fire."

Murmurings came from the crowd at that but he mustn't let himself be stopped. He curled back his third finger. "Breeches?" He shook his head and then looked at his knee. "Yes, torn." That was a present picture so he could be sure of it. He curled back his little finger. "Fat boy." He could see the round shape slide down the tree trunk, the pale blob of face looking at him. But sometimes dreams were as clear as that and it was obvious that nobody else had seen that picture. The only children he had seen in the crowd were thin and the little boy who had thrown the stone – his poor arms were like sticks. Speaking of a fat boy had made the people angry. He looked up at Sir John's frowning face and sensed the desperate impatience of the crowd. He shook his head. "Fat boy – a dream."

Cheering broke out and the sharp cruel voice shouted, "To the gallows with him. You are still the law here, sir."

Daniel looked up at the face of Sir John.

Sir John turned to the jurymen. "Do you find Daniel Wilson guilty or not guilty?"

They all yelled "Guilty."

He sighed. "Daniel Wilson, I would commit you to the care of a constable till the sentence be pronounced by a more regular court –" He got no further.

His son, Robert, of the sharp, cruel voice shouted out, "Do your duty, men. He has been condemned to hang."

There was not a second's pause. Daniel found himself manhandled out of the building, the crowd pressing on every side. His legs scrabbled along the ground as they ran with him across the green, out between the houses and up a hill. At the top he could see a gallows, a stark shape against the blue heaven. There was one just like it back home outside the nearest town. He had seen figures hang there and had hidden his eyes because he couldn't bear to think what it must feel like in the moments before you became a corpse. They were rushing him towards it.

He couldn't die away from Nat. Nat and he did everything together.

Surely Nat would come. He gave a scream. "Na-a-a-at! Na-a-a-at!"

"Is he saying 'not that'? But yes indeed that. You should have thought of that before you fired my stack."

Daniel had shut his eyes to the sight. He saw a picture of his father kneeling by a dying woman and forgiving her her sins. Her eyes had smiled through her pain.

I have to be forgiven if I am going to die. I know I am a sinner. We are all sinners. I have to pray. Father signs the cross over them as they are going.

All at once he felt his arm loosened. They needed the rope. His hand flew up to his chest and he made the cross as he had seen his father do. His lips cried out, "Father! Father!"

"By the Lord," voices cried all around him, "he's a filthy papist too." Something heavy struck him on the head. Stars. A rushing in his ears. Darkness. Oblivion.

He knew nothing of the moment he had dreaded.

Bel roused herself. She could hear horses' hooves in the stable yard below and the raised voices of her father and Robert. She flew to the window but then opened the casement gently so it wouldn't creak. She could see and hear plainly.

"I say it was bungled," her father exclaimed. "I am not comfortable in my mind. He was big but he was no more than a lad and simple at that."

"The only bungling was Turner clubbing him for a papist. He was knocked out so we couldn't see him squirm."

"He will have a family somewhere who will want to know what happened. We are not even sure whether he was in the army or where he came from. There could be an officer in whose troop he served – if I could trace him in all this chaos."

"If you found him he'd shoot him for desertion, so you've saved him the trouble."

"I will have the old dame's notes written over properly and the whole thing put in the judicial records. I have a reputation, my son, that I value and I hope to God that you will one day deserve men's respect yourself."

Robert laughed his thin high laugh which Bel loathed. "I think *I* was more in tune with the people today than you were, sir."

Peering down while keeping out of sight, she saw Tom the old groom come to take Lady's bridle and as her father dismounted he replied with sorrow, "Their baser instincts, indeed, Robert. Men in our position should seek to raise them to higher things."

Robert flung himself down, chuckling. "We certainly raised Daniel Wilson to higher things, but I wager he plummeted straight to hell."

Her father began walking to the servants' door, his shoulders stooped a little. She knew that dispirited look well. As Robert followed with a sharp word to Adam, the stable boy, to rub down Caesar properly, her father looked round.

"We must do something for Turner. He was hasty and vindictive but I can understand his anger. I will see to it he doesn't suffer for this. That lad of his is a fine, upstanding youth."

They disappeared below. Bel closed the window. She was smiling deep inside at the last remark. Oh true, true and my father knows it. Maybe he will be so pleased to be rid of an unmarriageable daughter that he'll give me to a tenant farmer after all. Then she sat down on the bed and, with nothing else to do, tried to work out what exactly had happened that morning. It seemed certain that they had hanged the robber but how could Farmer Turner have suffered when he hadn't even lost one hen?

The door key rattled in the lock and Nurse popped her dinner tray round.

"Don't go, sweet Nan," cried Bel leaping to the door. "Tell me what's been going on?"

"I'm not to speak to you, her ladyship says. But I daresay there's no harm in you knowing Farmer Turner's haystack was fired last night and they've hung the man for it. So you see how bad deeds gets punished. Eat your dinner now." She went out and locked the door.

Bel sank down onto the bed, her mouth agape. The haystack! My glowing stick – the flaming straw – the wind! It wasn't the robber. What have I done? I've killed an innocent man. He didn't even keep the hen and he was hungry – like the poor folk Sam spoke of. And now he's dead.

An hour later her dinner was still untouched.

CHAPTER 4

W<small>HEN</small> Nathaniel Wilson woke his head was clear. He felt a firm shape against his back.

"Dan?" There was no answer. He rolled over and found the two knapsacks pressed together behind him. He jumped to his feet and struggled to remember this wooden hut and how he had got here. Streaks of sunshine criss-crossed the floor from all the cracks, the largest a long thin triangle of light from the lopsided door.

As he stood staring at this gap and piecing together memories of Daniel being there in the night a figure appeared outside.

Nat took a step back. It was not Daniel.

Eyes, growing round with terror, were riveted at the opening. A choked off scream came from the lips. The figure scuttled away.

Nat leapt to the door and dragged it open. "Hey, you, come back here. Is this your hut? I meant no harm. I just slept here."

The figure, an angler he could tell from the rod over his shoulder, hesitated and with obvious fear turned round, poised to run off again.

Nat spread out his arms to show he had no weapon. "Forgive me for startling you, friend. I have just awakened. The sun is high but I was unwell and slept long. May I ask you, have you seen a man like me anywhere about? My twin brother."

At this the man stood very still, then suddenly scampered back towards him, hustled him inside and, following, pulled the door behind him to close the gap as best he could. He held his hand to his heart to still its pounding and when he could speak he gasped out, "Oh the Lord, I took you for a ghost." The colour crept back into his white face.

Nat, weak from hunger, began to tremble. "What are you saying, man?"

The angler leant his rod in the corner, set his back to the wall and slithered down to a crouched position. He motioned Nat to come down close beside him and put out a hand to his shoulder. Before he spoke he shook his head several times, his breathing still coming fast. Then he burst out, "You must run. They'll kill you too."

"Too? Oh God! Speak, man. What has happened to Dan?"

"They've hung him."

"No! *Hung* him?" A horrible coldness descended on Nat. He looked into the man's face. "Say that's not true."

The man had the sweet timeless look of one who had sat for hours in silence by gently flowing water. His eyes glistened with tears as Nat's sought in vain for hope. "I was there," he said. "God forgive me, I could do nothing, but I believed him innocent."

"Of course he was innocent," Nat gasped out. "Daniel could do no wrong."

The man seized his hands. "I believe you. I have a son myself who is slow-witted. When he spoke – your brother – I knew the signs. You say you were ill? Had he gone to seek food for you?"

Nat nodded.

"He took a chicken from the Turners' farm but the squire's son, young Robert Horden was passing and fired at him."

Dan's coming in the night burst into Nat's brain. "Yes, yes, my brother was here. He told me. He was shot at. He gave me fresh water. He was sorry he had dropped the chicken. We lay down together. I must have fallen asleep again."

"He *did* drop the chicken. It was unhurt –"

"Unhurt and they hanged him!"

"Nay, there was more. The haystack was fired and they were sure he had done it. He seemed to confess to it but the questions muddled him. And he spoke of a fat boy he had seen, but no one believed that. There are no fat bairns about here."

"There was – he told me." Nat withdrew his hands from the man's grasp and pressed them to his temples. Dan had fallen asleep first. He always slept speedily whereas he himself had lain a while with Dan's words going over and over in his head, puzzling his feverish brain. He could repeat them now aloud. "I know what he said, the very words. 'The fat boy saw me but he went away after the bang. There was some fire. The wind was blowing it along.' I asked him if he meant gunfire – the wind carrying the sound – but he said quite plainly, 'Fire on the ground.' I wasn't sure what he meant but I drank the water he gave me and he lay down to keep me warm because I was shivering. Then he fell asleep. Oh I will curse myself for ever for not waking this morning. He must have gone to find food again. There *was* fire. He saw it but he couldn't have done it. Why, his tinder box is here in his knapsack" He picked it up as the enormity of what had happened rushed over him. Dan had gone. He bowed his head over the knapsack and burst into sobbing.

The angler was shaking him. "Listen, man, you must get away. Grieve later. You are young. Save yourself. Think of your father and mother if they lose you both."

Nat's hands fell to his side. Father! No, there were no circumstances in life when he could not face *him*, but Mother! Daniel was her sweet babe who did all she said without question. Till he had grown too heavy she would take him on her lap and pet him and sing to him. When he became a great strong man she made him sit at her feet and she would stroke his head and massage his big shoulders. His big shoulders!

"What happened? *How* did they take him?" he demanded fiercely of the angler. "Tell me it all. I'll go nowhere till you tell me everything."

The story was dragged from him with many questions. He said he had just emerged from his own cottage to go fishing when he had seen Daniel knock at a door and begin to ask for food. "Peg Blakely should have told Sir John that," he added sadly. "Your brother wasn't trying to *take* this time, he was *begging*, but the trial all ended in a rush because of the fears the Scots were coming. They *have* come but only a small troop and their officer said your poor brother's body must stay as a warning to all that there is to be no more looting or violence on any side."

Nat recoiled in horror.. "Tell it straight," he cried. "There *was* a trial then."

The man told him everything he had seen.

At the end Nat repeated the names, "Sir John Horden, the justice of the peace who held a mockery of a trial, his son, Robert Horden, a vindictive beast, Farmer Turner, too angry at his loss to listen to reason, young Samuel Turner who surely must have failed to put out his bonfire, or else the mysterious fat boy blew it up again and fired the stack himself." He jumped to his feet. "I must find the fat boy and prove Daniel's innocence."

"Nay, I fear that's hopeless. Your brother admitted that was a dream. I'd wager the wind that got up after sunset did stir the fire to life and a spark could have lit the dried grasses round about. We've had little rain of late. Fire running along the ground. Ay, that was it. Some straw blew up against the stack. Look, man, the deed is done. Save yourself. Go home. Where are you from? You are not from round these parts by your speech."

"Darrowswick in Yorkshire, near the town of Easingwold. But how can I go back without Daniel? He must be buried at home." He broke into weeping again. "I must have his body."

"They'll kill you. They say our own soldiers beat to death one of their officers for being a Papist."

"I heard that, I was in the army, but we are not Papists."

"Your brother crossed himself –"

"I know, you said so. Our father is a parson. He obeys Archbishop Laud and holds to the old ways. That's why a passing rabble wrecked our church – tore out the rails, smashed the saints' windows. They even broke into the house and stole our goods with my mother following them about and yelling that we were faithful followers of the King and the Prayer Book. One of them said, 'We are not so sure o' the King with his French wife.' But they went away at last. No, we are not Papists."

The thought of Daniel crossing himself in his last moments cut him to the quick.

"You and your brother were both in the army? I'm afraid the mob took him for a deserter."

"It's true. I could feel this fever coming on and Daniel wouldn't leave me. But it was worse than that. Daniel had loved to watch the trained bands exercising in the Market Place in Easingwold and kept telling our mother he wanted to be a soldier. When a troop came through our village and the officer was calling all young men to the King's standard he was jumping up and down like a child. Mother said, 'Yes, go,' because she loved to give him his way. 'I have always longed to see Daniel fight the King's enemies. There will be no greater warrior.' That's what she said. I had to go too. We've always done everything together." He broke down again and sobbed. "How can I go back and tell her I made Daniel throw away his pike when we were left behind as the rest of our troop went on to Newburn. I was ill but it wasn't that. Daniel was never violent. He hated the training to use his pike to kill the cavalry horses or prod the riders off. So did I. I kept hearing my father say, 'The Scots are not our enemies. They only wish to worship God in their own way.' He was right."

"Well, son, I too am a man of peace, but I urge you to make your way home. This war will end when it's scarce begun. The Scots will not venture further south but if they take you you'll be a prisoner of war and if you are found by the local people who hung your brother they will string you up beside him. For God's sake, man, go."

"I'd be better to die by Dan and meet in heaven."

"Never. Your duty is here. Who will care for your ageing parents?" He pulled Nat to his feet and pushed him to the door. "Keep your hat down over that flaxen hair. I would say wait till dark but other anglers come here. No, you are best to head west as fast as you can travel. Make for the hill country before you turn south. Then cross the valleys where the rivers are but streams. The Tyne, the Derwent, then, I believe, the Wear and the Tees but I have never travelled so far. You may meet lawless folk but no one there will know of today's doings and the Scots will not spread that way. They will move east along the Tyne to the sea where all the coal ships go to London."

"But Dan – hanging on a gallows!"

"You cannot take him all that way home and you'd be slaughtered if you tried. Take the knapsacks. Have you food?"

Nat shook his head. "That's why Dan died," he choked out.

The man fumbled in his pouch and produced a hunk of bread and a piece of cheese in a scrap of cloth. "You have water?"

Nat picked up the water bottle from the floor. "I can't take your day's ration."

"Nay, I may catch a fish. The day will cloud after noon." He peeped out. "You'll have cover for a few miles in the woods but you must skirt the villages at first till you are well clear."

Nat clasped his hand. "How can I thank you?"

"By forgiving me for not saving your brother."

"You could have done nothing against a mob."

"Thank you, son, and God go with you."

Nat, tears streaming down his cheeks, stumbled out and headed, as the man had told him, west.

Bel sat with her arms clasped round her body and her chin pressed to her chest. It seemed the only way she could stop herself from disintegrating at the awful thought that she had caused the haystack fire and an innocent man had hung for it. The memory of her stick and the burning grasses seared her mind. And he had seen her. Wouldn't he have told his accusers he was not alone there? If he had would *Sam* believe she was to blame? That was a fearful thought. She had to know the whole truth of it. When had the man been taken? What had been said?

She paced her room, from the old-fashioned box chair in the window to the chest in the corner and back again. As she passed her dinner tray she kicked it in fury and frustration – just as Nurse opened the door and reached down for the dish.

"What's this, then?" It was still full of stewed beef, onions and chopped turnip. She took it up and held it out to Bel, "You're to eat it, Missy, every bit."

Bel screamed at her, "I *must* be let out."

"So you will be tomorrow morning. Now don't you waste good food!"

Bel dashed it from her hand, the earthenware dish broke and bits of food were scattered on the bed and the floor.

Taking advantage of Nurse's shock she made to rush past her out of the door, but her foot slithered on a piece of turnip. She landed on her rear and burst into tears.

Nurse turned and locked the door behind her and put the key in the deep pocket of her apron. She pulled Bel to her feet none too gently. "You bad, bad girl. What are your poor Mother and Father to do with you?" She picked her way over the spilt food to the chest and found a small bundle of clean rags used for dusting. Abstracting one she held it out to Bel.

"You will clean up the mess onto the tray along with the pieces of plate. It's lucky her ladyship doesn't allow you the porcelain with the family crest on or you would be in worse trouble. I shall tell her you're to have wooden platters like the kitchen maid till you can learn to be a good child." She sat down on the oak chair and directed operations.

Bel itched to refuse outright but the fear of having her imprisonment extended held her back. Somehow she must go tomorrow to see Sam Turner and find out all he knew or had guessed at. She scraped the food up without a word.

CHAPTER 5

NATHANIEL Wilson guessed he had been walking fast for about two hours, the pain of hunger and thirst helping to mask the agony of his grief. He was becoming lightheaded and finding himself passing under an oak he put out a hand to it, feeling comfort from its solidity. He must eat and drink or he could not go on. His shoulders were stiff and sore from carrying the two knapsacks. He sank down and with his back to the trunk he took out the angler's provisions and his water bottle.

A long drink cleared his head and at once the horror of his solitariness came upon him. He had never been apart from Daniel in his life except for study time with his father. Even then, when Daniel had completed his chores, chopping wood for the fire and tending Mother's vegetable patch under her supervision, he would come in and sit on the floor and nod his head as if he was following the lesson and then perhaps lie back on a cushion and fall asleep. It wasn't possible that he would never see him again. They were part of each other. When his father had said, "You are so good at your books, Nat, you should go to the university as I did," he had replied, "If I went away it would break Daniel's heart, sir."

But it would have broken *my* heart, he thought, and now how can it not be broken?

He tried to bite on the dry hunk of bread but it almost choked him as his mother's face, fierce as an eagle in her wrath, rose up before him. "You can eat with Daniel hanging on a gibbet?"

I were better to die here and now as face her with this horror. I should at least have Dan's body for her to hold and caress.

He leapt up, driven by a cry within, "Go back and get it." He had even taken a dozen paces along the bank stumbling in his weakness and with the crust of bread held out in his hand when his father's quiet reasonableness which was deeply embedded in his soul took over. He turned and walked back to the tree and sat down and swallowed the crumbs in his mouth and took a bite of the cheese. Then he sat very still with compressed lips trying to think calmly.

Father will accept that I was feverish. He will understand our quitting the army – letting it go on without us. He will see how Daniel would seek food for us both and fall into trouble from which he couldn't extricate himself. He'll listen quietly if I can just get through the tale without utterly breaking down. He will forgive me for leaving him on the gallows. I can hear his words. "Dan was bigger and heavier than you. You were weak from the fever. If they had let you take him down you couldn't have carried him. And you could have been shot as a deserter. After all what is a body but dust? Daniel's soul is with the Lord. He was a faithful servant of God all his life."

Nat put his head on his knees and sobbed for many minutes. Looking with his father's wider vision had moved him and there was some relief in tears but the pain of loss would never go away and his dread of facing his mother was undiminished.

At last he lifted his head and made himself finish the food. He must logically assess his situation. Following the stream had brought him to its confluence with a substantial river – presumably the Tyne again, flowing west to east. He and Daniel had crossed it after they had hidden their pikes and uniforms in a ditch. It seemed safer to hide in the woods they could see in the distance to the north. Now he must head south if he was to get back home. The Scots army would spread into the country for provisions round Newcastle but the angler was right that he should head west and find a ford or a bridge where the river was narrower. He packed everything necessary into one knapsack and pushed the other into the dark cavern beneath a holly bush.

Ninety to a hundred miles must lie between this spot and home. The immediate task was to earn his bread and travel the distance. From Daniel's knapsack he had taken the recorder they could both play. Dan managed simple tunes but he could never achieve the sweet, moving sound Nat could make. When they were alone in the hills near home Daniel would beg him to play to him and Nat would lap up his wonder and admiration but at home their mother allowed only Daniel to entertain guests. Now perhaps he could pass himself off as a wandering minstrel and if folk in the hill villages could spare him a bite to eat he might make his way south at last and reach home in less than a week.

Home, he remembered bleakly, had been sorely ravaged, leaving them in poverty despite the collections the parish had made for the whole family. But the sufferings they had had were nothing to the horror he would bring with him. The kind angler had spoken of him supporting his ageing parents but his mother could banish him from the house if he confessed the truth about Daniel's end.

No, that thought must be pushed to the back of his mind. He shivered and realised that the sun – as the angler had foretold – had given way to a mass of cloud from the west. He watched a flotilla of brown leaves float past on the grey water like baby ducklings. When they were out of sight he would resume his journey.

Bel woke next morning and found it barely light. Her punishment, she re-membered, was over but she felt no sense of freedom as she slid out of bed and opened the shutters. A chill mist filled the stable yard and hung over the woods behind. She couldn't guess at the time. She listened at the door but there was no sound of the servants moving about yet, so it must be very early. She tried the handle gently but the door was still locked.

A farm wakes early, she reminded herself. If I could get there I might see Sam.

No more thought was needed except that she would not try to saddle Paddy her pony as it might bring the boy Adam from his loft above the stables. Besides, her special short cut through the woods was quicker than the road. She dressed herself somehow, choosing a dress of green velvet which would keep her warm without petticoats. The bodice had lacings at the front that she could do up herself and she found in the chest her only attempt at knitting – a shapeless dark cap – which she pulled down over her cropped hair to just above her eyes. It didn't matter what she looked like but at least she would be inconspicuous if she hid among the trees.

Racing against time she dragged off her bed sheets and tied them together, testing the knot with all her strength. Then she drew one end round a leg of the heavy box chair, pushing it with difficulty close below the window. She tied a tight knot and, forcing open the casement as far as it would go, she lowered the other end through. Peering out over the sheets she saw they ended a good way from the ground but once over the stone lintel above the kitchen window she would be able to balance on the window sill below and jump from there. Her only fear now was that someone might be in the kitchen. She must take her chance.

Climbing onto the chair seat she squeezed feet-first through the aperture and twisting the sheet in her hands she began to let herself down a little at a time, her feet feeling for protuberances in the stonework. She was not in the least frightened, only driven by the desperate urge to be away. The lintel of the kitchen window gave her a foothold and she took one hand off the sheet and nearly fell as her other shoe missed the stone. Her hands were scraped as she let herself slither down and feel for the stone sill below the window. She was at the end of the sheet. She turned round with her back to the window and jumped. Landing perfectly with bended knees as she had seen tumblers do she was instantly running out of the stable yard and heading for the woods. No shouts pursued her.

The fronds of mist among the trees slowed her after a few moments as they obscured her marks. It was best to look down and follow where the summers' weeds were crushed by her own feet. There was enough light for that.

As soon as she reached the farm track she saw through the hanging silvery veil the horrid blackened boards where the stack had stood. How it must have blazed! She saw in her mind's eye her own glowing stick and the grasses it had lit. It must have been only a few minutes later when she was scuttling home that the evil wind had wafted that helpless little fire against the stack. Now that she saw it she was sure in her heart how it had been. She knew where her careless hand had tossed the stick. She remembered how she had not even thought of stopping to stamp it out.

Do I *want* to speak to Sam, she wondered. I can't ever confess about the stick. But perhaps he was beaten for having a bonfire. She looked to her right towards the plank bridge. No, his fire was far over there. *I* did it. My stick did it. But there was a trial of that poor man.. What was said? I need to know why they hanged him.

She glanced about in an agony of indecision. Nobody seemed to be stirring when she looked towards the farmhouse. All the same she skirted round the back of it through the trees. And then the cock crew, making her heart bump and startling her into a panic as if a devil was chasing her. She was past the farm and running now at the edge of the track to cover the ground more easily, but heading as she knew for the village of Nether Horden. She was sure it wasn't light enough for six o'clock but the mist was dimming everything. She mustn't be seen in the village but she knew now what she had to do. She must punish herself by going and looking at the gallows.

Crouched behind a wall and peeping at the village between the rough stones on top she saw the first sign of the new day. A grey wisp from a chimney curled into the whiteness of the mist which was thicker down here. People were lighting their fires. Bent double she scuttled behind the walls of the vegetable plots at the backs of the houses, till she came to the grassy slope of Gallows' Hill as it had always been called. Now she made a circuit to approach the crest out of sight of the village. The mist was a kindly cloak as she scampered into the open and began the ascent, her shoes slithering on the wet cropped grass. A few tethered goats and roaming sheep stared at her as she had to move on all fours in the steepest places.

Then her head was out into clear air. She stood up and right above her was the huge framework of the gallows against a brightening sky. And a body. Oh horror of horrors! She hadn't expected a body. It looked enormous, dangling towards her, but what made her flesh crinkle and her stomach shrivel within her was the discoloured face twisted down at her with one popping eye meeting hers. The other was a reddened hollow.

She dropped to her knees and covered her head with her arms, her eyes tight shut but still seeing the look of accusation in that one eye. Silently screaming she dare not move in case she saw the thing again. She had no idea how long she crouched there, horribly aware that it was still above her. Then a breeze came fluttering from the east and brought a sudden creak from the vast structure. In a panic that the thing would fall on top of her she squirmed round without opening her eyes and began to slide back down the slope, her whole body racked with panting sobs. Then she let herself roll and ended up in a heap, pressing her clenched hands against her mouth to hold in the sight that could never go away. She lay still.

"Why it's young mistress Arabella from the Hall! Goodness me, is she hurt?" The woman's voice was kindly but Bel dare not open her eyes. She feared what she would see. Was it possible she would ever see ordinary things again? The woman touched her, patting her shoulder and then trying to turn her over. "Here, Gideon. Pick her up, she's hurt."

Bel at once scrambled to her feet and opening her eyes a chink saw only a swelling bosom under the grubby bib of an apron. "I'm all right," she mumbled. "I'll go home."

"What are you doing out here so early on your own?" It was a man's voice. Bel could smell him. "Nay, little lady, you'll have to stop this wandering about. You had everyone a-searching two nights ago and that's when Farmer Turner's stack was fired for there was no one watching out."

"Ah, but she was at home all the time," the woman said. "Our Mary said she'd been hiding somewhere. The Hall's such a warren of rooms they'd never found her till she was tucked up in bed."

"Well, she still caused a deal o' trouble," the man answered. "And who is to see her home now?" He had gripped Bel's arm.

Bel lifted her eyes then. "I can go myself. Loose me at once."

"Nay now, young Madam, we'd be in trouble ourselves if you went a-wandering again."

There came the rattling of cartwheels on the track round the village green.

"There's the Turners' cart," the woman said. "She can go back on that as far as the farm and then maybe they'll spare someone to take her home from there. I'll just run in for the jug and do you bring her round the house, Gideon."

Bel found herself hustled past a cabbage patch and out onto the corner of the green where suddenly there was life and activity, children running across the grass with earthenware jugs, a few Scottish soldiers loitering about, and Sam Turner standing up on the farm cart ladling out milk from the churn. Fingers of sunlight stroked the green between the elongated shadows of the cottages. The mist had lifted. It wasn't how she had hoped to see Sam but somehow life was in progress again and the complete indifference of the people to the horrible thing above the village helped her to put on a show of normality herself.

Sam looked down at her with raised brows but lifted his hat in a mock salute and shrugged his shoulders when the man Gideon asked him to take her to the farm.

"Ay, when I'm done here. Who wants eggs as well?" He was collecting the pennies in a leather pouch slung round him and Bel, in all her torment of mind, found a little flame of admiration spurting up at his cool self-possession and handsome looks. What she would say to him she had no idea.

When he was finished with customers he held out one hand to her and she felt the man Gideon lift her up to grab it. She scrambled into the cart beside him. Sam clicked his tongue and the horse moved off round the track. Bel kept her eyes well averted from the hill behind them.

"So Mistress Arabella, why were you up so early?" he asked. When she said nothing he peered at her. "Of course you don't answer to that. So, Bel, what were you doing? You've been crying."

It was hard to speak when she couldn't wipe out the image on the hill. Her voice came out in a squeak. "They hanged that man. I saw him. Why is he still there?"

He shrugged again. "What did you go and look for? He's there as a warning. I daresay they'll take him down in a few days." He was looking at her again, a little curiously. "Whatever are you wearing on your head?"

She snatched off the cap. "I knitted it. Don't laugh."

He did laugh and she wanted to die.

Then he said seriously, "That evening – when the stack was fired – why did you not go home at once? The robber saw you He said there was a fat boy." He chuckled. "Of course I knew it was you though no one else believed him."

A coldness like a knife went down her spine. "He said that? Yes, I saw him. After he went away I took your breeches off. But tell me about it. What did he say?"

"Your father gave him a sort of trial with a jury an' all. Didn't you know that? I had to be a witness."

"How could you be? You hadn't seen *him*. But you knew *I* was there. Why didn't you tell? Then they might have believed him. Did you lie when you'd sworn on the Bible?"

"Never. I said I saw no fat boy, which was exactly true."

"Oh!" This was her honest hero! "But you knew it was me. If you'd said so you could have saved the man. You made him a liar."

He was looking at her in astonishment. "Did you want your father to know you'd been playing with me, worn my breeches?"

"I don't care about his anger. If you'd spoken up they might not have hung that man."

"Why not? What are you saying? *You* fired the stack?"

"Of course not!" She rushed the words out. "How could you think I would do such a thing?"

"Nay, I didn't. So I protected you. You should be grateful. I knew if he'd seen you he must have been hanging about – watching for the coast to be clear, hoping to get another hen even after he was shot at. But when he couldn't he took his revenge. Why should you speak up for him? I think he was a simpleton. He seemed to be trying to lay the blame on this fat boy but at last he admitted he must have dreamt it. I wondered where he saw you. Your brother Robert never knew you were there."

She shook her head. "I was by the beech tree. The man looked right at me. He frightened me. But he had two eyes then." She couldn't go on.

"You did see the bonfire was out, didn't you?" he demanded now.

She nodded. Then muttered, "I put more earth on to be sure."

He grunted. "I knew it wasn't a spark from there. Much too far. No, he did it – no doubt. Well, people are hung all the time. But little girls don't have to go looking."

She bit her lip. Then pleaded in a whisper, "But now he has only *one* eye?"

"What? Oh," he laughed. "Crows do that." He drew the horse up by the farm. "I suppose my mother could walk you home if she's not in the dairy churning butter."

"I'll run and I'll never come back."

"No, don't. I think you're trouble." He was still laughing. "Promise you'll go straight back then?"

She nodded, speechless again and took off. He had been hateful, almost as bad as Robert. He despised her like everyone else. Laughing! Oh, he was utterly demolished as a noble hero. He was a coarse uncaring farm boy.

She was hot with shame and anger. Hot too in her velvet dress. After the mist the sun was going to be fierce. Oh that it would burn up everything, herself included!

The picture on the hill was with her again. However hard she ran for the rest of her life she was never going to escape it.

CHAPTER 6

Nat made a late start on the second morning because the mist robbed him of all sense of place and direction. He had earned himself a supper the night before when he finally reached a ford which he could pass dry shod and found a few cottages clustered on the south bank. A group of girls were sitting in a ring on the grass cherishing something in their midst when three boys broke in amongst them and with shouts of glee snatched it up.

Nat saw it was a young thrush so he called out, "Nay, lads, don't hurt it." They looked up in surprise at the stranger and the bird fluttered to the ground and flapped along lopsidedly. "Let me see." He took it up and found one wing bent awkwardly. With gentle hands he straightened it and smoothed the feathers into place.

"We chased a cat from it," one of the girls said. "But the boys are worse than the cat. They've hurt it more." She glared at them.

Nat shook his head. "We'll not quarrel over it." He motioned them all into a ring, set the bird down in the middle and took out his recorder. "See if we can cheer it up. It's still not sure if it can fly."

He played a sweet lilting tune and after a few moments the thrush made a little run and flew into the air. The children clapped and cheered and asked him to play some more.

"Stand up then and dance," he said and played a lively reel. They took hands and pranced about to the music. Soon he saw women gathering from the cottages to listen and watch. Men were coming from the fields and in a few minutes he had the tiny hamlet all dancing. He was readily invited then to join the family supper in the home of the three boys.

"They're always teasing the lasses," their mother said. "If you can tame them like that, stranger, you must be an angel from God."

"Just a wanderer," Nat said.

Her husband questioned him about where he had come from and whether they were true rumours that the Scots were come over the border.

"Ay," Nat told him, "but it's mostly quiet now. I'm no fighter so I keep away, but I believe they'll only stay in Newcastle till King Charles gives them what they want."

"I hope that's not our sheep and cattle," the farmer said.

"I should have said rather if the King takes from them what they *don't* want."

The man scratched his head. "And what would that be?"

"Bishops." Nat laughed, expecting that in this remote spot the answer would be meaningless.

"Bishops! Ay well, I hear the Bishop of Durham lives fat and comfortable and he would never come this far, so if they dinna want them ower the border I reckon that's their business. It's not a thing we should be fighting about."

After supper they wanted him to sleep in the barn but while there was still daylight he pressed on south by the way they had directed him to a drove road. When dusk fell he turned aside and walked over the moor till he found a hollow where he could curl up out of sight in the heather. The kindliness of the people soothed his mind and he was soon asleep.

But finding thick whiteness about him when daylight came he dare not move in case he blundered further and further from the road. The delay frustrated him and because his body was inactive his mind worked feverishly, comparing these hill people with the village that poor Daniel had blundered into. Were they not all ordinary human beings? He went over the whole story the angler had told him, feeling his wretchedness at Daniel's loss turning to bitter anger towards those responsible for his death. Could Sir John Horden not see that Daniel was slow-witted? Why had he allowed his vicious son to incite the mob to hang him so peremptorily? Why had no effort been made to find the fat boy who could be the key to the horrible mistake?

Daniel said it was a dream. Ah but they didn't know him, he thought. I could always sort his dreams from reality and when he spoke to me that night in the hut he was telling me what he had just seen. It was no dream, for he was well awake with the pain of his wound. What sort of a magistrate is Sir John that he could allow a verdict of guilty on such slight evidence?

Nat worked himself into a passion as he paced about in the hollow to keep warm. He had water but no food to eat while he waited for the sunrise when the autumn warmth would surely suck up this cursed fog. His heart yearned to hear Dan's voice soothing him. "Don't be angry, Nat. Don't be sad." It always distressed Dan to see him give way to emotion, unless it was happiness, when he would laugh with him over the smallest and most absurd things.

Nat thought of their boyhood with stabbing pangs of regret for the times he had been impatient with Daniel, when he had wanted to study and Daniel had begged to play. Mother would shout at me, he thought. "Go play with him at once. How can you stop being the little runt if you don't exercise yourself!" How I hated her for that and my fury made me do everything in our play faster than Dan. I would be up a tree before he could haul himself onto the lowest branch. I always beat him in races and he never minded. And of course I could read before he even knew the letters. I had Father's praise but it was he who warned me not to gloat over Dan's slowness nor be jealous of Mother's special love for him. It was still hard to take but never hard after that to love Daniel because he loved me with such a passion. Ah, but did I ever show him enough how much I loved him. And now I never can.

Nat sank again into his heather hollow and gave way to a burst of weeping which he thought would never end. But at last he sensed through his fingers a lightening of the sky. The mist was thinning. The east was that way and so was the drove road.

"God be praised." He hoisted his knapsack and walked forward. He must complete his journey and face the horror of the homecoming. Beyond that he couldn't see. It was shrouded as the distant hills were still shrouded. Perhaps he could talk to Dan as he walked of all that he experienced this day and find comfort in the telling.

Bel sat on her bed and stared at the wooden bars that had been screwed into the window-frame in her absence. They didn't matter. Nothing did. Her hands were sore from the caning Nurse had given her on her mother's orders, but she remembered that monks and even nuns used to wear hair shirts and flagellate themselves in their cells. What a pity all those places had been wiped off the face of England! She could have run away and joined one.

Only I can't run away, she remembered, looking at the bars.

She was to have only bread and water and she didn't expect anyone to visit her but about noon her father came in and locked the door behind him. She stood warily by her bed while he sat down in the box chair by the window. He looked at her gravely while she studied him, thinking, he is all precise points – his beard, the lace collar over his doublet, the triangular seams at his narrow waist, and the V-shapes of the doublet below aiming at his boots. Even the bows on his boots come to points. Why is he so neat and clean and his grey hair so smoothly brushed onto his shoulders when that poor man this morning ...?

"I'm sorry you had a caning, Arabella," he began. "Such punishment is for children and I want you to start behaving like a young lady. In two years' time, you could be married to young William Horden, your second cousin. You know you have always been intended for him. He is seventeen now, a suitable age. My father and his grandfather were brothers. I am not in favour of girls being married before fifteen, but knowing it will happen should give you a sense of purpose and security."

She stared back into his eyes, furious. "Why are you talking about marriage when people are fighting and dying?"

He moved his hands in a dismissive gesture. "No, no, child. The fighting is over. The Scots have promised to pay for any provisions they need. Many in Newcastle welcome them. They say the Mayor has entertained the Scots General Leslie to dinner. This is not a conflict between barbarians."

"Oh and was that not barbaric – hanging a simpleton yesterday on no evidence at all?" Bel was glad to see his eyes became hooded with shame and anguish – till her own guilt reared up her gorge and nearly choked her. She shut her eyes tight and hung her head. But shutting her eyes was worse because she could see the gallows and the body and the face with its one eye ... She looked up, aware of her father's silence.

"I believe you went out to see the gallows, Arabella? Why did you do that?" His voice was quiet, gentle, even troubled.

She shook her head, unable to speak.

"There has to be punishment or evil would run rampant through the world. You are being punished now for breaking your last punishment."

Words burst from her. "That man didn't need to be punished. He was innocent."

"What can *you* know? He was certainly guilty of attempted robbery –"

"No, I don't know." Again the words came in a rush of fear that she was betraying herself. "I only know what I heard you and Robert saying when you rode back yesterday and what I learnt in the village. Why did you let them hang him?"

She could see he was moved but he rose up, shaking his head. "It is not a child's place to question a father. As always you are assertive and rebellious in spirit. I know not what we can do with you. They say there are fine preachers come, following the Scots army. I think I must take you to hear one of them. Maybe you will ponder some of their words in your heart. If we can tame that wildness you may yet be a fit bride for young William when the time is right." He unlocked the door.

"Which it will never be," she yelled at him and he almost ran out of the room.

She heard the key turn and threw herself on the bed in a paroxysm of weeping. They had been close to a real conversation.. He was unhappy about the mockery of a trial and the sudden brutality of the people. Who could he confide in? Robert had enjoyed the scene and neither her mother nor Henrietta would be interested.

She sat up. I am the only one he could have talked to. If only he had I might have told him what really happened but I mar all speech because I am still a child in his eyes and must be meek which I don't know how to be. I nearly had a friend in Sam Turner but he is not the hero I thought he was. And I could never tell *him*. He would despise me for minding about a robber. I am just a troublesome girl. He told me so. So now I can never tell anyone and it's inside me for the rest of my life. Awake or asleep that face, that eye will never go away.

She was let out next day and brought to sit at the table in the family dining-room which her great-grandfather had had constructed next to a small parlour at one end of the original medieval hall. It was this room that had been reduced in length when the priest's hiding-place had been built.

"A century ago," her father was saying, not for the first time, "the lord and lady of the manner were expected to dine in the Great Hall with their retinue before them. We live in more private times but I expect the same dignity of bearing at our family meals that would have been exercised then as an example to the lower orders."

Bel used to grin at this when Robert and Henrietta were younger and prone to snap at each other over trifles. Of late she had been the butt of them both whenever she opened her mouth, but neither Father nor Mother rebuked them. Mother would flourish her fan to ward off the argument with a sigh while Father warned Bel that she should listen to others until she was old enough to have opinions worth hearing. Now however she determined to keep total silence at family meals, having little appetite and only longing for them to be over.

Henrietta, a dark beauty and a younger version of their mother, upbraided her for "sulking."

Robert remarked, "But how pleasant silence is from that quarter," and then took no more notice of her.

She listened perfunctorily to talk between Robert and his father of the Scottish occupation. Already the storerooms in the cellar had been investigated and several cartloads of provisions taken away and no payment made as far as she knew.

"You will need to enrol again in the King's forces to earn your bread," she heard her father admonish Robert one day as they left the table.

"And when did the King last pay his army?" Robert countered and her father seemed to have no answer to that.

Nevertheless, though the Scots were increasingly unpopular and there was consternation at the news that Edinburgh Castle had fallen to the Covenanters, crowds were still apparently flocking to the Presbyterian preachers and Bel was commanded the next Sunday to put on a sober good dress and accompany her father to Newcastle to hear a sermon, after they had been to the village church for communion.

Robert said he would take Mass in their own little chapel as their mother and Henrietta were expecting Father Patrick to come.

When his father objected Robert said, "Sir, when you were married you allowed our Mother to make a vow to her priest that she would bring up her children in the old faith. You let it lapse with that little heathen," pointing to Bel, "but I ought to make a show of it now and again."

Bel knew he would almost certainly disappear into the woods and shoot rabbits but their father let it pass.

She went in the trap driven by Tom, and Mary, the housemaid, came since Nurse said she was too old to be bounced around for four miles. Her father preferred to ride beside them so conversation was difficult for which Bel was thankful.

When they reached the town they found it patrolled by Scots forces but otherwise at peace with a good proportion of the populace walking soberly to church. Leaving the groom on the quayside to mind the horses and telling Mary to follow, her father took her hand and they climbed the steps to the church.

Emboldened by this mark of kindliness Bel looked up at him and asked, "Why did you promise Mother that we would be brought up Catholics?"

Sir John frowned her into silence, shaking his head and looking about to see if anyone had heard her. As they walked into the building he hissed at her, "I have told you to curb your questions. You are always asking questions."

She thought, how do I learn if I don't ask questions but she said nothing, awestruck by the height of the church, its vaulted roof and stone pillars marching ahead of them. This was much grander than their squat Saxon village church where the only splendour was in the Horden family pew with its painted crest and tall sides. She was so bewildered by the vast space and the numbers of people that she didn't at first realise that the preacher was already in the pulpit and beginning to harangue the congregation in a penetrating voice.

He spoke of sheep and goats and wise and foolish virgins and Bel could work out that his theme was entry into the kingdom of heaven which was obviously denied to Papists. But as he went on this seemed to grow more difficult for everyone, till she began to fear there would be no one in heaven at all when she got there. Was the hanged man there now, she wondered. He had been caught in the act of theft, so it seemed unlikely. Was there really a purgatory, as her mother believed? And would the poor wretch be able to convince God he was so hungry he couldn't help it? Though she sat perfectly still with her hands clenched in her lap she was seeing the awful eye looking down at her. Suddenly her ears caught the next sentence.

"And ye know that no murderer hath eternal life abiding in him."

I am a murderer. I killed that man as surely as if I had gone out and shot him. I didn't *know* but what excuse is that? I have always been bad and rebellious as Father says and that's why I was out that evening. If I hadn't been I wouldn't have thrown the burning stick down and the haystack wouldn't have caught fire and no one would have bothered about the hen that got away and the poor simpleton would have gone home to his family. So I am a murderer and I can never go to heaven.

She continued to sit absolutely still as this dreadful truth sank into her soul. She didn't hear any more of the sermon. Her father looked at her once or twice as if astonished at her stillness and because he looked she felt tears brimming into her eyes. She had no one she could ever tell. Her eyes were shut against the tears, but one forced its way out and then another. She daren't draw attention to them by trying to wipe them away. She felt one roll down her cheek. When another chased it, it could no longer tremble on her chin. Both fell together onto her sleeve.

Her father had seen. He rose and eased her and Mary along so that they slipped out at the side and headed for the door. She was just aware that other people had come and gone during the long sermon. She needn't be too ashamed.

When they were outside her father said, "I am glad you were moved, Arabella. Perhaps you will try very hard from now on to be a good, obedient child. The sermon was long enough already and the horses are waiting."

They descended the steps from the church to the quayside The river moved steadily by, a brown stinking mass of water. The ships were silently tied up for the Sunday. Tom stood there seeming mesmerised by the sight till he became aware of their presence. Then he jumped to attention, helped Bel up and Mary after her and led her father's horse to a mounting block next to the wall. In two minutes they were on their way.

If I can never go to heaven, Bel told herself, why do I need to be good? The logic was fearful but inescapable.

Nathaniel Wilson had been seeing for the last two miles the square tower of his father's church above the village of Darrowswick among the autumn trees. He made his legs move on though the pit of his stomach felt locked in ice. The day was without wind and balmy. Under the window of the first cottage in the village an old lady he knew well was sitting on her bench in the sunshine. There was no way to avoid her.

She held up her hands in an attitude of prayer and called out as he drew near, "Nay, tell me not you have lost your brother." He could only nod. "Eh, the years I have sat here and watched those two fair heads come over the moor when you and he went walking and today I saw only the one. The sun picks you out miles away against the heather. My heart went down into my boots. Which one, I thought and then I made out it was not Daniel with his big loping stride. If one had to go it was well t'was he for he'd not have survived losing you, Nat."

Nat leant on her little gate. "But how am I to tell my mother?"

"They'll be in the church. I heard the bell but my legs is so bad I cannot walk as far now. If you slip in at the back your father will see you. He'll finish the service, if I know Parson Wilson, and what can your mother do before the whole village?"

Nat noticed that on the bench beside her was a bowl with apple peelings, half hidden by a kerchief she had thrown over it. She saw him looking at it.

"You won't tell I've been at these on a Sunday. The wee lad next door brought me a basket of bilberries and I need the apple peels to make the jam set. Parson won't mind but your mother's strict on such things."

"She's not going to mind anything when she hears my news."

"Nay, that's true. Was it a Scots musket bullet took the poor lad?"

Nathaniel just shook his head. How he was ever going to bring out the truth to all and sundry he had no idea. If he could only lie ... but that he couldn't do when he looked into his father's eyes. For now he could only say, "Thank you for your advice, Granny Woodman. I think I will just creep into the church."

He had drunk the last of his water hours before and was dry from thirst and the dread of this moment but he wouldn't stop at the village pump. He replaced his hat that he had been carrying to dry the sweat on his forehead and touched the brim to the old woman and walked on. No one else was about. They were all in the church and to go there now might at least prevent a myriad of different rumours from spreading. The path up to the church was steep in places and he could understand Granny Woodman not being able to struggle there. Shivering with dread as he was he broke into a fresh perspiration as he climbed with the September sun hot on his back.

The sight of the gravestones reminded him of Daniel's physical body. Why had he not lingered to demand it back and bring it somehow by a cart all this way he had travelled? The village would never understand that. He pushed open the heavy door. It creaked as it always had and the backs of heads became faces, breaking into welcoming smiles and looking, he could tell, for the lumbering figure of Daniel to follow him in. When it didn't and he pushed the door shut behind him the smiles faded to anxious frowns.

He laid his finger to his lips and perched on the rearmost bench. His father, he could see, was before the altar with his back to the congregation in the act of blessing the sacrament. If he had heard the door he was too engrossed to look round. He was vested which meant that someone, perhaps the Squire, had procured him some fresh robes to replace those the soldiery had torn up and burnt. They had wanted to drag the altar down to the crossing but finding it a stone block they had contented themselves with smashing the candlesticks. .

Nat's stomach tightened when he saw his mother in their box pew, her red hair partly hidden by the loose black hood she always draped over it for church. As he looked someone nudged her from behind and pointed but she appeared to brush them aside and keep her eyes forward for the most solemn moment of the service.

Now his father was turning to exhort the congregation to draw near and partake. Nat remembered with relief that he himself could not go forward. He had not been here for the confession and was not absolved. But had his father seen him? He kept seated as the people rose. Would someone tell him? His father took the service with such solemnity that perhaps they would be restrained. Nat watched him as he passed along the first row. He could see the bald pate as he bent over each communicant and the spiritual joy on his sweet round face as he lifted his head, a sunbeam falling on it from one of the windows on the southern wall. Dear father. How good to see him again despite the horrible news he had to impart!

And then a shriek pierced the reverent silence. His mother had risen from her knees and turning had seen him before she descended the steps. The people waiting to go up parted to let her through. She came like a black whirlwind down the church and faced him, her eyes darting this way

64

and that.

"Daniel? Where is Daniel?"

He held up both hands as if to ward her off, shaking his head, speechless. He could see that she had lost all awareness of her surroundings but he could hear his father's voice still murmuring the words of communion to the remaining people and those who had returned to their places were too overawed by their minister's steadfastness to stare at him and his mother. He must get her outside. He turned and pointing towards the stone porch he compelled her to follow, the heavy door creaking again as he dragged it open.

She was upon him then practically pushing him while her lips gabbled, "Tell me, tell me. He is ill? He is dead? Take me to him."

He couldn't help the door thudding behind them. Her eyes now scoured the paving outside, the churchyard, the path to the parsonage and the slope to the village. The emptiness left her with her mouth open and her ferocious eyes staring back into Nat's face.

"Daniel? Where is Daniel?" She gripped him by the arms, her nails digging into his flesh through his sleeves.

"Oh Mother, Daniel has gone."

"Dead?" she screamed.

He nodded again and she thrust him from her with such force that he staggered back against the church wall.

"It was your task to protect him," she yelled. "What have you done with him?" She was looking about again. "Have you taken him to the house? Take me to him."

Now he could hear the congregation repeating the Gloria. Soon they would be pouring out. His father would appear. It was cruel to leave him in the dark for even ten minutes but it was urgent to remove his mother from curious eyes.

PRUE PHILLIPSON

"Come home," he muttered to her and she started off at speed, taking the worn steps that led down to the parsonage path in great leaps, her skirts held up above her shoes. He caught her before she reached the door. The house, built for a married parson in the days of Queen Elizabeth, stood squarely across the hillside. Nat was stabbed by memories of Dan and himself rolling down the grass beyond the vegetable garden.

"He's not here," he told her as she thrust open the door but she ran into every room calling, "My baby, my Daniel, my sweet boy."

Nat stood in the familiar hallway as her desperate shouts filled the air. She will see no one's suffering but her own, he thought. This is how I knew it would be.

She came back to him, her features all drawn to the point of her nose as he had seen her, eagle-like, in his mind's eye. "Where is he? What happened? Why have you not brought him?"

"Let's wait till my father comes. I need to drink." He walked through to the kitchen where the water barrel was filled from the well every morning. Dan's task. He lifted a pewter mug from its hook and took a long drink.

She stood in the doorway still draped in her black shawl. She had dragged off her hood and her dark red hair streaked with grey was all dishevelled. "Where is he?" she demanded again.

Nat heard his father's measured footsteps. She didn't look round even when he came up behind her, came past her holding out his arms, his eyes brilliant with tears and exclaiming, "Our Nat is home. God be praised."

They were enfolded in each other's arms, Nat utterly broken down and sobbing.

"And Daniel is dead," she shrieked, trying to part them. "And he will not tell us how."

"Take time," his father murmured. "I knew it in my heart when I saw you alone but God gave me His service to finish and I found peace. Daniel is with Him. Whether it was with a musket bullet or a fever he is with the Lord. Come, let us sit down. You must eat, Nat. You look thin and gaunt." He gently disengaged himself and turned to the hearth where he took up the bellows and revived the fire and set on the trivet a covered pan standing ready.

"Where is Jenny?" Nat asked.

"We have no servant now. When our debts are paid to the workmen who have repaired the windows here and in the church and other restorations about the place, Jenny may come back to us."

"You answer him about *Jenny* and he has not answered my questions." His mother was standing stiff with disbelief. "He eats nothing till he has told us all."

They sat down at the scrubbed kitchen table and Nat, looking mainly at his father but with anxious darting looks at his mother, struggled to unfold the tale. Where should he start? At the doubts that had overwhelmed him of the rightness of the war? At his own disgust and Daniel's horror at the training to use a pike? No that was a detail, a distraction.

"I was ill with a fever," he began. "Daniel sought food and water for me."

"The Scots took him?" his mother burst in. "Do they kill their captives now?"

"Peace, Anne," said his father. "Let him tell the tale."

Nat told it then in a rush, the bare, horrific facts. Daniel was caught as a thief and falsely accused of firing a stack, tried and hung before Nat knew anything of it.

His father did then bow his head over his hands and weep but his mother leapt up howling. She tore at her hair, she scraped her nails down her cheeks, then came round the table as if she would strangle Nat with her bare hands. He pushed away his chair and backed to the window. His father tried to hold her arms from behind but she broke away, spat into Nat's face and rushed from the room and pounded up the stairs.

"Oh Father, have I sent her mad? Why did she ever let Daniel go for a soldier?"

His father shook his head. "It nearly broke her heart seeing you two march away with the troop and she has fretted herself out of her mind in your absence."

"But why, then, why?"

They could hear her trampling overhead.

"She always feared you two would grow up as feeble in spirit as I. That was what she used to say. 'They are nineteen now. They must be tried and tested as men. Nat is for ever at his books and Daniel is so sweet-natured he will let all men trample over him. They must be stiffened to face life.' Those were her words and when the King's standard was carried through the village and Daniel was so excited she said this was the chance. We had been raided by those Puritan devils as she called them and there was little food in the house. How were we to feed your healthy young appetites, I asked myself, and I didn't oppose her as I should have done. She was bursting with pride that her Daniel would be a great warrior and come back heaped with honours for his valour."

"I remember that too well. Oh Father I will tell you it all, every moment from when we left home, but God knows I would rather I had died than come back without my brother."

His father raised his hand. "Hush! She is quiet. She may do herself harm."

Nathaniel followed him upstairs and they could hear a low moaning coming from the chamber where the brothers had slept in one bed from boyhood.

She was lying on the bed, on the side where Daniel always slept and covering with tears and kisses the leather bound book in which he had written the alphabet and the few words he had learnt to spell.

Nat and his father crept away before she could hear them.

Downstairs they sat at the table and his father extracted the piece of boiled beef from the pan and insisted on cutting slice after slice for Nat. Once he had taken a mouthful he ate compulsively, having scarcely tasted meat since quitting the army. Then he answered all his father's questions till the whole story was told.

"Where will they have buried him, I wonder," his father mused, his cheeks still wet from the tears he had shed during the relation. He lifted his eyes to the room above. "She will need to go and see."

Nat shook his head. "That has tormented me through all my journey home."

His father nodded and rose to his feet. "I think I will go into the church for a while and pray for her, that this will not send her mad." He said it softly and went softly out. It seemed to Nat that all his childhood his father had become more and more quiet with every outburst of his mother's.

He took up the wooden trencher to clean it and then saw his mother standing in the doorway clutching Daniel's book. The look she gave him was one of loathing.

"Oh Mother, do not be angry with *me*," he cried out. "If you must be angry, be angry with those who put him to death. Be angry with the Horden family. Sir John and his son Robert. Let your anger rest on them. I would have died for Dan. Without him I *am* dead. Can you not forgive me?"

She marched over to the window, picking up the meat knife from the table. What was she going to do? She stood with her back to him. Then, using the sharp point she scored something into the bottom corner of the glass, making a harsh rasping noise. She turned and faced him. It read "Death to the Hordens."

"That is your task, Nathaniel – or my anger will be heavy upon you for the rest of my days."

CHAPTER 7

Some weeks later, Bel found to her surprise that the chapel was to be dismantled and she was to be moved back there next to Henrietta's bed-chamber. The room was really no more than a dressing-room to her sister's larger one. The girls should have shared the one big bed but Henrietta, five years older, would never have anything to do with her.

While the room had been used for Mass its only furniture had been velvet covered stools for the tiny congregation, a small table for an altar, a cross and religious paintings and statues round the walls. The trapdoor that led to the priest's room had been hidden by the rug before the altar. Now all this had been removed and the room was the same long bare rectangle Bel remembered when she had slept there as a small child. What she couldn't remove was the memory of Father Patrick's head appearing and the leer on his face when he reached his hand towards her.

"Why has this been done?" she demanded of her father when he took her there to watch two of the men-servants set up her bed over the trap-door which she was pleased to see had been screwed down.

"Father Patrick is going away from this neighbourhood to take up a position elsewhere and there is no other willing to come out here to say a Mass. It is too dangerous on the roads."

Bel hugged herself with glee but all she said was, "But why do I have to move? I like my room at the back."

"So you can escape from the window?"

"Not now you have had it barred. I don't want to be next to Henrietta. She can come in when she wants through the communicating door."

"Which she always keeps bolted so *you* can not disturb *her* things. Arabella, you are showing that rebellious spirit again. I thought you were making an effort to curb it."

"I just like to understand the reasons for things."

"Well, the reason is that I would like to keep you under my eye, supervise your reading, your prayers, your learning, your daily deportment."

A thought struck her. "What will Mother and Henrietta do for Mass now?"

"There are houses in Newcastle where Mass is said. I prefer not to know where they are."

This intrigued Bel but she knew from his clipped voice that he would answer no more questions.

"I will see your clothes' chest brought in and your books. I trust this move will mark the turning over of a new leaf."

He went out and she walked over to the tall pointed window and looked out at the open view of lawns and carriage way with, directly opposite her window, the rather crude statue of the first Baronet Horden, her great-grandfather who had bought the title in 1611 when King James was raising money by selling honours. The estate, her father occasionally warned Robert, had never fully recovered from his notions of grandeur. The statue had been sculpted at his orders in his lifetime and showed him on horseback, his right arm brandishing his sword as if to display the extent of his land. Bel always felt a little embarrassed when she looked at it. Here at the front of the house were no crowding woods into which she could escape. The window could not even be opened. It was as narrow as a church window and there was a lingering smell in the room that had hung about ever since Masses had been said there. She had heard it referred to as incense which was a thing out of favour with the national church. It was all very bewildering.

As she stood gazing out she asked herself aloud, "What if they are all wrong and there is no God at all? Could I be happy then? No God, no guilt?" She heard the click of a bolt and Henrietta stood in the connecting doorway from her room.

"*I* didn't ask to have you here," she announced.

"I didn't ask to be here. The other room was bigger and it had that great oak chair. I could curl up in it."

"That was made specially for the old housekeeper. It was the housekeeper's room when I was little. I suppose there'll be a housekeeper again, so they'll need it."

"Why will there be a housekeeper again?" Bel was pursuing this conversation with some amazement. Henrietta was *talking* to her. True she was still standing in the doorway and regarding her with supercilious eyes. She knew things which Bel didn't know and despised her ignorance, but her superiority had put her in a good mood.

"When I go to France, Mother will come with me." She said it casually, admiring a ring on her finger as she leant her hand on the door post.

Bel sat down on her bed and gazed up at a broken piece of plasterwork at the corner of the ceiling. "Oh, so you and Mother are going to France, are you?" Inside she was whooping with delight.

Henrietta stepped across and slapped her hard. "You unnatural little monster – pretending such indifference when you are bursting to know why. I am going to be married of course, something that will never ever happen to you, you ugly awkward thing."

Bel wouldn't lift a hand to rub her cheek. She continued to gaze at the ceiling. "*I* won't be married off to someone I hardly know. I suppose it's that French vicomte you were betrothed to in your cradle. Haven't they been arguing about a settlement for years? I hear these things talked about, but I lost interest long ago."

Henrietta slapped her again. "Well *you* are not coming to the wedding. You would utterly disgrace the whole ceremony. If I had had a sister I could be proud of she would have attended me. But I'd rather have a Barbary ape dressed up than you."

Bel was working it all out. Had the French wedding been brought forward because Henrietta had an unhealthy passion for Father Patrick? Was that why the priest had gone and why she was to be moved here where Father could keep an eye on her? But was Mother coming back? If a housekeeper was to be engaged, was it for a short stay or a long one? She wanted to ask but kept her mouth firmly closed..

Henrietta moved back to the doorway and posed there. She was wearing a new gown of oyster silk. Perhaps she was trying on what she would be taking with her. "It will be so grand an occasion," she said as if musing to herself. "Mother is related to half the French nobility. It was a terrible descent to be married to a mere baronet. Father was travelling in France when they met, you know. France is where my heart is. I have always felt I belonged there rather than this obscure English outpost. Father had to come back here with his bride, but France is where Mother belongs by right. I may be presented to the King and Queen."

Bel could see out of the corner of her eye that Henrietta was twisting one of her long dark ringlets round her fingers and gazing at her reflection in the cheval glass in her own room. I haven't even got a hand mirror in here, she thought. Why, if she is going away for good, can I not have her room? But would I want it? This is like a monastic cell, ugly and awkward like me. The smell of her scent bottles will never leave *that* place. I couldn't bear it. She got up and strolled to the window. "I suppose," she chuckled, "when you get to France you'll not have to hide your priests in holes." She had the satisfaction of seeing Henrietta turn round and stare at her. "Oh yes, I know all about the false wall in the dining-room and the boards covered up under my bed. I expect they'll get rid of the stair and the wall down below so the good Scots who are in charge now will never suspect we were harbouring treacherous Papists here. What a relief that will be to Father! Even Robert doesn't want anyone in the army to know he has a Catholic Mother. That's all he cares about your precious Masses."

While Henrietta looked as if she would boil over it struck Bel that Robert was not going to his sister's wedding. That was a pity. Alone with Father and a new housekeeper she might find life bearable – if she could only blot out the gallows and the face and the one accusing eye. Suddenly weary of provoking her sister she flung herself on her bed and pulled the curtains round her.

Henrietta marched in and pulled back the one on that side. "You *are* a monster. I think there really is a devil in you, always has been since you were born. How glad I will be to see the last of you!" And she turned round and marched out of the room and slammed the door.

For once I can agree with Henrietta, Bel thought. I do have a devil inside me. He makes me do things that end with terrible consequences for other people, innocent people. But at least the devil can help me pay back Henrietta for years of scorn and meanness. The thought excited her and she began to plan what to do and look out for an opportunity.

They were to leave in early October and her chance came a few days before on a day when Henrietta had left the communicating door unbolted.

Seeing underwear spread out on her sister's bed she took a pair of scissors from her drawer and turned with glee to the pile of clothes. She would like to have chopped up her stays since Henrietta was so proud of her slender waist but the buckram in these proved too solid and resistant. The chemise was easy work and that was soon in shreds on the floor, so were the stockings of Chinese silk. There was a collection of lace collars and cuffs, lying apart from the gowns, ready to be folded into a white silken bag their mother had made for them. The scissors went through bag, collars and cuffs with delightful results, scattered like snowflakes about the room on chest and writing desk and the travelling trunk already standing in the room. Bel was about to start on the oyster silk gown but hesitated since its colour would spoil the snowy effect she had unwittingly created. She was sitting on the bed eyes screwed up to see it as a room transformed by a snow storm when Henrietta walked in and shrieked with horror.

Bel threw down the scissors and jumped away from her sister's flailing arms.

"Mother!" Henrietta was screaming, "see what the monster has done. Mother, mother!"

Father and Mother both appeared and took in the scene with increasing dismay as they realised where the flakes of white everywhere had come from.

"John! She is truly evil." Their mother had her arms round Henrietta who was sobbing with rage.

"Oh wretched child," Sir John cried. "How could you do such a thing? Think of the cost of replacing all those items."

Bel could see just what she must look like to all of them, her hands clasped in front of her face, thumbs pressing on her lips to hide a grin, mischievous eyebrows raised. She longed to find some satisfaction in their discomfiture but her initial glee had shrivelled away like a withering flower. Self-loathing sprang up in its place as she saw the bewilderment in her father's eyes. She bolted into her own room and shut the door. Keeping tight hold of the handle she put her ear to it.

"John, she's not fit for a Christian household," her mother said. "When I come back, I don't want her here. Send her away to a boarding establishment for girls till she has learnt – if she ever can – to be a civilised young lady."

"There are few such places. Are you thinking of Cranmore House in Yorkshire where Father Patrick has gone?"

"Why not? I could secure her a place there. I am only ashamed that anyone should know we have produced so fiendish a creature. Your preaching man seems to have roused the devil in her. Let us try other influences."

"Do they not charge twenty-five pounds a year?"

"Sell her pony," came Henrietta's voice still choked with tears. "She must pay for all my lovely things."

Bel shrank from the door as she heard her father step towards it. He plucked it open.

"Are you repentant yet, Arabella?"

She shook her head.

He sighed deeply and fingered the precise triangle of his beard. "I cannot have you here in your mother's absence. There are too many trials coming upon us. I have weighty matters to deal with. You will be sent to Cranmore House in Yorkshire as soon as it can be arranged."

"If Father Patrick is there it must be a Popish place."

"You have been listening at doors," cried her mother. "No, it is not Popish as you call it. Father Patrick may minister to a few girls from Catholic homes, but the place is a regular boarding school for young ladies."

Her father silenced her with a gesture and went quietly on, "You will not see Father Patrick. You will study there and also contribute by working at whatever tasks they put you to since I will send no money with you for your own spending. The fee they charge for your keep and teaching is as much as I can afford and we will see if the sale of your pony will defray the costs of what you have here so wantonly destroyed. Meanwhile, you will be locked in your room until you are prepared to apologise to your sister. She and your mother leave in four days' time and I wish to see a true reconciliation before they go."

He withdrew and bolted the door. She sat on her bed till she heard him come round to the passage door and bolt that too. She saw there was water in her big pewter jug and books on her shelf. How long, she wondered, can I hold out? Would they happily let me die here? Then she began to think about going away. She had never been away anywhere before and the prospect excited her. That Father Patrick might lurk about was a pity, but she would be safe among all the other girls and teachers.

I will meet so many new people, she realised. Here I am so alone and have too long to think. There I will be far away from the gallows and I may not see the corpse any more. That would be a miracle. Would the devil leave me then? But I would still be a murderer. I can never escape from that as long as I live even if I could be very good which I can't. So I must add lies to murder. Lies are not important. I'm sure all murderers tell lies.

She jumped up and banged on the door to her sister's room hearing their voices still in there. "I'm ready to say sorry," she called out.

Her father opened the door himself, beckoning her in and fixing her with that straight earnest look that she dreaded. "Truly sorry?"

"Yes, truly." She saw no effort had been made to clear up the mess. Henrietta would feel humiliated if she had to show her maid what had happened. "I'll pick every bit up." She swept the top of the trunk clear with the flat of her hand.

Their mother summoned Mary to fetch a brush and shovel.

"But how am I to get new collars and cuffs?" cried Henrietta. "And dear Mother made such a beautiful silk bag to put them in. How could you do such a thing, you wicked girl? You're jealous of my going to France, aren't you?"

"I believe she is sorry now," their father said. "And no doubt you are right, Henrietta, about her momentary childish fit of passion. We will see what a spell of discipline and hard work will do, Arabella. When times are peaceful again you may be allowed to visit your sister in her new home, but that will depend on your behaviour and the circumstances of the time."

Bel just managed to hold back an exclamation that she never wanted to go to France at all. Mary handed in the brush and shovel and went away surprised that she wasn't needed to use it herself. Bel found the little pieces of fabric flew about when she swept them but she stopped frequently to empty them into a leather bag which Henrietta wordlessly held out to her. When she thought she was finished there would be another and another pointed out with an outraged finger.

At last no more could be seen and Henrietta turned to her mother who had been watching from the bed. "I am not buying my lace in Newcastle. We must stay longer with Cousin Clifford Horden in London before we take ship for France. I must have time to choose, but what am I to wear on the journey? *She* doesn't have anything fit for me. Her cuffs are plain linen and always dirty."

"I shall spare you something of mine, my love."

Bel heard the endearment. Never had her mother said that to her. And they were to stay with the London Hordens, were they? This Cousin Clifford was the father of her own intended, young William Horden. He had visited Horden Hall when she was five or six.

I put my tongue out at him, she remembered, because he called me pig-face. Henrietta knows I'm meant to marry William, but nothing to do with me is of any interest – unless I force myself on her notice with my wickedness. I won't marry him, of course. I'm too ugly and Father won't be able to pay the dowry the London Hordens will demand, wealthy as they are already. She thought for a moment of her brief time of loving Sam Turner. She still saw him fleetingly in church on Sundays and on some weekdays when he delivered produce from the farm at the kitchen door. But he was all bound up with the horrible night of the stack burning and she could hardly bear to look at him.

Cranmore House, whatever it was like, would be new and different. The sooner she went the better. She backed to the connecting door and said, "I am really sorry and I hope my pony will fetch enough to pay for the new things."

Her mother and Henrietta, with raised eyebrows that expressed complete disbelief, watched her retreat.

When she was back in her room she splashed water from her jug onto her lips to wash away the taste of her apology.

The early October day was sharp and sparkling from an overnight frost as Nat fetched firewood from the shed under the parsonage eaves. He was carrying the axe and began to split the larger logs when his father came out with his finger to his lips.

"Just bring what's ready. Your mother is sleeping still and I believe she has slept the night through for the first time since ..." He had no need to finish the sentence.

Nat piled up the basket as his father went on, "It is the writing of the letter that has calmed her. She feels action has been taken at last, but I still have misgivings on your account about making an appeal to the authorities. In their eyes you are a deserter from the army and I would rather not have drawn attention at all to what must seem to them a minor incident amidst these great matters that are afoot at York."

Nat straightened up. "I know, Father. I understand. But there was such chaos in the army after the defeat at Newburn that I am not anxious on that account. If you had not written, Mother was threatening to borrow a horse from the Squire and ride to York herself as soon as she realised the King was there in Council. 'The King!' she shouted at me yesterday when you were visiting Granny Woodman. 'I will force my way into his presence and throw myself at his feet. Justice for my boy! He will have to listen to me. I swear I will go tomorrow if your father still refuses to do anything."

His father shook his head and drew a long sigh. "She said as much to me. To tell you the truth, Nat, she has worn me out with her pestering. At first she wanted me to write directly to Sir John Horden and I would have done that but when I consulted Lawyer Pinkerton in Easingwold he said a legal document from the Court of the North would be more likely to elicit a response from the baronet. For myself I only wish Daniel to rest in peace. All our friends here are sure of his innocence. He was not a great figure in the world's eyes whose name must be cleared for posterity."

"But, Father, they do think we should demand his body for burial in the graveyard and I believe the Squire would write to Sir John Horden as one baronet to another on your behalf if you asked him."

"All in good time. First the trial and sentencing should be investigated and shown up as a sham. If that is established, we cannot be accused of pleading for a felon. We will await the outcome of my letter to Lord Strafford first." Then he laid his hand on Nat's arm and indicated he should set down the basket and withdraw into the woodshed. "I cannot speak of this other matter in the house."

Nat felt something of great import was coming. His father's eyes were no longer hooded with sorrow but bright with excitement.

"I not only wrote a letter yesterday. I received one. I have not spoken to you of this, in case it came to naught, but I have been in correspondence with a friend at Queen's College, Cambridge."

A thrill of joy engulfed Nat's whole body. He looked over his raised clasped hands into his father's eyes and saw the same delight reflected there.

"I was a student with this man – Anthony Sparrow – and he has held a fellowship there for some years. I sent him examples of the theological studies you have done at home and of your proficiency in Latin and Greek. He says he is impressed but would wish of course to examine you himself when you come –"

"When I come! Oh father! But how? The cost –"

"I have been plain with him about my circumstances but there are sons there of other poor clergy. You would not be alone among the sizars and he is prepared to enter you for a bursary after your first term if you show promise."

"Sizars?"

"They are the lowliest rank of student, below commoners. They make a living waiting upon others. This is a regular practice and no disgrace –"

"Oh sir, never suppose I would object to that. To be at Cambridge. To study! You knew well that if anything could ever help me to bear the horrible loss of Daniel, this was it. And you have been secretly working for it since my return, amidst your own sorrow." Tears overcame him and he flung his arms about his father's neck. They clung together for a long minute till Nat relinquished him and asked "But, oh, sir, can I leave you alone with my mother and no servant?"

His father's moist eyes beamed at him. "Nay, I can take Jenny back now that my stipend has come and the workmen have been paid off and I will not have a hearty young man to feed. Only love the place and your studies as I did and I will be happy. It will be hard, but you are not used to luxury like some young men and I am certain you will avoid the drink and gambling which are the curse of student life."

"I can promise you that on my life. But how will I get to Cambridge? I would walk the whole way, but if I am truly to take up a place there I should arrive soon, should I not?"

"You will hire a horse. I have had a small sum of money laid up for that purpose ever since I saw you were good at your books. You should have gone two or three years ago but for your own reluctance to leave Daniel."

"And my mother's reluctance to have anything spent on me that could not also be spent on Daniel."

"I acknowledge that, but be not bitter towards her on that account.

She needed to lavish love on him and he repaid it a hundredfold without question. You were so forward as a small child that you swiftly outgrew her ministrations and I think she felt almost intimidated by your sharpness."

"But I was afraid of her anger. I always have been."

"But you didn't resent her love for Daniel?"

"No, because Daniel was so devoted to me."

"Indeed, he almost worshipped you. He marvelled at your cleverness and when you loved him back he was for ever grateful."

"I did love him. I loved him with a passion. I hope he knew how much –" Nat's voice shook. He grabbed the log basket again and moved outside.

His father checked him a moment. "I may be mistaken but I think that that intense brotherly love and constant companionship kept you from looking at young women by way of love. When you are away from home you will have many temptations in that direction, but I trust you can keep yourself chaste till you can enter the ministry and take a suitable wife from these parts."

Nat smiled through the tears in his eyes. "I would lie if I said I have never lusted after a woman, but I will endeavour to keep your council with God's help."

He opened the kitchen door and found his mother standing bewildered in the middle of the room still wearing her bed gown.

"I have slept long," she said. "I think I am befuddled with sleep." She looked about the room and out of the window. "Where is Daniel?" she asked.

CHAPTER 8

B‍EL sat on her travelling trunk in the hall, waiting for the coach to be brought round. She could feel nothing, neither regret, fear, curiosity nor excitement. She was a parcel, a mere lump of the life of this place called Horden Hall which was to be removed, carted away and set down in a strange place called Cranmore House.

Her father appeared holding a letter in his hand. His eyebrows were drawn together. "I regret, Arabella," he said, standing in front of her but with his attention hardly on her at all, "that a matter has come up demanding my attention. I will not be able to accompany you to Yorkshire. Robert has agreed to be your escort." Hearing her little snort of dismay he met her eyes briefly. "It may be that you will come home at Christmas time, but that depends a great deal on yourself." With difficulty he gave her a smile and a pat on the head. Then he crossed the hall and walked into the room he used as an estate office and shut the door.

That's it, she thought. That is my farewell from my father. She recalled the day he had waved off his wife and Henrietta with great ceremony. I am nothing, an encumbrance. And to have Robert for the journey!

She could hear the horses as the coach was brought to the front door. Nurse came bustling down the stairs with a coarse linen bag containing Bel's winter mittens and a short hooded cloak. "Keep it with you inside. It's mild enough this morning but it may turn. Stand up, then. Here's Tom to carry your trunk out." She looked her up and down. "Eh, well, you seem harmless enough just now, but I pray God they'll never let you near a pair of scissors. Go on with you. It's a happy day for me, for I'm to retire with a pension to my own wee cottage." She gave her a little push to follow Tom and the trunk. "I suppose I should see you tucked in, since you're the last through my hands, but you've been the hardest. Maybe I'm getting too old for bairns."

Bel clambered in and took the bag from her. If a word had been said about a goodbye kiss, she thought she would have burst into tears, so she said nothing and Nurse just leant in and pulled the rug over her knees and exclaimed, "Now, where's Master Robert?"

Robert came stalking round the house from the stables. "I thought we were to ride," he said to Nurse. "She could have got up behind me on Caesar and the trunk could have gone by carrier. I hate sitting in the coach." He got in, all thin elbows and knees, and scowled at Bel.

This protest was nonsense she knew because his own bag was already on top for the overnight halts that would be needed before they reached their destination. With no more fuss they trotted forward. She turned her head where the drive swept round and looked back at the Hall trying to feel something for the place, even with its ugly ostentatious statue in front. The tall rosy brick chimneys were catching a gleam of sunlight between clouds but the rest of the house, built of local stone to save money she had been told, looked sombre and forbidding. As well as the internal work Sir Ralph had had a new façade built and Bel had often heard from their father that his ancestor had sought his baronetcy on the strength of his improved mansion.

"We'll be giving this up, I shouldn't wonder," Robert said, twitching impatiently on the seat.

"What? The Hall?" she was surprised into asking.

"No, goose, the coach. It costs seventy pounds a year for farrier's charges and Tom's wages and livery. It's devilish being short of ready money for necessities."

"Are we poor suddenly, then? And of course my fault I suppose – twenty-five pounds for this school."

"That's a pity, too."

"Is there more trouble in the letter Father got this morning?"

"He's anxious about it, yes. But I've advised him to do nothing yet. In truth, I am minded to deal with it myself. I might seize the chance when we're in Yorkshire."

"I suppose you're not going to tell me what it is." As she had with Henrietta Bel marvelled that Robert was holding any sort of conversation with her but she was afraid that the very rarity of the event and the prickliness of their relationship would soon bring it to an end.

He shrugged. "It's of no import, really. It's just unlucky that the father of the villain he hanged for the rick-burning turns out to be a parson."

Bel felt her skin creep and crinkle. She fought with all her might to show no reaction. But Robert was insensitive to the effect of his words.

He went on, "They've appealed to the Court of the North in York for a commission of some sort to investigate the circumstances."

The coach went over a stone in the road and he swore. "You see, Caesar would have avoided that."

Bel had shut her eyes but swiftly opened them again to stare at the blur of hedgerows passing by. She knew now from long nights awake, that darkness conjured up the gallows picture too well. She saw her brother's sharp nose and chin pointed towards her.

"What do you care about such matters from a man's world? I'm only telling you because Father may be fined for not following due legal procedures. So don't start writing home for feminine fol de rols, laces and ribbons and perfumes and such. I know you'd chop them up if they were Hen's, but in a year or two you'll be wanting them yourself, if I know anything about young women." His sneering laugh implied he knew a great deal.

Bel took several slow breaths to get her voice under control. Then she brought out in a rush, "Does this parson live in Yorkshire, then?"

Robert raised his thin black eyebrows. Everything about him was thin and sharp. If he grows a beard when he's older, she thought, it'll be a little spike of a thing.

He shrugged again. "I believe so, but Father is hoping the King's business will take everyone's attention at present. He's minded to do nothing till he has talked to his lawyer, but I say this is as good a time as any. Lord Strafford will hardly look at it himself and if I can grease the palm of some lesser official, it will never go higher. Father is useless at managing these things. He thinks he must send a copy of the transcript of the proceedings, but it was that old Dame Leary in the village that wrote it down and who was she to have a hand in any law business, they'll be asking."

Bel was bursting to say that it was Robert himself who had incited the mob to the hanging and taken the outcome out of their father's hands, but she was afraid to betray how much she knew. All the same, she must keep Robert talking.

"What is the King's business you speak of?"

"What d'you think, numbskull? Getting the Scots' army out of England, of course. He's called all his peers to a Council in York to work out a peace treaty. Lord Strafford had to hot-foot it from Ireland, but he is Lord President of the North as well as Lord Deputy in Ireland. Can you imagine a man like that – in conference with his King on state matters – taking any notice of a letter from some country parson about a dim-witted son who got himself hanged for looting and rick-firing?"

"I see," she murmured. But she was not convinced that nothing would be done. One thing her father had conveyed to her all her childhood was the sanctity of the laws of England. He regarded his duties as a magistrate with great solemnity and his troubled face that morning showed plainly that he took the letter he had received very seriously indeed. She was sure that if some law commissioner from the Court of the North was sent to find out the whole truth of the incident, they would eventually unearth the identity of the fat boy and a constable would be sent to Cranmore House to arrest her. Perhaps that would be a huge relief. Perhaps they would hang her and she wouldn't have to go on living in this present hell. Unless the hell afterwards was all too real and horrible ...

When she lapsed into silence she realised after a while that Robert had too. She peered at him and saw his head inclined back into the padded corner and his eyes shut. She had never seen him asleep before. It was disconcerting but faintly exciting, giving her a strange sort of power over him. To keep her thoughts from his news she studied him. His short travelling cloak lay open showing his doublet of soft kid leather, embroidered with a fine black pattern of flowers and leaves in satin stitch. She was sure it had been expensive. The shirt showing in the front and through the slashed sleeve seams was of the finest linen and the falling collar was trimmed with the best lace. Protruding from it his scrawny neck and prominent Adam's apple looked slightly disgusting. The thinness of his legs was hidden by his breeches which were tied above his boots by purple ribbons. New shirts, ribbons and laces would be the necessities he had spoken of just now. As she considered him he shifted about and settled again with his back to her which seemed to express perfectly the relationship they had always had.

He is my brother, she reflected, and I really loathe him. What is the verse in the Bible? He that hateth his brother is in darkness. That's me, I am in darkness. And as a murderer I can never hope for anything else. She longed to sleep too, if only it could be without nightmares.

Nat had been a week in Cambridge and was still overwhelmed by the size of the city and its College buildings of such antiquity and beauty. He gazed up at the intricate timber roof of the hall of Queen's College, in awe at the workmanship. What was he, a poor parson's son from Yorkshire, doing in this magnificent place? And what am I doing anywhere without Daniel, he asked himself constantly, especially at morning prayers in the College chapel as the familiar liturgy washed over him. Father hoped new scenes would soothe my grief, but I need to feel Daniel's hand creep into mine and that smile light his face as he asks, "Daniel safe now?" I was his bulwark in strange places and his trust was my happiness, my confidence. Can I endure it here, alone, without him? And how did he endure those last hours of his without me? Why did I agree to join the army with him?

If only Mother hadn't called me 'the runt' and said I would grow up a "helpless weakling" like Father! I hated her to say that but I think she made me despise Father sometimes – God forgive me. Now I despise myself. Perhaps I am a coward. I couldn't bear the thought of a man impaled on my pike. I could feel it entering my own guts. I could feel it for Daniel. If I had said the Scots were evil men maybe he would have fought them but noise and conflict bewildered him and I believe he would have sat down and covered his ears in the midst of a battle. I knew that and yet I was too afraid of Mother to refuse to go. If I had been brave enough to take a stand against her, Daniel could be alive today.

When his thoughts reached this point he looked about him at the bowed student heads. So many new people about him and none of them Daniel. Despite the wonder of Cambridge and the relief of escaping from his mother's anger a pang of home-sickness for his father's steadfastness, for the shabby vicarage and the wide Yorkshire landscape gripped him.

I must not be afraid of this new life. If Daniel had not been taken away I would not be here, he thought. I can't wipe out the past but I can overlay it with the joy of study and I must seek new companions.

He had been allotted a room shared with another sizar, a lad of sixteen called Benjamin Hutton. At their first meeting Nat had been glad to find that there were others as lowly as he. Above them were ranks of pensioners, then fellow-commoners and finally noblemen. Benjamin's youth had also made Nat feel, at nineteen, old and experienced which compensated a little for his sense of awe and of his own insignificance in his new surroundings. But already he was aware of a seething rebellious spirit in Ben which had begun to make him feel uncomfortable.

"Will you endure this long?" Ben had demanded of him at the first dinner in College when they found that sizars had to wait till all the other students had eaten and then sit down to the left-overs.

Nat had responded as his father would have done. "Let us be thankful we are here. If we wait upon these noblemen's sons we can purchase books and writing materials."

"I can't eat paper," the boy grumbled. "And who are they that they should account themselves so much better than we?"

Nat had looked at him anxiously. Was he closeted with a revolutionary? All his life he had witnessed his father's humility. Of late he had seen how his mother's passion tore her apart. He had no wish now to be sucked into festering discontent with his lot. To be here at Cambridge University was almost a miracle.

Kneeling in the chapel he added a prayer for Benjamin Hutton, the opposite in every way from Daniel. Help me to see your purpose, Lord, in all this. This prickly youth may be the thorn I have to bear along with poverty and the loss of Daniel. Is this to be the test of my courage in a way my poor mother could never begin to understand?

Bel said a perfunctory goodbye to Robert as he left her at Cranmore House to proceed to York, where he said he would take a lodging for a night or two while "I deal with my father's business" as he put it – as if Sir John was not her father too.

Tom had set her trunk down in a bare passage and lifted his hat to her. "Ay, well, I hope you find a new life here to your liking, my little lady," and he turned to follow Robert out.

Compressing her lips to stop their trembling she watched him disappear. Then she sat down on her trunk, a parcel again that had been dumped here. The servant girl who had let them in had gone to fetch "the Mistress or someone" so she presumed something would happen soon. Meanwhile there was nothing here to look at but stone and the heavy oak door in front of her, now shut against the outside world. The walls and floor were all stone with slits of pointed windows so narrow that from her angle she could only see the thickness of the walls. Turning her head she saw that in the wall behind her were some low arched doorways, all closed. Total silence prevailed. How could this be a school? Where were the girls? It was exactly her idea of a nunnery, chill and Spartan.

Didn't I wish I could run away to a nunnery but I knew they had all been abolished? Maybe God has saved this one as a punishment for the devil in me. Maybe there is no one here at all. That servant has vanished now I am inside. I will sit here and freeze to death. Worse! Father Patrick will come, gliding round that corner. Alone with her thoughts, she felt a rising sense of panic. The cold striking up from the stone floor seemed to be entering her soul.

She was on the point of leaping up to try and open the solid front door when she heard pattering feet and a diminutive female figure came running from the passage where the maid had retreated. She wore a grey wool dress with white collar and cuffs and a bonnet such as Bel had never seen before, with a brim coming over her forehead and flaps at both sides so her face in the dim light was quite obscured. But what was even more strange was that she was holding out both arms and exclaiming, "Oh my poor child, sitting here alone. Where are your family?" The voice though curiously indistinct was that of an elderly woman though she was no taller than Bel.

Bel stood up as she approached, not sure if she was a nurse or a lower servant. She tried to make out the face. There seemed to be something odd about it.

"Did not your father bring you? You *are* Arabella Horden? Where is Sir John?" Her blurred voice had trouble with the name Arabella.

Now the person was so close she could reach out and seize Bel's hand; now Bel could look into her face despite the starched linen surrounding it. She recoiled in horror. There was almost no chin, the mouth was all twisted to one side and the face covered with blotches. All the horror of the hanged man's face came back. This was alive but almost as revolting.

The woman was not disconcerted by her reaction. In fact a weird cackling noise came from her. "Oh my pretty, you will get used to Old Ursula. I wear this bonnet so I can run by quickly and not frighten strangers but all the household know me and you will soon. I was born with my funny curly mouth and no chin to speak of and getting the small pox made it no better." The cackle came again and Bel, beginning to look with genuine curiosity, saw that the eyes were bright blue and twinkling with a fan of smiling lines at each corner. If she looked at them she need not notice the wreckage of the face below and something about them went straight to her inner cold. She felt the blood rush up her face and her eyes fill with tears.

The woman took her in her arms and hugged her tight. "My sweet precious, lonely little girl." Then she held her at arms' length and asked, "*Are* you Arabella Horden?" Again her lips had trouble framing the syllables.

"I like to be called Bel. Just B-E-L."

"Well, and isn't that a blessing for me! I can manage Bel." She laughed so much at this that Bel started to laugh too.

They were in the midst of this when the inner door nearest to them opened and a tall angular woman stood in the opening. Behind her Bel glimpsed rows of girls' heads lifted above desks and staring at her. It seemed unbelievable that they had all been there before in the silence.

"We are studying here and this noise is unseemly. I will deal with our new arrival, Ursula. She is the Horden young lady, I presume. Where is Sir John?"

Bel dropped a curtsey. "My brother brought me but he has gone on to York on urgent business." She was sorry to see Ursula backing away and then scurrying off round the corner of the passage.

The new lady turned to her class and motioning Bel forward she announced, "Young ladies, this is Arabella Horden, from Northumberland."

The girls rose, very straight-backed, at their desks, recited "Welcome, Arabella Horden," and sat down again just like puppets on strings.

I will never, ever, be like that, Bel thought. No one can make me. But she was now following the Mistress who had closed the door on her class and was stalking along the stone passage in the opposite direction, Bel was sorry to see, to the way Ursula had gone. It was soon obvious that the single-storey building formed four sides of a square and the dormitories led off the passage on the far side. She wondered who would carry her trunk all this way round. The Mistress stopped beside a bed. One of the narrow pointed windows was next to it and Bel looked out onto a quadrangle bordered by a walkway marked with stone arches at intervals but no roof.

She was so used to blurting out questions whenever something curious struck her that she found herself demanding, "Isn't that a cloister? Is this a nunnery?"

The Mistress opened her eyes very wide. They were a steely grey Bel noticed, not a sunny blue like Ursula's. "Of course it is not," the Mistress snapped. "You know perfectly well it is Cranmore House, an establishment for the education of young ladies. I am surprised that your father has not come with you. Did he give you the fee? It is customary to hand it over at the commencement of the year. I am unable to make any allowance for your late arrival."

"Oh, Robert did give me something." She drew a leather pouch from where she had stuffed it up her sleeve. One of the sovereigns dropped out so she picked it up and handed the pouch to the Mistress. She took it with apparent distaste but eagerly enough, Bel thought, and, turning her back, counted it out.

"There are only fifteen sovereigns here." She inserted the money into a reticule on her arm and faced Bel with eyebrows drawn into a single grey line.

Bel felt up her sleeve and looked down at the floor but there was nothing else. Robert must have taken out ten pounds for his own purposes.

"I don't know where it all is. What will you do, send me home again?" Now that she had seen Ursula she suddenly didn't want that to happen.

"We will trust it is an oversight. Write to your father tonight. Writing materials are provided on that table for letters home." She pointed to a long narrow table with benches each side down the middle of the dormitory. Bel had a vision of the girls sitting at it and all lifting their pens simultaneously, writing their letters, finishing at the same second and rising as one.

Patting her reticule the Mistress now looked at her with a more genial air. "I will have your box sent along. You have a cupboard there for your things. It was your mother who wrote to me, but I understand she was about to go to France for your sister's wedding. I trust they have had a safe journey."

"I suppose so. My father was expecting a letter soon."

"He was not going himself to give his daughter away?"

"Oh one of my mother's brothers was going to do that. It's to be all the French family and a Roman Catholic wedding so my father said he would be a fish out of water. I think that was the phrase he used."

The Mistress's eyebrows now arched and all but disappeared under the low curls she wore on her forehead. "You talk pertly for a young child, but now I must say to you what your mother asked me to say." She sat on the bed to be on Bel's eyelevel and looked at her very searchingly. "We are not, as I said emphatically, a nunnery. The girls go in procession to the parish church every Sunday, but there are *some* – of which your mother hoped you might be one – who are given the privilege of a Mass according to the old religion privately in a small room which you may hear referred to as the chapel. We do not call it that. This is simply a school, teaching young ladies deportment, needlework, the rudiments of music and other subjects, but for the sake of the consciences of a few we allow Father Patrick to visit. Your mother thought you needed to make confession of – I am sorry to say – many misdemeanours and Father –"

Bel's anger boiled over. Home was pursuing her and she would not stand it. "If that's *our* Father Patrick no, I shan't see him at all. He used to come to Horden Hall with his face hidden and creep about the place and hide in a hole if strangers were about who might report on us. I don't want anything to do with him."

The Mistress rose in shock and withdrew several paces from her as if she was a leper. "Control yourself, Arabella. Alas, I can see you are indeed going to be a troublesome child, as your mother feared." She looked up as two girls struggled into the dormitory with Bel's trunk. "I will speak to you later. Our evening meal is at five and there are two hours of Bible study and prayers before bed at eight o'clock for the younger girls. You may unfasten your box, but one of the teachers will come to inspect your things to see that nothing unsuitable has been brought in." She lifted her head and swept out into the passage.

The girls set down Bel's box and stared at her.

"How old are you?" one of them asked.

"Thirteen. How old are you?"

"Oh we are both fourteen." They wore their own dresses not the pupil dress of blue serge she had seen on the younger children. One was plump and the other skinny.

The plump one said to the other, "What a pity she doesn't want to see Father Patrick. He's so be-yooo-tiful."

"You were listening in the passage!" Bel shouted at them.

"Everybody does that here. It's how we find out things. Did you have Father Patrick visiting your house? You must be Catholics."

"My father and I are *not* Catholics. Are you?"

"Doesn't she ask a lot of questions for a new girl?" the skinny one giggled. "No we're not, but many girls are. We suspect the Mistress is, but if she admitted it the school would be closed down. Old Ursula is and she told us her great-grandmother was a nun here when King Henry's men came and all the nuns were thrown out."

Bel didn't want the loving Ursula to be tainted with Popery but she was pleased to be vindicated. "I *knew* it was a nunnery, but how could her great-grandmother have been a nun when they're not allowed to marry?"

"She was a novice, of course. She hadn't taken her vows. I wish they'd let the priests marry. I'd have Father Patrick any day."

"Is Ursula a teacher?" Bel asked. She had no wish to talk about Father Patrick.

"No. The mistress keeps her here out of pity. Old Urs always says she'd be a nun if it was allowed." She laughed. "She knew she'd never marry anyway. The bonnet thing she wears is a little like a nun's, but of course that's to hide her dreadful looks, poor thing. She just helps out all over the place, in the kitchen or if anyone's ill. When the weather's fine she takes girls into the gardens to tend the vegetable beds. Did you get an awful fright when you saw her?"

"Not at all," Bel lied defiantly. "She has such kind eyes."

A stout lady, with grey curls and a few hairs on her chin which Bel looked at with distaste, bustled in. "I am Madame Buchon and I teach French and needlework."

Bel just managed to stop herself from saying 'I can speak French already, but I *loathe* needlework.'

"Let's see your things now, Arabella Horden," she said and plucked at the cord round her box. The other girls retreated with grins and winks. Bel decided she didn't like them but perhaps it was because being in the company of other girls was a totally new experience. Looking at the row of beds she realised that the hours of solitude she had had at home were now over for what might be a very long time. It was good if she ceased to be plagued with nightmares about the hanging body. And then she remembered that Robert might soon be in York and the whole business could be brought to the light of day.

She sat down on her bed and helped with uninterested hands the stout teacher as she unfastened her trunk.

CHAPTER 9

November 1640

'*My dear Nathaniel,*

'*Your last letter gave me great delight, bringing back my own memories of College days in your pen-pictures of the roof of the Hall and the splendid President's Lodge, such a fine timbered building from the last century. I remember it well. I commiserate at your description of serving the Earl's son at the high table with so many and varied dishes and then finding so little left for the sizars. I am sure if you carry the platters into the kitchens the cooks will find you more to eat if it is only bread and cheese of which I recollect there was always a plentiful supply. I do not wish you to return to the spare figure you made on your sad return from Northumberland. Much work of the brain I know gives the stomach a hearty appetite.*

You ask whether I have yet received an answer to my plea to Lord Strafford and through him to the King's Majesty. I have indeed and enclose a copy of the letter which I am afraid will distress you, but I know you would rather be told the whole truth. I have so far managed to keep it from your poor mother. She speaks of going on foot herself to see Lord Strafford if he fails to give us satisfaction. We understand he has not removed to London yet, but is resting at his Yorkshire home.'

Nat at once cast his eyes on the enclosed paper headed with great flourishes from The Court of the North.

'*To the Reverend Joseph Wilson at the Parsonage of St Wilfrid's, Darrowswick in the County of Yorkshire.*

'*"Sir, your petition to the Earl of Strafford is to hand and a copy has been forwarded to Sir John Horden at Horden Hall, Northumberland, for him to make representations upon it as it concerns his actions as Justice of the Peace in the case of your son Daniel Wilson on the charges of looting and rick-burning.*

'I have to inform you that Sir John Horden has responded with great promptness by sending his son in person to York to show his willingness to report fully on the matter. It appears that the felonious activities of your son occurred after he had basely deserted the English force which had been sent to confront the invading Scots army at Newburn on the Tyne.

'Although beset with advancing enemy troops Sir John held a trial with witnesses and a jury of twelve men and gave your son full liberty to speak in his own defence. A verdict of guilty was pronounced and as Sir John was desirous of showing to the Scots army an example of firmness in the suppression of looting and ravaging of the country, the sentence of death was carried out without undue delay. This action greatly impressed the Scots commander, whose troops were already occupying the whole region, and he gave orders to his own men to behave with circumspection to the population, a commitment which has been fulfilled to the benefit and comfort of all.

'You will appreciate that the great matter of the peace treaty which has been occupying my Lord Strafford in the King's Council until the last week has delayed the sending of this answer to your petition till now.

'Inquiries have however been made among the commanders of the troops stationed here in York to confirm that your son, Daniel, had served in his Majesty's forces and his senior officer, having been traced, declared that both Daniel and his brother Nathaniel had been trained as pikemen but had been reported missing in the confusion following the skirmish at Newburn. Unfortunately many bodies from both sides of the battle were robbed by local marauders and remained unidentified. If you are aware of

the fate of your son, Nathaniel, Captain Carter would be pleased to hear of it but regrets he can offer nothing of himself with certainty.

'I trust, reverend sir, that you will accept that your petition has been dealt with in all fairness and justice and that I as clerk to the Court of the North have reported fully to my Lord Strafford and laid before him all your concerns, in proof whereof he appends his own signature to this letter.'

Nat looked with sinking heart and saw that it was indeed signed Thomas Wentworth, Earl of Strafford. Had the great man been shown the whole matter? Nat doubted it but the thing was done and as far as he could see there was nothing more his father could or should attempt, especially as his own name was involved.

He went on with his father's letter and found this was indeed his view. 'Stay quietly at your studies and come not home at all until I deem it safe for you to do so.'

Nat desired nothing more now than to stay in Cambridge. Although he longed to see his father, he was deriving such inward joy from the expansion of his mind that he wanted no interruption to his studies. Daily life was physically uncomfortable, with the cold and wet streaking in cutting winds across the fens and overwhelming the wretched fire which was all that he and Benjamin Hutton could afford to keep in the small grate. Hunger was harder to bear, but he had made a friend in the kitchen, a boy whom he was teaching to read, and he would slip Nat a raw carrot or piece of turnip at the end of the lesson. This he would secrete to his room under his gown and chew on slowly as he read so that something lay on his stomach for a while longer.

He took up his pen to reply to his father, but what most gripped his mind was dread of how his mother would behave when she realised that the petition had been rebuffed and his father intended no further action. She had not ceased to reiterate the task she had set for himself. Her farewell wave to him when he left for Cambridge was a tapping on the window where she had scratched the words 'Death to the Hordens.' "You know I can never call you a man until you have avenged your brother," were the last words she had said to him.

He laid down his pen. There was no need to write yet to his father. The cost of sending letters must be rationed out over the term and Christmas too if it was unwise to return home lest the army track him down. Am I afraid of that? Am I afraid to see my mother? He picked up a volume of Eusebius from his desk. Study of ancient texts was very comfortable, but this time the intrusive question went on pricking his mind as he read: I am a lover of peace. Does that make me at heart a coward?

When Bel had been three weeks at Cranmore House she received to her surprise a letter from Robert. So far she had had one brief letter from her father, enclosing without comment the missing ten pounds and hoping she was being very well-behaved but for Robert, lazy, cold, vindictive Robert to write ...!

'*Greetings, little sister*,' she read, '*You looked somewhat woebegone the day I left you and dashed off to York, but I must tell you my business there was most successful. The clerk at the Court of the North forwarded to Father a copy of the official reply he had sent to that old parson whose son we strung up.*'

Oh no! Bel slapped the letter down on her knee as the one-eyed body came swinging into view. Why does he have to write of that? But of course she must learn the outcome for she had never lost the fear that a constable might come for her here. She made herself read the next sentence.

'*It exonerated Father completely and he was delighted with my success. The fact is, I know how to deal with these things. I would have studied for the law, but of course Father needs me on the estate which I will inherit one*' *day. We are managing as best we can with the levies the Scots army makes upon us. The tenants are in arrears, of course, and I have to go round and stir them up. Turner never really recovered from the rick burning, though Father bought some of his cattle. The boy Sam has gone to work for a Scots captain who took a fancy to him and he sends money back to help the family. It will be a lean Christmas all round, I am afraid, but we have a pig fattening so you will not starve. Mother and Hen are living in luxury, of course, amidst mighty preparations for the wedding. We, in sad contrast, have given up our own coach. You will have to arrange to have your trunk sent by the carrier and I will come on Caesar to collect you. Pray don't suppose I am going to make a habit of this if you go back after Christmas. On winter roads, it is not a pastime I enjoy.*

Your affectionate brother,

Robert Horden.'

Bel noticed with astonishment the 'if' in the penultimate sentence. Is there some doubt that I will come back here? Father has paid a year's fees. I must come back to Ursula. I don't *like* it here, but I have no one at home I can talk to or who listens to me the way she does.

She wrote back to Robert. '*Thank you for your letter, Robert.*' She couldn't bring herself to write 'Dear Robert.' '*If it is a great trouble to you to come for me at Christmas, perhaps I should stay here which would also save you a journey back with me. A few pupils whose parents are abroad stay during the holidays and I enjoy helping out in the kitchen. We walk to the parish church in Easingwold, our nearest small town, every Sunday and round the courtyard every day unless we have rain. So it is like being in prison but not an unpleasant prison. Neither Mother nor Henrietta have written to me, but I suppose they don't want to remember I exist.*'

She decided not to allude to Robert's business in York. He had only been boasting about his own cleverness and she was sure some of the ten pounds of her fee money had gone to bribe the clerk. If it was all smoothed over she was glad for her father's sake, but bury it how she might the black guilt would never go away from her.

It was hard to know what else to put in the letter since she had never written one to him in her life. She couldn't comment on news of the Turners because Sam was linked with the ghastly event that had put an end to her childish belief that she was in love with him. What else could she write about Cranmore House? Robert would only think her proud if she wrote that because she had read all the books at home she knew much more about everything than the other girls, except in needlework where her stitches were big and her thread kept knotting. She couldn't tell him about Ursula, who came seeking her at least once every day with her eyes bright and her comical voice exclaiming, "Here's my lovely Bel. How are you chiming today?" It didn't matter if girls within earshot repeated, "Lovely! Bella Horden?" in voices sharp with scorn. She was used to scorn from Robert himself about her looks. How could she explain her joy in seeing Ursula happy behind real ugliness?

She finished it off with her loving duty to her father and scrawled her name at the bottom. As she expected she received no reply and the routine of Cranmore House closed round her till a day in late November brought unexpected excitement.

A sudden snow storm had blown over the moors and drifted into the quadrangle, cancelling the usual compulsory cloister walk. Bel was sitting on her bed drawing a picture, while many of the others in the dormitory were writing an extra letter home. She looked up to see Ursula approaching.

"Come into my cell, Bel," she chuckled. "You've never seen my cell, Bel, have you?"

Bel jumped up, tucked her drawing under her arm and followed her to what was indeed a cell, a bare stone room, narrower than her own chapel bedchamber at the Hall and a quarter of its length. There was a bed, one corner shelf with a crucifix and a rosary, and a chest for Ursula's few possessions which also served as a seat.

"I have a free half hour," Ursula said, "and who better to spend it with than my Bel." She perched on the bed and Bel sat on the chest, their knees almost touching.

"They knocked all the nuns' cells down but I begged them to keep one for me. Of course if any strangers are shown round, my poor dear Lord goes under my bed cover. May I see your drawing?"

Bel showed it her readily. It was of the village at home, Nether Horden, on a Midsummer Day festival. She had hoped by trying to recall a happy day there to blot out the horror of the gallows. But it had only reminded her of the indifference of the people to the dreadful structure on the hill above them. She was glad of Ursula's interest in it as a charming scene.

"You draw well, my pretty. Are you homesick for your little village?"

"Not a bit. It was just something to draw." She took it back and laid it on the stone floor at her feet and looked expectantly at Ursula, feeling there was a special reason for this summons.

Ursula's deformed mouth curled into what Bel now knew was a loving smile. "Now, my sweet girl," she began, "you and I have had many a talk together and I've rattled on about myself and my comical history and you've told me a little about your home, so I can guess why you are a lonely soul and why you find it hard to make friends. But there's something else, isn't there? I see a grey cloud in the air above you that's keeping the sun off my Bel and stopping her from shining as she should."

Bel looked up at the air above her. She certainly felt the cloud all the time but it astonished her that Ursula could *see* it. "You can't see what's *in* the cloud, Ursula?"

"I wish I could."

"No you don't."

It was easy to contradict Ursula because taking offence was no part of her nature. She could have added, "It would give you nightmares," but again Ursula's contentment would not accommodate such things. Everyone seemed to know she had been a bad girl at home and that was why she was here, but Ursula always dismissed this with, "You're not a bad girl with me."

So, she had already resolved, I can never tell Ursula I am a murderer. She truly loves me, amazing as that is, but if she knew I am possessed with a demon that would change. No one has ever loved me before and I am not going to throw that away.

She looked into Ursula's eyes to see how she took her abrupt reply and saw the yearning in them to reach her. No, she mustn't be reached. Even sitting together as close as this was almost frightening. She lowered her eyes and shook her head. "There are things –"

Ursula put out a hand and just touched her knee. "You could speak to the priest."

Bel jumped as if a snake had bitten her. "What! Father Patrick?"

"But he came here from your family. Did you never speak with him at Horden Hall?"

"No, no. Well, once." She couldn't lie to Ursula. "I don't like the way he moves like a shadow. I have glimpsed him here too, hooded like a monk."

"He has to be secret but I believe him to be wise, young as he is."

"Some of the girls call him beautiful."

"He has fine features indeed, but I set no store by that." She chuckled her merry laugh and Bel, who had grown hot and uncomfortable, gave a little smile of relief.

Ursula chuckled some more. "I'm obliged to set scant store by looks, am I not? But it's true enough that the good Lord looks inside and I think

He likes what He sees in Father Patrick."

Bel twisted her hands in her lap. "I could never – I don't *want* to speak to him."

"But speaking to a priest is like dropping a stone into a bottomless well." Ursula's lips had trouble framing 'bottomless' and she laughed again but Bel knew she was in earnest and when she brought out the next words it was with great emphasis on the sharp consonants. "Your cloud would be *gone*."

"I don't believe in priests."

"Then talk to the Lord."

Bel shook her head again. She had tried prayer but the demon in her lay between her and God. All the same, she was thinking, I could see Father Patrick if Ursula was there. It would break the dreadful monotony of school. I must not be wary of young men. Who do I know but Robert, whom I hate, and Sam Turner, who laughed at me that horrible day and Adam the stable boy, who loved my pony more than me and wouldn't have cared a jot if Paddy had thrown me. She lifted her head. "Would this Patrick come dressed as an ordinary man? I might see him then."

Ursula's bright eyes opened wide. "*Father* Patrick."

"He's no father to me. And I don't see why a young man should skulk about in long robes and a hood because he's a priest."

"But there are gangs about calling themselves Pym's Men who want to be rid of all priests. I hear the news from the market men in Easingwold who bring our provisions. And today they said the Puritans in town are roused because we failed to celebrate Gunpowder Night here. They want to know why."

"So Patrick – if he's here today – should dress like a man not a priest. But these fools should know that not every Catholic wants to blow up Parliament. My mother and sister didn't and I don't suppose this

Patrick does."

"Indeed he doesn't. But there are folk who believe every Catholic would like to bring a French army over here or a Spanish – I'm not sure which –" Ursula chuckled at her ignorance and indeed Bel had never heard any talk in Cranmore House of the outside world, except when one girl, whose father was a lowly official in York, read out in a letter from home that the Scots army was to be paid over eight hundred pounds a day while they stayed in the north of England. Bel was fascinated and wondered whose money it was that the Treaty of York was giving away so lavishly to the enemy.

"Well," she said, "if they think Patrick is spying for a foreign country he should do an ordinary job, like a gardener, and throw them off the scent."

Ursula laughed again but seeing Bel was serious she said, "And would you talk to him if he came to you in doublet and breeches?"

"Oh yes. Do you mean this morning? Will I miss lessons?"

Ursula jumped up. "I will see. The Mistress always accommodates young ladies wishing to –" She hesitated and Bel knew she would have said 'make their confession' but that the term might have provoked a rebellion.

To herself she said, Ursula hopes I'll unburden myself to this man but I won't of course. Never.

"You stay here, my precious," Ursula said at the door. "I won't be long."

Bel sat on, staring round the cell, clutching her arms across her chest for the cold. She could hear the wind moaning and when the light from the small window grew dim she got up and peered out. The sky had darkened and as she looked, another show shower began, one or two flakes at first drifting against the far cloister, but soon a wild flurry of them dancing in swirls about the quadrangle. She watched, delighted, until a male voice said behind her "Arabella?"

She swung round and in the doorway stood a young man in a plain dark

107

doublet and breeches, a very white shirt free of lace or any ornament except for the exquisitely chiselled face above it set off by dark hair curling onto his shoulders.

Bel almost laughed. This was her Satanic angel.

"You wanted to see me?" His voice was soft and low.

She could see Ursula hovering behind him just outside the open door.

I am not afraid of him now, she told herself, only what can I say to him? "Ursula suggested it," she muttered and, letting her gaze drop, she saw her drawing on the floor and picked it up as a distraction. He peered at it upside down.

"Nether Horden, is it not? A fine drawing but you have left out the hill and the gallows."

She shivered. "Yes," she said, in a tiny voice.

"Not in keeping with the happy scene?"

She nodded.

"And have you something you would like to speak to me about, not as a priest but as a friend of your family?"

Hot and cold went through her. The question had followed the picture too quickly. What did he know? Had things been found out and he was here to interrogate her? Report to her father about the night she was missing? She had fallen into a trap. But surely Ursula was innocent of laying it?

She just shook her head. "I've nothing to say."

His low murmur persisted. "Something has been weighing you down. Have you not a burden that you would like to cast off and make a fresh start. You may speak of it and it will go no further I promise you."

She glanced quickly up at him. His eyes were grey and probing. I don't believe him. He is not in his vestment and stole, hiding behind a grille, so a promise means nothing.

"Arabella," he said and she detected a steely authority in his voice as she had once before, authority coming all the way down from the Pope. But, she told herself, it shan't touch me. "Arabella," he said again, more gently, "your mother wrote to me. She wanted me to be in touch with you."

Mother! Bel thought. What does *she* know of the letter Father had, or Robert's visit to York? There was something strange here. She looked at him boldly at last and demanded, "Why?"

"Before your sister marries she would like you reconciled. Was there not a dreadful deed done," he paused, "with *scissors*?"

Bel stared. The fearful gallows shrivelled down and became a pair of *scissors*! She couldn't help it. She laughed aloud.

Ursula's face immediately appeared round the door, her eyebrows exclaiming, "Is all well?"

Bel nodded and grinned at her and she disappeared.

"You laugh about it?" Patrick had now sat down on the bed and Bel tried to push back the chest to get further away but it was too heavy.

"That was nothing. I was cross. I cut up some of her clothes. They sold my pony to pay for them and sent me here."

"But you were not sorry and Henrietta wishes to be at one with you as sisters should be before she is married."

"I *said* I was sorry."

"Were you?"

"Not a bit."

"So you lied, too."

"Yes." She was now recklessly speaking to him face to face. As an emissary from her mother and Henrietta he had become nobody special, despite his beautiful profile. Besides, she could see him glance at her budding breasts in a way no priest should.

"I am sorry you treat the matter so lightly," he was saying when the sound of heavy running feet echoed along the passage with girlish squeals and the Mistress's voice exclaiming, "What means this intrusion?"

Ursula came tumbling in, scrambled past Bel and grabbed crucifix and rosary and pushed them under her bed cover. With her hands over her mouth she stared at Father Patrick and mumbled, "Pym's Men."

He had jumped to his feet when four men appeared outside, three carrying staves and one an axe.

"This is he," the axe man cried. "Seize him."

Bel saw his face was ashen. The axe blade was two inches from his cheek.

One of the other men called out in agitation, "Have a care to the child."

Bel had leapt up, thrilling with excitement, and now she fixed the axe man with a ferocious glare. "What do you want with the drawing master, you foolish man? Can't you see he's giving me a lesson? Put that axe away before you do a mischief with it." She held up her drawing just as the Mistress came panting round the corner of the passage.

The four men looked at each other and the axe man lowered the axe.

"Drawing master?"

"Madam," Bel cried to the Mistress, "make these horrible men go away. They're interrupting my drawing lesson."

The Mistress's features, all awry with terror, struggled back inside her habitual mask of composure. "How dare you break into the peace of a school for young ladies, brandishing weapons? Have you no shame?"

"We heard you harbour a Popish priest here. And where was your bonfire on Gunpowder night and your festivities for that great deliverance from the Papists?"

The axe man was still eyeing Father Patrick with deep suspicion.

The Mistress replied, "We had long prayers of thankfulness." That was certainly true, Bel thought, very long. "But we have no wood to spare for bonfires. So get you gone."

"Let us see if he is truly a drawing teacher," one of the men said who had so far been silent. "Show us how you would improve the child's work." He made a sudden snatch at the picture from Bel's hand and thrust it under Father Patrick's nose. "Sit and make it better."

Patrick sank down again onto the bed, the men crowding into the doorway so that the Mistress was blotted out of sight in the passage behind. Ursula who had been all this time trapped at the window end of the cell handed over a pencil without showing her face. The axe man lifted the axe head again so that it gleamed at Patrick's eyelevel.

Bel saw how his hand shook as he took the pencil and his eye shifted to the blade inches away. What would he do? Why had Ursula co-operated so readily? She was exultant about her own part till now. But now it would go wrong and violence would be done right here and she would be to blame again.

But he was drawing. He had gained control of his voice too and he spoke as he worked. "To give the picture vitality there must be more light and shade." He was addressing Bel just as if it was a lesson. "Let us make the sunlight come from here. Then this gable and the side of this tree will be in shade and shadows will be cast here and here." A few rapid movements of the side of the pencil filled in the darks and it was true, the picture was coming to life.

Bel was back in the play-acting. "Thank you sir. I will remember that. Light and shade." She met the eyes of the axe man with a sweet smile.

The men looked at each other. "Where is the priest then?" said one.

"They will have a secret room," said another.

"Shall we search now?" said the third.

They turned to the axe man but his mouth had dropped open in horror and he was staring at Ursula who had lifted her face and pushed back her bonnet. "Don't you put the evil eye on me, you hag," he cried.

"And don't you bring axes into god-fearing folks' homes," she cried. "If you had taken life would not the Lord have required it of you at the day of judgment?"

He turned, growling, "Let's get out of here." There was a frantic struggle in the narrow doorway as they all tried to escape together and then they were pounding away past the Mistress, their boots ringing on the stone floor.

"I'll just see them off," Ursula said quietly, pulling her bonnet flaps round her face again.

"And bolt the outer door," the Mistress cried, her voice shrill with relief. "Jane Wyndham was sweeping snow as a punishment for hiding pastries on her book shelf That's when they broke in."

She came back to the door of Ursula's cell and looked from Bel to Father Patrick and back again. For once she seemed lost for words.

He said, "What can I say to this quick-thinking young lady? I believe she saved me from a horrible death." He had laid an arm across Bel's shoulders.

She wriggled it off, not caring for the feel of it there. "You were quick to scold me for lies before, but you didn't mind *that* one."

The Mistress clasped her hands together. "Oh Arabella, pert as always. But indeed you were bold to some effect there. If you can ever learn that there is a right time also for humility, you will become a great character one day. But we will not let your words remain lies. Father, I appoint you drawing master to Cranmore House, beginning today at nine in the morning, which I believe is some three hours ago."

Bel looked up at her and grinned just as Ursula came scuttling back.

"They ran away with their tails between their legs. Eh, Father, what think you of my precious Bel?"

"Arabella has the courage of a lion." He was looking her up and down with genuine admiration. Bel's flesh tingled as if he had stroked her.

112

"We will not use the word Father any more, Ursula, if you please," the Mistress said. "Master Dawson is our drawing teacher."

Ursula peered up at him and clapped her hands. "Eh, now that is a wonderful thing, for it's what you wanted to be before the Lord called you to something higher. Your mother told me that."

"Indeed. I travelled abroad and studied some of the great masters. But now, should I ... do I dare to spend more time here, putting you all in danger, Madam?" He was looking at the Mistress and Bel thought he had gone pale and trembling again at the thought of the mangled corpse he might so easily have become only a few minutes ago.

"If you were to disappear now," the Mistress said with great emphasis, "we might indeed be under suspicion. Ursula, I shall have to address the pupils before dangerous rumours fly about. Will you see they are all called to the refectory now, though the dinner hour has not quite arrived? Arabella, you will accompany me and Fa – Master Dawson, you also." She sailed forth with one hand on Bel's shoulder, propelling her along.

Bel was experiencing the strangest thoughts. She had pictured this young man hacked about with an axe but here he was beside her, whole and untouched, because of *her*. Have I dispelled my black cloud? Is it possible that saving this life has made up for the one I took away? I am about to be publicly commended, a thing that never happened to me in my life. Can it wipe out the guilt of my unrelated sin? But when they reached the refectory the Mistress just waved her to her own class and she found nothing was to be said at all about her part in the incident.

The Mistress chose her words with extreme care. "Young ladies, you will be aware of a disturbing incident just now. Not one of you was ever for a moment in danger and there is no need for any of you to report this outside these walls. You would only alarm your families, who were unable to see that it was all dealt with in a few moments and was entirely due to a misunderstanding. Some men acting on a false report believed some wrongdoer had taken refuge here. As soon as they realised their mistake, they left. Stand forth Jane Wyndham." A damp-looking girl stood up. "You will complete your punishment of clearing snow for fifteen minutes *within the courtyard,* not outside the front door, but you do not need to do it until the present fall has ceased." She glanced at the pointed windows where moving whiteness was all that could be seen. "No pupil is to keep food among her books. It is a disgusting habit. You may sit, Jane. And now I wish to introduce to you Master Dawson, who is here to give drawing lessons. He will take the lowest class for an hour after dinner today. You may stand and welcome him."

The girls rose as one. "Welcome, Master Dawson."

As they sat down again Bel sensed the buzz of talk bursting to break through the disciplined silence. Eyes darted, lips twitched. No one has been fooled for a second, she thought, but I have lost my eulogy of praise and now that the exhilaration of the moment has passed, I feel a little sick and I can't look at Master Dawson without seeing his beautiful face cleft through with that shining blade. It didn't happen. He's standing there alive and well and only looking embarrassed. But that horrible strangulation *did* happen. One minute there was a big, healthy young man and the next he was a ghastly dangling corpse and then the crows came ... Oh, it has become more real than ever. It should have been prevented, as today's killing was, but it happened. I was the cause of it and I was the only one who could have stopped it. What was the use of my cleverness just now when that is still for ever hanging over me? She wanted to weep into her dinner when it came.

At mealtimes the girls were allowed to talk quietly. Today the whispers were like a swarm of wasps about Bel's ears. Those at her table hissed questions at her.

"You were *there,* Bella, weren't you?"

"What happened?"

"Why are you sitting on your drawing?"

"Did Father P want to see it?"

"Is he really going to take us for drawing?"

"The men wanted to seize him, didn't they?"

"Why won't you tell us?"

At last Bel rounded on them. "I only went to see Ursula's room. It seems strange men break into people's houses these days for very little reason. They went out again and that was that."

The girls tut-tutted with frustration till one said, "Never mind, we'll find it all out from Ursula."

They did soon enough but Bel knew that her obstinacy and aloofness left them torn between fear and admiration. Some said she was a witch and only someone as hideous as Ursula, who must have been cursed at birth, could find delight in her.

In bed that night she found herself reliving the excitement of staring the axe man in the face. I didn't do it for Patrick Dawson. I did it because I was angry with the men and their silly weapons. I had no fear for myself. Maybe my devil makes me bold. If I am damned already what else is there to fear?

She waited to see if the new drawing master would try to speak to her alone again but her presence seemed to trouble him and he would only glance at her work and murmur, "Very good, Arabella," and pass on. He owes me too much, she reflected, or I remind him of how close that axe was to his precious face. And then she would remember the constant hovering of her own cloud, which touched not her present existence but her eternal life and she would cease to feel sorry for him.

CHAPTER 10

ONE chill morning later in November Nathaniel was crossing the quad with other students when a pamphleteer who had come in off the street accosted him to buy his news-sheet. Nathaniel shook his head but Ben Hutton who was more prodigal of his meagre funds bought one.

"Ah, ha," he cried, standing still to read it, "Lord Strafford has no sooner arrived in London from Yorkshire and taken his seat in the Lords than he has been impeached by the leader of the Commons, John Pym. He is in custody now."

Nathaniel, drawing his threadbare gown round him against the cold, peered over his shoulder. It was not so long since he had received his father's letter. So ends any hope of further appeals in that direction, he thought. How easily these days the great can fall from grace!

Ben grinned at him as he read on. "It seems there are moves afoot too, to abolish the courts that give the people direct access to the King, even the Star Chamber Court. Now is that not right and fair? The law rests not in the King alone but in the King through Parliament."

"You are in a minority here, Hutton," another student cried. "Queens' stands for the King."

Some cheers went up and Nathaniel sensed that the noblemen's sons in particular were dismayed at the news about Lord Strafford. Although the Earl was not popular in the country, they were shocked that things should have come to such a pass for the King's favourite. Nathaniel, who appreciated more and more as he had grown from boy to man the wisdom of his father's gentle tolerance in the face of his mother's fanaticism, struggled to understand what was happening to his country. Why were these gulfs opening up between factions? Of course, if the Earl had intended to quell the invading Scots and their puritanical sympathisers in England with an army from Ireland, he must answer for it, but his impeachment was only one of the divisive topics that had begun to infiltrate even this aloof centre of ancient learning.

There were a few Roman Catholics in College with their own tutors, although the law actually banned them from both Universities but they kept themselves apart and the other students didn't find their presence a threat. Since the crushing of the gunpowder plot, Roman Catholics were lying low and now it was the Bishops and ceremonies of the Church of England that were arousing extreme loathing even among intelligent young students. To find here the same attitudes as those of the rabble who had ransacked his poor father's church was a shock.

After morning lectures when they next met up in their room, Nathaniel tried to share his plea for tolerance with Benjamin, but he only became more aggressive. No doubt he was spouting the views of his father, who was a tailor and had, according to Benjamin, joined one of the London mobs that had hurled eggs at the coach of the Archbishop of Canterbury.

Nat exclaimed, "Would our Lord have done such a thing?"

To which Benjamin retorted, "Did He not call the Pharisees a generation of vipers? Did He not overthrow the tables of the money changers? He exhorted his followers to worship in spirit and in truth. Everything that comes in the way of that must be eradicated. Bishops in their fine robes, idolatrous images in churches, stained glass that distracts the eyes from the preacher; sweep them all away."

"Nay," Nat protested, "let us all live peaceably together. Has not this country had enough of religious strife in the reigns of Mary and Elizabeth? We have settled into a largely Protestant nation. Surely to God we are not going to split again."

"And we will not when both church and state have been purged of the trappings of power. The Scots Covenant is one step on the way, but the goal is the humbling of all Archbishops, Bishops, Kings and nobles and the proclamation of the equality of all men under God. Only then will there be peace and contentment throughout the land."

Nat leapt up from his desk and faced the boy. "You are spouting the seditious rubbish you have heard from the pulpits of some of the preachers that followed the Scots commissioner to London. I have read of them ..."

"Ay," jeered Benjamin, "and they were heard by thousands when the churches were nearly empty."

Nat considered the boy. He had all the self-assurance of the Londoner who believed life began and ended in the capital. What he had said might be true. Nat had heard his father remark on the strength of the Puritans in London, but to speak against the King himself, however obliquely, surely that amounted to treason.

"Ben," he said gently, "you and I have to share this small room. Can we agree to keep our opinions to ourselves on contentious matters?"

"Ha! You're afraid my arguments are too strong for you. Well, you'll see. If it comes to war, you'll be on the losing side."

"War! Do you mean *civil* war?"

The more Nat studied the boy's cheeky white face under his close-cropped black hair, his slight frame and jaunty assertive air, the more he yearned for Daniel's height and breadth and untidy flaxen thatch above his round rosy face and smiling eyes always ready to signal acquiescence. The gentle giant had gone, to be replaced by this pernicious goblin. Is this my trial? Is this a punishment my mother has cursed upon me for not avenging Daniel?

He turned and sat down at his desk as Benjamin gabbled, "Why not civil war? The King will not listen to his people. In the end a fight may be inevitable."

Nat half turned his head. "Have you no studies to do? You told me your father wants you to take your degree and enter Parliament. How will you do that if you don't attend to your books?"

"I'm too cold and hungry," Ben said, suddenly sounding like a little boy.

Nat laughed. "Put some of your ideas on the fire and make a blaze. Here!" He opened his desk and threw him a hunk of bread he had had been saving for later. "Chew that and hold your peace for a while."

"Thanks, Nat. That will be remembered in your favour on the day of judgment."

Nat bowed his head over his book to hide his mirth.

December began as cold and wet in Yorkshire as it was in Cambridge. Bel began to long for the comforts of Horden Hall. In winter there fires were lit in all the bedrooms. The Christmas table would be laden with the fattened pig and probably a goose and some pigeons. Here, meat of any sort was meagrely dispensed and as she had heard that the Mistress would be returning to her own family home in the holiday and the grim Madame Buchon left in charge, she feared the festivities would be kept to a minimum. Why did I write to Robert to excuse him from coming for me? she thought. Why hasn't Father written again? She had just sat down at the table to pen a letter home when a bundle of letters was brought in and there was one for her from Father himself. She opened it eagerly.

'*My dear Arabella,*' he wrote, '*Robert has shown me your last letter and I am pleased to see your readiness to consider others before yourself. You understand the expense and inconvenience of sending Robert for you on the very bad winter roads and indeed such travel is not at all advisable for the health of a young girl.*'

Oh what a fool she had been! Anger seethed up from the pit of her stomach against herself and against the coldness of his words. He was 'pleased' with her compliance, but still glad to be rid of her. She was inclined to tear up the letter and read no more but she had seen that it filled the page so she read on out of curiosity.

'*As you can be accommodated at Cranmore House without further expense, we will accede to this arrangement and trust that you will continue to give satisfaction by your diligence in study and in acts of helpfulness about the school. I have received a letter from your Mistress hinting that you have shown exemplary behaviour on an unspecified occasion and I am very gratified by that.*'

That irritated her. The Mistress had written to him but managed not to describe what had really happened. She felt cheated of approbation on all sides. Without much interest she looked at the next paragraph and found to her surprise that her very reserved father was writing about his own health.

'*I have not been well myself with a troublesome cough and have been obliged to commit many of my estate duties to Robert. These cold wet days I have stayed within doors and have written to resign my office of magistrate, which I feel no longer able to undertake. With the Scots forces still quartered here and no immediate prospect of their withdrawal, I feel keenly that our traditional and settled system for the administration of the law has been disrupted.*'

Oh yes, she thought, he always treasured the sanctity of the laws of England. He was distressed about that sham trial he conducted. I am older now and I see him from afar as a man, not just an inadequate father. Fancy him confiding all this to *me*. She began to feel a little sorry for him and turned to the last paragraph.

'*It is sad and lonely here without your mother and sister, now of course a Vicomtesse, but I shall hope for a visit from them in the Spring and also from you, my dear little one.*

Meanwhile I remain,

Your affectionate father,

John Horden.'

Bel covered her face with her hands. She could feel tears welling up from deep inside her. The words 'my dear little one' were so new and strange. Her shoulders shook. She couldn't fight it. An uncontrollable paroxysm of weeping broke from her, shocking and shaming her.

Jane Wyndham came over to her. "Have you had bad news?"

Bel shook her head.

"But you're crying?"

Another girl called out, "Some of you said she's a witch but witches can't cry."

"Maybe they can, for nothing," Jane giggled. "Truly, Bella, what's up?"

Bel squirmed off the bench clutching her letter. "Just leave me alone." She scurried out of the dormitory and went to seek Ursula but before she reached the kitchen door she managed to choke back her sobs and ask herself the question; why should I cry because my father might after all love me a little? Is it because Spring is so very far away and suddenly I want to be with him now? She stood still, struggling against another outburst, and the stone passage above, below and all round her struck icy cold into her bones. Then she heard scampering feet and Ursula appeared round the corner from the kitchen.

"I was sure it was you, my Bel." Ursula had the sharpest hearing. "Something must be wrong to upset you so."

Bel tried to laugh. "After all this time, I feel homesick." She held out the letter.

"Oh Bel, I can't read writing like that. I can read big print but that's just spiders crawling across the page."

Bel read it to her, though she felt she was laying herself bare as she did so. Ursula will know why I cried. I mustn't do that again. Even she must not get too far inside me.

Ursula just hugged her tight. "Maybe it needed that waterfall to empty the grey cloud. We'll be very jolly here and you shall go home for Easter. Your father calls you his little one, but by then you'll be quite the young lady. You are already slimmer and taller than you were when I first saw you sitting on your trunk, such a lonesome soul. Can you be happy now?"

She was so comical, the way she poked her head on one side in her absurd bonnet, that Bel managed a laugh to please her. But she was thinking, Ursula couldn't ever have really seen a cloud over my head, or she would know it's still there and always will be. She sniffed and drew a shuddering sigh and countered Ursula's question with her own. "Would you not think that my mother and sister might also write?"

"Oh I feel sure they will." Ursula's lopsided smile and twinkling eyes seemed to suggest a secret confidence and the very next day a packet of letters arrived from France.

"You are a soothsayer," Bel challenged her. "How did you know this was coming?"

"I was sure it would come before Christmas. And now you can answer it too. Then there will be happiness everywhere." She gave a little skip of glee and ran back to the mincemeat she was making.

She has had something to do with it, Bel thought, wandering back to the dormitory. She has told Patrick Dawson to write to France. Well, let us see if Mother and Hen can also become human beings like Father.

The first missive she read was from Henrietta, a long account of the wedding with every detail of her gown and its trimmings down to the last flower in gold leaf that adorned her silk gloves. This was followed by a description of the family home of the Vicomte, where they had their own suite of rooms in one wing of the chateau. 'Mother will stay with us till the Spring,' she concluded, 'and then we may both make a visit to England when we hope to see you at Horden.'

There was no inquiry about Bel's life, no plea for reconciliation, not a mention of *scissors*.

Bel turned to her mother's letters. Again they had been written over several weeks and covered much of the same ground as Henrietta's, though she also became lyrical about how beautiful Henrietta had looked as a bride. It was this that led her on to a more personal note.

'*I look forward to seeing you too as a bride, Arabella, perhaps next year. Though you cannot aspire to beauty you can, with care and good deportment, make a very presentable young lady. I had hoped and Henrietta hoped too that we could have made a loving parting from you if you had shown yourself truly sorry for the upset you caused, but now I wish us to put that behind us as I believe you are become quite a different person under the benign influence of Cranmore House. You were a petulant child and now you are a young woman of courage. I always felt when you were born that you were meant to be a boy and would have been happier as a boy but you must accept your lot in life and learn feminine ways. These are not incompatible with bravery and resourcefulness. Indeed with grace and modesty they become a young woman. I look forward to seeing you in the Spring and finding you a dutiful companion as a daughter should be to her mother. Although life here is so charming and civilised compared with the bleak north of England I intend to stay by your dear father's side at least for the summer to see him well again. Perhaps I can persuade him to return with me to France for his health's sake during the harsh winter months. Pray give my greetings to your Mistress and the other teachers, including the drawing master, and may the blessings of Christmastide rest upon you.*

Your affectionate mother,

Maria Horden.'

Bel folded up all this paper without any tears and stuffed it in her trunk.

The only thing that moved her was the allusion to her father's health. Perhaps he was more ill than she had imagined. I suppose I must write back to Mother and Hen, like a dutiful daughter and sister, she thought, though how do they think I can pay for a letter to France?

But when she gave her mother's message the Mistress handed her writing materials and told her, "Master Dawson will be going to France, Arabella. You may bring me your letters and I will see that he takes them."

So Bel took care that her reply was beautifully phrased and spelt, expressing her gratitude for the long account of the wedding and telling them of the excellent teaching she was receiving and what pleasant companions all the young ladies were. They will not believe any of that but they will be pleased to see that I have at last entered an adult world of courtly hypocrisy, she thought, as she folded the letter small and sealed it down.

But she felt a little guilty when Ursula danced her joyously round the kitchen on hearing that their letters and her reply had been all friendliness.

"My Bel is chiming pure and true now with no muffling cloud. Now we can indeed sing God rest you merry to one and all this Christmas."

The girls were saddened though at the news that the drawing master would be away. They all declared they were violently in love with him, but Bel could conjure up no reverence for him as a priest and little respect for him as a drawing master. Since the few moments when under threat of death he had managed to show her how to improve her picture he had not inspired his pupils. He seemed always distracted and nervous, eying their figures rather than their drawings and glancing anxiously at the schoolroom door in case death came stalking in again.

It was the day of his departure and Bel was helping Ursula change the linen on the beds of the girls who had already gone home when they found among the pile of fresh linen a pair of coarse sheets, grey with age.

"Oh bless me, those are mine," Ursula exclaimed. "Can you run with them to my little cell and just leave them there? I'll see to them later."

Bel strode off with the manly walk she always assumed in defiance of the 'elegant young lady' she was supposed to be and cannoned into Patrick Dawson, carrying a travelling bag towards the front door.

"Arabella! I beg your pardon," he exclaimed.

"And I yours," she laughed. She loved to look at his perfect features but felt almost nothing for this man whose life she had saved. She grinned at him with most unladylike ease, till she noticed a strange yearning expression in his grey eyes.

"Where were you going with those?" he asked looking at the sheets.

"To Ursula's room."

"I'll walk along with you. I wanted to speak to you before I left."

"But you are coming back after Christmas?"

"No, no, I really can't stay here now." He was breathless. They reached the door of Ursula's cell and he came in after her and pushed the door to behind him. Bel laid the sheets on the bed and stood very straight and stared him in the eye.

He was between her and the door and she didn't trust him an inch.

"Yes, you see," he rushed on, "you know better than anyone that I am a danger to this place. It has been very good of the Mistress to let me stay, but I feel I must leave the country and if I go I may never be able to come back. All is changing here. The King has had to dismiss the Queen's people. We are never going to be safe here while this Parliament ..."

Bel broke in, "Why are you telling *me* this? It's nothing to me what you do or where you go."

"I hoped it was. No, I mean, I am going to France. I will visit your mother and sister. I wrote to them what you did, that you were my saviour. Oh, if I could come back ... if I could renounce my office ... I should never have become a priest. Why do you think your mother brought on so swiftly your sister's marriage? Henrietta had a passion for me and I for her. She was so beautiful. I had to leave, but here it is all young women and you ... you stand out from the crowd. You are young but you have such character. You never mingle with the others. You carry yourself proudly. You are aloof. At the same time you have a look of her ..."

"Her! You can't mean Henrietta!"

"But I do. I know she is beautiful ..."

"And I am ugly."

"No, you are not. I see you with the eye of an artist. That square jaw you think ugly ... no, the line is strong and as you grow into womanhood that fine bone structure of your whole face will have beauty. Oh if I could come back in a few years without the burden of priesthood ... but we know not what lies ahead for us. What can I say?"

"You have said more than enough, Father Patrick."

"No, not that, please. Master Dawson if you will, or just Patrick."

"If I understand this nonsense at all, it is that you would like to give up being a priest, come back when I'm grown, marry me and be close to Henrietta again without suspicion. Now, may I please pass and go back to Ursula, who will be wondering what I am doing and will be very surprised when I tell her what has passed in here."

"But you wouldn't? And you have misunderstood me. Henrietta is married and for ever out of my thoughts. It is you I have observed. There is a quality about you which she lacks. You do not set out to please or charm as she does. There is nothing false in you. You do what you have to do, but it touches you not at all. You are only happy with Ursula for she is pure love. But I could love you as a man; a love you will need one day if you do not seek it yet." He put out a hand and touched her breast.

She smacked the hand hard, punched his midriff and when he shrank back, bolted past him and out of the door. She ran furiously back to Ursula, bursting to tell her all, but the moment she saw her, bent busily over one of the beds, tucking in the quilt and then looking brightly round at her with those eyes shining with smiles she knew she couldn't speak of it.

How could I hurt her? she thought. She thinks ill of no one. She has never had a man touch her. She never will and nor will I ever again if I can help it. I hate men. All except that poor innocent hanged man who was only hungry when he took that hen. The world says I am old enough to be married. When I was still young, I thought I was in love with Sam Turner, but that was when he was good fun and before the THING happened. Now I see all the bad in people, as I did in him. He became scornful, callous, shallow. More like Robert. And this hollow, lecherous priest is the same. What would the other girls have given to have him touch them, or say the things he has just said to me! As she tucked in the next sheet she surreptitiously rubbed her breast where he had touched it. The place was defiled.

Her thoughts still seethed. I am sure as anything that the devil is still inside me. Henrietta said I had a devil and she was right. I see evil in everyone except Ursula. Henrietta and Patrick! Did Henrietta suffer when he was sent away and she was whisked off to France to be married? She showed no sign of grief or torment. She loved his pretty face as these girls do. Patrick is flattering himself. He can't keep his eyes away from all this female flesh around him. But whatever the truth of it I can never love my sister enough to feel sorry for her.

Bel was so deep in her thoughts that she started when Ursula said, "Next bed, my precious. You have tucked that one over and over again." She was chuckling in her gladsome abandoned way as if the grim grey room and the grim grey day outside were a flowery meadow under a summer sun.

Bel laughed with her and moved over beside her. She could tell from the expression of the poor twisted face that Ursula guessed that the cloud might be hovering again. *She can sense that but she is too innocent to see how evil I am. I must never destroy her happiness. She must never know my dark secret. Let her sing all day long. She has no devil in her. I suppose she is actually a saint, a beautiful hideous saint, and I need her always beside me. How will it be when I go home for Easter?* Suddenly she was fearful of the prospect.

Benjamin Hutton came bounding up their staircase and burst in upon Nat. His pale face was glistening with the effort and alight with joy at the news from London.

"They've arrested the Archbishop of Canterbury."

Nat looked up. "Poor man. He's old. They could have let him die in peace."

"But did I not tell you that the petition last week would succeed? There were fifteen hundred signatories demanding the abolition of 'the ungodly institution of Bishops root and branch.' Root and branch. Is not the Archbishop the root and all the rest the branches? You said it was too extreme and nothing would come of it."

"Where have they taken the sad old man?"

"To the house of the Sergeant-at-Arms, but it will be the Tower presently."

Nat felt nothing but disgust that this peevish youth should exult over the fall of Laud. Maybe the Archbishop had pushed the Church of England too far back towards Rome and provoked these so-called purgers and purifiers, but he never abandoned the prayer book which Nat's own father had stood by through thick and thin. "Pray keep silence, Benjamin, for a while if that is possible for you. I have received a letter from my father which I am anxious to finish reading."

Benjamin slouched out of the room saying he would find someone with the right notions. "They will be rejoicing at Emmanuel."

Nat had heard there was a large Puritan faction there and he heartily wished Benjamin would enrol there and leave him in peace. He turned back to his father's letter. The first sentence expressed his joy that Nat had been awarded a scholarship but reiterated the sad advice that he should not return to Yorkshire for Christmas.

He read on, seeing a name which filled him with apprehension.

'*I have had a visit from Captain Carter inquiring about your whereabouts. I told him the truth but I fear it was only partial truth – that you had been seized with a fever and left behind when the regiment went forward and that you were stricken with grief on learning what had happened to your brother. I acknowledged that you should have reported to him when you were recovered, but in the retreat of the army from Newcastle you were never reunited with your troop. I pointed out that you had since received a place at Cambridge and it was necessary to take it up or lose it. He seemed to accept that and I don't believe he will take things further. Indeed the army may well be disbanded as he admitted that pay was seriously in arrears. All would then have been well but as he was about to mount his horse your mother came running from the house and laid hold of his sleeve. "Where have you buried my Daniel?" she demanded, not understanding I suppose that he could have no knowledge of that. "Do you not care for the men under your command? Are you satisfied that they should be falsely accused and hung? When will you lead a troop to Horden Hall and arrest those murderers?" I disengaged her with difficulty and murmured to him that her mind had been turned by grief but this she heard and seized upon. "My mind is clear that we have had no redress, we know not even where he is buried." Anxious to ride away Captain Carter assured her he would make inquiries but she shouted after him, "I writ to Sir John Horden myself to demand the body of my son but he has not deigned to reply." That was the first I heard she had done so but I recalled her speaking one day with a tinker at the door. She bought some thread and gave him a few coins and something which he put in his pocket. It might have been a letter to deliver but of course he would take the money and throw the letter away. I would myself write to Sir John but I have so longed to let Daniel's memory rest quietly on my heart that I have shrunk from stirring trouble about him. He bore no ill will to anyone all his life and in death he would want no revenge. He is at peace. I long to be at peace too.'*

Nat lowered his head then and wept for his father. I should go to him, he thought. Why did he ever marry that wild beautiful red-haired Irish girl, as he once described my mother in those days? He told me she had lost her parents in an uprising of Catholic peasants. So she came to stay with an aunt who lived in our parish when he was first appointed there as a young vicar. They fell in love, a state I am still ignorant of, but I can see how he was taken with her striking looks and the lively nature that had helped her overcome her sufferings.

He gave her a position in the community and she loved him with her whole passionate soul till she found his quiet, submissive nature tedious. I know she lost some babies which embittered her till Dan and I were born and then she lavished all her love on Dan, believing I was too much of a weakling to live. But I did live, Mother, and proved too clever and studious for you. But Dan loved her and she found solace in his devotion. Oh I can understand how his death and above all my guilt in it has twisted her brain. Between the lines of Father's letter, I read his dread that my coming will inflame her further. There is not much to fear from Captain Carter but I believe my father is going through a living hell and hopes to spare me from it and alas! perhaps from fanning the flames of it.

Nat sat a long time more, not looking at his books, oppressed with sorrow for his father and guilt that he himself was too far away to be able to help him.

CHAPTER 11

Spring 1641

BEL'S heart lifted as Caesar turned into the gates of Horden Hall and she saw the daffodils bordering the drive and the old, unloved house squarely ahead of them, the twisted red brick chimneys afire from the sun's beams and the whole scene alive with light and springtime. Even the statue exuded a cheerful look as if the old baronet were saying, "See what a lovely day it is."

The place wants to be loved, she thought, and I'll try to love it. I'll love Father too if he'll let me get close to him.

She was thankful that the road to the Hall didn't pass by Nether Horden or the Turners' Farm and she resolved never again to use her childhood shortcut through the woods to the village. She wanted only bright memories of home to share with Ursula.

She and Robert had passed two nights at inns where they had been eaten by bugs and she had wept for the parting from Ursula. Robert had had to prise her off as she clung to her, saying, "Oh Ursula, how will I live without you?"

"Why easily, my lamb, it's only for three weeks."

Robert had plucked at her arm. "Let us be on our way. Caesar is impatient to start for home."

Caesar knew he was home now and trotted happily round to his stable.

Tom appeared and held up his old arms to Bel. "Why, little Mistress, how you have grown in not much above half a year!"

And then, who should appear at the kitchen door but Bel's old nurse "Ay, I'm here again. They couldn't do without me. Well, well, you'll be worn out with riding but you're young. Come away in."

In fact Bel had found it exhilarating to be out in the countryside, to see lambs in the fields, to smell the wind off the moors. Uncomfortable as it was to ride behind Robert on Caesar's broad back it was wonderful to be released from the greyness of Cranmore House where the stone walls seemed perpetually to enclose winter. If it had not been for the brightness of Ursula's friendship, she thought, she would have run away long ago.

"Where's Father?" she asked Nurse.

"Why, in his bedchamber but he has risen and dressed for your coming."

"What ails him, Nan?"

Robert had dismissed her questions on the journey. "You needn't fret, Bella. It's nothing with a name. The old give up on life."

"Father is *not* old."

"If he's decided he is, he is." And that was all Robert would say.

Nan was as bad. Instead of answering Bel's question she took her cloak and bonnet and said brightly, "Happen you'll cheer him up. There'll be some supper for you when you come down."

Bel ran up the stairs and tapped at her father's door. His "Come in" sounded husky and when she peeped round the door, his pallor and emaciation was a shock.

He was reclining on a couch by the window with a rug over his knees and cushions at his back. He gave her a wan smile, but when she ran to him and stood questioningly by his couch, he held out his hand and clasped hers and gazed at her with what looked like longing.

Her dismay at his appearance made her demand abruptly, "What is this, Father? Are you ill? It's a lovely spring day. Why are you not taking the air?"

He glanced at the sunlit window and then back at her. "Still the same Bella. Always asking questions." His eyes were wistful. "Your mother and sister are afraid to come. Robert is just waiting for me to die. Now I have only you. But you are grown. You look well. You are not a child any more. You do not need to go away again. You will stay now." He still grasped her hand and though his voice was thin it carried authority and confidence.

She stared back at him, taking this in. Suddenly he needs me, she thought. I was sent away an unwanted package but now I am to be picked up and planted back here to become his companion. That was the meaning of his 'dear little girl' in the letter. So am I never to see Ursula again? That cannot be.

She slid her hand out of his and sat herself down on the window seat.

"What are you saying about Mother and Henrietta?"

He shook his head with a sort of sad impatience. "Tales are carried to France of the persecution of Catholics here. There have been terrible attacks in London but in the main they have been on priests. I am sure that two distinguished ladies could pass safely through the country with their servants. But what can I say? If they were set upon and murdered, I could never forgive myself." He reached a hand towards her again. "I am oppressed, Bella, with the evil in this world of ours. Will you not come closer and give me a kiss?"

She wriggled along the window seat till she was close to him and leant over and pecked his cheek. Would he sense that she too held evil within her, the devil which only Ursula could keep at bay? Here it was again, holding her back from loving her father. She let her arms go round his neck as she murmured, "I'll go back to Cranmore House till the end of the school year, won't I? You have paid the Mistress till then." That would surely be a vital argument.

He shrugged it off and gently drew her hands from his neck as if the pressure were painful. He held them between his own which looked pale and felt cold. "That money is of no consequence now. It is paid and cannot be reclaimed. We are in some straits you must understand and every needless expense is to be avoided – even overnight in an inn and the stabling of horses. Robert finds it hard to economise. What will come of Horden when I am gone I know not. We must arrange your marriage sooner than I thought. You are fourteen now. Fifteen will not be too young. If I mortgage the Hall, I can raise money for a dowry."

Bel pulled her hands away. "You are speaking of my second cousin William Horden, who could be a wastrel for all you know. You needn't raise any money to marry me to him or anyone else. I have no intention of marrying at all."

"Oh Arabella, have you not learnt obedience yet? Of course you must marry and he's no wastrel. He is eighteen and already learning his father's business, the correct way as ordinary apprentices do, and I believe he would be in a position to marry in the summer of next year as long as you lived at first under his parents' roof. His father has been in touch with me about it and is willing to take an interest in the Hall as dowry payment. At least we can then keep it in the Horden family."

"So, if I understand aright ... the poor Hordens must borrow from the wealthy Hordens on the security of their home in order to pay money to the wealthy Hordens, so that I, against my will, can be married to their son, who has no notion of what a horrible monster I am. This is what you, my father, have been planning to greet me with after my long absence." Her throat swelled and she almost choked on the words. This was so far from being the start of a new bond with her father that she could not even pay heed to his hints of his impending death. She stepped round the end of his couch with the intention of leaving the room to hide the bitter tears she felt rising up.

"Arabella," he cried in his old authoritative tone, "you will not walk out like that. Come back here and sit down."

Very slowly, with clenched lips, she walked back into the window and sat down.

He gazed at her with sad eyes. "I broached this subject because it was in the forefront of my mind, having only received my cousin's letter today. I believed, too, that you were a changed girl since your time at Cranmore House."

"I am changed. I am older and wiser because I have met so many people and because I have made a friend."

"What friend? Not a man?"

"Not a man. What little I have seen of men has not endeared me to them."

He looked relieved. "So you have a friend among the girls? Only one? I hoped you would make many."

"Not the girls. They were so ... different."

He shook his head. "It is you I fear who is different from them. You are not like most girls. Your interests are not the same. So, it is a teacher with whom you have struck up a friendship?"

"No, a servant."

"A servant! Oh Arabella, why do you always have to do the odd thing? Why can you not be ...?" He struggled for a word.

"Ordinary?" she offered.

"Pliant, conforming. You must know that daughters are expected to marry as their parents choose. Affection will follow later."

"Tell me about you and my mother then. Did her family select *you*?"

He flushed and there was an uncomfortable silence. Then he spoke, slowly and with obvious reluctance. "I must make some things clear to you about your mother. She was not perhaps as grand as she may have let you and Henrietta imagine. She was an orphan and only the *ward* of a French aristocrat. I had been given an introduction by my Grandfather to a Count Rombeau, who had been page to the French ambassador at the Court of Queen Elizabeth when Sir Ralph was a page there."

"That's the one outside!" Bel turned her head and pointed to the statue.

"Indeed. He had the notion I should travel abroad and then seek a place at the court of the young Prince Henry. The Prince liked the people about him to have knowledge of foreign parts."

"Yes, yes, but you and mother?"

Her father sighed. "Count Rombeau was your mother's guardian. He loved her, but was eager to have her married. Her beauty overshadowed his own daughter. When he learnt that my grandfather had been created baronet by King James, he thought I might do. So, yes, in a sense I was acceptable to her family. But it only happened because I, having just attained my majority, acted alone as I should not have done. I engaged myself to her without reference to my family. It was the worst thing in their eyes that I could do; to marry a Catholic ..." His voice tailed off, his chin sank onto his chest and he looked so unutterably woebegone that Bel was moved.

"You were in love," she said. "And you still are I believe. Is this why you talk of dying? You are pining because Mother has been away so long and is afraid to come to you. Do you think you will never see her again?"

"Don't Bella. Don't probe the wound."

"But you know about love, then, and happiness. Should you not want *me* to be happy?"

"I do, Bella. I do. But I am in poor health and you must be provided for. If my cousin Clifford Horden owns a part of this property, he will have some control over Robert, who is not as wise in the management of it as I would wish. William is quiet and steady and you will grow to love him.

They are also inclined to the Puritan way of thinking, which will make you and Horden safe from the suspicion of Popery which still hangs about it. My parents and my grandfather wanted to choose for me among the neighbouring gentry. He was particularly angry because I had spoilt his plan for me. Prince Henry would have no Catholics at his court, but that mattered little because we were married in France in the summer of 1612 and the poor Prince took typhoid fever and died in the November. But if I had left it to my parents, I would not have suffered this separation from wife and daughter. Life would certainly have been easier. So, you see, it is not always wise to succumb to the passions of youth."

She gazed out at the spring sunshine that had seemed so happy. His speech saddened her deeply. Here she was, truly conversing with her father for almost the first time in her life and still they could find no meeting point. Without turning her head she said, "I have no passion for anyone, only a passion not to be married at all."

He tut-tutted and his impatience turned it into a cough which racked him for a few minutes till he could sip some cordial that stood on the low table beside the couch. Then he looked at her, shaking his head in the old way he had when she was naughty as a child. "How can you say such a thing, Arabella, at fourteen years old?"

"You didn't make Henrietta marry till she was eighteen and Robert is twenty. Where is the heiress for him that would solve all our troubles at a stroke?"

He sighed. "There is a family in Newcastle who have made their money from coal and would be happy to ally with a baronetcy like Horden, but Robert has not endeared himself to the young lady."

"She is proving difficult, too, is she, like me? We young women will have to stand together and not agree to be sent hither and thither like parcels

138

and married off against our will." A thought struck her. "You didn't say *Mother* was in love. Did *she* have to do what she was told?"

It was a tactless thing to ask as she realised at once. He winced as though in real pain but angrily blustered it out. "Oh Bella, she was fifteen as you will be. She never questioned it. Marriage came to young ladies and she liked me. As only the *ward* of a count she had not expected to marry well. Love came later when she had ceased to be homesick."

That told Bel a great deal. Perhaps her mother had never ceased to be homesick. She had instilled in Henrietta a passion for all things French. The thought prompted Bel into another question. "How did the Count accept Henrietta as his grandson's bride? We are poor I keep being told and yet you must have paid a dowry."

"The Count's own daughter had married by then and given birth to a son, so as he was always very fond of your mother he hoped to draw her back into their family circle by this marriage. I set money aside for Henrietta at that time. Well-invested it accrued over the years." He shook his head as if to be rid of that subject.

It *is* a pain to him, she realised. He believes he has lost Mother for ever.

"But you and William," he hurried on, foiling more questions, "he is not only English but our own kin. No homesickness there. Love will grow easily and naturally between you." He leant back against his cushions. "Now I am weary of this talk. I so longed to have your company believing you to have changed at Cranmore House ..."

"Yes," she cried eager to find a different subject and keep him talking. "What did the Mistress write to you of my good behaviour? You said in your letter my *exceptionally* good behaviour? Did not my mother write to you what *she* knew?"

He looked startled. "Why, no details ..."

"Then I shall tell you." And she recounted the whole incident of the attempt to seize and probably murder Father Patrick, but she checked from mentioning his subsequent declaration to herself.

He listened with growing alarm and his hands went up over his open mouth.

When she was silent and gazing expectantly into his eyes he lowered his hands and clasped hers. Then he spoke the same thought that her mother had expressed in her letter. "Ah, my little Bella, you are the son we should have had. We had a boy you know, before Robert, and another after Henrietta but neither survived infancy. When you were expected we hoped for a son ..."

She broke in vehemently, "Is that why I was unloved? If I'd been pretty like Hen I might have served, but to be plain and boyish and a *girl* was unforgiveable."

"Unloved? No, my child, how can you say that?"

"I never felt loved. I know I was a horrid child and that's why no one loved me, but maybe it was the other way round."

A knock came at the door just as she saw in his weary eyes that he was struggling to work out what she was implying.

Nurse looked round. "Arabella, your supper's waiting, and will I bring yours up here, Sir John?"

"Yes, yes, please. I am very tired."

Bel rose and went silently out. She was tired too. Tired and frustrated. There was so much to come out between herself and her father but it was twisted and turned aside as much by her own devilment as by his weakness and lack of understanding.

Am I not capable of keeping the devil in and holding a friendly conversation that will make progress towards love? she thought. And if

I am as brave as the son he wanted why can he not love me though I am a girl?

When she descended the stairs she found two places laid in the family dining-room and Robert already eating greedily. How he remained so gawky and stick-like she had no idea but anything like a friendly conversation with him was impossible.

I don't believe he lives up to Father's hopes, she thought sadly, so why can I not be a substitute son? She began to eat silently, but he seemed inclined to talk.

"Nurse is standing in as housekeeper, you see. To save money of course, but if my own plans work out, I'll soon bring a very capable and very rich young lady here as mistress. She can choose what servants she likes and you can go back to school. We'll be all right then, eh?"

Bel just looked at him and looked away again.

"What did you think of Father?" he asked next.

"He looks ill. Has he seen a physician?"

"Oh yes, he gave him the cordial for his cough but reckons he won't mend."

"Why? When did this start? When he heard Mother was afraid to return?"

Robert shrugged. "That made him worse, but he was brooding before that. You know he resigned from his magistracy. God knows why but he took to heart that rick-burner we hung ... even though I put it all right for him at York. He guessed I'd had to bribe the clerk when your ten pounds was missing but, as I said to him, that's common practice. Then before Christmas we had a letter from a Captain Carter telling us the man's family wanted the villain's body for burial. Father tried to find out where it went, but of course it was the Scots took it down and the commander had been replaced since then. It was likely in some field where they put other felons, but who can say where? It won't be a pretty sight now."

Bel who had tried to cover her ears pushed away her plate and leapt up. "How can you speak of it so lightly? Father is cursed. We are all cursed. It was a man's life." She ran from the room. The image was there again, stark as ever, leering down with its one eye. And yet they wanted the body. He was someone, real, their son, a person who had lived a life till it was horribly snuffed out.

She ran up to her narrow room and found the door to Henrietta's open and her own travelling trunk in that room. No, she thought, I need to be enclosed, shut in. This smells still of Henrietta and she will come and haunt me in the night and demand to know why I am sleeping in her bed. She dragged the box back into her own room and ran to the old housekeeper's room where she had slept when the Catholic chapel was in use. There she found Nurse in the big box chair with her feet on a stool.

"I want my old bed, Nan. No, don't get up. I'll change the sheets myself."

Nurse had shown no sign of getting up. She only said, "Sir John said you should have that room."

"I'm not used to it. The old chapel will be easier for Mary to keep clean."

"Mary's our only maid now. She has to be kitchen maid too and she's not so pleased at that. Tom and Adam do the fires as well as grooming the two horses. You'll have to clean your own room, my girl."

"All the better if it's small and nothing much in it. I don't care about that, but I can't stay here for ever. I have to go back to Cranmore House."

"Eh, you're in your old moods are you? You'll do as your father says." Nurse lay back in the chair with her arms folded across her substantial bosom and closed her eyes.

Bel stamped back to her own room and lay on the bed digesting all she had learnt from her father. For the first time ever she felt some sympathy with her mother. At fifteen she had been whisked to a foreign country and into a household that didn't approve of her. The old grandfather, Bel recalled, had not lived long to enjoy his baronetcy. He had seen his statue erected and had had an apoplexy shortly after, but her father's parents had lived till Robert was two years old. Then they had died within a few months of each other, before Henrietta was born. That was when her mother became Lady Horden and at last mistress of the Hall. But she must always have hankered after a return to France and now her own daughter was settled there, why should she ever come back?

"I don't mind if she doesn't," Bel said aloud, trying to believe it. "When I have Ursula I don't need a mother. But I haven't got Ursula. How," she cried, grinding her teeth, "can I get back to Cranmore House?"

Cambridge was a revelation to Nat in the springtime. The meadows, the river, flowers bursting in all the gardens, the rosy buildings burnished with sunlight. He wanted to be joyful but the news from home and the news from London were all disturbing. His father's last letter had described how his mother had left the house at dawn one day and set off to walk northwards with little knowledge of the way and been found after a hue and cry thirty-six hours later in a state of exhaustion, wrapped in her cloak and curled up under a tree. She was quiet and resting now, but he never knew when the urge to break out and take action on her own would suddenly come upon her.

From London came news of Easter riots, of the trial of Lord Strafford and how the King, under duress, had dismissed all Papists from the court. Ben Hutton found all this very satisfactory. His father, with other members of the Guild of Tailors, had been on the streets again protesting, but Ben seemed sorry that he had not been part of the rabble that had tried to break into the Spanish ambassador's house during Mass.

"I'm glad to hear it," Nat said. "Violence is abhorrent to me and those who commit it in the name of a right cause are sinking to the level of the evildoers."

"No," Ben cried, "evil must be wiped out or how will God's kingdom come?"

But Nat found himself quoting again and again from his father, for whom his love and admiration grew the longer he was away from him. "I stand by 'Blessed are the peace-makers'. So let me hear no more of your rebel talk." And he would bury his head in his book and ignore the rest of Ben's ranting.

What he found most hurtful and disgusting was Ben's glee in May when the Earl of Strafford went to the scaffold. That so powerful a nobleman and a favourite of the King should suffer so was deeply disturbing. Where was the country heading? He began to fear that Ben's prediction of a civil war might not be so wide of the mark. Scuffles broke out among students from Queen's and Emmanuel and Ben, finding himself branded a loyalist as a Queen's man, applied to be enrolled in Emmanuel and changed his studies from Classics to Theology to start again as a freshman.

Nat was much relieved and even more so when his tutor told him that with his new status as a scholar he was entitled to a room on his own. He was allocated a room next to that of a young nobleman, Edward Branford, who as a younger son was destined for the church. Edward had come up the same time as Nat, but was only sixteen now and had often come to Nat for help with his Greek exercises. He was an engaging boy, not very clever, and Nat had to explain things to him many times over, but his company was a pleasant change from that of Ben Hutton.

Edward was fresh-faced, taller than Nat and gangly but he looked up to Nat and had none of the airs of superiority that some of the young nobility assumed. "You'll be given a Fellowship, Nat," he often said, "when you have your Masters' Degree."

"And since I am far from a Bachelor as yet you are speaking of years ahead," Nat would laugh. "Besides, all I hope for is to be a country parson like my father."

"No, no, you will go on to be Archbishop of Canterbury."

"That I will not. There may be no Bishops at all if Parliament brings the Scots Covenant to England."

"Will they, do you think, Nat? I can't say I understand it at all."

It was amicable conversations like this that raised Nat's confidence and proved so delightful after the sharp arguments with Ben Hutton. If he had not been anxious about home and the divisions in the country, these weeks as spring grew into summer and the University began to empty would have been unalloyed peace. He could lie out on the grass with a book, absorbing sunlight and knowledge at once. But he knew he must return to Yorkshire and see the state of things there for himself.

It was August before he finally made the journey home. The meeting with his father was overflowing with love but, as he had feared, his appearance in the house filled his mother with horror.

"Why is *he* here and not Daniel? Where has he been? I thought we had seen the last of him if he could not bring Daniel back with him."

He was shocked at her gaunt face in which her eyes looked larger and more fierce than ever. Until his return, his father said, she had gone about in their daily life in an apathetic daze which was at least bearable. He had Jenny to do the cooking and cleaning, a stalwart woman who accepted what life brought and managed her mistress with tolerant cajolery as if she were a child. When she was rewarded with occasional bursts of petulance, she disregarded them with a grunt of amusement.

"I couldn't have kept my sanity without her," his father confided to Nat. "But do not be distressed at your mother's greeting. Most of the time now she hardly seems alive. It is as if a part of her died with Daniel. I knew there was a danger that your presence would revive her passion but if you are here for some weeks she may sink again into a sort of torpor."

Sadly this failed to happen. Nat had grown stronger and broader and even added an inch to his height in the months since he had been better fed and more comfortable without Ben Hutton. With his distinctive flaxen hair and bronzed cheeks from long hikes on the moors he was more like Dan than he had ever been. His walk was neater and more brisk but sitting in a chair he could rouse his mother to a frenzy when she came into a room behind him and shrieked that her Dan was home. This was very painful and Nat often longed to be back at his desk in Queen's.

One balmy morning in September he had decided to walk to Easingwold to purchase a quire of paper and some ink when his father drew him to the bench outside the vicarage saying softly "Jenny has got her occupied in the kitchen. Let us speak of the situation in the country. In Cambridge you are nearer to London and must have some sense of the lengths to which Parliament will go now that the King is in Scotland."

Nat sat down willingly enough, though he was unsure what to say. "It's hard to predict, sir. Parliament has taken advantage of the King's absence to make peace with the Scots and they have withdrawn their forces from the border counties. All that happened since I left Cambridge, but I would guess that since London is hot for Parliament and cool towards the King, Mr Pym will feel strong enough to push for more reforms, as he calls them."

His father sighed and ran his hand through his thinning grey hair.

"Surely, son, the land can be at rest now. Cambridge is peaceful, is it not? When you return, I trust you will learn that London too has quietened . No more riots, no more arrests, no more horrible executions."

Nat had to confess that Cambridge was far from peaceful. "Students and dons all take sides, sir, and I fear Parliament is set on testing its strength against the King to the limit. I can but pray that here at least, you will be spared from any more trouble."

"I thought we would but Pym's men have eyes and ears everywhere. They object to my taking a prayer book service, but just now they are determined to root out the last poor skulking remnants of the Catholic faith hereabouts. They even raided Cranmore House lately, for no reason but that it was established in a former nunnery. The vicar in Easingwold tells me the girls walk in procession to his church every Sunday without fail. But I believe the Mistress drove the raiders out empty handed."

Nat stood up. "I am glad of it. But speaking of Easingwold reminds me. I must go there for paper and ink. Can I bring you anything, Father?"

"Nay. I believe Jenny stocked up on provisions from the market. But you go. I will accompany you as far as Granny Woodman's and see how she does."

When he left his father there, Nat walked sadly on. His father was too gentle for this world. It was a cruel fate that had given him turbulence in his own home when he longed for all mankind to live at peace. Nat felt his own guilt keenly, but his father was not free from blame himself. He had abdicated his headship of the family for peace and quiet. His mother had had free range for her excesses, for the partiality of her love which had left Nat himself out in the cold. If I ever marry, he thought, slashing off the heads of the long grasses with his stick, I shall rule my household and my children will be treated with scrupulous fairness.

As he walked, enjoying the motion and the benign air, his spirits rose. His present life was study which he loved and he had no need to delve into the future. He would not allow the turmoil in the country to fill his mind with foreboding. But as he strode into the small bustling town of Easingwold, he noticed three men of puritanical dress accosting every passer-by, apparently demanding signatures as most people scrawled something on the sheaf of papers that was pushed under their noses.

Sighting Nat, they advanced upon him.

"A scholar by his looks. No labouring man. He must sign."

A chill of apprehension shot down his spine. They were three and the square was emptying of people.

"A petition to Parliament, young man," the tallest of the three said.

Nat's quick eye glanced over it and found it was demanding the closure of a girls' school in the county which was described as 'a viperous nest of covert Papists from the Mistress downwards, offering an ill example to the pupils under their charge.' The paper was headed Cranmore House.

"Well!" He smiled round at them. Here was a chance for sweet reason to confound bigotry. "I heard this place mentioned only today. My father spoke of it as a well-run school, where girls are turned into young ladies. I believe a recent investigation cleared it of Roman associations."

"Perhaps your father himself is a secret Papist." They began to gather round him menacingly.

"Certainly not. He is the vicar of Darrowswick." As soon as he had said it he wanted to bite back the words.

The tall man who seemed to be the leader laughed evilly. "There are some doubtful vicars about. Is he not Parson Wilson and was he not found in vestments and with candlesticks and images in his church?"

Nat had thought that as soldiery had ransacked the church these men would know nothing of that incident. It seemed his father was right that nothing escaped Pym's spies. He was managing this badly, but now he gritted his teeth and determined he would not sign their paper. He was sure his father would refuse. He glanced about hoping to see some friendly onlookers. He had been crossing the paved square to the jobbing printer's where he knew he could buy writing materials. He was known there, but they were almost certainly the people who had printed this petition. These days all businesses were glad of work whatever it was. The printer appeared at his door at that moment but when Nat met his eye he ran inside and shut the door. A few-passers by looked in his direction but hastened past.

One of the men jostled him, thrusting the petition under his nose. "Sign, vicar's boy!"

He gave the man his most courteous smile. "I cannot put my name to something when I know not the truth of the matter."

"Take that then!"

Under the paper the man's hand punched him in the stomach and he doubled up, only to be knocked sideways to the ground by the other two. One kick landed in his ribs and the thought flashed through his brain that the next might be on his head and that this was a stupid thing to die for. But before the next blow came he heard a shout.

"Hold off there. What has the man done?" His attackers ran and a constable was helping him to his feet.

He was bruised and shaken but exultant that he was alive and had not given way. Miraculously the square was now full of people proclaiming that the attack was completely unprovoked, that these men had been bullying everyone into signing and even if Cranmore House was a nest of Papists, it was no way for folks to treat freeborn Englishmen.

"They are not from the town," one man said. "They rode in from York this morning."

As there was no sign of them and the constable was obviously on his own it seemed sensible for him to remark, "They'll be riding out again then, I warrant. They are under orders not to flout the law. Are you in need of medical help, sir?"

Nat shook his head. There was a sharp pain when he took a deep breath but he could stand and walk. What he feared now was that the men might turn aside on their way back and pay Darrowswick a visit. "I am not hurt. I must make my purchases." He pointed to the printer's sign and the Constable let him go and ordered the crowd to disperse.

The printer, a small wizened man, acted as though he had seen nothing. "Well, it's Master Wilson. You'll be providing for your next Cambridge term, no doubt."

Nat escaped from him as quickly as he could and began to walk the painful two miles home. Freeborn Englishmen, indeed! The population was cowed and fearful.

He was much relieved to see no horses tied up outside the church or the vicarage. His father was weeding the vegetable patch which had always been their mother's interest with the enthusiastic help of Daniel. She had had to instruct Daniel anew each season, but she took delight in watching him and checking him with laughter if he was uprooting young lettuces instead of weeds. Seeing her drooping on the garden bench and staring unseeing at his father Nat was moved with pity at the change in her from those happy days.

His father looked up. "Nat, are you all right? Your cheek?"

Nat touched it. "Nothing. A scrape." He sat down on the bench and put his hand to his side. "I think I have a broken rib."

His mother made no sign that she had heard. He remembered all the times Dan had had tumbles as a boy. Every tiny bruise was lovingly rubbed with ointment. She cradled him and crooned over him. When he was too big for that, she would put him to bed and make him her special herbal brew.

His father of course wanted to know what had happened. Nat told him and finished, "I wish I had not mentioned you. These Puritans take note. They have lists of names. Ben Hutton told me they aim to purge the realm of all wrong thinkers, Church of England men as well as Papists. Even the poor old Archbishop is still languishing in the Tower."

His father laid down his trowel. "But I am of no importance. Let us go in and see if this rib should be bound up."

Nat stood stiffly and they went inside. His mother never moved.

"Father, was I foolish? Should I have signed their paper to save trouble? If the constable had not appeared they might have killed me."

"I trust others would have intervened. No, we should not encourage their vindictiveness. Even if the place did have Catholic leanings, that is no reason to close it down. You had the courage to do right. I am proud of you. I only hope I would have been brave enough to do the same."

Nat absorbed this praise greedily. It soothed the painful memory of throwing his pike and Dan's into the ditch.

In the kitchen his father unbuttoned his shirt for him and exclaimed, "Eh, you will have a colourful bruise here." He ran his fingers with tenderness along the rib. "I think it is cracked. I will bandage it with wet cloths but you must take care how you move your arm." Again he said, "I am proud of you, Nat. When you left the army you were saving yourself and Daniel from taking life in an unworthy cause. That took courage of a different kind. In these dreadful days, when strife in the name of God is breaking out all over, we will need both courage and wisdom to know when and how to take our stand."

CHAPTER 12

Late September 1641

BEL was polishing the big silver fruit dish with the Horden crest to be ready for the coming of the London Hordens.

"They'll not believe the bride did the polishing herself," Nurse chuckled as she carefully washed and dried the few rarely used pieces of porcelain, similarly adorned.

"Don't call me a bride," Bel snapped at her. "Whatever William is like, I am not marrying him. Father knows this, yet he persists with the charade of entertaining them. What needs the ridiculous expense of sending for 'exotic fruits freshly landed at the port of Newcastle' as the billboard said?" She held the dish to the sunlight and then laid it on the kitchen table. "I can see my ugly face in it, but who will notice how shiny it is when it's covered with fruit. All Father is doing is getting deeper into debt."

"Nay, you'll come round to the idea when you see the lad. You've had no experience of young men, that's all it is. You don't know what it is to be courted."

"Who says so?" Bel flashed back. "A man courted me at Cranmore House." As soon as the words were out she wished them unsaid.

Nurse laid down the plate she was drying and stared at her open-mouthed. "A man? At Cranmore House! What men were there? Some outside workman teasing you I warrant!"

"Well, it wasn't. It was our precious Father Patrick, so there!" She was too far in now to hold back.

"A priest propose marriage! You must have misheard him. Come, get on with the work. Those tankards are still to be polished."

Bel took one up. Unused for so long it was badly tarnished. Like Patrick, she thought. Why should I care for his reputation? He is in France still, I suppose. She began work on the tankard and grinned sideways at Nurse. "He was ready to cast off his priesthood and come for me when I was older. But it matters little now. He is abroad and not likely to come back."

"No he won't, for Cranmore House is shut up now."

Bel set down the tankard. "Cranmore House shut up? When did you hear that?"

"Lately. A commission came from Parliament, so the master told me. You couldn't have gone back there, for all the fuss you made when you first came home."

"But what will happen to the teachers and ... everyone?" Bel had suppressed all summer her longing for Ursula, hoping that if she rebelled over William Horden she might be sent back there.

"I daresay they'll have families to go home to." Nurse was musing with her hands caressing the porcelain she had now finished. "Maybe some parent complained Father Patrick had a roving eye to the girls. He must have looked at many beside you, such a contrary little thing that you are."

"But he went away long ago. At Christmas. Oh he did look. He looked at them all but I was different, he said." She didn't know whether her father had told Nurse of the threatened attack. It didn't seem so. But her mind was now only engrossed with the fate of Ursula. Where could she go? She had no family. The thought that she might never see her again was agony. Mechanically she picked up the tankard again and resumed her polishing. Nurse was talking away to herself, digesting what she had heard about Father Patrick.

Bel caught her sister's name and realised Nurse had said, "Ay, well, he did cast an eye at Henrietta but I dismissed it at the time for everyone looked at her. She was a beauty."

When the tankards were finished and the silver spoons too, Bel went back to her own room to escape any further interrogation. She had after all been allowed to keep the former chapel room and now that the London Hordens were expected the parents, Clifford and Celia, were to have Henrietta's old room as the smartest of the bedrooms, while William would share Robert's. This would keep down the number of fires that must be lit and conceal the fact that furnishings from other rooms had been sold months before to help pay the levy that had been laid on all landowners for the upkeep of the Scots army.

Bel sat on her bed and yearned for Ursula's bright eyes and spontaneous hugs. That summer had been desperately frustrating. The visit of the London Hordens had been planned and postponed several times, sometimes because of riots in London, when Clifford Horden was reluctant to leave his home and business and then because the Scots army was still in the north and he thought it dangerous to be on the roads. Once the King had safely travelled north, actually stopping in Newcastle and hosting a dinner for the Scots General Leslie, Clifford must have realised the north was not as barbarous as he had supposed. Then at last, a treaty was concluded and all but four thousand of the Scots troops departed and Parliament went into recess. Clifford decided all was quiet, they had set off and were expected next day.

If only I had Ursula! Bel moaned to herself. We could laugh about William afterwards! She would giggle and tell me I did well to refuse him. I can hear her funny, blurred galloping voice. 'My Bel has a lot more chiming to do before she's hitched up.' It was impossibly cruel to think she would never see her again, not even know what had happened to her! The hope that had sustained her all these months died inside her and life was as dust.

She lay on her bed choking with dry sobs till she heard Robert bounding up the stairs calling for her. Surely the Hordens hadn't arrived already. He banged on her door and called, "Are you in there? Can I come in?"

This was unheard of. "If you must. What's happened? Have they come?"

He stalked in. It was a dull day and the room was dim enough for him not to notice anything amiss about her. "No, no, but I wanted a word with you about them. Nurse seems to think you'll have to agree to young William after all. It's been talked about so long, but now it's almost here so it's really pretty urgent for me to see you do the right thing." He sat down on her clothes chest and placed his hands on his thin knees and glared at her.

If she had not been so desolate about Ursula she would have been curious. It seemed to be the first time in her life that he had ever taken any interest in her future. It was unprecedented even to have him in her room. She curled her legs under her on the bed and decided to be very wary of him. "And what do you call the right thing, brother?"

He lifted his shoulders to his ears. "Refuse him, naturally. Send him packing."

Now he had astonished her. She untucked her legs and perched on the edge of the bed, shaking her head. "You don't want me to marry him?"

"Of course not. Father will have to raise money on the estate to pay your dowry. Hang it, Bella. It's my estate. I know the old man's been much better in the summer months but he may not live through another winter ..."

"Oh I see. It's your future you're concerned about. But if you are so sure Father is dying, don't forget you'll have to find me a dowry ... if I ever marry."

"Oh you'll marry. Girls do. I'll find you a rich widower looking for comfort in his old age and by then I'll have this place out of debt through my own marriage. No, what I don't want to see is Clifford Horden getting a foothold in here and thinking he can take charge. I'm the heir. Father talks about keeping the Hall in the family, but he's not going to do it this way. Cousins they may be, but we hardly know them and I don't see why he should be giving away my inheritance to them when they've money of their own. So mind you stick to your guns, and say no to young Will."

But then she thought, what if William is nice-looking and well-mannered, as Father keeps saying he is, and there is no legitimate reason in anyone's eyes for me to refuse him? They won't believe that I never intend to marry. I have that within me that makes marriage unthinkable. How can I explain that to them? Of course I can be utterly obnoxious to him, which will bitterly anger both my father and his parents who are making this tremendous journey to seize me into their family.

"I intend to say no," she told Robert. But in her heart she was dreading her father's distress. She had tried to get closer to him in the summer. She had made him take short walks on sunny days. She had tried to cheer him about the state of the country.

It had been hard to lift his gloom. "We were to be one happy land," he said often, "when King James succeeded Queen Elizabeth. I was only a little lad but I remember when he rode south with his courtiers and we cheered him on his way. And now his son has stirred up strife with his burdensome taxes and trying to force the prayer book on Scotland. But he is still the King and I do not trust these Parliament men." He usually finished his musings by saying, "It is all the more urgent, Bella, that your future should be secured in these troublesome times." He had been more cheerful since the King had gone to Scotland to deal with the grievances there but she knew how he longed to see her 'settled' as he put it.

Robert got up, running his hands through his black locks which he was wearing longer than ever now in defiance of Puritan fashions. "That's settled, then." He gave her a wide grin which almost split his narrow face. "So all I need to do to help," he added as he went to the door, "is tell young Will that you are an untameable wild beast and he certainly wouldn't be happy with you."

She smiled wanly as he left the room. Did she want this reputation? Had there always been a devil in her urging her to be rebellious? How was it that Ursula's presence kept him at bay? Ursula was there when I defied those three that were certainly the devil's men. But I was angry then and if I had had a pistol in my hand I would have shot them all. So I would have been a worse murderer than ever and she wouldn't have loved me any more. But now I have lost her for always and I have no way to find goodness and peace. Where is it to be found? It can't be right for me to marry William and yet that is just what my father expects of a meek, dutiful girl.

A fresh passion of tears overwhelmed her again. "I need you, Urs. I need you."

It was late afternoon the next day when she heard the sound of hooves and the crunching of wheels on the gravelled drive. She peeped from her narrow pointed window and saw the fine equipage pass the equestrian statue of the first baronet and a man's hat poke out to admire it. Tom and Adam came hurrying to take charge of the horses and Father himself emerged from the front door below to greet his guests.

He had told her to put on her best dress, without reflecting that she had never been into Newcastle since she had come back and had had no new clothes for a year. It was Nurse who had emptied Henrietta's closet of the old or outgrown gowns she had left behind and who helped Bel to find petticoats and bodices and over-skirts that could be altered to fit her enlarging breasts and increased height. For this meeting, Bel had insisted on the plainest gown of blue with no decoration but a fine white stripe. Nurse said she must soften it with the best of Henrietta's collars and cuffs that had escaped Bel's scissors because they were not good enough for France. They were however of the finest Italian needle lace and "all the mending won't show," Nurse declared, "because I did it myself. But why will you have a blue gown when you have green eyes?"

"Just to show how contrary I am," Bel said and Nurse lifted her eyes to the ceiling.

"We'll do your hair nicely at least."

It had been cut only once at Cranmore House when it had finally grown out of Bel's own hacking it about, so it was now long and thick and Nurse twined it up onto her head with clasps and ribbons and let a few dark ringlets fall each side of her face.

"Eh, now, you could look seventeen," she said, holding up a glass.

"Oh, dear," Bel said, gazing at herself in surprise. "I don't look nearly ugly enough." She was secretly excited to see that what Patrick had said seemed to be coming true. Her too solid, square-chinned face had fined down to show the strong bone-structure under a skin that, without any art, looked flawless.

"Nay, you look quite a picture," Nurse said.

And now the moment had come. Three figures had emerged from the coach: a tall father, a small round mother and a slender son only an inch shorter than his father.

Bel was dismayed to find that her heart was thumping as she ran downstairs. What do I care for any of them? she reminded herself.

They were already inside the wide hall to which the front door gave direct access and Mary was bobbing in a snowy apron and collecting the travelling cloaks. Though it was still September there was a raw gale blowing and all that they were saying to Father was about the bitter northern weather and the trials of the journey. A fire was blazing in the wide hearth and they quickly congregated round it before they noticed Bel's presence.

"My daughter, Arabella," Father said and Bel curtseyed with her eyes fixed only on William. She saw at once that this disconcerted him. He had the narrow Horden face, like Robert, but his cropped hair was a neutral brown and his eyes not nearly so dark and sharp. Altogether he made little impression on her, so she looked at the father whose hair was greying like her father's, but cut straight all round just below the ears. He was also clean-shaven. They look like Puritans, she thought. Father won't care for that. The mother was a very different breed, not in dress, because that was dark and plain, but in shape and height. Bel found herself looking down on her and saw plump cheeks dominating the small eyes, nose and mouth which seemed crowded together in the centre of the hummocky face.

She smiled and held out her hand but Bel sensed wariness rather than warmth. "You have certainly improved with the years, my dear," she said which seemed to Bel a dubious opening compliment.

Her father requested that she should show them their rooms so she went ahead up the stairs and led them first to Henrietta's room. "This is for you," ushering in Clifford and Celia Horden.

The lady looked around and went at once to the connecting door. "And my boudoir in here?" Finding it fastened she looked round in surprise.

"It has been closed up. My room is next door."

"Is there only one room for us both? One bed?"

"It's a large bed," Bel said. She couldn't help smiling. It was a splendid four-poster and curtains that had never been hung before had been brought out of storage.

"It will do very well," Clifford Horden said curtly. "Where is William to go?"

"This way, the other side of the stairs. The first room is my Father's and then Robert's. We thought it would be less lonely if William had Robert's company."

Robert, she noticed, had now followed them up and he took William by the arm in a very free and easy way. "We'll keep each other warm but take note I prefer the right hand side. The footman will bring your things up.

He's just helping your man lift them down."

Footman? thought Bel. We have no footman.

And then to her astonishment who should come up the stairs, dressed in the old Horden livery which had not been worn in the house for years, but Sam Turner. He gave her a brief grin and with the visitors' servant carried the travelling trunks into the appropriate rooms. In her amazement she couldn't help also a pang of yearning. He was so much more a man than William. His cheerful rosy face under his chestnut curls and his open straight, confident look were just as she remembered them from their game by the stream. That he had disappointed her later was all mixed up with the horrible sight of the hanged man, which still came back to her as sharply as ever in nightmares or suddenly in her waking thoughts as it did now.

Telling the visitors that a meal would be served in the dining-room off the hall below in half an hour she ran down after Sam. "What are you doing here in our livery?" she challenged him as he headed for the kitchen where she could see Nurse pouring mugs of ale for the Hordens' men.

"Helping you north-country Hordens show off to your southern cousins."

"But the last I heard you were serving a Scots officer."

"And so I was but you must have noticed that most of the Scots have returned to Scotland. I came back to the farm and Sir John has borrowed me for as long as your visitors stay. He knew I had learnt how to wait at gentlemen's tables, but if you fix up your marriage quickly, Bel, I'll get back to the harvesting where I'm needed."

"Well," she said, "I too want to get rid of the visitors as soon as possible. I'm not ready to wed for a long time."

He shrugged his shoulders and gave her the comical look she remembered from their brief journey in his cart. He was laughing at her again.

She bit her lip and thought, I told him to call me Bel because I never wanted to be the young lady from the Hall, but now I am no longer a little girl and he is a footman!

She hung back at the kitchen door as he went in with his eyes on the third mug of ale Nurse had poured, but then he turned to murmur to her, "Tell you the truth I feel a fool in this rig, but you look like a princess." He gave her a little bow and she fled from the room when she caught Nurse's disapproving look at seeing her there.

He's still teasing me, she thought happily, but if Cousin William should turn out like Sam, I might find my resolution a little harder to keep.

Fortunately over the next week William showed no such signs. He was uncomfortably shy, which made her the more bold in asking him questions about himself and his work in his father's business. He only grew more nervous and monosyllabic. At mealtimes she was conscious of Sam's amusement, though he remained impeccably formal. Once she was also conscious of glances passing between him and Mary. Had they an understanding? A stab of jealousy infuriated her and she renewed her questioning of William with an impatient, "Why won't you tell me what you do, Cousin, when you go to work in the morning?"

"I have to learn all aspects of the business," he mumbled, head down.

His father came to his rescue by explaining that his business was buying and selling. What they bought and what they sold depended on the markets and Clifford Horden by his own account had a very good eye for where to make a profit.

Celia Horden defended her son more volubly.

"You have to understand, Arabella, that William is too modest to boast of all he has done. He has been down at the docks to see the loading and unloading. He has worked in the warehouses. He has been round the markets to see what is selling well. He has studied the trade routes to find the safest and speediest ways to the farthest countries on the globe. He knows the worst places for pirates and he can estimate risks and how to cover them. At present he is working directly under his father's eye in the office, learning all about keeping the ledgers. You can have no conception of the complexity of the work. Every load, every package is recorded and can be traced from first order to safe delivery. He is mastering it all." She smiled fondly at her son. "Such a clever boy!"

"That's very interesting," Bel said, "but I wanted him to tell me himself."

Sometimes her father frowned at her to stop talking so that he could himself question Clifford about the political situation and how unrest and rioting in London affected business and the ordinary lives of law-abiding citizens.

Clifford made light of his own delays in coming north and seemed to assume Sir John was anxious on Bel's account. "Your daughter will be safer in London than any other part of the kingdom. What is important at present is to be in good favour with the Parliament. I have close friends there. I know Mr Pym personally, the leader of the House. I have done him little favours. Parliament is now the power in the land."

Bel hoped this kind of talk might make her father disillusioned with the idea of allying their families.

"I like not the way he speaks of the King," she heard him mutter to Robert that evening after their guests had retired for the night. "You heard him. He said the King must bow to Parliament in everything and Parliament cannot be dissolved without its own consent."

Robert snorted. "They are a bunch of Puritans. Have nothing to do with them."

"And yet it would secure our lands if there was wealth like theirs behind them." He turned to Bel when he noticed she was still in the parlour. "What say you, child? You can object to nothing in young William, can you?"

"I object to him because he is nothing."

Robert laughed. "Ay, that is William in a nutshell."

Sir John stroked his beard and frowned. "Nay, he is in awe of his father, who is his master too. Take Nurse with you tomorrow, Bella, and walk with him about the grounds and he will be more forthcoming."

"I walked with him this afternoon on my own and told him he was too young to think of marriage yet and I would not in any case be right for him. He seemed to agree; if I could make any sense of his mumblings."

"Oh Bella, you thwart me at every turn. You are so bold in your talk and to go about with a young man unchaperoned! He is rightly frightened of you."

"And so he should be," Robert laughed. "Can you imagine any man willingly taking on our Bella? If she's a dragon now, what will she be in ten year's time? I have told you, sir, that I am making good progress with my own marriage prospects and I am sure there is as much wealth behind my girl as this merchant has."

"You have been telling me this for many months, Robert, and still her family have not resumed negotiations. I fear it will all come to nothing and the only hope lies with our cousins." He passed his hand across his eyes. "I must to bed. I am weary and I can only pray that we can bring things to a resolution tomorrow. They are anxious to return to London as soon as possible. Arabella, why will you not see that a meek, quiet, sober and hardworking husband is just what you should have? You will be the strong partner, the support, the driving force. I do not see you as extravagant so if in due course he can set you up in your own home and defer to you in household management, I believe you will make wise decisions and not waste his substance." He went out then without giving her time to reply and she watched how slowly he climbed the stairs.

Robert grabbed her arm. "Listen, I tell William every night that you are a young vixen and had to be sent away to school because of your tantrums. He's terrified of you."

"But he will do as his father tells him because his whole life depends on pleasing him. No, I can see I will be the one to take all the blame for it coming to nought."

"But you won't give in at the last minute for a grand house and fine dresses?"

"No, I'll run away first." She pulled her arm from his grasp and ran up to her own room and flung herself on her bed, gripping the covers as if she would tear them to bits.

I only want to be loved and to love, she sobbed to herself. They are all using me for their own ends and see nothing at all wrong with that. I know I am wicked, but I loved Ursula and she loved me. I'm sure she did. I believe I could love a man too, if I could be rid of my cloud. But that I can never be, so how can I ever be loved for myself?

She was sobbing aloud now, her face buried in the pillow so that no sound would carry to the Hordens' room. She dreaded tomorrow. Clifford Horden had been closeted with her father in his private room for two hours, but she was sure the outline of a marriage settlement had been drawn up already by lawyers and they were only discussing the details. After Christmas she would be fifteen and in her father's eyes perfectly marriageable. William was nearly nineteen, but seemed much younger. Many young men were married by seventeen. But I can't surely be dragged screaming to the altar. Truly, if they try to make me I'll do what I said to Robert; I'll run away.

Her dreams that night were full of foreboding.

Bel woke early the next day and saw a white mist against her window. Jumping up to look she was reminded of the day a year ago when she had escaped from her room to find Sam but had instead gone on to discover the body on the gallows. Sick at heart over all the intervening months of joys and disappointments and the ever present black cloud, she longed to disap-

pear altogether under cover of the fog. But where would she go? Older
now she knew that aimless running achieved nothing. As she watched, her
great-grandfather's statue began to loom through the whiteness. She was
oppressed by the generations that had come and gone, the women endlessly bearing children so many of whom did not survive.

"Is this what I am doomed to?" she said out loud. There is a world out
there but I am fixed in the lineage of Hordens and have no way out. She felt
the Hall and its lands as a great load about her neck. Why must it be saved?
It could be shared among the tenant farmers.

By the time breakfast, at which everyone was very quiet as if all sensed
a crisis point approaching, was over, a brave sun had sucked up the mist and
it promised to be a beautiful September day.

Robert said he must exercise Caesar and would William come riding
with him? William declined.

His mother rushed in with, "He doesn't know your mounts and we have
only our carriage horses here. He rides well, though, does he not, Clifford?"

"Tolerably," he said.

This naturally spurred Robert to go to the stables and come prancing
round in front of them all on Caesar as they stood on the front steps. "You
won't see a better horse than this in the whole of London," he called out to
them and galloped off round the park.

Sir John, frowning at this bravado, invited Clifford to his study,
presumably, Bel thought, to complete their deliberations.

"Will you walk, cousin," she said to William, "as far as the fishpond?"

He nodded and his mother descended the steps and trotted after them.
He hung back so she could join them and she immediately took Bel's arm
and became very confidential. "Sir John doesn't look at all well. Has he
seen a physician? We have the best in London, of course. What I would
really like is for you and your father to come back with us. If you saw

London you would never want to leave. All young people need to see life and have wholesome pleasures."

"We have life in Northumberland and I know no pleasure greater than walking in the country."

"But we have a fine house in the Strand, between Westminster and the City and we can stroll by the river or in St James' and not much above a mile away is the splendid Hyde Park, which was opened to the public some five or six years ago. Our house is not as large as the Hall here, but the space is much better used and it is so much warmer. We have water piped in and such conveniences as you wouldn't believe. Clifford would like of course to have a country estate. It is just unfortunate that this is so far north..."

"So he would really rather not have a share in it, as my father suggests."

"How you do jump in, Arabella! You are lacking a mother's training of course. But no, you don't understand the position. We are not seeking a share. It would be a purely business arrangement. I can't see us ever wanting to travel so far again, but if we can help your father out at eight per cent we are happily in a position to do so. You two need to become better acquainted. William is rather quiet and you are just the opposite, so I should say you are well-matched."

They had reached the fishpond where several branches and twigs were floating that had been torn from the ancient oak in this corner of the grounds by the recent gales. More were strewn about the grass and the place had a neglected look which would certainly upset her father. Bel reached down and drew out a branch, half expecting William to do the same but he just stood watching the fish slipping to and fro in the sunlight.

Bel fixed her eyes on him sternly. "Do you like fish?" she demanded, determined to make him speak.

"Oh," he said, surprised, "to look at or to eat?"

It was at that moment that Robert galloped past and called out, "I spy an intruder – a beggar by her looks." He was brandishing his whip.

Bel looked and could just make out a small, ragged figure venturing along the drive. For a few seconds she stared, unbelieving. There was no white bonnet but she knew only one person who had that peculiar scuttling run.

"It is!" she shrieked to an astonished William and his mother. Then she was running across the grass shouting "Ursula!"

But she was still a long way off and Ursula had now seen and heard the horse and was scrambling to the only shelter she might hide behind, the statue of Sir Ralph. Robert was upon her, thrashing out with his whip, circling the statue, yelling with the excitement of the chase as his quarry tried to escape.

Ursula was bobbing round on the plinth but Bel saw the whip catch her two or three times across the shoulders.

"Stop it, Robert," she screeched in a fury.

The branch was still in her hand and she hurled it as soon as she was close enough at Caesar's huge haunches. He reared up, forelegs flailing in the air, turning on her. Robert was hurled off backwards, his head cracking on the corner of the plinth. Bel dived out of Caesar's path under the stone hooves of Sir Ralph's horse and found herself clasping the small slight body of Ursula nestling under its belly. They looked into each others' eyes.

"Oh my sweet Bel," Ursula squeaked, "are you hurt?"

"You, you ... what has he done to you?" cried Bel.

"Nothing, nothing. I have covers enough on me." She was in fact in rags but they were bits of old blankets, thick and coarse. "But the horseman? Is he hurt? I am so sorry to have caused such a rumpus."

"You cause it! He is a brute, a ..."

She got to her feet and seeing Robert's inert legs protruding from the other side of the plinth she muttered, "If he has knocked himself out it is all he deserves." She stepped round and looked at him. She stared. The life seemed to go cold within her and drain out at her toes.

His neck was broken.

That much was instantly obvious from the angle of his head and his staring astonished eyes. Then he must be dead, her brain told her, but she still crouched down and lifted his head and called his name.

"Oh my Bel!" Ursula was beside her. "Who is he?"

"My brother."

She had never seen Ursula's face twisted with such shock and horror. She had never seen her whole head before, her pale ears and sparse grey hair. She had no bonnet and the shawl that had covered her as she scurried along had slid off. Her poor distorted features were all too plainly exposed to view and now as others came hurrying up Bel wanted to hide her from their sight just as much as she wanted to hide the sight of Robert.

All she could think was no, no, no, this hasn't happened. This can't be real. Time must go back.

But now all the Horden cousins were there and her father.

Celia Horden was crying, "Sir John, Sir John, where is your man to ride for a surgeon?"

Bel thought her father now truly looked an old man, white and haggard.

"But he is dead," he said hopelessly. He looked about. "How did it happen?" And then his eyes lighted on Ursula and he shrank away. "What is that?"

"Oh the Lord!" Celia Horden screamed. "It frightened the horse. It's a witch."

William was just staring in utter terror, unable to move.

Clifford at last spoke. "She must be locked up before she can do more mischief. Have you a cellar?"

"Don't look at her, William," his mother cried. "She can put a curse on you."

Bel surrounded her with her arms. "Father, don't you dare lock her up. She is my friend. My only friend in the world. How she came here I know not, but Robert was whipping her and now he has fallen off Caesar and he's dead."

"You hit the horse," William said. "I saw you."

Bel stared at him. So he had come to life, had he? "Yes," she shouted at him. "I hit the horse. I'd have hit Robert if I could have reached him. So call me my brother's murderer if you will. At least you won't want to marry me now." She glared at them all, her arms still round Ursula. "It is not this lovely one who has a devil. It is I."

Her father was moving his hands about as if to brush all this away. "We must carry him in. He's my son. I've lost my son, my only son." He bowed himself down then and took Robert in his arms and sobbed. The head lolled horribly and he moaned as he closed the eyes and tried to support the head against his shoulder.

Now at last other figures were emerging from the house and stables. Old Tom and young Adam, with the visiting footman and coachman, Nurse and Mary trailing behind them. Bel knew Sam had been running home between his footman duties to help his father so he was not there. If I have to run away to save Ursula from them all, she thought, that's where I'll run; to the Turner's farm.

Ursula had now wrapped herself up in her pieces of blanket with as little as possible of her face showing. Bel was clutching her tightly round the waist, aware how skinny she was and just beginning to realise that she was almost fainting from shock and exhaustion.

Still she could lift her head and murmur, "Let me just creep away, my Bel. I only came because the sweet Lord seemed to be telling me my girl needed me; but this you did not need. Maybe I mistook His word, for I have caused a disaster for you and your whole family. Let me go."

The servants were lifting the body onto a blanket and taking the corners. No one, for the moment, was looking at Bel or her companion.

"If you go, I go with you," Bel said. "Need you? I have been dead without you. I am the witch. I am the bringer of disaster."

"You just saved me as you saved Father Patrick. The Lord took your poor brother. If he had fallen on the grass he would be alive now. I am wretched for you, Bel, but you are not a murderer and though my coming was the cause of this, I do not believe I am either. But I should go while they have for the moment forgotten me. Let me slip away."

"You will come inside and have some refreshment. How did you come here?"

"I have walked, begging my way or working so it has taken a long time. I only knew Horden Hall was somewhere near to Newcastle."

Bel was walking her round the house to the courtyard where the stables were and the back door to the kitchen. Caesar had prowled about, pawing the ground, lost without his master, but now he followed them, seeing figures heading for where he knew hay would await him. Young Adam took his bridle. He peered at the strange being Bel was clutching, but Ursula held her blanket shawl close about her face and he asked no questions.

Bel could see he was bewildered with shock like them all and glad to seize upon something he could do that had any sort of normality. She told herself that her immediate task was to find food and drink for Ursula. Yet all the time there was a shout in her head. "You have killed Robert. Robert is dead."

A few minutes ago, she realised, he was laughing on Caesar's back and now he is a corpse, like that hanged man. No wonder he looked surprised. His soul flew off, ping, just like that; if he had a soul. Do any of us have souls?

She was looking in the larder and saw the pewter milk jug on the stone shelf. She took it out and cut a hunk of bread and spread it with butter.

How could his soul go anywhere but hell, she asked herself, when he was lashing out at a helpless woman when he died? I hated him. I wished him dead when I saw what he was doing. Please God, let there not be a hell or a heaven. Let there not be judgment or I am lost. But I am lost. That preacher said 'no murderer hath eternal life abiding in him.' What have I done but make my black cloud blacker still?

She sat Ursula on a stool and set before her the food and drink, telling herself, just keep caring for Ursula and never let her out of your sight again.

Nurse came into the kitchen. She had the same look as them all. She needed to be busy in the face of this horror; that the young master was dead. The heir to Horden was no more.. "What's all this then? Who is this?"

Bel saw that Ursula's back was towards her and she didn't turn round. "This is the poor woman Robert was trying to chase away when he fell. I know her. She was at Cranmore House. She is the best soul in the world and we must care for her."

"I'll see to her. You go to your father. He needs you."

"Nan," Bel whispered, stepping close to her, "she was born deformed. Do not be frightened of her. She is an angel."

Of course Ursula had the sharpest ears. Putting her head down she slipped off her stool and turned round and bowed herself almost to the ground before Nurse.

Bel saw Nurse frown in disgust.

In her thick, cramped voice Ursula brought out the words, "I'll work at anything, Mistress, but if I'm not wanted I'll go away."

"Nay, sit and eat," Nurse said sharply. "There's vegetables stewing in a good beef broth on the fire." She stepped to the hearth and taking the ladle from its hook and a bowl from the dresser she served Ursula a good portion.

Bel gave Nurse a hug, something she had not done since she was a small child.

Then she ran to find her father.

CHAPTER 13

NATHANIEL, buoyed up with excitement at the prospect of returning to Cambridge, brought down from his room the last items to go in his box. He knew he must put off no longer the news that his friend, young Edward Branford, had written to invite him to spend Christmas at their London home instead of returning to Yorkshire. To his sorrow and disappointment he found his father seated at the kitchen table, his head bowed over his hands and his shoulders shaking.

"What has happened? Where is mother?"

His father sat up abruptly and brushed one hand across his eyes. Nat saw a printed paper lying on the table. "No, no, son. She is sleeping late after one of her restless nights." He slapped the back of his hand on the paper. "It is this. For a moment it overcame me. Is there not sorrow enough in this life without the High Court of Parliament reaching down to meddle between us and our God?"

Nat reached for the paper.

"Can you believe it?" his father said. "They are telling me I am not to bow my head at my Lord's name. You know I have always preached peace and love, but now I am striving against anger and I am failing. I *am* angry. Who are they to think they can control such things?"

Nat saw that the paper was headed 'An Ordinance on Sabbath Keeping and Idolatry' and glancing down it he read that no games were to be played on Sunday, all images were to be removed from churches, the communion table was to be set in the middle of the church and finally that bowing at the name of Jesus must cease.

"How can they enforce such things?" he cried. He was bitter that it had come on his departure day and he must leave his father to face this trouble on his own.

"Oh they will come. You still bear some bruises from their methods, but how am I to command the necks of my parishioners? Will I be cast out of my living if heads that have lowered reverently all their lives at Jesus' name still bow? Will I myself remember to venerate in my *heart* only? Oh Nat, the world has gone mad."

Nat was overcome with pity. Had his father not had enough to bear with his mother's near madness but this also must be thrust upon him? He was angry too, thinking of Ben Hutton and his like, pig-headed in their self-righteousness. "I will speak out against this folly at the University. There are many there who believe in tolerance and will abhor this. My friend, Edward Branford, whom I have mentioned to you, is certainly one of them." Then he slipped in quickly the news of his invitation. "Will you mind if I accept, Father? He is a good youth and as a younger son is destined for the church. He seems to look on me as a sort of mentor. He is only sixteen."

His father rose and embraced him. "Of course go with him. In this world we cannot despise rank and an acquaintance like that may help you in your future. But the higher thought is that your faith and diligence may be a shining example to him. I thank God always that he has left me a son like you. But do not seek trouble by speaking your mind too freely on matters of religion." He was looking at the document again. "Maybe this will all pass. You have a life ahead of you. Bide your time and keep to your studies."

Nat smiled and nodded but he was telling himself the time might come when right must be striven for. He felt certain his courage would be put to the test again in the days ahead. The thought excited him and when, an hour later, he loaded his box onto the carrier's cart and turned to take his farewell of his father he tried to cheer him. "You are right, sir, that anxieties pass with time. We need no longer worry that my quitting the army will be held against me and Mother's obsession with vengeance on the Hordens may fade with the passing of the years. Even Daniel's death is now over a year past and the pain is perhaps a little, a very little, dulled."

He wished he had not mentioned that as he caught in his father's eyes a fleeting look which seemed to say, "The pain is still sharp for me, but you are young and your head is filled with new and absorbing study."

Nat could only hug him, glancing behind him to the house door to see if there was any chance his mother would come to bid him farewell but there was no sign. There were tears in his father's eyes as they separated.

"Yes, be happy, son. And I too will rejoice in the Lord always. I have long since forgiven the Hordens. Bitterness was not a burden I wished to carry. Indeed I pray for them nightly. May God be with you on your journey."

Nat climbed up beside the carrier who would take him into Easingwold on the first stage on his journey south. His father stood and waved till he had passed the village and was out of sight.

Only then did Nat fully appreciate how bereft his father must feel and how fearful – as a kindly traditional priest – of all the strife and oppression that he saw coming upon the country.

Bel found her father alone in his study. His face was grey as his beard, his body sunken in his chair. When he realised she was standing before him he looked up and to her surprise his eyes were gentle.

"I fear you will be blaming yourself for what has happened, Arabella. I know how it was and I believe it is something Robert brought upon himself." She was taking comfort from this when he suddenly clutched at her arm and cried, "But to strike a horse! You must have known it would endanger the rider. And did I not hear you say you would have struck Robert if you could have reached him? Who or what is this creature you were trying to protect?"

Still scarcely believing that life was going on, that she was standing here and the body of Robert was lying screened off in a corner of the great hall, she struggled to answer in a steady voice. Keeping Ursula was all that mattered now. "Father, she is the one I told you of, my friend from Cranmore House. She is destitute but she came here not to beg but to help *me*. She is the only one who can. Say she can stay. She will work for nothing. There is no household task she cannot do. Robert was treating her as he would a thieving vagrant. That was cruel, horrible."

Her father was shaking his head as if he could shake away the hour that had brought this catastrophe. "I know, I know, he could be cruel but he was my son, your brother. What is to become of us all? This woman, for whose sake he lies dead, you say she can do anything. Can she turn you into a dutiful daughter? I will see her, but not now. There are servants' rooms empty. Give her one for tonight at least. I will send for her when I can collect myself."

Bel slipped away to the kitchen before he could change his mind and told Nurse what he had said.

"Very well, but we must wash her first." Nurse spoke as if Ursula was not present. "Some of your outgrown dresses would fit her, she's such a little thing."

Bel ran to find one and brought an armful of underwear and a nightgown as well. Poor Ursula was now undressed and standing in the wooden tub. She clutched a length of old sheet about her as Nurse washed her down with a piece of flannel. The woollen rags were in a heap on the floor.

Bel was horrified to see that there were red weals and bruises across her shoulders.

"They were not all from your brother," Ursula murmured, and added with a hint of her old humour, "It was all I expected, when people saw my face."

"Oh Nan," Bel cried, trying not to imagine the horrors of Ursula's journey, "where do you keep some soothing ointment?"

"I'll get it," Nurse said, handing her the flannel. "Here, you finish her."

"I can manage, my precious," Ursula said. "She's very kind, but I can manage. If you'll hold that sheet as a shield. One of the men came in before, but he went out quickly, bless his heart."

When Nurse came back Bel had Ursula out and standing on the sheet wrapped in a warm towel from the clothes line above the hearth.

While Nurse applied the ointment vigorously Bel asked her, "Dear Nan, could you find some pieces of linen for her to make a bonnet with flaps at the side. When it's starched it's stiff enough to hide her face. She wore one at Cranmore House."

"Ay well, that sounds a good idea, for if she goes in the larder she'll curdle the milk. Put the nightgown on her, for she's dead on her feet and I've made the bed in the first attic. I reckon it's afternoon now and she can sleep a few hours or the night through if she wants."

"Eh, Mistress, you're goodness itself," Ursula cried.

Nurse grunted and turning up her nose manoeuvred the pile of dirty rags out of the backdoor with her foot. "They can be burnt tomorrow."

Bel helped Ursula up the back stairs and saw her tucked up. She didn't know where Mary was or whether Sam was coming later to serve dinner. Did people go on having regular meals after what had happened?

The attic was bare and cold but there were thick blankets on the bed and Ursula said it was luxury she didn't deserve after what she had done. Bel began to protest at that but she saw Ursula's eyes close and heard her murmuring a prayer of thankfulness. There were a thousand questions she wanted to ask her but a few minutes later she was fast asleep. Bel stood gazing at her. What a joyful miracle to have Ursula with me again! But why should I be blessed and cursed in the same moment?

With no immediate task to complete there was no escaping the thing that had happened. What were their guests doing? She didn't want to know but she couldn't hide herself away. She went down to the parlour and found the three Hordens there huddled over a decaying fire and talking in whispers.

They looked round as she came in and Clifford stood up. "This is a terrible sorrow, Arabella. Your father is writing letters to your poor mother and sister, though he is hardly in a state to do it."

Bel realised she hadn't given them a thought. It was strange to think of Mother receiving news of her son's death when she hadn't seen him for almost a year. All her childhood she had thought Mother adored Robert, but she had left him happily enough and Henrietta had done no more than tolerate him when they were grown, though as children they had united in teasing and hounding their little sister. Would they be devastated in the midst of their comfortable French life? She supposed they would feel obliged to come.

"Of course," Clifford was saying, "letters travel uncertainly to France. It may be weeks before we hear from them. The funeral sadly must be held without them and we believe it would be better to hold it as soon as possible. We cannot burden your father with entertaining visitors much longer at such a time."

"Oh," Bel said, much relieved, "so you'll be leaving us."

"Not till after the funeral of course, my dear," Celia broke in, rising too and taking her hands. "What we wish is that you and your father should follow us as soon as he can arrange it. A change of scene will do him so much good. And if your mother and sister and her husband too should come from France, it will be so much easier for them to visit in London than travel this dreadful journey north."

Bel didn't know how to withdraw her hands since Celia held onto them firmly and was looking searchingly into her eyes.

When Bel said nothing, Clifford went on gravely as if he had not been interrupted. "Your father knows of course that Robert's tragic death has made even more necessary the concluding of our business here. The marriage between you and William is the only thing that will save him not only from grief and despair, but from financial ruin too."

Bel looked from him to his wife and then at William who still sat hunched with his back to her. "Financial ruin?" She repeated the last words because she could find no other way to express her astonishment that he should revert to this at such a time.

"You do understand, Arabella, that your father has lost his heir. Of course he wishes his estate to stay within the family ..."

"So William's to have it, through me?" She pulled her hands away from Celia's and marched over to William and prodded his shoulder. "Is that what you want, William? You want to come here to Northumberland and be a squire and manage an estate?"

He scrambled to his feet in alarm. "I ... well, we ... I suppose we would live in London and I would work for my father in the business, but we could appoint a bailiff to look after things here."

It was the longest speech she had heard him make and she wanted to laugh in his face, but this was no laughing matter. "This, William, is my home. This is where I live with my father. I'd be wretched in London. If he needs any help managing this place *I* will do it. He told me himself Robert didn't do things the way he wanted. I can learn all about the farms and the crops and the leases. I *know* the tenants. I can see my life ahead now and it's good." She was bubbling suddenly with excitement. Ursula had come to her. Everything now was possible. She had a goal in life. Maybe if she could do some good here the black cloud, made blacker still today, could lift at last. She would help the poor, she would ...

William was looking away, embarrassed. His father and mother were both talking at once.

Bel wanted to walk out and leave them to it but instead she moved away from them and sat down on the couch below the window and folded her arms.

To her annoyance Clifford followed her and took a seat beside her. "Arabella, you are a child –"

"Far too young to marry, then," she snapped at him.

"I was about to say 'a child in these matters'." He was exuding an air of strained patience. "I can put this estate on a firm foundation. It is burdened with debt largely because of the Scots occupation. The farms have been plundered and the tenants cannot pay their rents. We hope the situation in the country will now settle down. The King is making concessions to the Edinburgh Parliament which we trust will bring lasting peace. Now all that remains is for our lawyers to approve the final settlement, so that you and William can marry in the spring. A six month interval after this tragedy is all that is necessary. Then the two families will be happily united."

Bel was fighting tears. "Robert didn't want you meddling in his inheritance," she burst out, thinking of how he had sat on the clothes chest in her room, one of the few times he had been pleased with her. Her only ally in fact. How alive he had been! She knew she could never grieve deeply for him, but this sudden snatching him away from her life was a fearsome shock. She stood up, afraid that she would give way to sobs. They were all looking at her. She choked out, "Can you not let us alone to get over this? William doesn't want marriage and neither do I."

"But William will do as he is told," Clifford Horden said as she fled to the door.

She heard Celia exclaim, "Oh Cliff, she is upset," and then she was running up to her room, determined to come down no more that day.

Nurse came to seek her eventually and said Adam had ridden to

Newcastle with her father's letters to speed them on their way. "Sir John is too worn out to sit at dinner, but he said you should go down."

"Oh Nan, I can't. Let me see if Ursula is still asleep and if she is hungry let me take another bowl of that beef broth to her and have some myself. The cousins speak of nothing but my marrying William and I can't stand it."

Nurse shrugged her shoulders. "You'll come round to the marrying business, but they shouldn't press it now. Well, slip down the back stair and take two bowls up. There's the doctor come to see how poor Mr Robert died – as if it wasn't plain to everyone his head hit the statue and his neck broke. But it's for the coroner I suppose. Your father never liked that statue. I was here when it was put up, you know. I thought it a grand thing, though the likeness to Sir Ralph was not so good." She went out still talking to herself.

She has seen so much of our history, Bel thought, births, deaths and marriages. What is one more death in the catalogue of the past?

Ursula was still deeply asleep so Bel finished both the bowls, returned them to the kitchen and took a mug of ale and some oatcakes up to the attic and left them by Ursula's bed. Not much later she put herself to bed but sleep was far from her until the early hours of the morning.

When she rose next day she found out that Ursula had been up in the early morning and had found the wood basket and the coal store and had cleared and relaid the hearths downstairs, swept the kitchen floor, lit the fire there and boiled the big kettle before either Mary, Tom or Adam were up.

Nurse went to inform Sir John of this when he appeared, white and haggard, before noon and she told Bel afterwards what had passed. "I said to your father, 'We know nothing of her, sir, except she has a face nobody would want to look at, but if you'll keep her on she could be a godsend, especially as Mary will want to leave soon to wed that Turner lad."

Mary and Sam! Bel thought with a bitter pang. Of course, why would they not wed? He is a fine young farmer's son and she is a capable pretty girl from the village. They have no hateful baggage round their necks, no dowries, no settlements, no estates, no lawyers and they are attracted to each other. How sweet and right and simple that is! Marriage is in the air. All I have to do is follow suit.

"What did my father say?" she asked Nurse.

"Eh well, he's not saying much at all, but he waved his hand at me and nodded so I reckon he's leaving it to me to decide. Poor soul, I suppose her family cast her off when they took a look at her. But if she can cook too, I'll be happy. All this work is not how I expected to live out my last years.. Will there be many mouths to feed after the funeral, do you reckon?"

"I don't know, Nan. I don't know what's proper. We'll have to let all the tenants drink at The Crossed Swords I suppose." Overjoyed though she was at Nurse's acceptance of Ursula she was exasperated by her question. Is father so helpless now that I must be in charge as the mistress of the house but at the same time I am still a girl who must do as I am told?

But it was her father, despite his brittle state, who gave orders for the funeral. Though there were to be hangings at the windows and yards of black ribbons on the horses and two hired carriages, the trestle tables were not to be laid out in the medieval hall for the tenant farmers and their families to be feasted. As she had supposed, some money was distributed after the service of burial for the mourners to go to the inn, but her father was not prepared to go any deeper into debt, so it was only the Hordens and the vicar of the parish who were to dine afterwards.

Small as the numbers were, several courses were prepared in the kitchen and Sam was there in his livery to help Mary serve. Bel took note of their glances as she watched them lay out the best silver she had herself polished and it was obvious that they were in complete accord. She would have tormented herself watching them during the meal but her father, having asked the vicar to say grace and waited till the first dish had been served, sent the servants out.

"We will call you when we require your services."

As soon as the door was shut he declared, "I have to tell you that when Adam took my letters to Newcastle a ship had just come in with letters for me from France. Knowing they were likely to contain only frivolities I couldn't bear to look at them but I resolved to do so when I had said farewell to my son." His voice shook and he took a sip of wine and continued. "I find they do in fact contain news which ought to lift our spirits. My daughter Henrietta is with child. Let us toast the unborn infant and pray for a safe delivery which is expected in early March."

Amid the exclamations of congratulation from the others Bel sipped her wine and studied her father's face to see if he was taking comfort from the prospect of a grandchild. It was hard to tell, so drawn and pale he still appeared. Her own mind was busy with speculation. How did this affect her situation? Surely it would lift the pressure to marry William. There would be a direct heir.

Clifford seemed to have read her thoughts. "We thank God for this, John, and will pray for a son, but of course he will be brought up a young French nobleman. It is most unlikely he would ever come to England to manage this property."

Her father drew a sharp breath and winced. He laid his hand momentarily against his left side. Bel watched him in alarm. "You are no doubt right, Cousin," he said huskily. "And I know too well the fragility of infants. Maria and I lost two sons."

Celia cried out, "And our William is the sole survivor of our four. Three girls succumbed to sickness."

In healthy London? Bel itched to say.

Celia reached a hand to her across the table. "This is why I long for a daughter."

Bel stared down at the table cloth. What wretched suffering lies ahead for married women, she was thinking. They become bloated creatures, they give birth in pain and like as not their child is dead or lives a while only to be taken from them. I had rather die an old maid than go through such torment. She began to feel very sorry for Henrietta.

The vicar now intervened. "Alas, our thoughts are morbid, after today's sad ceremony. Let us rather rejoice in the glad tidings of a new life. I am sure, Sir John, that your daughter, who I remember as a fine strong young lady, will have the best care. No doubt you will be making a journey to France in the spring as she and Lady Horden will not be risking a sea voyage themselves."

Bel saw her father smile wistfully. "I cannot look so far into the future." He clapped his hands for Mary and Sam to clear the dishes and bring the leg of mutton. Bel saw it had been dressed with fresh mint just as Ursula presented it at Cranmore House when they had meat on Sundays. She was sure the dear soul was very busy, but keeping in the background behind her newly-made bonnet.

The presence of the vicar kept the talk from the marriage controversy, but when it turned to the political situation it seemed unlikely to be any more harmonious.

Clifford was certainly in favour of Parliament and what he called 'our precious English liberties' while her father and the vicar spoke up for their duty to the King.

Celia raised her hands in mock despair. "Oh if the men are going to speak of these things, Arabella, we shall have no peace" but as Bel would give her no help she was unable to make any other conversation on her own. William of course said nothing but he ate well, especially of a handsome apple pie that was brought in.

Bel wondered if plans had been made for their leaving, now that the funeral was over. Her fear that the marriage negotiations would break out again, despite the news from France, spoilt her appetite when she would have loved to match William mouthful for mouthful.

It was the next day that her father sent for her to his study in the middle of the morning and she thought, this is the moment. I am once more to be told my duty and will have to hurt and disappoint him all over again.

She stood warily before him and he said, "It is time I saw the new maid. Nurse speaks well of her. Will you bring her to me?"

She almost skipped with relief. "Oh yes, Father, at once." And off she ran to find Ursula who put on a clean apron and adjusted her bonnet.

"Will I do, Bel?" She was calm and composed. In the study she bobbed very low and with eyes down waited to be spoken to.

"Look at me," he said and she lifted her face. He studied it a moment with knitted brows. "Can you speak?"

"Oh yes, sir. But I try to keep away from long words."

"What was your position at Cranmore House?"

"I did what I was asked. The Mistress took me in off the streets when she started the school. I can cook, clean, make fires, do the beds. I can read if it's writ large and write a little."

"My daughter is very fond of you. I am ashamed at the way you were treated when you came here."

Then Ursula became her animated self, "Oh sir, I am ashamed at how I looked that I provoked your son. It is terrible what happened and I am so very, very sorry."

He waved this away. "No, no. It has happened and that is it. I believe you are called Ursula. Have you another name?"

"I never knew one, sir."

"Very well. I would like you to stay with us, but as you may know already my daughter should marry her cousin soon and will leave us. She calls you her friend. Would you stay here if she went away?"

Bel who had waited by the door sprang forward. "No one is to separate us ever again."

He held up his hand and she thought he had never looked so sternly at her. "Be silent, Arabella. Pray answer me, Ursula."

"I would be happy to serve you, sir, as long as Bel lived here, but if she went away and wanted me, I believe the good Lord would say that was my duty, my duty and my joy, if I may say so, sir, because I love her."

Bel felt tears choking her.

"You call my daughter Bel?"

"I beg your pardon, sir, but my lips are not good at Arabella."

"Well, I let that pass. You must understand if my daughter goes away, any decision about her bringing a servant would be as her husband and his family wished since she would live with them."

"Oh father," Bel burst out, "Ursula is my *friend*, not my *servant* and I am not going away anywhere, so she doesn't have to choose at all."

"I have told you to be silent." He leant back in his chair and Bel saw red spots of anger glowing in a face that suddenly appeared white with exhaustion. "You leave me no choice," he began after a few moments in a voice grown faint and husky. "If you do not consent to the marriage I will have to send Ursula away. If you comply I will do my best to persuade my cousins to accept that she accompanies you."

Bel stared at him, open-mouthed, and then hugged Ursula to her. "How could you be so cruel, Father!"

He made a shooing motion with his hand. "You have wearied me to death with your obstinacy. In my poor health and after the blow that has so lately fallen upon me, I think many people would call your disobedience cruelty. Now leave me and consider carefully what I have said. You too, Ursula. And, as my daughter appears to value you more than her father, if you can give her wise advice I will be for ever grateful to you."

Ursula bobbed deeply again but Bel clasped her hand and pulled her outside.

"To my room, quickly." She bounded up the stairs still clutching her hand and didn't release her till they were safe inside the narrow room.

"It used to have a bolt inside when it was a chapel but they took it away. Now it only has one outside. Well, Urs, all we can do is run away together. I will not be forced into marriage. We had better wait till after dark."

Ursula's bright eyes were twinkling with love. "Oh my Bel, I am not worth a break-up with your father. You shall not be forced into a marriage you hate, but you will not tear yourself from your family and go into a life of homeless wandering. I am well used to that. I will go quietly away and you will stay and love your father. I can see he is a man in need of love. Much, much love."

Bel stamped her foot. "How could I love him now? I hate him. You speak of my family. I have not seen my mother and sister for a year and they never loved me. My brother is dead. That is still the strangest shock, but I never loved him. You are the only person I love and who loves me. You will *not* go away."

Ursula smiled. "Now come, sit on the bed and we will think together. What you have just said is so very sad. It is a story of hate when there should be love. Are you going to add the young betrothed to your list of hates? And his parents too?"

"*He* is not worth hating, but I think I could hate *them* very easily. They think only of money and possessions."

"But they are people with feelings like all of us. If you are loving to them, they will come to love you. If you show all the sweetness you have in your nature to their son, he will open to you like a flower. He will begin to love you and then you will soon find you love him too."

"Oh Ursula, when you say it, it seems so easy. You do it. You are sweet and gentle and cheerful to everyone. But I have that within me that holds me back. I only want to be here with you and that those people should go away and Father; oh I am sad for him. He looks ill, but how could he put so dreadful a threat upon me?"

"But he is wounded by the loss of his son. It is so new and raw. All else about him should be peace but you are fighting him."

"So you would have me say yes to what he asks! Is that really what you are saying?"

"Sweet Bel, you could say no *gently*. You could be soft-spoken. Ask that it should be put off while you are all grieving. You could be loving with him and he might long to keep you by his side since he will now be so alone."

"You don't understand. It's already dragged on since the very first day I came home. They are all set on it being fixed now. But I shall never marry. I told them yesterday that I would learn about managing the estate to help Father." In a sudden flash she recalled Robert's word that Father might not survive the winter. A wicked, wicked thought reared up that she and Ursula could live happily here with no one to bully them about anything.

Ursula had slid down off the bed and was assessing her expression.

"My Bel, I must go and do my duties. Think and pray, my precious, and the good Lord will put good thoughts into your heart." Bel was about to burst into protests but Ursula just gave her a loving smile and slipped out.

I do believe she guessed what I was thinking about father, she thought. She doesn't know how hard it is for a murderer to have good thoughts. She put her hands together in an attitude of prayer and looked with her mind's eye at each of the four people in turn who could influence her destiny. A few pitiful thoughts floated in her father's direction but bounced back, hardened by the horrible dilemma he had put her in. As for Clifford Horden, it was a struggle to send any good thoughts in *his* direction. His sharp face and Puritan haircut positively repelled her. His manner was cold and imperious. Whether William would turn out the same she couldn't possibly tell, because as yet he seemed to have no character at all. To send good thoughts his way would be like shooting at a wraith. But then there was Celia. Ursula had suggested everyone had feelings and Celia had shown glimmerings when she had reached across the table and said she wanted a daughter. Bel felt quite moved when she thought of the three little girls she had lost, whether in babyhood or later she didn't know.

She fired off some kindly thoughts to Celia Horden and found herself thinking, but she was putting on a show to win me; she *is* under Clifford's thumb. All she's ever said to me was to persuade me to do what he wants. She's not interested in me as me.

"You see, Urs," she said aloud to the empty room, "it's no good."

She went to the window and stood looking out. There was Sir Ralph on his horse, totally indifferent to the death that had happened right there below on his stone platform. Bel shook her fist at him. "You killed your great-grandson, don't you know, you stupid old man." She became aware of a figure coming into view and waving a hand to her. It was Celia Horden. "Oh heaven, she thought I was waving to her. Why, she's alone. Well, I do feel *something* for her so I must catch her now. She's my only hope," and without putting on a shawl she flew downstairs and dragged open the big front door.

Celia was sauntering past the statue, pausing to look up at it, but she heard her footsteps and turned to greet her with a smile.

She's such a funny little round figure, Bel thought. I'm not in the least afraid of her. It's the first time I've spoken to her on her own.

But Celia in her voluble way didn't give her time to speak. She tucked her arm through Bel's and began, "Now my dear, I must apologise for my shy boy. Here he is, for the first time in his life, coming a-courting and what does he say to his lady-love? Absolutely nothing. Of course you can have no impression what he's like and I don't at all wonder at your reluctance to say you'll marry him. But I really must tell you that he is not only most industrious, but actually clever. Any subject he applies himself to he can master in the time it would take most people barely to learn the rudiments. What he hasn't had the chance to master is how to talk to young ladies. If his sisters had only lived, what a difference that would have made! He would have met all their friends from an early age and he wouldn't be afraid of anyone in skirts."

When she paused for breath Bel managed to say, "I don't want to be thought of or talked to as a young lady. When he was about eight and I was five you came to visit and he called me Pig-face."

"Gracious, my dear, I hope you've forgiven him for that. I had no idea!"

"It was good. I put my tongue out at him. At least we were communicating."

"Ah, I can see it is as I suspected. You want to get to know him and he's making it difficult. I have had words with him this morning and he has promised to try harder."

Bel felt the conversation was taking the wrong turn. "No, truly, Ma'am, I don't want him to. I do not want to marry, not now or ever."

"Ah well, of course that will change, but I see how it is. You are unusually young for your age, even childish I may say. Some young ladies of almost fifteen are quite grown and sophisticated but you run about and speak out of turn just like a little girl. Not your fault, I am sure, for you have lacked a mother's care for a whole year and the school they sent you to – well! Never mind, it is closed now."

They had walked round the lawns and arrived at the fish pond again. Bel took the chance to disengage her arm so she could stoop and clear more of the twigs that had gathered at the rim near them. "I don't know why they closed that school," she said. "I've no other experience of schools, so I can't say if it was better or worse than another."

"It was a *Popish* establishment. Dreadful contamination for a good Protestant girl."

Bel shrugged. "I didn't notice. We went to the Parish Church on Sundays."

"You had to, by law of course, but never mind that, you are away from there now and Sir John very wisely didn't send you back. What I am thinking, my dear, is that you and William should consider yourselves betrothed now but wait till you are sixteen and he is twenty before you marry."

Bel stood very still, oblivious of the bunch of wet twigs clutched in her hands, thinking furiously. She had come out to try to convince this lady that she could never be her daughter-in -law. But could this be a possible compromise? A betrothal was generally considered binding, but it was not a marriage. And Ursula would not have to go away. They would gain precious time, a whole year together. Who knew what might happen in a year! If Father is better he might expect to take me to France to see Henrietta's baby and Ursula could go as my lady's maid. We might all be drowned on the way back. Perhaps if I drowned with Ursula she might get me into heaven despite my devils. Oh anything could happen in a year! William might even fall in love with someone else!

"You're quiet, Arabella. What think you of my suggestion? I am quite prepared to tell the gentlemen that neither of you are ready for marriage. William would certainly have conformed to our wishes, but as his mother I do believe he is not quite ready."

Bel nodded vigorously. "He is not and neither am I."

"Very well, let us walk back to the house. This pond must have sad associations for you since it was from here you ran so hastily to spare that odd little creature, we sometimes see flitting about the Hall. And what a tragic outcome that was! I think it was then I realised how very young and impulsive you still are. But a year will work wonders and you shall spend much of it in London where you will see how society conducts itself. Come, let us go in."

Bel reluctantly set her feet in motion. She wanted to stay rooted to the spot watching the little fish flash hither and thither, young and carefree, and not obliged to go to London. That had not been part of the bargain if indeed a bargain had been made. But she knew her father would not want to go to London – if he was indeed well enough to make the journey. He had never liked the smoke and noise and smells.

So she slowed to Celia Horden's pace back to the Hall, while plans darted about in her head. I must submit to the betrothal. I must show myself sweet and dutiful to my father so he will agree to this delay. I will find Ursula and tell her and she will help me to be good. I will behave like a young lady – but not too much so or Celia will forget how childish I am. But oh if I have escaped from the impossible choice Father gave me –! She could hardly restrain herself from skipping ahead and running to Ursula with the news.

It was of course the dinner hour and nothing was said or done till afterwards when she knew the elder Hordens were closeted in the study with her father. William had disappeared to Robert's room which he now had to himself and Nurse had gone to have her afternoon rest in the housekeeper's room.

Sam had returned to the farm till he was needed again and Mary had walked him part of the way because she knew Ursula would do all the clearing up. Bel had Ursula to herself in the kitchen and was able to hang up for her the brass pans and kitchen tools which she had to climb on a stool to reach.

"So you think the horrid knot is untangling, my Bel, and you can see a straight way ahead."

"If Cousin Celia can make the men see reason."

"And you are ready to plight your troth to young William?"

"We will buy time. You and I will not have to run away."

"But you don't expect to marry him?"

Bel looked at her doubtfully. "You *are* going to stand with me in this, aren't you, Urs? I am doing this to keep you. Nothing else matters."

"My precious, I will never leave you if I can help it." She put her little arms round Bel's waist and hugged her. "But if you make a promise you don't expect to keep, I will think my Bel is not chiming as clear and true as she might."

"Is that all?" Bel chuckled. "You know I can never live to your standards."

She whirled her round the kitchen till her bonnet was awry. Then she stopped. She had heard footsteps. Ursula adjusted her bonnet and began scrubbing the table as Bel hastened to the door. Her father was at the head of the steps to the kitchen.

"I thought you must be here," he said, glimpsing Ursula at work. "I believe we have peace at last." He stretched his hands to her as she came to meet him. "You have agreed to a betrothal and we have settled your marriage to William Horden for the Spring of 1643, God willing."

Bel swallowed hard. Was this what she had done? She let her father lead her to the parlour where they were now all assembled. A little ceremony was performed in which she and William repeated words to each other and momentarily held hands. All the time she was saying in her head, it is only October 41. April 43 is an age away. Where will we all be by then? Where will the world be?

Two days later the Hordens departed at an early hour in the morning. Her father who had come down in a bed-gown to wish them 'God Speed', said, "I will to my bed again, Bella, but I have secured your future. God be praised. I can sleep now."

When he had gone upstairs Bel stood in the centre of the great hall and looked about her. "All this is mine. I am free. Nurse has said she will go back to her cottage and resume her retirement. Sam will go back to the farm for good and take Mary soon. Old Tom will stay on in the room above the stable and do the heavy work and he will only have Father's horse to groom when Caesar is sold. Adam wants to join the King's army. So Ursula and I will be left to look after Father. I shall go and see what is growing in the kitchen garden. With only Nurse's pension and Tom's wage to pay surely we can live well enough. Yes, I am free."

She was dancing all over the hall when she suddenly stood still and asked herself if the black cloud had gone. Deliberately she let herself look at the picture in her head, the huge hanging body, the distorted face, the one eye. No, it was there with the guilt that she had never confessed. I fired the stack and he died.

Strangely Robert's death, so recent, was not as sharp a pain. I hit Caesar and Robert broke his neck. But people saw it and though they know I did it they are saying only that I am a wild, impulsive child.

I will always have my cloud. I am for ever a murderer and can never inherit the Kingdom of God but I can eat and drink and be merry here as long as I have Ursula.

And she went into the kitchen to find her.

CHAPTER 14

Christmas 1641

NATHANIEL, overwhelmed by the sights and smells and above all the noise of London, could hardly believe the change when the Branfords's liveried footman admitted Edward and himself into a spacious hallway and closed the heavy door behind them. There was sudden quiet, order, cleanliness and polish. Straight ahead was a gleaming oak staircase, intricately carved and with finials of heraldic beasts staring down their leonine noses at him. He found his travelling cloak silently removed and Edward ushering him towards the stairs, a little shyly as if Nat's speechlessness made him unsure of the impression his home was making on his visitor.

They walked up past several huge portraits of Elizabethan Branfords to the first landing, from which several panelled doors led off.

"They've given you this one, Nat, next to mine. I hope it'll do."

Nat saw furniture such as he had never seen before, an ornamented hanging cupboard in which his short cloak, one spare doublet, two pairs of breeches and three very plain linen shirts would look miserably insignificant, and an inlaid chest of drawers which he couldn't possibly fill with his few stockings, collars and cuffs, but it was the bed that dominated the room. It was at least eight feet high to the canopy and almost as long, every inch of its four posts and top carved with flowers and scrolls. The curtains were of crimson velvet ending in tassels of gold cord and the coverlet was of white silk with a gold and crimson embroidered border. He fought down an urge to echo Ben Hutton's levelling philosophy. 'We should be all the same, no high, no low, no rich, no poor.'

"It's magnificent, Edward," was all he murmured.

"Oh well, I'm pleased. But I apologise for the lack of welcome. You'll meet the family at supper, except Henry of course, who is in the army. Father is at the Lords and I suppose my mother and sisters are visiting a neighbour. They weren't sure when we would arrive, but for once we made good time on the road from Cambridge. We don't stand on ceremony very much. I hope you don't mind."

Nat didn't mind at all but the mention of sisters filled him with apprehension. Young ladies were a total mystery to him. He had heard Edward speak of an older sister who had been married to a cavalry officer, killed in the very battle of Newburn on Tyne that he had avoided. She might be out of mourning, but still very subdued. Hot and embarrassed at his own guilt, he would scarcely be able to look at her. The other sister was Edward's twin, so would be coming up to her seventeenth birthday, a terrifying age. Nat had never spoken of Daniel to anyone at the University. How could he fend off inquiries as to his fate? But knowing Edward was also a twin had further endeared him to him. Meeting a charming female Edward would be another matter altogether. He expected to be horribly tongue-tied.

"I'll knock you up when it's time," Edward said, peering into the silver gilt basin and ewer set out on a marble-topped table. He tested the water with his fingers. "That's right. It's warm. I'm in the next room if you want anything."

When he'd gone Nat perched on a chair and gazed up at the plaster ceiling, more intricate patterns, cherubs, flowers and birds. What am I doing here? he wondered. I should be at home in the room Dan and I shared all our childhood. I should be supporting my poor father and trying to pacify Mother.

When Edward at last knocked and said, "Thank goodness, it's feeding time," he had reached a spurious state of indifference to the family he was about to meet.

This was gone within the first five minutes. No one could be indifferent to Lord Branford, large and florid and apparently in a state of simmering anger. His lady made less impact although she was also large. Her manner was friendly but casual; just another friend of Edward she seemed to be thinking as she gave him her well-beringed, flabby fingers. But the girls, introduced as Hermione and Penelope, made Nat lower his eyes in embarrassment. Both wore very low bodices, though a flimsy piece of lace offered partial concealment. Both had shining fair-hair in dazzling ringlets and wide blue eyes. At first he was confused as to which was the older but he soon found that Hermione, far from being a sad widow, was flamboyantly beautiful and brimming with confident charm while Penelope had small, plain features and the resemblance to Edward was slight. She was quiet and Nat thought she looked sulky. Perhaps it was because her sister instantly took charge of him.

Hermione sat herself next to him and though her father was obviously bursting to describe his day in the House of Lords she wanted to know Nat's impressions of London, how did he like Cambridge, where was his home and was he as brilliant a scholar as Edward kept telling them?

All this was very flattering and helped to dispel some of his nervousness, as she appeared genuinely interested in his answers. But he was aware that Lord Branford wanted him and Edward to listen to what he had to say and at last he managed to cock an ear in his direction.

"I am sure, sir," Lord Branford addressed him directly, "that you are a King's man." Nat nodded with enthusiasm. "But I have to tell you his majesty has done a very foolish thing." Nat moderated his expression. "He has appointed to the Lieutenancy of the Tower a man that is a brute and utterly intolerable to the Commons and many in the Lords. Who is advising the King I ask myself? Anyone could do better than those he has about him."

"You, my dear, would be perfect," Lady Branford said in a tone that suggested she had said such things regularly throughout their marriage but with little conviction.

"And then there are the Bishops. There is a move to put them out of the Lords altogether. The King can't protect them if he has lost the people's trust. There are apprentices in the streets shouting, 'Down with the Bishops' and 'No Popery.' It's such a turmoil that the Commons are not going to recess for the usual twelve days of Christmas. They will be back in two or three and I daresay we in the Lords will have to do the same to counter some of their excesses, but none of us will stand this new appointment to the Tower. He must go." He sighed deeply. "Apart from church, I would advise you all to stay indoors till things are quieter. I fear you have left a peaceful Cambridge, young man, for a turbulent capital."

"We have known turbulence even in remote Yorkshire, my Lord," Nat ventured to say and he recounted the episode of the Puritans and their petition in Easingwold. He was delighted with Hermione's reaction.

"You stood against three of them and refused to sign! Oh the bravery of it. Now, Father, do we not need men of such principle in high places today? You are for ever bemoaning the corruption both at Court and in Parliament."

Nathaniel, embarrassed now, felt his cheeks grow hot.

Lord Branford permitted himself a smile in his direction and said, "I think our young friend will at least wish to graduate before he is elevated to high places. And we can but wait and see, all of us, the outcome of these struggles. At least the King has made a measured reply to the so-called Grand Remonstrance that Parliament had the effrontery to put before him. We will hope moderation prevails when sittings resume. But I am doubtful, very doubtful." He shook his heavy-jowelled head, as if gloom and frustration had again set in.

Cards were produced in the evening and the four young people were expected to sit down and play. Hermione insisted on partnering Nat who had never played cards in his life.

"We only gamble with buttons," Hermione said. "But it's fun to pretend it's real."

Nat supposed that couldn't be sinful and concentrated on learning the rules of the game, which he did so quickly that Henrietta screamed out to her mother, sitting on the sofa with her embroidery, "Oh, it is as Edward said; his brain is as sharp as a needle."

Nat attributed this to his moderation over the freely flowing wine. Unused to that as he was to cards, he kept covering the glass with his hand when the footman came to refill it. He was glad he had because the others became merry and careless and soon a pile of buttons had accumulated in front of him to which Hermione had contributed very little.

"How thoroughly we have trounced them," Hermione cried and Penelope looked more sulky than ever.

When they were all tired the servants carried candles and warming pans to the bedrooms and goodnights were wished all round.

Hermione laid a hand on his arm. "You are by far the most interesting of Edward's friends. Very strong-minded I can see, fearless and self-controlled. I think you quite frighten me." She gave him her most ravishing smile and vanished to her own room.

This was so unlike Nat's own image of himself that he lay long awake thinking of her full lips and startling blue eyes with their air of surprise and delight turned constantly on him.

On Christmas Day they walked to church in the next street, the Branfords all wearing dark cloaks over their rich clothes, though Nat thought their large feathered hats rather gave away their status. He saw several coaches pelted with horse manure and rotten fruit, but they were not molested.

Afterwards an enormous Christmas dinner was served, which would have fed the whole of Darrowswick for a week. Then there was music. Hermione sang and played on the virginals. Edward and Penelope sang a duet and when Nat was called upon to perform, he played them a medley of carols on his recorder.

"A humble instrument but mine own," he grinned feeling more at ease than he had imagined possible on so brief an acquaintance.

"I'll wager you have a better instrument than that," Hermione whispered to him, "hidden away."

He felt himself flush and turned away his face. Surely she couldn't mean what he thought she meant!

For the rest of the day he tried to keep his distance from her, but they had not long been retired for the night when he heard a tapping at his door. It must be Edward or a servant come to see if he had all he wanted. Taking his candle he opened the door a crack. She had pushed it open and whisked inside before he could stop her. She turned and locked it and stood with her back to it, smiling at him. She was in her nightgown.

"This is what you have been wanting, Nathaniel Wilson. Very cunning the way you kept apart from me these last hours, to throw them all off the scent."

Nat, dismayed and horrified, set down his candle and retreated several paces, but where could he run? "Madam, I assure you," he began. "It would be ill repayment for Lord and Lady Branford's hospitality if I had ever had such a thought ..."

"Oh we can take all that as said. They'll never know and you can have no fear. I have come prepared," and she drew from her sleeve what looked like a tube made from an animal's skin.

Nat could only guess its purpose as his horror at her behaviour deepened.

His expression made her manner change. "Oh I do believe you are a total innocent. How charming! From the remote wilds of Yorkshire without an idea what goes on in high places, even at court. Goes on discreetly of course. Charles' court is not like his father's or so I am told. Nevertheless, we all have human nature."

She sidled closer and he retreated again. If he could lure her to the other side of the bed he might leap through it and unlock the door. He had already drawn back the curtains. It would be painfully embarrassing but he might escape to Edward's room and say he had had a nightmare. Surely she would slink away then. But first he would be plain with her. And once again he was drawing on courage he didn't know he possessed. He held his hands in a stop gesture and said as sternly as he could, "You speak of human nature, Madam, but that is the very thing we are to keep under. You commended me for my self-control. So pray leave my room."

"Self-control fiddlesticks. You are desperate to find out how good it is. And with me it is. I can tell you."

There was certainly a temptation to find that out but he had vowed chastity till he should marry and the idea of performing with this woman for whom he had begun to feel a deep loathing was abhorrent to him. Beautiful she might be in an abandoned way with her golden hair falling about her shoulders, but she made him think of the sirens of Greek mythology and how Odysseus had escaped them.

"You lapped up my praises like a little dog," Her tone was wheedling now.

"I was gratified by your interest. No more than that. I am sorry if it meant more than friendly courtesy. No ..." as she made to jump on him.

He turned and plunged through the bed as she tried to grab his bare foot. Leaping off at the other side he ran to the door. She was almost as quick in running round the bed. He had unlocked the door and was pulling it open when she reached up her hand and scratched her nails down his cheek. Her lovely face was distorted with rage, reminding him agonisingly of his mother. "I will go, you beast. And I hope you never have a second's pleasure with a woman in your life." She dragged the door behind her with what sounded to him an echoing bang and he heard her footsteps running away down the passage.

He locked the door and put his hand to his cheek where he could feel blood trickling down. He had hardly begun to bathe the place at his silver basin when a different knock came and Edward's voice called softly, "Nat!"

Holding a handkerchief to the place he opened the door though how he was to explain the rumpus he couldn't imagine.

That proved unnecessary. "Oh Nat, she didn't, did she? I'm so very sorry," was Edward's greeting. "It's hard to know what to do because I made a fool of myself once butting in. The fellow said I spoilt his pleasure."

"Merciful heaven! Does this happen often?"

"Usually they are older. I thought you would be safe. She's quite old – twenty-six. I'm afraid she misses her late husband. He was a dashing cavalry officer and I suppose ... but you understand."

He sat down on the end of the bed and looked sadly at Nat. "She's quite a problem, because he was a terrible spendthrift and she's been left with debts. Father would love to get her married off, to anyone steady. She's already cost him one dowry and I suppose he'd have to find another. Well, she certainly took a fancy to you."

Nat held up his hand in a stop gesture. "No thank you, Edward. Much as it would delight me to be your brother that would be too high a price."

"There's Penelope of course but they're fishing for an Earl's son for her, who would bring a good marriage settlement."

"Whereas I would bring nothing. No, Edward, I never aspired to marry into the nobility and I will certainly not marry at all until I can take a wife home to a cosy parsonage. And I'm afraid at present I have a low opinion of the stability of womankind." He refrained from saying it but he was disappointed too with the whole family, including Edward himself. All he wanted now was to get into bed and, if possible, sleep.

Edward sat on, musing, "Will there be any parsonages left for you and me with the country taken over by these ranting Presbyterian preachers? When my father said it was the church for me, he promised a well-endowed parish where the vicar was quite a figure in the community. Mother hoped I could get one of the fashionable London churches. But now ..." He looked mournfully at Nat.

Nat wanted to pick him up and shake him, shake off the family and have his fellow-student back. Instead he shrugged and yawned. "Let us not be anxious; the morrow will take care of itself." He said it lightly but the thought of meeting Hermione on the morrow sickened him. He looked at his handkerchief. "If I have stopped bleeding, I'd like to get into bed but I must not stain this beautiful silk cover."

"I'm truly sorry. Father and mother don't know about Herm's little ... what? ... escapades, so we'll think up an excuse for your scratch. *She* will probably not speak to you again till we go back to Cambridge."

"Perhaps I should go sooner."

"I must show you London first, whatever Father says. But we'll go soon. My tutor expects me to have read that new commentary on Aristotle by Thomas Hobbes. There are too many distractions here."

Nat gave a wry smile. "There certainly are."

For the next few days all was well as Nat and Edward breakfasted early and none of the ladies appeared then. Lord Branford said that if the young men walked or took Hackney coaches rather than the Branford carriage, they might be safe to look about a little. In the evenings Hermione simply ignored him and pretending a headache refused to play cards. As no one else was eager, Nat made it his business to learn as much as he could of what was going on in Parliament from Lord Branford.

"The King has agreed to replace that brute at the Tower," he told him.

"I think he has been frightened into making concessions so Pym's men in the Commons see their chance to oust the Bishops."

Nat said that he and Edward had seen several attacks on coaches believed to be carrying Bishops to the House.

"Yes indeed," his Lordship said, "which means that many of the Lords Spiritual dare not venture to take their places. The Archbishop is getting up a protest. He says if they are not able to sit in the Lords, any law passed without them will be invalid. We can't have that. It's an interference in the powers of both Houses and I wager Pym will rouse the Commons to a fury."

It was December 30th, the day after this conversation, that Edward took Nat to see St Paul's with its sprawling market stalls, beggars and rogues operating around its walls. The filth and clamour appalled Nat. He longed for a quiet evening reading in his room, but when they returned they found Lord Branford had more startling news.

"Pym called for the impeachment of all the Bishops who signed the protest and when he had got the Commons to pass this it came to us. *I* couldn't bring myself to assent to that but there were enough – and not just Pym supporters – who felt the protest had gone too far and they endorsed the impeachment. What shocked many though was that the twelve bishops were arrested immediately and where do you think they are now? In the Tower. Never was such a business conducted so fast."

"Why are all the bells being rung?" Edward asked. They could be heard plainly within the house.

"It's the apprentices," his father growled, "expressing their joy. They were starting bonfires in the streets too, as I came home."

Lady Branford exclaimed, "Bishops in the Tower! Surely we must think again about putting Edward into the Church. It is becoming as dangerous as the army is for our poor Henry. With Nathaniel to help Edward with his studies, he could stay in Cambridge and become a great figure at the University. I believe the Deans of the Colleges live very comfortably."

Lord Branford's sneer at this showed Nat plainly what his Lordship thought of his wife's opinions. "You will find," he said, not glancing at her but addressing them all, "that appointments to high places will soon be made directly by Parliament."

The next day Edward asked Nat if he still wanted to see the sights in spite of the unrest. Rather to his own surprise, Nat was keen to go out. It was not enough to hear the news at second-hand from Lord Branford.

The nearer they walked towards Westminster the greater became the feeling of tension. They could see officers exercising the Trained Bands and some excited onlookers said the King had ordered the Lord Mayor to use them to put down rioters. Others equally vehemently said Mr Pym demanded them to guard Parliament.

"I wouldn't like to be the Lord Mayor," Edward said. "Shall we get off the streets and go on the river?"

He led Nat down a set of steps to one of the many landing stages where wherries could be hired. The boatman, seeing Edward pull out an expensive looking purse, charged what Nat thought an exorbitant fee, but once they were on the water he could only marvel at the buildings crowded along the waterfront, at the amazing sight of London Bridge covered with houses and shops, and the Thames itself creeping sluggishly to the sea while across its brown slimy surface hundreds of boats of all shapes and sizes scuttled like beetles or clove their imperious way. The immensity of London's business stunned both his mind and his senses.

"I wouldn't have missed that for anything," he told Edward when they were set down at another set of steps and found their way home by a different route. "My eyes are exhausted with looking."

Edward laughed, pleased, and promised to show him more every day, but on January 3rd they heard on the streets, before Lord Branford could bring the news home to them, that the Attorney General on the orders of the King had accused five Members of the Commons including Pym himself of High Treason.

"The King will have his revenge for the Bishops," a costermonger commented.

"If he sends armed men to Parliament there will be war." A tailor with a needle threaded through the sleeve of his coat had come to the door of his workshop. There was something familiar about his small wiry figure and elfish features under cropped black hair that puzzled Nat till he saw below his signboard the painted name, Saul Hutton.

He pulled Edward quickly past. "I think that's Ben Hutton's father."

"Should we not stop and greet him."

"Have sense, man. If Ben is about, he will start yelling that we are King's men."

"By heaven, you're right." Edward nearly broke into a run but Nat grabbed his arm.

"Hurrying draws attention."

Already he felt that Edward's hat with his long curly hair emerging onto the furred collar of his cloak was attracting unwelcome glances. Nat kept his own distinctive flaxen hair short enough to be mostly hidden by his very plain black hat.

They made their way onto a broader thoroughfare where they saw another of the Trained Bands drawn up. At least that was authority of a kind. And so little by little they reached the Branfords' house in safety.

But next day they were too curious about what would happen to stay in and against Lady Branford's advice they set out again, Edward at Nat's suggestion wearing much plainer clothes. Lord Branford had already told them that the King had published the articles of treason against the members and there was a tremendous air of excitement and expectancy in the streets.

Nothing happened in the morning and they bought some pies from a pastry cook and mugs of ale to stave off hunger.

In the afternoon they were walking down Whitehall when they began to hear shouts of, "The King, the King is coming."

Hemmed in by crowds surging from all sides, Nat and Edward could do nothing but wait as rumours flew about that the King was bringing an army to arrest Pym and his friends. Presently the chattering hushed and a sound between a groan and a roar swept through the mass. A gap opened in the road and looking up, they saw the King himself on horseback and behind him a large body of armed guards.

Nat drew in his breath. It was the first time he had seen the King. How imperious he looked, how resolute. The crowd fell silent as he rode by but shouts soon broke out.

"To the Parliament."

"Save Parliament!"

Edward kept his hand on his sword hilt under his cloak, more to conceal it than be ready to use it. With their backs against the building behind them, they didn't try to move as the more vociferous of the crowd were randomly hurling sticks and stones after the soldiers.

"We'll hear soon enough what happens," Nat said, thrilled at being so close to events. This was history happening before his eyes.

A butcher in an apron, clutching a meat cleaver, struggled past to get back to his shop before thieves stripped his hooks of poultry and rabbits. A stink of blood, sweat and horse manure assailed Nat's nostrils. His ears rang with the clamour of a thousand voices. It is not two years, he reflected, since the days of country ramblings with Dan and quiet study with Father! I knew few people, I knew nothing of the teeming world beyond a few square miles of Yorkshire. I am years older. I am running to catch up with life and hardly getting my breath. He shared a grin with Edward as their eyes met and then suddenly there came a great roar of cheering passing from street to street.

"What is it? What's happened?" neighbour demanded of neighbour.

The cry came. "The birds have flown."

This was amplified in the next few minutes with the news that the five members of Parliament had slipped away by river, forewarned of the King's coming.

"That'll teach His Majesty," an apprentice boy yelled, "bringing soldiers onto our streets!"

This seemed to be the general feeling of the crowd and Nat could sense the proud and independent spirit of the capital which left him an outsider. Londoners would guard their streets, their Parliament, even from the King, perhaps especially now from the King. The quiet, devout, loyal country in which he had believed for most of his life was being rent in two. He should feel utterly grieved, as his father would be, and yet he was stirred and exhilarated by all this new experience and, thankfully, not in the least afraid.

Edward grabbed his arm and whispered, "I can see a way through. Let's get home and tell them what's gone on."

Lady Branford was relieved to see them. News had already flown round London like wildfire while they were struggling through the excited but generally happy crowds. Nat noticed how her ladyship's demeanour had changed since his first meeting with her. Until her husband was safely home and the doors shut and barred, she was a frightened woman.

Lord Branford had plenty to say when he did arrive and Nat was eager to hear his assessment of the situation. "Their escape," he said, his chins and heavy cheeks quivering with emotion, "is a disaster for the King." He paused and looked round at the whole assembled family, shaking his head and seeming to revel in his own gloom. "But that he should have attempted it at all has done the real damage. He has horribly inflamed the Commons. 'Privilege, privilege' they have been shouting. Armed men at the very doors of the House! That was the grossest affront. They will never forgive that."

"But if he had succeeded, sir," Nat asked, "would his own supporters have triumphed?"

"If he had sent Pym and his cronies to the Tower as they sent the Bishops? No, I do not believe so. He has outraged the moderate voices and the staunch royalists in the Commons are too few in number now. Many are staying in their home counties, frightened to come up to London to take their seats. If they vote against Pym they fear arrest." He ran his hands through his thick hair, mostly dark still and curling on his shoulders. "That it should come to this! What did the King gain by being conciliatory before? Who advises him to these sudden rash acts?"

He frowned all round as if challenging for an answer. Nat could tell from all their faces that the scene was unprecedented. When no one spoke Lord Branford went on, "Pym and his friends will lie hidden till the danger's passed. I tell you the Lord Mayor knows not who to answer to. He is being told by both King and Parliament to muster the Trained Bands ready for action. Who will they fight?" He bent his thick brows on his son, who looked, Nat thought, white and startled. "You know, Edward, that your brother is with loyal troops near Oxford. Will the King go there and raise more men from the shires and lead an *army* against London? As things stand now, it would not surprise me. I would like you and Nathaniel to slip away to Cambridge as quickly as possible and I will send the ladies into the country."

Nat knew the family seat was in Hertfordshire. It wasn't far from London but if the capital was to be the focus of bloodshed he supposed it was far enough.

Hermione looked up then and protested that the country was too quiet.

"Quiet" said her father "is what we are all going to want very soon and find it has vanished from our lives. We will start on our preparations after supper."

Nat had little enough to pack up and could have left at once but it was decided their boxes should go first by the carrier and he and Edward should ride out as inconspicuously as possible the day after.

When he said his farewells to the assembled ladies they received his thanks for his entertainment with brief courtesy. Lady Branford had a distracted air and only Penelope gave him a tiny smile. Hermione put her hand to her own cheek in a significant gesture and her eyes and mouth were full of scorn. He merely bowed. His cheek would have a slight scar for a long time.

As he and Edward rode out on the way to Cambridge they passed more and more of the Trained Bands exercising in the streets. Parliament had put their own choice of leader in command without reference to the King and it was evident they expected an assault on London. Apprentices were building barricades and digging ditches and the two young students would have found it hard to pass if Edward had not thrown a purse among them.

Once clear of the straggling outskirts Nat expected to heave a sigh of relief. Instead he felt a strange regret that they were escaping from the turbulent centre to the quiet backwaters. But I cannot be involved, he told himself, because I know not the rights and wrongs of it now. The old certainties have gone. Father would say, leave the squabblers be and continue with your studious life. But if the whole country breaks into strife is it possible to stay on the sidelines? He recalled Ben Hutton's prophecy of civil war. Would that poisonous little fellow be proved right after all? And was he so poisonous?

I have seen how Lords and Ladies live and I have not been impressed with their morals or the values they truly hold dear, he thought. I have seen a little too of the poverty and squalor of London. I have heard the King's wisdom doubted and his name profaned on the streets. Would I have done better to go home to Yorkshire and draw strength from Father's quiet steadfastness? I have avoided inflaming Mother's sad state by staying away, but where did my duty lie?

He rode on, unsure of many things and disinclined to talk when Edward who hated silences tried to draw him out.

CHAPTER 15

September 1642

It was a September day of warm wind and small scuttling clouds that briefly interrupted the sunlight flooding the cropped grass before the Hall. With no one to keep the lawns trim, Sir John had bought sheep from Turner's farm and Bel through half-closed sleepy eyes was watching the white blobby shapes as they moved slowly over the green expanse. She had worked hard all morning weeding the vegetable garden and Ursula had said after dinner, "Rest for have half an hour on the bench, my precious. Read that book on husbandry you wanted to study."

The book now lay on the gravel path beside her and she was stretched out along the bench with her head on a cushion, noticing nothing but the sheep and the brief chill when one of the cloud shadows passed over her. The book with its cheerful advice about harvesting and saving the gleanings for the poor had at first turned her reluctant thoughts to the devastation that hostilities were bringing to the countryside. Here it was the King's troops plundering, there it was Parliament's forces. All over England fights were breaking out which seemed to Bel utterly pointless and which left ordinary people hungrier than ever and many homeless. Then, when she had turned a page and seen a drawing of a well-constructed hayrick, her mind flew back to the fire she knew she had started just over two years ago. She visualised the wayward flames creeping to the base of the stack and triumphantly rising up the sun-baked straw. Over it all she saw again the hanging body and its one accusing eye. Would that sight never leave her?

At that point she threw down the book and tried to send her thoughts anywhere else to escape the vision. She even sent them to London where her betrothed and his parents must be struggling with the effect of the unrest on trade and commerce. They had written nothing for months now about the Northumberland cousins coming to visit. Sir John said, "They are ashamed that they represented the capital as so safe."

Despite the state of the country he was sleeping better, his cough was less troublesome, his face less drawn. Perhaps her consent to be betrothed to William had had something to do with it, but Bel believed in her heart that as long as Ursula was with her she had some sense of peace and could communicate this to her father. The cloud had not gone but usually it lay on the horizon of her mind.

She was annoyed that the Book of Husbandry had brought it sharply back. She had set herself to learn everything her father could tell her about the estate, its history, its farms, the extent of arable land and pasture. His delight at her interest was touching and she was moved to tears the day he said, "If only Robert had troubled himself to know so much he would not have made hasty and foolish decisions when I was not well enough to control him. He enclosed some of the common grazing land and provoked dispute among the farmers over the rest. He raised rents – which I fear we had to do – but he did it unequally and with no heed to the family circumstances. We are going to put things right now." That 'we' gave Bel the same thrill that his 'my little one' had done in his letter to her at Cranmore House.

As she lay on the bench she reflected on their simple daily lives since Robert's death and the departure of the London Hordens. Ursula had grown strong again and she and Bel with Tom and Mary's help managed the work of the Hall, shutting off all the rooms that were not in use. Bel soon found her father didn't like to see her performing any domestic duties, so she made sure she helped with the cleaning and washing before he rose in the morning. He was happy for her to bring him a small breakfast in bed and he didn't inquire if she disappeared for an hour before noon. If he guessed she was helping prepare the dinner that they ate at twelve he never commented, except to say, "Tell Ursula that was very good."

Bel had at first shocked him by demanding that Ursula as her friend should eat with them in the dining-room, but Ursula went to Sir John herself and said, "Such a wish would never enter my head, sir. Mary and I and Mistress Nurse when she sometimes drops in for company are very happy in the kitchen. If I may still call your dear girl Bel to spare my poor lips it is all I would ever presume to do."

And so, despite the disturbing news which arrived by word of mouth and in news-sheets and pamphlets distributed in Newcastle, the reduced household at Horden Hall, with backs turned to the probability of outright war, experienced a peace and harmony it had not known for many years.

It still seemed to be assumed that she would marry William in about six months' time but she avoided the subject with her father for the sake of peace. When her thoughts had reached London she let them cross the Channel to France and rest wonderingly on her baby niece whom she seemed unlikely to see for a long time. Henrietta's letters said the child was beautiful but she could not bring her to a hostile England. Her mother's letters suggested Sir John and Arabella should come to them and stay till England was at peace again. But Father will never leave Horden Hall to the looters, Bel reassured herself.

Today was so peaceful it was unbelievable that only a few miles away Newcastle was heavily fortified for the King, but there were rabid Puritan factions within the town ready to join a siege by Parliament if that should happen. Still anxious to keep away the sight of the hanging body, Bel concentrated her gaze on the sheep and half-heartedly counted them. Now her eyes were closing and her limbs relaxing on the warm wood of the bench. She was asleep.

It was again a passing shadow that stirred her senses. But this one didn't pass. Why was it stationary over her? She wanted the sun's warmth again. Did she dream that a voice said 'Arabella.' She opened her eyes.

A bearded man in a wide brimmed black hat was leaning over her. She screeched and swung her legs to the ground so suddenly he had to jump backwards.

"I'm so sorry I startled you."

"What ...? Who ...?" She was still befuddled with sleep.

She heard Ursula's little running steps. They stopped abruptly at a short distance and she exclaimed, "Mother of God, Bel! 'Tis Father Patrick come!"

Now Bel peered hard at his shadowed face under the hat, heavily masked with this dark beard, and there were his grey, searching eyes looking out at her, already, she felt to her disgust, undressing her. She had a well-shaped figure now and she rose and held herself fiercely upright before him.

"Whatever brings you here?" she snapped at him.

"Oh Bel, that's no way to greet Father," Ursula cried and held out to him the ale she had been bringing to Bel in a pewter tankard. "'Tis a thirsty day, sir. How far have you travelled?"

A poor nag, weighted down by panniers and a leather roll behind his saddle, was standing a few paces off on the gravel path, eying the grass but hardly able to summon the strength to walk to it.

"He could do with some refreshment too, Ursula. We've come a long way today." Patrick had taken the tankard and held out his other hand to her. "It's good to see you. We were so happy to know you were here after Cranmore House was closed down. I'm afraid Arabella is not so pleased to see me, but I have come from France at the urgent request of her mother and sister and at a grave risk to my own life."

"You'd better take him in to Father, Ursula," Bel said. "I'll send Tom to see to the poor beast and prepare some food."

"Oh Bel, will you not take Father Patrick in?"

He laid a hand on Ursula's arm. "I am a travelling artist, Patrick Dawson. Forget the priestly title unless we are totally alone. The King is under a terrible necessity to show antagonism to all things Catholic. He had two priests hung in York and one was nearly ninety. They had done nothing but minister to small flocks adhering to the old religion. I am carrying sketches and paintings done abroad to sell at market fairs or to show in schools for a few days' teaching to hopeful pupils. I have now been given safe-conduct papers from both parties, but every patrol I encounter, whether royalist or parliament, has been suspicious I might be a spy for the other. I may not be allowed to return to France if they fear I have been spying for a Catholic country. Several times I have believed I was being followed."

"Let us get you indoors then," Ursula cried, looking towards the gates.

He followed her glance anxiously and Bel, smiling a little at his nervousness, said, "They are never locked these days because we have no gatekeeper to open them. There is not the household of servants you will remember here and we have done away with your escape hole. But come in. Father will have wakened from his afternoon sleep."

When Ursula saw that Bel was leading the way she slipped round to the stables to alert Tom to the arrival of a strange horse. Bel shrugged her shoulders. She wasn't sure what they were to do with their visitor but they could hardly send him away after feeding him so she supposed he would have to stay the night. He could sleep in Robert's room.

Father must be in his study or he would have heard the goings on at the front of the Hall. He had a couch in there where he could rest and be close to his small library and the shelves where the estate books were kept.

Bel tapped at the door. His "Come in" sounded startled as if he had just wakened.

"We have a visitor, Father. Mr Dawson, the art teacher."

She just glimpsed his bemused face and his lips mouthing "Art teacher?" and then she beckoned Patrick in and nipped out herself, closing the door behind her.

It was not till the three of them sat down to the meal Ursula had prepared from the meagre store in the pantry that she learnt why Patrick Dawson had come, or at least the reasons he gave which she suspected did not tell the whole story.

Her father had his grey sunken look which always aged him. When Mary had served the vegetable broth with a few morsels of chicken in it and returned to the kitchen, he said, "Mr Dawson has brought sad news. Henrietta's child is sickly and not likely to live. Your mother wanted him to make clear to us that she is not passing her time in idle luxury but supporting her sorrowing daughter. Of course I had never found fault with her remaining in France. She is safer there and we understand how much her presence is needed. I trust, sir, that when you return you will make clear to her that I wholly endorse her staying where she is."

"I beg you will say that in your letters, Sir John, for it may be that I will not try to return to France. If I can make a living and see out this wretched war I may secure my future here in the North of England. In the south, especially in London, they are saying Northumberland is riddled with Papacy. Those are their words. Perhaps I can resume, secretly at first, my calling as a priest."

Bel couldn't hold back. "You told me once you should never have become a priest." She had the satisfaction of seeing alarm in his eyes and high colour in his cheeks above his beard.

He murmured, "Much has happened since then."

Her father chided her for impertinence and deftly turned the subject. "You call these outbreaks of hostility a war, sir. Is that what we are now afflicted with – a civil war which may last months or even years, that you speak of seeing it out?"

"You may seem peaceful here, Sir John, but as I passed through Newcastle I saw it well fortified for the King, under the Earl of Newcastle, and as you must know Parliament took upon itself control of the armed forces with its Militia Ordinance. It can raise troops and command the Trained Bands, and for that the King has restored the old Commissions of Array where he can order landowners to muster men and pay towards his army. We have had all this news in France and there is no doubt there that King Charles is fighting his own Parliament."

Bel looked at her father. She knew how he had tried for months to ignore what was happening in the wider country and think only of how he could keep his estate solvent by more and more stringent economies.

Now he answered Patrick Dawson with some asperity. "I am aware of all these developments. I have had to send several young men to the King's muster who are badly needed on the farms. Without my poor son to put in charge of them, they are led by Sam Turner, the one young man, barely eighteen, who can read and write fluently. He is enthusiastic at the prospect of becoming at least a sergeant, but his betrothed, our maid Mary, is grieving. So our lives have indeed been touched by these great events. But I still hope that a compromise may be reached before it comes to a clash of whole armies."

Patrick Dawson merely inclined his head.

Bel wondered what had passed between them in their first interview. Certainly her father was not delighted at his arrival.

Nevertheless after supper he ordered that a fire should be lit in Robert's old room and heated bricks placed in the bed to air it. Bel was checking that all was ready for their guest when Patrick himself appeared at the open door. He came in and quickly closed it behind him, exactly as he had done at Cranmore House when he had caught her in Ursula's room.

She set her jaw and glared at him. "You haven't changed, have you, Patrick Dawson?"

He smiled, a smile which his beard made positively sinister. "If you mean do I still admire you, no, I haven't changed. As I prophesied you have become a splendid young woman, strong of face and body, but I know you are betrothed to your cousin, William Horden. Your sister told me the wedding is to be in the spring and she is deeply saddened that she cannot be there for it. She truly wanted you there for hers, but you were a child then and behaved childishly. Now she is sure you are a mature young lady. Your father has written in his letters of your great help in managing the household."

Bel's spurt of delight at hearing this did not distract her from her inquisition. "So you are saying you have no hopes of me because I am betrothed and you will therefore continue as a priest, presumably till some other lady takes your fancy. Let me tell you I have no intention of marrying my cousin. Now what do you say?"

He took one step towards her and his eyes were greedy. "I say I would like to hold you, kiss you, caress you, but I may not. I have been an unworthy priest and have suffered much punishment on the way here which I have not described to your father. I have repented in jail cells and after beatings. I do not wish to sin any more against my calling."

His vehemence amused her a little. If I encouraged him, she thought, he would have me on that bed in a trice. But she was also curious about what he had endured on his journey. "Why were you beaten? Why were you put in jail?"

"I was set upon and robbed of the money your mother had given me for my journey before I had even reached London. I walked into one of the Trained Bands and they said they had orders to arrest all vagrants or press them into their forces. When I refused, they beat me and I was thrown into jail for the night. There were too many prisoners there, so they told me I could go next day. But it happened again a few days later when a band of Royalist soldiers decided I was a Puritan spy. I only escaped from their custody by offering to draw a portrait of their commander. He was a fat German and very vain. He let me go and even gave me a little money for the portrait, which helped me further on my way. It has been a few weeks of hell, but I was determined to reach Horden Hall."

"To see me?"

"To fulfil my mission. But yes, of course to see you, to see how two years had changed you. But you are not changed inside. You are as fierce and forthright as ever. And as admirable." He took another step towards her. "And adorable."

She laughed in his face. "Lust is one of the seven deadly sins, is it not, Sir Priest? I am sorry for your jail and your beatings but I do not like you and will not tempt you any further by my presence."

She stepped up to him and gave him a push so that he tumbled onto the bed. She had her hand on the door latch when he scrambled to his feet and protested, "I am not tempted. I wouldn't touch you. Stop one moment. I have to ask a favour of a very different sort." She would have ignored this but he added, "For Ursula."

"What then – for Ursula?"

"She has been deprived of the sacrament for a long time. Indeed she tells me she has had to attend the parish church and receive there so as to bring no discredit on your father. You know that rite is worth nothing to us, is worse than nothing. I can shrive her and say a Mass for her which would give her great joy."

Bel shrugged her shoulders. "Do so, if it makes her happy, though how it can do her good from one such as you I know not."

"Ah, it is not the man but the office that is sacred. Only I have no pyx with me. I dare not carry anything so dangerous. I can improvise with vessels from the kitchen if I bless them first and she can bake a little unleavened bread. But I know she would want your permission."

Bel waved her hand at him. "Do what you want." She didn't like to think of Ursula having secret needs that set her apart. I should be all in all to her as she is to me, she thought, bitterly. "Do it," she said again, "but privately."

"I am well used to that," he said, "but I thank you, Arabella."

He gave a little bow and she slipped out, feeling uncomfortable and with an unpleasant taste in her mouth.

When Patrick Dawson had been at Horden Hall three days, Sir John asked him straight out at dinner on the Saturday, "What are your plans, Mr Dawson? If you hope to teach drawing for your living you should be in Newcastle demonstrating your skills in the schools or to private patrons."

Bel was delighted with her father's bluntness. He had never had a great store of patience and he was not prepared to house and feed an uninvited guest any longer.

"You are right, Sir John," Patrick said. "Now that I and my poor horse are rested, I must trespass on your kindness no longer. Tomorrow is Sunday and I will take my leave on Monday morning. I trust I can find at least a small attic room in Newcastle suitable for a poor artist."

Bel saw her father frown uncomfortably. He would hate to be made to feel churlish and inhospitable and they all knew that with the Royalist garrison billeted there the town was overflowing.

"Of course you must come back here for a bed if you are unsuccessful," he said. He was stroking his own neat triangle of beard and eying Patrick's shaggy dark outcrop. "I suppose that is your disguise. The Puritans of course are very sparse on hair. You feel that is necessary?" He had already in an uncharacteristically intimate comment told Bel, "I can't bear to see all that unkempt vegetation opposite me at table."

Patrick only smiled, "Yes, sir. I know it is a little odd, but artists are forgiven a degree of eccentricity. I found it uncomfortable at first but have grown used to it. It is very generous of you to offer further hospitality, but I will endeavour not to trouble you again."

In this state of mutual but cool politeness they arrived at Sunday morning, Patrick keeping to his room when they all walked to the village church. Ursula followed her usual practice of accompanying them and Bel didn't ask whether she had received Mass first.

Bel noticed four Puritanically-dressed strangers apparently strolling casually about the village but she was sure they were noting the people going into church. The vicar had long since stopped wearing vestments and the communion table stood in the centre of the aisle. What could they be spying on? she wondered.

Settled in the Horden pew she closed her eyes. She felt that Ursula beside her was praying, though she made no sound. Nurse was the other side of Ursula. Father had wanted them both in the pew because he said it was too big for him and his daughter alone. Bel knew it was the time when he felt most keenly the absence of her mother, Robert and Henrietta. The closest he had come to confessing this was the previous Christmas when he had said, "I little thought to be without Robert too, but he is no more dead than they are when I know not if I will ever see them again."

Tom had a sister in the village and sat with her and Mary joined her widowed mother. The village was there Sunday by Sunday but now there were gaps where the young men had sat. The Turner family were the other side of the aisle and Bel remembered how she had watched them through much of her childhood and gradually looked only at young Sam as he grew tall and handsome.

What a child I was then to suppose I was in love, she thought to herself.

I wonder what it would be like to be truly in love, not looking at the outside but at the inner man. When I first saw Patrick Dawson I marvelled at his angelic features, but I soon found the man beneath was flawed. I can't make him out. Perhaps if he had not become a priest he would have loved a woman and kept only to her but he has become obsessed with the thing he cannot have. Poor man. I was sorry for him at Cranmore House among all those girls, but I hated him when he touched me and since he reappeared I have treated him with scorn and laughter. I am older but I am not a good person. I have tried with father and he has had to love me a little, because he has no one else, but the years of rebelliousness and disapproval lie between us and neither of us dares to mention this impending marriage. I'm afraid I only truly love Ursula, but even with her there are things I cannot speak of. She sees only the good in people and I see only the bad. I shouldn't be here in the house of God.

The words of the epistle edged into her brain at this point. Why she had begun to listen she didn't know, but they were telling her that they that partook of the Lord's supper unworthily, brought condemnation upon themselves. Weary of herself, she mentally shrugged her shoulders. I am a murderer. I am condemned already.

When the time came, she ate the bread and sipped the wine and went back to her place, wondering what Ursula felt performing this ritual if she had already received the real thing from Father Patrick, perhaps daily since he came. And what effect did this so-called sacrament have on all the other participants? Nurse repeated the responses in a clear voice, but her corns and stiff joints had more influence on her temper than the services of the church. Father seemed to draw some comfort these days. He was always quiet on a Sunday and gentler of speech, so maybe his soul was moved. If we have souls, Bel mused. But he is a hard man to get to know because he is so reserved. He is afraid of his own emotions.

They were standing up to sing the closing hymn. Soon they would be walking back, not her woodland shortcut but along the track, Bel keeping her eyes averted from Gallows Hill as she always did when she was in the village. They would find Patrick at the Hall. I'm glad he's going tomorrow, Bel thought. I'm uncomfortable while he's in the house. His eyes; I don't like his eyes but perhaps they are those of a troubled, frightened man. He's afraid of himself and afraid of the persecution he has suffered for his calling.

"I'm sorry for Patrick Dawson," she said aloud to Ursula as they walked.

Father was a few paces behind with Nurse so she could speak freely.

Ursula said, "You have a soft heart, my precious. Yes, he has had a hard time of it, but your mother urged him to come and he came. It was a brave thing to do."

"Yet she could have written to Father all that he told us. I don't understand it at all."

"I suppose she felt word of mouth was important. I was praying for her and your sister and the poor babe. I expect you were too, in the prayers for the sick."

Bel shook her head. "I didn't think of them. I'm wicked."

"But you were praying for Father Patrick, that he will be safe when he goes to Newcastle tomorrow. You are a much better girl than you pretend to be." She wagged her finger and let fly her chortling laugh.

When they reached Nurse's cottage Bel turned to see if Father would ask her to join Ursula for Sunday dinner as he sometimes did but she saw Nurse shaking her head. Then she scurried in quickly and shut the door. They heard her putting the bolt in place.

"Odd," he said joining them. "She was worried about those strangers in the village, yet she preferred to be alone. They look sinister in all black with those tall hats pulled over their ears. I suppose they are from some

Parliamentary commission to persuade young men to join their forces, but they would see we have none left." He sighed but smiled at Bel and added, "If our young men had been about, I think they'd have thrown the Puritans in the duck pond for their pains."

Bel was pleased to hear him speak lightly of the matter. The church service must have lifted his usual gloom. They followed the village track another hundred yards to where it ended in the rear courtyard of the Hall.

As they approached Bel tensed and looked up at her father. "Something's wrong. Look at the stables!"

She ran forward. The stable doors stood open to emptiness. Sir John's fine chestnut mare and Patrick's miserable old nag were both gone. So were the saddles.

"Surely he cannot have robbed us! A priest!" Sir John gazed at the vacant spaces in disbelief.

"The kitchen door's open," cried Bel and stepped inside. "Oh father!"

There were signs that someone had been eating and drinking here no, several people. Pewter mugs stood about that had been neatly on their hooks. There were crumbs across the table and the remains of a ham roughly hacked. Knives lay about and the biggest, the meat knife was on the floor.

An icy hand went down her spine. Were the intruders still here? She listened. There was no sound, but a creepy feeling made her shudder. Her father and Ursula had now come in. Bel picked up the meat knife so they wouldn't trip on it. As she laid it on the table in the light from the window she let out a gasp of horror. There was blood on it. She set it down quickly and looked at her own hands. The blood was still wet.

Ursula plucked at her arm as she was leaping to the steps to the passage.

"Don't look, Bel. I know what it is. It's Father Patrick. They have got him at last." She was crossing herself.

"God in heaven!" cried Sir John. "Have they taken him away?"

In a scramble they all went to look. Bel, pulling from Ursula's grip, was the first to emerge from the kitchen passage into the great hall.

She stood stock still, spreading out her arms as if to prevent them from seeing what she could see. Of course they saw it. Her father groaned and put out a hand to the hall panelling as if he might have fainted with the shock. Ursula let out the tiniest of little screeches.

Patrick Dawson's body lay sprawled face-down at the foot of the stairs, his legs trailing up the first two steps. A dark pool surrounded his head.

Bel stared. She could think of nothing but the attack in Cranmore House which she had prevented. This is how it would have been but she would have witnessed it herself, the hacking, the screams, the crash to the ground, the spreading blood. Here it was. It had happened. Where was the sense in my saving him? she asked herself. For what has he lived to come to this now?

Ursula was telling them both not to turn him over, not to look at his face. "I have seen many horrors, sir. He is surely dead. Let me deal with him. When I have covered him up we can carry him from here."

"And lay him where Robert was laid," Sir John said. He was white and shaking, making no effort to step any nearer.

Bel grasped Ursula's hand. "I'm not afraid." She looked into Ursula's twisted face and saw her poor lips were moving at a great rate. She is repeating the prayer for a departing soul. I must wait till the right words are spoken.

When Ursula bowed her head and crossed herself, Bel said, "You believe he is at peace don't you? He was a very fearful man, but now he has nothing more to be frightened of, does he, so why should we be frightened of a lump of mangled flesh?"

She crouched down but couldn't bear to risk the blood touching her gown. She closed her eyes, realising what she had just said. It's true. I should not be frightened but for two years I have been afraid of a dead body. But that was my doing. Surely this is not? I saved him once, but today I was wishing him out of my life. I have just taken the sacrament unworthily. The devil is inside me and somehow he has done this thing. I stared at the strangers in the village and the devil has put them up to this. I am not safe to be among people. Did I not kill my brother? Where I am people are cursed. One a year, this very time of year. She straightened up and clutched at her throat.

"I can't, I can't touch him." She turned and ran back to the kitchen and vomited into the tin wash bowl. Her vision seemed impaired. She groped her way, shivering to the back door and pulled it open and gulped the chill damp air. The paved courtyard, the empty stables, the crowding woods behind all came back into sharp focus. She stood, swallowing slowly with a hand on the doorpost, ashamed of herself.

Behind her she heard voices. Ursula was saying, "Oh Sir John, she is not yet sixteen. She is only a child."

Then her father cried, "She took her brother's death calmly enough and it was her fault." His voice was on the edge of hysteria.

"No sir, no sir. It was an accident. This is a horrible murder. Did she never tell you how she prevented just such an attack on the poor priest at Cranmore House?"

There was a pause and then Bel heard her father say in a flat voice, "I had forgotten that. Did she love him, do you think?"

"What! Unlawfully?" Ursula cried. "Never!"

But Bel turned herself round and faced her father who seemed to think she couldn't hear him with only the width of the kitchen between them. "Father, I hated that man. I hated Robert too. Blame me for their deaths if you will, but don't accuse me of love." She sank down onto one of the kitchen stools and bent her head over the table and broke into a torrent of weeping.

Ursula was beside her in a moment, an arm round her shoulders. "Hush, my pretty one. We are all shocked and know not what we are saying. I have covered the body and we must wait for Tom to come back to help us move him."

Tom and Mary were allowed to eat their Sunday dinners with their families.

"No." Bel stood up and brushed her eyes with the linen sleeve of her bodice. "We can't leave him there till then. There are three of us. I am sorry, Father. I can do it now."

To prove it she ran past both of them and up the steps and along the passage. Ursula had covered him with an old carriage blanket from the carved chest in the hall. Avoiding the pool of blood Bel went round him to the bottom stair and feeling for his legs under the blanket she pulled them round so that the body lay flat. She remembered how they had laid out Robert on a table in the far darkest corner of the great hall with two screens enclosing him completely.

The screens still stood there as they had for a whole year, just somewhere to leave them, she supposed. She went to look and found the table still there and a candle in the centre of it. Did Father come and light that sometimes and pray for Robert and grieve? She was astonished. She had had no idea. He hardly ever mentioned him.

She crossed the hall to the stairs again where Ursula was trying to work another blanket beneath the body so that it could be carried. Her father was standing by the open chest gazing into it.

"The moths have got in," he said as Bel came up. "The rugs are ruined."

"Then I'll spread one on that table in the corner. We can carry him there."

Her father murmured, "Robert's corner?" He shrugged his shoulders.

"What does it matter now? What does anything matter?"

Bel took another rug. Wool flakes and dust shook out of its many holes. She ran across the wooden boards, set the candle on the floor and folded the rug to make a reasonable covering on the table. Then she ran back to Ursula who had mopped up most of the blood with rags from the kitchen and the body was now on the blanket. She must have rolled him to achieve this but she had left him face down.

Her father came to life then when he saw the two women prepared to lift the head end. He went to the feet and bending down grasped the two corners. Bel saw from his almost green colouring that he was struggling not to vomit as she had done.

They staggered across the hall where Bel had left the screens turned back and laid their burden down. At once, her father closed the screens and stood momentarily gasping for breath with his back against them.

"What are we to do?" he muttered. "Who can we tell? Is there any law now to bring the murderers to justice?"

Bel was moved with pity. He had himself been the law and carried out every case that came before him with precise attention to detail, until the ghastly hanging of that poor idiot. The weight of Patrick's body had brought home to her how heavy must have been the big lad so cruelly hoisted up, alive and fit one moment and the next a dangling corpse. She wanted desperately to run away from that image that suddenly hung before her eyes.

Ursula had fetched mop and bucket and was trying to clean the stain from the wood floor.

Father walked over to her shaking his head. "It will never go away. Perhaps a mat . . ."

"Father," Bel said, "I will run to the village and borrow a horse. Someone must ride to Newcastle and tell the authorities of this deed and the theft of your mount. The men may be hiding there. We might get Lady back for you."

He nodded slowly. "The coroner still functions, I suppose. But you can't go, a mere girl." He straightened his spine. "I must ... I understand the processes. Did he have any family I wonder."

Ursula paused in her mopping. "I knew his mother. She taught needlework at Cranmore House in its early days but she's dead now. Patrick would have liked to teach drawing there, but his mother sent him to a seminary. She told me he was so beautiful only the Lord could have him. 'No woman is worthy of him,' she said. Eh, it's sad, for if he'd stayed a humble drawing master he might have been alive today. But if there is any other family, Sir John, it would be in Easingwold in Yorkshire. That's where his mother hailed from, but she was a widow when I knew her."

"Perhaps he will have to be taken there for burial and I will have to meet the expense. It's a dreadful business. In our house. It seems ... violated."

At least, Bel thought, he is forming plans, he is thinking again. He won't mourn Patrick Dawson as he does Robert.

Nevertheless the next few days were a terrible trial for him. Farmer Turner let him have a horse and he rode to Newcastle. He reported the whole matter to the Earl of Newcastle himself, who was commanding the Royalist garrison. He also arranged for a surgeon to come and look at the body and report to the coroner. He ordered a coffin maker to send a coffin.

"But, Bel," he told her when all this was done, "the murder is not to be pursued in law. I was interrogated for hours. Were the men we saw in the village armed? I told them no. If they were the murderers, they used our own knives. But then they wanted to know why a Catholic priest was a guest in my house and who knew that he was there? Well, of course, Tom and Mary knew who he was, but I told them not to speak of it. I said he feared he might have been followed on his journey and he kept within doors. I held nothing back, the whole truth of it, why he had come, everything. Then they said I should have detained him myself and brought him before them. Did I not know that the King had passed a law that no Catholic priest could enter the country on pain of death? 'Yes,' I said, 'I had heard of such a thing, but the man was a messenger from my wife.' They made light of that. He had met his due fate and though they disapproved of the manner of it, they were not prepared to take it further. They were more concerned at the theft of the horses. That a group of the enemy should come boldly in and seize our property was an outrage. But we are at war. They said the very words. If our troops could seize their horses or cattle, ransack their houses, return resistance with violence, they would do it. They are doing it all over the country. They said Patrick Dawson must have resisted arrest and got what he deserved for breaking the law. If they had got hold of him themselves, he would have been hanged. Bel, we are in chaos. The country is broken up. The beautiful thing I held so dear, the sanctity of our English law and its due processes, has been set at naught." He left her abruptly, went to his study and closed the door. She knew he was going to weep.

"Oh," she said to Ursula in the kitchen, "why is he so afraid to let me comfort him?"

"He is a man, my precious, a very private man."

Mary was cleaning out the bedroom Patrick had slept in, so Bel and Ursula were alone.

"Someone else may need your comfort, my Bel," Ursula went on. "Mistress Nurse was very distressed when she knew what had happened. Indeed all the village knows. She has not left her cottage since. Perhaps you could go and talk to her."

Bel sighed. She thought Nurse was tougher than that. Comforting Nurse had never come into her experience, but she threw a shawl round her shoulders and ran to the cottage and knocked at the door.

"Who is it?" came a scared cry.

"Only Bel."

"What do you want?"

"Just to see if you are well."

The door was opened a crack. "Who said I wasn't?

"Oh come, Nan, let me in. I haven't seen you about. I've come to inquire."

Nurse stood away from the door but went into the dimmest corner and sat down with her back to the one small window. The cottage only had two rooms and Bel was surprised at the untidiness of both, the door to the small bedchamber being open. It was not like Nurse to have so much as a ribbon out of place.

Bel perched herself on the stool by the table, where a bread board and the heel of a loaf lay next to some rolled up grubby stockings. She swivelled round to face Nurse, who kept her eyes averted and her hands clutched tightly in her lap.

"Nan, if you feel frightened here after what happened ..."

"I don't, I don't. I'm quite well. You can leave me be, Bella."

"So come and see Ursula and have some dinner with her, like you used to."

"No, no, I don't think so."

"But you and she are friends, aren't you?"

"Oh yes. Well, she works hard." Then Nurse suddenly lifted her head. "I didn't know she was one of them – a Papist." She almost spat the word out.

"Oh Nan, what does that matter?" Bel was surprised, then curious. "When did you find out?"

"That day she baked the special bread. I asked her what she was doing, what it was for. She said Father Patrick had come. I'd seen the strange horse in the stable."

"But he used to come and hide in the priest's room. You didn't mind him."

"Oh, I did, but what could I say? He came for your Mother's sake. Who was I to question that, but I was mighty glad when he went. The Hall was purged of him."

Bel was astonished at her vehemence. "So you are not upset at his death?"

Nurse made shooing motions with her hands. "Don't speak of it, girl. Forget it. It's over. I don't think of it. Has he gone? Have they buried him?"

Her confusion, her agitation gave Bel a sudden chilling thought. Father had been asked, "Who knew of the priest's presence in your house?" Had Nurse spoken of it to someone? To those strangers? On the Sunday she had been tense and nervous.

Bel answered her questions first, "Yes, the authorities buried him in a field outside Newcastle where felons are buried, poor man. No one was concerned to trace his family if he had any and Father has no one to send to make inquiries. So it's all over, as you say. The villains who did it must live with their consciences as best they can. Like you, they believed they purged the kingdom of a Popish priest."

Nurse leapt to her feet, her hands over her face. "Why do you say like me?"

Bel stood up too and looked her in the eye. "Nan, did you betray him?"

She screamed and fell back into the chair. "No, no, no. Never. I never knew. They asked me questions. How could I know what they'd do? They kept asking me."

Bel stared at her, absorbing her words. Oh dear God, she's done a foolish, wicked thing, not thinking of consequences. Just as I did. This is her black cloud and it will settle about her for the rest of her life.

"Oh, Nan!" She flung herself down at her feet and tried to put her arms round her. "Don't cry, Nan." She had never in her life seen Nurse cry. Her solid body was shaking with harsh gasping sobs.

She didn't clasp Bel in return. She almost seemed to be pushing her away.

"Nan, I'm not angry. Of course you didn't know. How could you?"

At last Nurse choked out, "You won't tell? Please don't tell Sir John."

"Of course I won't. It has hit him hard enough already."

"Or Ursula. You are so close to that woman."

"No, nor Ursula. It's finished. They won't come back."

Another icy thought struck her. She pulled away and stood up and looked sternly down at the broken woman that had been tough old Nurse, now staring up with terror in her eyes.

"You didn't tell them about Ursula, that she too is Catholic?"

The fear faded from Nurse's eyes. She breathed again, deeply.

"Not a word. She was never mentioned. They asked only about a Priest. They had followed him and lost him, but they were told Horden Hall had Catholic sympathies so they came asking. I said, no, no, no. We were all the reformed religion now. But he had visited here in olden days. We didn't want him, but Sir John was too much of a gentleman to throw out a poor, sick man. I said he was sick." Nurse was gabbling now. "They said they had orders to know where the priests were, that was all, just to make sure they weren't making converts, polluting the young. They spoke of God's truth ... oh, Bella, they were fine preachers."

Bel leant over her and gave her a kiss. "All right, Nan. It's over. It really is. You won't fret any more and you'll come back to us like you used to?"

She felt the cloud was still hovering, but Nurse gave a curt nod. Bel went to the door and looked back at her. She had picked up the stockings from the table and dropped them in the washing basket. She took the lid off the bread crock and put away the heel of the loaf. She met Bel's eyes as she opened the door. "Fancy you seeing my place like this." She grabbed the hearth brush and began to sweep the ash from the rug.

Bel couldn't help giving her a roguish grin before she ran off. It was a weird reversal of the roles they had always played. Nurse could never dominate her again.

Next day brought rumours of a great Royalist victory at Powick Bridge, where the King's nephew, Prince Rupert had charged with his cavalry and slain at least a hundred and fifty Parliament men.

A hundred and fifty corpses, Bel thought. We had only one and I never did look to see if his face was cleft in two. She tried to imagine a whole mass of mangled bodies. We are going to have to be hardened to this. Death will become unimportant. But she didn't say this aloud to her father.

He sat with her in the small dining-room and pecked at his dinner. That the news spoke of a success for the King had not cheered him. "Bella," he said, "I believe our cousins must come here for your wedding, though God knows we can lay on no festivities. Let us pray the fighting is over by Spring. Clifford has servants and his own carriage and as a man of business he is not a threat to either party."

Bel gritted her teeth. The wretched topic was back. He looked up and met her eyes. She knew he could see the rebellion in them without a word being said.

"Bella, I can only be at ease when I know you are married to William. You will have a life ahead of you, security, children. No, don't say anything. This war may drag on and I have no heart for a struggle now. If I mortgage a good part of the estate to Clifford ... he has money and to spare to put into its recovery. If we can bear to go on living here after what has happened and if I survive this winter, we will appoint a day after Easter for the marriage. Please make no difficulties. I am too tired. We will finish our meal in silence."

Bel complied. He was like a stick so brittle it could snap at any moment, but what will life be like, she wondered, from now on if we are not to speak of this, for I will run away with Ursula rather than be married to William Horden.

CHAPTER 16

April 1643

Nathaniel was in his third year of study at Cambridge. The Cam continued to flow and the students to swim in it or row on it, but the University had not escaped the war. The Colleges had collected their plate together to send to the King. Some had reached him to pay his motley army, some had fallen into Parliament's hands, and to punish the royalist sentiments at Queen's an up-and-coming officer, called Oliver Cromwell, had the previous summer brought a troop of soldiers and arrested Dr Edward Martin, the president, and marched him off to prison. These events were very shocking but for those students who had not joined either army, the study of ancient texts and languages continued with quiet absorption.

The war was finely balanced, the battle of Edgehill in the previous October having been indecisive for both parties, and during the winter there was a yearning all over the country for peace.

Ben Hutton, however, believed the King must be comprehensively beaten and he came to say goodbye to Nat before abandoning his studies to enlist with the Trained Bands, "fighting for freedom" as he grandly informed him.

"What sort of freedom is it," Nat retorted, "for Dr Martin and so many other distinguished men languishing in prison? Did you know that my friend Edward, has just learnt that his father, Lord Branford, is in the Tower? His crime is that he refused to support the impeachment of the Bishops. Mr Pym thinks he can purge the Lords and Commons of all who might hinder his plans. Your freedom means all men must think the same, or suffer for it. What is the point of your precious Parliament if no one can speak his mind? How can there be honest, fearless debates?"

"You would rather have one man raise taxes at a whim," retorted Ben, "give preferment only to his friends, wage war at his say-so and order foreign armies in to massacre his own people. When we are rid of the King we will all be equal and then we can all be free. Even Lord Branford and the Bishops can be freed if they drop their empty titles and become ordinary citizens. Well, Nat, it was amusing knowing you for we never agreed about anything, but I promise to speak up for you on Judgment Day for the crust you shared with me when we were starving."

Nat laughed and clapped him on the back. Ben was to go with a group of recruits to London first where he would join the Trained Band operating in his part of the City. Nat told him he had seen his father outside his tailor's shop on the day the King tried to arrest the five members of Parliament. "I don't think the King was wise that day," Nat admitted, "but I do believe God set him in his office and we should help, not hinder him in being a better king."

"Go back to Aquinas and Augustine then and see if that helps." And Ben rattled down the College stair chuckling.

Edward came in, his young face solemn. "Good, he's gone. I can't abide him, but he has the courage to go and fight for what he believes in. I would follow my brother and answer the King's muster, but Mother goes frantic if I so much as hint at such a wish. I am the only man left and she wants me at home in Hertfordshire in the vacation. Would you believe it, she went to see Father, to take him books and some wholesome food and they wouldn't let her in. They said they'd give him her gifts, but she doesn't trust them. It must be hell for him. He's a man of action."

"I do grieve for him and for your mother, and I am sure, Edward that for her peace of mind you should do what she wants."

"Even if she's wrong to ask it? You don't obey *your* mother. You told me."

It had been a relief to Nat to share the story of Daniel at long last. At College Edward was a genuine close friend, interested in everything about Nat and very proud and honoured to be the only person away from Darrowswick who knew about his great sorrow.

"I can't say I'd pine for either of my sisters," he admitted. "Pen never has much to say for herself and Herm has too much. We rub along but we're not inseparable like you and Dan were." Now he looked earnestly at Nat. "But don't you think it would put your Mother right if you did bring those Hordens to justice? You wouldn't need to... you know... *murder* them, but couldn't you bring an action in law? You're so much older now, you would know how to set about it."

"I told you we did try due processes but nothing came of it. And now there is killing and looting and pillaging every day which is never addressed by such law as still runs. There is no hope of redress. Besides, my father thinks my mother will never now regain her full mind. I dread going home for Easter, but I should go, since it is so long since I saw them. Only I fear the sight of me will upset her again. Father's letters say she is mostly docile except when she has bad dreams."

"You could *say* you were going to exact vengeance, couldn't you? Go to Northumberland but not *do* anything. It would be a kind lie if you told her you'd polished everyone off who was to blame for Daniel's death."

Nat smiled wistfully. Edward was young and ingenuous but he loved him. He needed a close confidant. He had always had Daniel at his side and though he couldn't exchange ideas with him, they had shared a delight in the country and the wild life and the Bible stories which Nat used to read aloud to him. The new experience of Cambridge had helped to salve the wound at first, but now that was familiar he felt the ache of loss more sharply and he was glad of the sweet devoted friendship of Edward.

"Well, I will tell you all that happens," Nat said now, "when we return for the summer. And I trust they will set your father free, for there are so many being sent to the Tower there will be no room left soon."

Two days after this conversation Edward returned to Hertfordshire for the Easter vacation and Nat set off for Yorkshire. As he rode on a hired horse Edward's suggestion began to take root in his mind. Would it be possible to convince his mother that he had taken some action but without telling a lie? Who knew what might have happened to the Hordens in the two and a half years since Daniel's death? Could he at least give an honest report to her about them? Could he talk openly with her of his reluctance to do personal injury to anyone? He had never tried to convince her it was against his conscience, because she leapt in so fiercely with her accusation of cowardice. Was he not old enough now to set aside the years of fearing her displeasure, of knowing he could never please her?

On the journey, despite the many interruptions by patrols who sneered at the travel pass his College had given him, he had many hours of solitary riding to brood on those years, to face how his lack of a mother's love had affected him. He yearned for it still. If she could only look on him with some small mark of favour what would he not do? But he must not earn it by deceit or it would mean nothing.

By the time he reached Yorkshire he was fired up to achieve this. He left his horse at the stables of the inn in Easingwold and, arranging for the carrier to bring his saddle bags next day, he set himself to walk the last two miles to Darrowswick. The April evening was chilly after a clear bright day and he walked fast, imagining all the possible scenes that might meet him at home. When the hilltop church came in sight with the upper story of the square vicarage on the slope behind, all picked out by the low sun, serene and peaceful, his heart ached for his father.

In the village he saw Granny Woodman at her window. She hobbled to the door.

"Eh, Master Nathaniel, is it you?" she cried. "My eyes are not so good. You've come just in time. Your mother is very ill. She was bit by a stray dog when she was on one of her wanders about and her leg swelled terrible they tell me. The physician from Easingwold says she's not likely to live."

Nat hastened his steps. Was this to be the release for her, after all her torment, and for him from her demands for vengeance? He had not anticipated this and he hardly knew whether he felt relief or deeper sorrow at the futility of all her passion.

His father saw him from the bedroom window as he breasted the hill. A minute later and they were in each other's arms, struggling against tears at the joy of meeting and the sombre circumstances.

"How is she?" Nat asked at last. "Granny Woodman intercepted me."

"Come and see," his father said simply and led the way upstairs.

Nat followed and peeped round the bedroom door. He frowned in dismay. The white pillows set off her yellow skin like old parchment. Her nose that had always been sharp was a thin bony ridge separating closed eyelids. Her hands lying flaccidly on the cover were skeletal. Was she dead already?

But his father went close and said gently "Anne."

The eyes flew open and fastened on Nat.

"Oh, Mother," he murmured, dropping to his knees by the bed. "I am so sorry to see you like this. Are you in pain?"

Not expecting an answer he was astonished when she spoke quite plainly in her old strong tones.

"You'll do it now, Nathaniel, so I can die happy."

He looked up at his father and mouthed, "Is her mind clear?" He nodded but Nat couldn't guess at all what he would like him to say. It's up to me. Edward was right. I must do something.

He turned back to her. "I will, Mother. I will go tomorrow. I will find

241

the Hordens."

Her lips cracked in what must be a smile. "And kill them," she said. It was a fearsome moment. He looked again at his father but her hand had gripped his wrist like a vice. "Kill them," she repeated. "Say the words."

"If it is God's will, Mother."

"Oh, it is," she said. She released his wrist and patted his hand. "I will rise early and watch you go. When you return you will have my blessing, Nat."

It was the first time she had used his name for what seemed years. He stood up and hurried out of the room and into the one he had shared with Daniel. He could hear Daniel's voice saying, "Come to bed, Nat. If you are cold, I'll warm you." That was how it had been in the angler's hut when Dan had lain down by him and held his shivering body until the fever left him. Nat sank onto the bed and sobbed.

His father was standing over him. "No, no tears. It was a good answer, son. She is lying quite content now."

Nat sat up. "But I will go. I must know what has happened to that family. If Mother is still living when I return, I will tell her honestly."

His father shook his head. "She will not last. You must wait and rest from your journey and then there will be no need to go anywhere."

Nat stood up. "No, Father. I have told her I will go tomorrow and go tomorrow I will. For so long she has asked of me this one thing and I have done nothing. Did she not give me a smile just now? My whole life I have longed for some sign of love from her. If she dies now, at least I can treasure that smile."

His father put his hands on Nat's shoulders. His eyes were full of sorrow. "Oh, Nat. I don't think I understood what a terrible void that was for you. You were so happy day by day with Daniel and you seemed to love our hours of study together. I should have rebuked her for her partiality. I fear I have been weak and shirked my duty. I knew not how to manage her strong passions."

"No truly, sir. I *did* love our study. I *was* happy with Daniel. Your love and his were wondrous. It is perhaps since I became a man than I have felt what I missed. The young men at College, some no more than boys, it is their mothers they pine for. But let us go down and speak of other things for I will hold to my purpose and set off tomorrow for Northumberland."

It was a month away from the proposed wedding when letters came for Bel and her father. They were in his study looking over the household accounts.

"Ah, this is from London," he said. "It is Clifford's hand. At last it will be his reply about the arrangements for the wedding. He has indeed left it late but maybe in the confused state of the country his letter has been delayed. And here is one for you from France – Henrietta's reply to yours on the death of the poor babe."

Bel had no wish to stay in the room while he read his from Clifford so she took hers to the bench outside the front windows.

Dear sister,' Henrietta wrote, '*your sweet letter of sympathy took weeks to reach us. I suppose it is the fault of England's horrid war. The one in which you wrote of the death of that wretched priest arrived with the other, so it had been even longer on the way. I believe all letters from England to France are being opened and resealed which is a frightening thought, though you and I write only of personal matters. Maybe when you get this you will already be married to William, but as our father wrote to Mother that the ceremony might be at Horden I am sending this there, not knowing at all when it will reach you. I wish I could be with you. There is so much now that you and I could share as sisters, so much I want to tell you about my own marriage to prepare you for yours, but it is hard to write it when we have not seen each other for so long. If only the fighting would stop,*

Mother and I would come since it seems our father doesn't feel able to undertake the journey to France. But we hear such tales of the persecution of Catholics, of the terrible oath which everyone who is anyone is supposed to take to abjure their religion and against their conscience, that we simply dare not set foot on England's shore till the nation has come to its senses and will tolerate all people believing and worshipping in their own way.

Enough of that. I am in good health and spirits again after seeing my poor little girl fade away of some unknown infection. Maurice has been very kind. But now I want you to know that I have no feelings of grief about Patrick Dawson. He was neither a good man nor a good priest. He tried to be both but he had a great weakness. You wondered in your letter why we sent him to you with messages we could and did put in letters. We did not send him. We dismissed him from our household and let his behaviour be known to the church here. That is why he went to England. He said he would teach drawing and not practise as a priest. I am sorry he troubled you and that his fearful death happened at our dear old home. When he left Cranmore House after the attempt on his life from which you saved him, he came to us as a refugee and proclaimed himself a changed man. He spoke often of you as a wonderful young woman which was how we knew you had changed but he hadn't changed and after quietly carrying out priestly duties for a while he again showed his true colours. My baby was sickly and he came to me to pray over her but... well, you can imagine the rest. I am glad you were spared his ill intents.

When I was a silly young girl I thought him so beautiful but then Mother found out his feelings for me and as you know my intended marriage to Maurice was soon brought forward. I was excited about going to France. It was to be all wealth and gaiety and happiness, warmth and colour after drab old Horden. Well of course it wasn't but believe me, Bella, when you accept your lot in life and a new husband and settle down to it you can find a deal of contentment. The old man who was Mother's guardian has taken a real liking to me, reminding him of Mother as a young girl and we both spend much time in his company. You will find that Clifford and Celia Horden will love you if you make their son a dutiful wife and I'm sure you will enjoy London life when the King and Parliament come to a truce as they surely will or the country will be ruined.

Give my duty to dear Father. I trust his health has not declined in the winter months. I wish you all happiness in your marriage and in your future life and long to be with you as sisters should be.

Your loving Henrietta.'

Bel put down the letter. She felt a yearning not for the Henrietta of her childhood, hard, sneering, self-confident, pleasure-loving, but for the one revealed in this letter. There was self-knowledge, doubt and much less assurance, even something she could call love. If Hen were here beside me, she thought, I believe we would be in each other's arms in a moment.

She wanted to sit on in the fresh April morning, absorbing all she had learnt, but reluctantly she got up to seek her father. The hour of final confrontation over her marriage had arrived. Pleased as she was at her sister's interest she was never going to be persuaded to change her mind.

Crossing the great hall to her Father's study door she could hear him moaning. What could that mean? Was it that the thought of losing her to her cousin had finally come home to him and he grieved at her loss?

She knocked and called out, "Father?"

The sound stopped. There was a brief pause and then he cried, "Yes, yes, come in, Bella. You will have to see the letter."

Puzzled, she slipped in. He motioned her to sit down. He gazed at her, shaking his head.

"It's the end of everything, Bella."

"How? What do you mean?"

He picked up the letter from the desk in front of him and as he reread the first paragraph anger took over. He slapped his hand on the page and barked, "He has gone back on his word, broken the agreement. My cousin, my own flesh and blood!"

Bel sat up. "What! I am not to marry William?"

He looked at her. "Oh I knew you would rejoice. But wait till you hear why. I told you, it's the end of everything; Horden, our home, our livelihood, everything."

"How is that possible?" She had seen him sunk in gloom many times but never looking as white and haggard as he did now.

He slapped the letter again. "Clifford is closer than ever to Parliament and has seen the latest lists of condemned properties. They call it sequestration. Horden Hall is one of them."

"Condemned?" The word had horrible associations with execution.

"Seized by Parliament. So he writes that as *I* can no longer fulfil my part of the bargain it is null and void – as if *I* have reneged on our agreement. I cannot mortgage to him what doesn't belong to me. Horden Hall will be sold to fill Parliament's coffers."

Bel jumped up, enraged at the injustice of it. "Why? How can they do that?"

"We harboured a Catholic priest here. We correspond with France. We are tainted. That apparently is enough."

"That's madness." She was pacing about the small room. "Can you not appeal?" She suddenly remembered Nurse's part in it of which Father was still unaware. He didn't even know that a private Mass had been celebrated within these walls. He was a complete innocent. Another thought struck her. If he found out would he want to be rid of Ursula?

He answered her question. "I believe I can appeal. What then? If the sequestration is lifted and my bargain with Clifford restored, would you

246

agree to marry William?"

"Would you want me too, after this?" She picked up the letter.

He shook his head. "I am deceived in them all. As a family member, could he not have told the men who compile these lists that we are not and never have been Papists? I believe he will have shown them a copy of this letter to prove that he has divorced himself utterly from any connection with us. He is buying and selling for them. He is making money from the war. But oh, Bella, how can I secure your future? This blow will kill *me* but you are only sixteen – a young woman cast alone into a hostile world. How are you ever to be married?"

Bel sat down again beside him. Now that there was no barrier between them of the looming wedding, she felt wonderfully free and very close to him. "I am only thankful to have nothing to do with men. I am content just to be with you, Father." As she had helped him with her interest in husbandry perhaps she could also help him over an appeal. "May I read the letter?" she asked.

He nodded and she glanced quickly through it. The tone was regretful but patronising. Father's foolishness had jeopardised his whole property, which now had no value on the open market. Sir John could not fulfil their bargain; therefore it was at an end. Clifford was sorry that the Northumberland Hordens had taken a stand against the cause of the lawful Parliament of England to which he and his family were devoted and so there could be no further communication between them.

Bel felt free to hate and despise the lot of them when she read this, though she had an inkling that neither Celia nor William would have sent such a letter. There would at least have been some reference to herself, some message of good will. But there were no hypocritical courtesies from Clifford. Father was probably right that he would show a copy of the letter to his Parliamentary friends, so that his name would not be tainted by association.

She laid down the letter. "He deserves no reply. Father, let us go to Newcastle and see what the authorities there say about this sequestration. Surely all is being decided now by force of arms. Newcastle is for the King. How can any Parliamentary writ run there? Could we not ask for a troop of horse to defend us against any attempt to seize the Hall and the land?"

He smiled wanly and took hold of her hand. "You should have been a son. This is how my son should speak. I wish I had your health and energy. Well, we will go in a day or two if we can borrow horses in the village. So many have been seized for the army."

"Can we take Ursula? She and I could ride together. After this I fear for her, left in the house."

"She would be a burden. She can hide in Nurse's cottage."

"Oh, no, Father. I mean, they would look there."

"In the village then?"

"I trust no one. Let her come. It gives us status. A young lady should travel with her maid."

He sighed. She could see he was too tired to argue. "Oh very well. I will send Tom to see if he can procure horses and saddles. She can ride pillion behind you."

Bel lifted his hand which still clasped hers and putting it to her lips kissed it.

She decided not to show him Henrietta's letter just now. She doubted if he could take it in, but she put it carefully away in her writing case. There was comfort in the knowledge that she had, after all, a sister.

CHAPTER 17

NAT had no travel pass for his journey from Yorkshire, but he carried the one from his College and hoped it would not be examined too closely. Before he left, his father had prayed for his safety and given him his blessing. Nat felt his anxiety at parting from him again so soon. What astonished him was to find his mother up when he went to say goodbye to her. She was in her nightgown with a shawl close about her and sitting on the window-seat. He could tell there were heavy bandages about her right leg which was so swollen she could not wear a slipper on her foot, but his Father said a great deal of discharge had come from it in the night and she had determined to watch Nat set off.

"I never thought this day would come," she said to him. "I thought the University had swallowed you up for ever under its mountains of books. But maybe you are a man after all. Now go and do your duty to your brother. I will wave to you and go back to bed. I do not wish to die before you return with my blessed Daniel's body and the deed accomplished, but the Lord's will be done."

Nat had been to see Sir Bertram Lauder, the Squire, the night before and he had generously lent him a horse from his stables and also written a letter for him, saying he was on family business with his approval.

"But for God's sake bring Jed back, Nathaniel. He is a good mount and will take you there in two days. I have been stripped of most of my horse and cattle."

Nat turned at the church and looked up at the windows of the vicarage. There she was waving her arm. What a transformation from all those days he had set off to Cambridge! His father said the pain of the dog bite had roused her from her apathy. She was aware of the doctor lancing her swollen leg. She had heard him ask if the son was returning soon, as she was not likely to survive the fever. So she had been alert to Nat's expected arrival and all her mind seemed to focus on what he must do then.

"But she has spoken of my bringing back Daniel's body. How can I do that, Father?" Nat had asked. "You inquired and there seemed to be no record of his burial."

His father shook his head. "Nat, I do not believe she will be living when you return. I am certain this sudden spurt of energy will sap her last strength. Just go and the Lord be with you."

Now that he was riding northward through the fresh Spring green of the countryside Nat had leisure to wonder how it would be if he tracked down the Horden family and whether there was even a grain of hope that he could find out Daniel's burying place after all this time. He had only funds enough for the journey and nothing to spare to pay for the return of a body. Let her think it possible. Perhaps she would not be alive when he returned, if indeed he managed the hazards of the journey.

It was two days later on a fine crisp April morning when Bel and her father, with Ursula, set off the four miles to Newcastle. They had no documents to see them safely past patrols, but Sir John had in his pocket book the letter from Clifford Horden.

Bel had had to rouse him that morning and he said he had lain long awake the night before anxious for her future. Now he looked almost too frail for the trying business of the day. The chill air set him coughing and Bel insisted on him tying a woollen scarf over his mouth before he mounted.

Bel herself was in a state of excitement. This was a mission in which she was determined to play an active part. She was ready to confront any authority on the justice of their cause and framed passionate arguments as they rode along. Ursula, unused to horses, clung onto her and said nothing, so Bel guessed she was frightened but would not want to distress her by admitting it.

Their own track joined the road south leading to the Pilgrim Gate of the town and soon they began to meet small troops of soldiers. Bel was sorry that they always addressed her father, demanding to know his business. When she called out that they were lawful citizens seeking justice, he turned round and silenced her with a frown. The soldiers were all Royalist and were willing enough to let them through, though one rough-looking group without an officer leered at Bel. Ursula in her bonnet kept her face hidden against Bel's back.

The officer of the last patrol they met volunteered to escort them to the Pilgrim Gate so that they would not be shot at accidentally from the walls. He spoke with the officer on the gate and learnt that the Mayor and Aldermen were at a funeral at the Church of St Nicholas, but if Sir John and his party made their way there they could speak to him presently.

Bel from the vantage of horseback took her chance to look about her as they clip-clopped the length of Pilgrim Street, lined by very elegant houses. When they had been to hear the Puritan preacher, they had approached the town through the Sandgate, a much poorer area of dense housing by the river and from there had mounted to a different church where she had been told that the Kingdom of Heaven was for ever closed to her. Her memory of that church was how large and intimidating it had seemed, but when they reached St Nicholas her father told her this was the largest in the town. She gazed up at it and thought it the finest building she had ever seen.

"We must stable our mounts," he said, "for I know not how long I will be closeted with the Mayor, if indeed he is the official who should send a petition to Parliament on my behalf. I have no hope that he has powers himself to help me."

Bel was alarmed at her father's use of "I" and "me". Was she not to accompany him?

They found a hostelry in a back street prepared to stable their horses and Ursula dismounted with relief.

"Eh, Bel, my precious, it's good to be on firm ground," she laughed with relief and stamped her feet.

They walked back to the church as the congregation was dispersing.

Bel soon spotted the Mayor and was boldly making her way to him when her father seized her arm.

"I met him over the Patrick Dawson affair last autumn," he reminded her. "He will remember the circumstances. He knows I never welcomed the man. You and Ursula can take a walk or stay in the Church. If you do walk, return to the church in an hour and wait for me there. Be careful to keep in main thoroughfares where people are going quietly about their business."

"But I wanted to help you, Father."

He shook his head. "Men's work. There, I can catch him. He is disengaged for a moment." And he pushed his way through the people to the Mayor's side.

"Well, Urs, we are dismissed." Bel was hurt and angry. "Why did God make me a woman? We will go down and look at the river. It must be that way."

Ursula gave her a comforting smile and held her hand, keeping her head bent down to avoid stares. Bel forgot her anger in pity that she missed so much. They came to the wide river and for an hour she could watch the soldiers patrolling the bridge and on the water the coming and going of the keels that carried the coal to the colliers moored downstream. There was so much to see, but at last she said, "I suppose we should be finding our way back to the Church. That narrow street called The Side that we came down was very steep and it will be hard work for you going back."

Ursula just grinned her twisted grin and scuttled up it as easily as Bel.

There was no sign of Sir John in the Close around the church, so they went in and sat down. Although there were people walking about it was quiet, and Bel studied the pillars and vaulted roof with a sense of awe but when she tried to copy Ursula in praying she found nothing would come, either for the souls of her brother and her baby niece or more immediately for her father's health and his present enterprise. She wanted to be in the centre of things, not waiting to see what would happen.

The hour had long since gone and she was feeling very hungry when a liveried serving-man stopped beside her.

"Excuse me, my lady. Are you the daughter of Sir John Horden?"

Bel jumped up. "Has my father sent for me?"

He made a rueful face. "He is not well, my lady. If you will follow me ..."

Ursula, head tucked down, trotted behind.

Bel was not too anxious. She was remembering how tired her father was even *before* their ride. Talking will have brought on his cough and he needs me to speak for him. She was thankful to have a part to play at last.

She was surprised to find that after only a few minutes' walking they were entering not a municipal building of some sort but a tall stone house in Pilgrim Street. The footman led them straight up the stair and Bel had an impression of glossy wood everywhere in the wainscoting, the bulbous balusters and the polished floors. The owner must be well-to-do, although they had come straight up a few steps from the street. Bel was unfamiliar with grand houses which had no land about them.

They passed the door of a long drawing-room with windows onto the street and turned a corner of the upper hall to a closed door. She began to feel apprehensive.

Before knocking the footman said, "Your maid could remain below."

Bel turned and grasped Ursula's hand. "No, no, please." The man must think Ursula's bonnet very odd but in the dim light he hadn't noticed her face. He inclined his head and tapped at the door.

A lady opened it. "Ah, is this his daughter come?" Bel heard her say.

The footman nodded and retreated. The lady who was of middle-age and dressed in an elegant day gown stood aside. Behind her, Bel saw an elaborately carved four-poster bed and on it lay her father, whiter than she had ever seen him and with his eyes closed.

"Oh," she gasped. "Is he dead?"

The lady took her hand. "No, no, my dear. Resting. We brought him here when he became ill since our house was close by. My husband is Alderman Johnson; he was with the Mayor at St Nicholas. They were listening to your father when he took a fit of coughing. Then he brought up blood and a doctor in the crowd said he must lie down at once. With support he was able to get as far as this, but he seemed very weak afterwards. He was able after a glass of wine to describe you and your maid to us and tell us you would be in the church. Now, pray sit down by him and I will send you up some refreshment." She touched Ursula's arm and added, "If you will come down to the kitchen, you will find the servants just having their dinner and you are welcome to join them."

Ursula had to look up then and thank her. Though the lady's eyes registered shock she was too polite to comment. With regret Bel saw Ursula retreat. She wanted to plead that she was a friend, not a servant, but Ursula would have been embarrassed, so she watched her go with the lady who closed the door after them.

Bel, sick with fear now, approached the bed and took the ornate carved chair beside it. She saw it was upholstered in blue velvet with a gold fringe matching the bed hangings and little gold studs. It was too incongruous, when the hands lying on the bedcover were so sad and colourless. There were no lace cuffs at his wrists and she realised his shirt had been removed.

It must have been bloodstained.

"Father?"

His eyes opened at once. "Bella?" She saw he was looking beyond her at the unfamiliar room. "What happened? Where are we?" His voice was weak and husky.

"In Newcastle. You were taken ill. They brought you to Alderman Johnson's house and sent to the church for me."

He tried to sit up and she saw they had put a woollen nightshirt on him. How was she to get him home? She remembered their horses stabled at the inn. He was far too weak to ride. What was she to do?

"I recall it all." He passed a hand across his face. "I was so ashamed." His voice grew urgent. "Bella, if I die they can't take the Hall and the land. I am the named delinquent. They knew about it. They had had a letter. The law here is supposed to act for Parliament. They said they were going to have a meeting but had not resolved on any action. They know we are for the King, but they also know your dear mother and sister are Catholic and they believed our house might still be called a Papist cell. I was in the midst of explaining to them how things have changed ... I couldn't ... it was all too much ..."

His chest heaved as if he were gasping for breath.

"No, stop," she begged, looking frantically about. On a carved chest was a pile of linen pieces. She jumped up and grabbed a few and ran back to him just as a cough racked him and a trickle of blood appeared at the corner of his mouth. She held the linen close and more blood came. She managed to contain it with difficulty, but at that moment a maid tapped and put her head round the door. She was carrying a tray, but seeing Bel's predicament she quickly set it down on the chest and brought more cloths, laid them on the bed and took the soiled ones.

"How thoughtful! How quick! Thank you," Bel cried as her father lay back on the pillows exhausted.

The maid dropped the bloodstained linen into a basket and brought a bowl of water. Bel moistened a clean cloth and wiped his face. He closed his eyes.

"My lady," the maid said now, "would you like the Doctor fetched back? He lives quite close."

Bel looked at the ghostly figure on the bed. "Perhaps we could wait. The doctor could be dining now." She saw there was a steaming bowl of something on the tray and smelt a wonderful savoury aroma.

"Very well, my lady. If the poor gentleman is peaceful, would you care to partake of some refreshment?" She moved the pile of linen onto the foot of the bed and placed a padded stool next to the chest. It matched the chair in blue velvet and also had a gold fringe and studs. "I shall wait outside, if you require me."

Bel shook her head. She felt tears coming at all this kindness. The girl was about her own age and her deference shamed her. She slipped out now with a little curtsey.

Bel choked down her emotion and fell upon the broth and cut bread and butter. When she had eaten the chopped meat and vegetables in the bowl she wondered if her father could drink any of the liquid. He had had no nourishment since breakfast and it must be far past noon. She went close but he didn't move. If he was sleeping it might be the best thing. She finished everything on the tray including the mug of light ale.

Then she opened the door and there was the maid sitting on a stool at the corner of the upper hall. She jumped up at once and Bel handed her the tray.

"That was so good. Thank you."

"Mistress Johnson wishes to know how the gentleman is."

"My father is sleeping I think. I will sit by him."

The girl gave a little bob and then, biting her lower lip, asked, "May I take the liberty of asking what awful accident befell your old servant?"

Bel smiled. "She's more of a friend than a servant and she was born like that. She is a truly wonderful character, so I hope you will all be very kind to her."

"Oh yes, my lady. She has already asked what she can do to help us so I thought ..." She bit her lip again.

Bel smiled. "I'm not 'my lady' though my father is Sir John. What is *your* name?"

"Molly, Ma'am."

"Well, thank you, Molly."

She was a plump girl and Bel remembered that the footman had had well-rounded legs in his white stockings. She had had a good sight of them as he led her up the stairs. This is a rich household, she thought, returning into the room. Everything is of the best. They will have no idea of our poverty.

She looked at her father, ascertained that he was still breathing, and wondered what was to happen now. These people seemed to have accepted that they would care for him for the moment, but she could hardly expect them to do so indefinitely. Her father had paid for stabling for the day. Did he have any more money in his pocket? There was a door in the room and Bel peeped inside. As she expected it led to a dressing-room where her father's doublet, riding coat and breeches were hanging up. They must have taken away his shirt and stockings to wash.

After the years of having no servants but Mary and Tom, Bel had grown used to caring for her own and her father's clothes with Ursula's help. It was strangely comforting to feel that there were many pairs of hands here to deal with such matters at a word of command. In his riding coat she found a purse with some silver and six gold sovereigns. In his pocket book was folded the letter from Cousin Clifford. She re-read it and then put it and the money back. Was it true what Father had said that Horden Hall could not be sequestered if he died? She went back to his bedside. She wanted Ursula's comforting presence. She felt hemmed in and helpless in this strange house and in the face of this totally unexpected calamity.

Presently she heard footsteps and voices and a knock came at the door. She was much relieved to find Mistress Johnson with a strange man who she was sure by his dress and bag was a physician.

"Doctor Harcourt has come to see his patient."

"He's asleep," Bel blurted out, "but please tell me, is his condition serious? He has long had a cough but never brought up blood. Or if he has he hasn't told me."

The doctor was a tall, spare man with a severely professional face.

"That is likely, young lady. He has been ill for years. It was I who came when your unfortunate brother died. I thought your father in poor health then, but he would not acknowledge it. I am afraid there is little I can do for him now. His lungs are diseased. He may recover from this bout, but I would not expect him to live long. I take it he is past fifty?"

Bel nodded. "I believe so." Surely he was allowed a greater lifespan. I need him, she thought. I'm too young to be abandoned. Her zest for independence had swiftly evaporated. "How can I take him home?" she asked.

"He should not be moved at present." The doctor looked at Mistress Johnson.

"No indeed," she cried. "We have plenty of room. My sons are with the King's forces. I will have the next bedroom made ready for you, my dear, so that you are within hearing."

"Oh pray, let me stay beside him. I can't bear to be so much trouble to you. But I am worried about our horses at the inn. They were borrowed and our groom at home will wonder where we are if we don't return tonight."

"They can be sent back with one of our men and perhaps your lady's maid could go with him and show him where to go. I will lend you our Molly while you are here and when Sir John is fit to go home, of course we will put our carriage at your disposal."

Bel didn't want Ursula to go, but Mistress Johnson's kind but authoritative manner seemed to leave her no alternative.

The Doctor who had been examining her father rejoined them by the door.

"His pulse is very weak. If he regains consciousness he should have fluid. Some beef broth perhaps, strained. Asses' milk if you can obtain it. Wine is good, but it may be mixed with boiled water and not given for a few hours after milk. Honey, a few spoonfuls, is also very soothing."

Bel looked after them as Mistress Johnson saw him downstairs. She felt her father was condemned and she herself cast alone onto a strange shore.

Ursula came up later for orders before she left and Bel hugged her and cried over her. "I don't want you to go but I suppose you must. How will you manage?"

Ursula reassured her that though she wouldn't ride a horse alone she was perfectly content to sit behind a strange groom and the other horse could be led. "These are all kind people," she said simply.

When she had gone, Bel gave all her attention to her father, who woke rather breathless and had to be propped up. Whatever Molly brought on the doctor's orders, she tried to encourage him to take, but he had little appetite. He seemed anxious to talk about her future but she begged him to be quiet in case he started to cough again.

Later in the evening, Mrs Johnson invited her to join them for some supper. "My husband will be happy to meet you."

Bel begged to be excused. "I had rather sit here." The room with all its furnishings was now familiar to her and she felt she dare not venture out.

At bedtime two servants wheeled in a truckle bed since she still refused to leave her father and she was thankful to lie down as soon as it was dark outside. She had not slept long before he had another bout of coughing and so it went on all night. She would rise and hold the linen before him until he had coughed up blood, then he would have a short rest while she waited for the next interruption. By morning she was utterly weary and after Molly had brought breakfast and her father had fallen into a deep sleep she asked Mistress Johnson if she could go out and get some air.

"Of course, my dear. We will watch your father and send for the physician if necessary. You have been confined in here for a long time. I'll send Molly with you."

'Confined' was certainly the word. Bel knew she had none of Ursula's patient endurance. The sick room had become a prison and she could see how the houses on the other side of the street were aglow with sunlight, the windows reflecting it back to her, dazzling her eyes.

"No, please. I have been used to walking alone from a child."

Mistress Johnson raised her eyebrows but Bel almost ran down the stairs, hoping to meet no one else. A footman appeared to unfasten the heavy front door. She smiled at him and descended the five steps to the street.

Immediately her nose was assailed by the smells of the town. She had forgotten that the air would not be fresh like the country air about Horden Hall. All the same, the sunshine was welcome and the cold wind of yesterday had vanished. Instinctively, she moved towards the river. She would have sought open country but it lay beyond the gates. Amidst the bustle on the quayside she had felt safe yesterday, though Ursula's strange bonnet had drawn curious eyes. I should have carried a basket so I might be supposed to have come for produce, but no matter, I am walking and the exercise is good. She walked briskly with her swinging country stride until she came to the bridge. Near here there was a bench against the wall in the sunshine. She sat down and unfastened the short cloak she had brought for riding yesterday and putting it over the back of her head she was able to lean against the wall and close her eyes against the bright sun. Her mind was suddenly empty of everything but weariness. In two minutes she was asleep.

Nathaniel Wilson riding on Jed approached the bridge over the town from the south side. He was intensely excited by the sight of Newcastle rising before him on the opposite bank. Until a few years ago the busy river Tyne would have amazed him and the tall narrow houses along the quay, the steep bank and the spires of several churches, one very large and splendid shining in the sunlight, would have thrilled his eyes. But he had seen Cambridge and above all London. What excited him now was his nearness to the end of his journey. Somewhere here he would find directions to Horden Hall and then his quest would surely reach some kind of resolution.

Vengeance was not in his heart but how could he tell what emotions he would feel if he looked upon the faces of the Hordens, father and son, who had combined in the cruel death of his brother.

He swallowed hard and rode up to the guard on the bridge. "I have a pass to my home from the Master of Queens College, Cambridge. I am a student of that University." All that was true. Everything depended now on the mood of the soldier.

"Dismount. Have you weapons?" the man demanded.

Nat jumped down and spread out his arms, turning back his short cloak to show he had neither sword nor pistol. The soldier rummaged in his saddle bag, but finding only a change of clothes and a few books which Nat had put in for show, he shrugged his shoulders.

"He's harmless enough," he commented to his mate nearby.

"But that's a fine horse for a student."

"It was kindly lent me by a friend, Sir Bertram Lauder, as I came through Yorkshire. He is for the King, as I am."

"You should be fighting for him then, not stuffing your head with words."

"Oh, let him go," the first soldier said.

"Walk your horse across the bridge, then."

Nat led the horse and, passing the houses and boarded up shops on the bridge reached the other side. The guards there, satisfied that he had been allowed on, waved him through. He stood on the quayside of Newcastle and looked about him.

The first thing that caught his eye was a young woman asleep on a bench against the wall. She wore a light green gown, the skirt open to show a paler green petticoat sprigged with yellow flowers. Her sun-bronzed country face, tilted up to the light, was quite large and square, a strong jaw and a bold forehead, her curly hair having fallen back from it. The darker green shawl behind her head framed her like the leaves of a flower. The whole effect sang of Spring.

As he gazed at her with delight, she stirred, perhaps conscious of his scrutiny, and though she didn't wake she moved and her head slid along the wall overbalancing her. She would have fallen off the bench if Nat, dropping Jed's rein, had not leapt forward and caught her.

Her eyes flew open and she squealed at finding a man's arms gripping hers and pulling her upright.

"Oh ma'am, I'm sorry," he cried. "You nearly rolled to the ground."

Other people crowded round. A voice yelled, "Hands off her, you villain."

Another cried, "He was trying to rob her."

The girl was laughing. Her eyes, instantly alert, had now focussed on Nat's. His whole body tingled. She seemed to be looking into his soul.

"Nonsense. He's no robber. I was asleep. He saved me from falling."

Nat marvelled at how smartly she had assessed the situation. She was no hysterical young lady. She stood up now, adjusting her shawl, still with her eyes on his.

"I thank you, sir."

The small crowd was beginning to move back when someone shouted, "Man, you'd better look to your horse."

Nat looked round in alarm and saw that Jed, startled by the commotion and finding himself loose, had cantered off along the quay.

"Please stay there. I'll come back." Nat surprised himself by addressing the girl. He ran off after Jed. Why had he said that? Was it the feel of her sturdy torso between his hands? Was it her bright intelligent eyes? Was it her free, joyous laugh?

For the moment, he concentrated on reclaiming Jed. People were scattering. A runaway horse was a danger. Nat was desperate not to lose him. Suppose he leapt off the quay in his fright and landed in the river or worse, broke his back against the many boats moored below! He saw a burly waterman reach out and grab Jed's reins. Thank God for that! But when he came up the man demanded a reward.

"What's he worth to you, young man? He's a fine beast."

"My thanks for your swift action."

"Let's see your silver before I hand him over."

Nat had stayed two nights on the journey so that he could be in Newcastle early in the day and he was not sure how much he had left of the little money he had set out with but he fished in his pocket and found a sixpence.

The man bit it with a scowl.

"I am a poor student," Nat said, "and the horse was lent to me."

A voice spoke at his elbow. "Come friend, this gentleman loosed his horse to help me. You are well paid."

Nat turned in astonishment. The girl in green and yellow, his Spring maiden, stood beside him.

The waterman yielded Jed's rein, grunted a little and rolled off to the alehouse.

"Why, I am for ever in your debt," Nat began.

She laughed again. "Nonsense. You saved me from a bump. I saved your horse. We don't need pretty speeches. So you are a student? I envy you." They were walking Jed back along the quay as people resumed their occupations after the small diversion.

"You envy me?" Nat wondered where his terror of young ladies had gone. She was at ease with him but not as Hermione Branford had been. He could speak to her naturally as to a casual acquaintance, while all the time his heart was quickening as he noted her well-packed bodice, neat waist and the flowing movement of her skirt.

"Yes," she said with passion, "I think I would love nothing better in the world than to be a student. I always wanted to be a boy."

That would have been a waste, he thought, but didn't dare say it in case it was called a pretty speech. But he glanced sideways at her and gave her what he hoped was a smile of sympathy and understanding. She smiled back readily.

"I need to stable this beast somewhere," he said, facing the immediate practical problem. "I have inquiries to make and that will be done better on foot. Can you advise me? Do you live in Newcastle?"

"For the present," she said and a shadow seemed to pass across her face. "But I can show you where to go. We'll walk up The Side and round behind the big church where there is an inn which should accommodate your horse reasonably."

Leading Jed who came quietly enough now Nat walked up with her.

"What are you studying?" she asked.

"Theology, which with my tutor includes the whole history of philosophy as well as Greek and Latin."

"Are you going to be a priest?"

"I do hope to be ordained; in the Church of England, what's left of it if the Puritans have their way."

"So you're neither Roman nor Puritan. A compromise."

Nat smiled, not sure if she meant it critically. "Our beliefs are stated in the creeds – the essence of the Christian faith – about which most Romans *and* Puritans agree." This was the most extraordinary conversation to be having with a very brief acquaintance, especially a lively and attractive young lady wandering on her own round a garrisoned town.

"You say they agree," she stood still at the top of the steep bank. "If they do, why are they all fighting?"

"Why indeed? It is madness. My dear father, a parish priest himself, always taught me peace not violence, love not hate."

She nodded and walked on. Then she asked suddenly, "Did you have plenty of love as a child?"

Her questions were astonishing but he would answer with the same directness and complete honesty. "From my father, yes, not my mother."

"You were fortunate. I didn't have much from either." She brushed her hand across her eyes and pointed ahead. "There, that's the inn. Get rid of your horse and then come back to the church door. I'll wait for you there."

"You can spare me some time?" He felt he was gazing at her with too much intensity.

She laughed and shrugged but her eyes were moist. "If you are to be a priest, perhaps you can teach me to pray."

She turned away and he walked on with Jed to the inn stables. He was so taken aback by this encounter that he could hardly collect his wits to arrange for the stabling of Jed till he should come for him later. As soon as the bargain was made he hastened back to the church. Would the extraordinary girl still be there?

She was, a bright patch of colour in the back pew. He sat down by her with no idea what he was going to say.

She looked up brightly, with eyes still glistening with tears and she resumed their conversation as if it had had no break. "I must not malign my father. He is ill and has been tender to me lately."

"Your words reproach *me*. My *mother* is ill and has also smiled upon me lately. But she always loved my brother more."

"Ah, both my parents cared more for my brother and my sister. I felt that keenly when I was young. Have you a sister?"

"No and my brother is dead, so they have only me."

"My brother also is dead and my sister is married and is far away with my mother, so my father has only me."

"We have much in common." He desperately wanted to put an arm round her. She looked small and woebegone now.

"Ah, but we don't," she burst out almost savagely, "you are studying and have work ahead of you. I have nothing. And you believe in God and I don't. That's why I said teach me to pray."

Oh, this was sad! This was a new view of her. He thought for a moment, meeting her challenging eyes. He said gently, "You can't pray to a God you don't believe in."

"No; it is because I can't pray that I wonder if there is a God."

"How old are you?" he ventured.

"Sixteen. How old are you?"

"Twenty-two." He had thought her older until her last petulant outburst.

"You think I am a child. If I'd been willing, I could have been married a year ago. By now I might have been a mother."

He was ashamed. So much maturity was expected of girls when they were hardly ready for it.

Her big green eyes were staring defiantly up at him.

"No, you are not a child. I must be honest and admit I have no experience of talking to young ladies. In fact I have never spoken so long alone with one as I have with you now and I don't even know your name."

She cocked her head, thought a moment and grinned. "There's another thing we have in common then. I have never walked and talked alone with a young man as long as this. Not even the one I was supposed to be betrothed to. I don't think we'll trouble about names, as we're unlikely ever to see each other again. But I was serious when I said, teach me to pray. If you are going to be a parish priest one day you should be able to do that. I truly want to pray for my father but I feel only emptiness."

The thought of not seeing her again saddened him, even more the thought that she was indifferent to their meeting again. Could he help her now? He was overwhelmed by diffidence. He bowed his head and began in a low murmur to ask God to bless and heal her father, then he added his mother too. "And help your dear daughter here to pray. Surround her with your love. Surround us both with your love and ..."

"All right," she said, standing up. "I can see how to do it. What you don't know is that I am a lost soul. The clock is chiming noon. I must go."

"Jesus came to save the lost. Please tell me your name."

"Just Bel, B-E-L. I like only three letters in a name."

"And I am Nat, N-A-T."

"Oh good. I like that. Then goodbye, Nat and thank you for bearing with my silliness." She gave him a smiling wave and ran off into the sunshine.

He stared after her, utterly unable to place her in the web of society. A lost soul! She speaks well, she dresses well though her clothes looked crumpled and a little grubby when I was close to her. Did her planned marriage come to naught because she was found to have been with another man? She had great boldness certainly, speaking to a stranger, yet her frankness seemed without guile. She said she had never spoken so long alone with a young man. I have to believe her. And her childhood? She was unloved as a child. That has wounded her.

He got up slowly and looked about the church before leaving it. It was a vast and beautiful building. He drew a long breath and wandered outside. Where could he go to make inquiries? This strange and disturbing encounter had put his purpose completely from his mind. He paced the streets looking for any public buildings where he might seek information but secretly hoping to see a green and yellow figure flitting along. Coming upon an ale house advertising best mutton pies he realised how hungry he was and went inside.

While he was enjoying his pie he asked the landlord, "Have you heard of a mansion called Horden Hall somewhere in the country round about?"

The man shook his head. "If it's not within the walls I don't know it."

"Ay," said a man at another table who by his bloody apron was a butcher, "there's little villages with the name Horden beyond the Liberties. There's a Nether Horden and an Upper Horden. The Hall's that way I reckon."

"How far is it?" Nat asked.

"Be four, maybe five miles from the town gate, northards."

"Thank you." Nat paid his bill. Should he walk or go back for Jed? Or should he make further inquiries.

He was hesitating outside when a carrier's cart drew up and the man handed in some parcels for the innkeeper.

"My good man," Nat accosted him, "you know your way around. Do you know a place called Horden Hall."

The man looked startled. "Ay, it's on my regular route. What do you want with the Hordens?"

"To speak with Robert Horden or Sir John."

The man shook his head. "Ay, well, sir, I fear you're behind the times. Mr Robert fell off his horse and broke his neck. It'll be two year gone or more."

"And Sir John."

"Died this very morning. My daughter Molly told me not an hour ago. She was running an errand so she couldn't stop. I'm sorry if you was acquainted with the gentleman, sir, for you'll not be speaking with him now in this life."

Nathaniel looked him in the eye.

"You're sure of this."

"Ay, that I am. He was staying where my daughter's a housemaid. Why, she's been helping nurse him. She's a good lass. She would never make up a tale like that."

"Your pardon, my good man, I believe you. And I thank you." Nat moved off and the carrier gee'd up his horse and was gone.

Both dead. Nat stood absolutely still absorbing this. Mother will say she cursed them. And Sir John died today! It is indeed uncanny, as if my arrival in the town had conjured it. But my task is done. I can go home. He felt strangely numb and irresolute. His mother imagined he could bring Daniel's body back. That could never be. But even to learn of his burial place was hardly possible after all this time and with both the Hordens dead! Rather than leave at once though, he thought, now I could see where he died. A trial was held at Nether Horden. I would like to look at that place. Newcastle's gates are shut at sunset. I must fetch Jed and ride.

Once he had made up his mind he almost ran to the inn stables, mounted Jed and was on his way. Only then did the huge relief enter his soul. No act of vengeance was to be required of him. His mother could call him what she would. He had left it in the Lord's hands and this was the outcome.

CHAPTER 18

B**EL** reached Alderman Johnson's house just as Molly returned from her errand to fetch the doctor. He was two paces behind her, grave and intimidating as he had been before.

"Oh my lady," Molly cried, seeing Bel on the steps to the front door. "I'm afraid he's gone. We didn't know where you were."

"Gone?"

"Now then," the doctor said, as the door was opened. "No one has 'gone' as you put it until I have pronounced death."

Bel, sick that she had not been there, that she had been laughing with that odd young man, lifted her skirts and took the shallow stairs two at a time. Mistress Johnson was at the door of her father's room.

"Oh my dear, I sent to the church but you weren't there. We're not quite sure when he slipped away, but it was very peaceful. He never woke that we saw at all."

The doctor put them all aside and went in.

Bel stood in the Upper Hallway, transfixed, not looking at Mistress Johnson or Molly but at a tiny chip in the wainscoting by the doorway. *Father is dead...he fringe of my skirt is dirty...I have worn this gown two days...I even slept in the petticoat...Father is dead...I only untied my corset. I was too tired to remove it though there was a pretty nightgown laid out for me...Father is dead.*

The doctor came out. "I would say he died an hour ago." He laid a hand on Bel's shoulder. "I am very sorry for your loss. If I had been called earlier it would have made no difference. He was worn out. I will send a good woman for the laying out, but if you wish to go in he is very peaceful."

He was speaking to Bel. They would expect her to go in. She had neglected him all morning. He might have wanted her even though his eyes were closed. He might have said her name in his mind or just murmured it and she was not by him to catch it, to hold his hand or wipe his brow. She went in. The doctor had turned the sheet to cover his face. She could see where the point of his nose was.

"No," she cried, "he is not there. He has gone and left me. I didn't say goodbye."

Mrs Johnson's arms were round her, drawing her to the bed. "So say goodbye now. You'll feel better. Give him a kiss."

"No, I have seen too many dead. I am not fit to be around people. I have a devil in me. They die. They all die."

"She's hysterical," came the doctor's voice. "Give her this sleeping draught I will prescribe. She will feel better in the morning."

"No, I must have Ursula. If I have Ursula I will be well."

"She speaks of that poor little deformed creature. She could be sent for. Benjamin who rode with her yesterday could go for her."

"Oh, yes, please, ma'am."

Mistress Johnson took her into the next room, the one she could have had the previous night. She was shaking in every limb and could hardly sit on the bed. They brought wine which she was unused to, but drank eagerly. She was aware that everyone was being very kind. She was even aware that this was a family that had not known of her existence the day before yesterday but was now cumbered with a death in their house and an hysterical girl. Bel Horden can do better than this, she told herself. Bel wanted to be a man. Then she remembered the extraordinary morning she had had. Her guilt was extreme and yet she didn't want to forget that young man she had met. There was something about him; honesty and gentleness but an innocent humour too. She had never encountered these qualities together in a man. She lay back on the bed and thought about everything they had said. It wasn't he that was odd. He must have thought *me* quite preposterous. Giggling a little, she curled on the bed as the wine flew to her brain. When Ursula was brought in later she was deeply asleep.

Nat rode north after showing Sir Bertram's letter to the guard at the Pilgrim Gate. "I will not be long. I am going to see the place where my brother died. That is the family business his letter refers to. I have to satisfy my mother about it. She is very ill and I must return home as soon as possible. Yes, I will be back long before you lock the gate."

The guard seemed to assume his brother had died in some skirmish on the King's side and made no demur.

Jed had been well fed and rubbed down at the inn and was happy to gallop so the miles were soon covered. A cowherd at a field gate told Nat that if he kept straight on he would come to Nether Horden. If he turned right on a gravelled track he would come to Horden Hall. He was keen to see the Hall, but the village was where it had all happened. He was still some way off when the gallows on its hill came into sight. Then he did draw rein and the thought of Daniel hanging there made his gorge rise. He closed his eyes and tried to let his mind cling desperately to his father's vision of immortality. We will have eternity together. What are the sufferings of this life compared with that? The track into the village skirted the hill with a duck pond on his left and brought him down one side of the village green. He drew rein again and looked round, spotting the low school building where the 'trial' was held.

People were staring at him, he realised, and he was glad that he had tucked his over-long flaxen hair under his hat which he had kept well pulled down all day. He had not removed it even in the church knowing it was now often seen as Popish to take off one's hat as a sign of reverence. Well, he had seen the village now and he had no wish to excite too much curiosity. The people in remoter places were very jumpy and he knew from Daniel's experience how quickly they could turn violent if fearful or angry. He turned Jed and rode back, passing the hill with his eyes down, and then saw that riding towards him was a lad in the uniform of a Sergeant in the Royalist forces.

"What are you doing here, stranger?" he demanded.

The truth will serve best, Nat thought. "My brother died here. I came to look at the place, that's all. I am returning now."

"There have been no battles here. How could he have died? You're a Parliament spy, aren't you?"

"Nay I am not. I am for the King, like you."

"Not like me. Where is your uniform? We have had Parliament men sneak in here and break into houses and commit murder."

"I am unarmed."

The Sergeant pulled his horse close up to Nat and in a sudden movement snatched off his hat. Nat's flaxen hair fell down.

The Sergeant stared. "I thought you had a pistol hidden there. Hold! I've seen you before. Where have I seen you before? That light hair!"

Nat considered the lad and made a wild guess. "You are not Sam Turner are you?"

"Sergeant Turner. God in heaven. You are a ghost. You fired our stack, we hanged you."

Nat shook his head, smiling sadly. "You hanged my twin brother. I am no ghost."

Sam's colour came back into his face. "Man, you gave me a start. Ay, I see it now. You said you came to see where your brother died. You are not here to stir up trouble, are you? It was all fair and square. He had a trial. He must have done it. I know it was hard, because he was a kind of idiot, wasn't he? He may not have known what he was doing."

"He spoke of seeing a fat boy. Why was he never found and interrogated?"

Sam's eyes betrayed fleeting surprise. "Your brother told you that? How could he? You were not there."

"I was not far away, sick of a fever. He told me he'd seen a fat boy but he left me again to seek food."

"There was no fat boy," Sam said quickly. "It was ... no, there was no one could have done it. It's all in the past anyway. You are like him but he was broader, quite a big man."

"I believe there *was* a fat boy. Maybe he fled the scene when he saw what he had done. Daniel would never have fired a haystack, nor was he capable of lying, but I am not here to plead his cause. Only we – my family – would like to know where he was buried. We made inquiries without success."

Again the lad's eyes – he looked no more than eighteen – looked surprised and wary. "I never knew of any inquiries. No one asked me."

"Do you mean you knew?"

"Ay, but I was told to keep quiet. I was only a boy, you know, and the Scots army were in charge."

"Where then? Tell me. I won't blame you. What happened?"

Sergeant Turner dismounted and motioned Nat to do the same. He led the horses to the edge of the wood where an upward pointing tree branch had been pruned to clear the track. They threw the reins over it and went a little way into the wood.

"It's somewhere about here. The Scots left him hanging a week as a warning. They were strict at first about looting and suchlike. When they took him down I was at the foot of the hill getting blackberries for my ma's jam and puddings. They had put the body in a sack but they were foot-soldiers and had no transport. They saw I had a spade. I'd brought it to beat down some of the tangles to get at the fruit behind so they shouted at me to help them dig a hole. I dug a bit and they all took turns. When it was big

274

enough they threw him in and filled it up and pulled some of the brambles over the top. I asked them if the landowner had given permission. They were threatening then and said, 'If ye dinna tell he willna ken.' Their talk was so broad I mostly couldn't understand it but I remember that."

"But you won't remember the spot now?"

"I do because there's a stream further on and when the soldiers had gone I went and fetched a big stone out of it and dropped it on the place. With the edge of the spade I scratched a D and a W on it because I remembered he was called Daniel Wilson. See there it is. I'm sure that's it but moss has covered the letters."

Nat ran forward. He snapped off a sharp twig and scraped at the moss. Sam Turner came up and drew his sword. "Let me."

How easy to kill me now, Nat thought, and lay me beside him. But the young Sergeant soon scraped the stone and the very rough D and W could still be seen.

"There it is then. You're not going to dig him up, are you? There was no coffin."

Nat felt unable to speak. He just shook his head. Sam seeing how moved he was, sheathed his sword and mumbled something about leaving him then.

Nat grasped his hand and then, breaking into sobs, embraced him. "I thank you a thousand times. Thank God I met you."

Sam grinned with embarrassment. "I was given some leave to see my family at the farm. Life has been hard for my father without me, but Sir John had to send a troop to the King's muster. He was too ill to go himself and his son was dead so I got the charge of them," he finished proudly.

Nat said, "You won't have had news of Sir John today?"

"No. Why do you ask? He went into Newcastle on business yesterday. My father lent horses."

"I have been in the town. I heard a report – and I believe it – that he died this morning."

"What, Sir John dead? Just this morning? Ay, well, last time I saw him in church he looked fit to drop. I must tell my folk. My God, this is a sad day for his tenants. He was a good man and tried to spare us hardship. What in the world will happen to us now, I wonder."

"There is no heir, then?"

"Just his daughter, Arabella. She was to be married to a London Horden, a wealthy merchant's son but their maid, Mary – she and I are to be wed when the fighting's over – she said it was called off. The poor young mistress will be desolate. Her mother and sister are in France and like to stay there for they're Catholic."

A strange feeling came over Nat. "What did you say her name is?"

"Arabella." He laughed a little. "She likes to call herself Bel, just B-E-L. A canny lass. A mind of her own."

Nat nodded and held out his hand again. "Well, Sam Turner, I must let you go to your family. Thank you again and God bless you for what you did for Daniel."

Sam, obviously fearing tears were erupting again, retreated to his horse and unhooking the reins, sprang lightly into the saddle, waved his hand and was gone.

Nat stood by Daniel's stone, not for the moment thinking of him but of the astonishing fact that he had been talking for an hour or more with a member of the Horden family and had not known it. Poor young mistress indeed. Everything she had said to him fitted and yet her demeanour was so strange; a mixture of merriment and deadly earnest. I must find her again, was his first thought. But how? He had no idea where she had been staying and if he had he couldn't intrude on her grief. I know what I can do. I will write to her when I return home and express my sympathy. What that might lead to he didn't dare to think. Now all that mattered was getting home in safety.

He looked down at the tangled overgrown spot that hid his brother's body and couldn't help dropping on his knees and remembering the loving guileless soul that had been his hourly companion all his youth. He prayed and then, noticing some windflowers growing among the new green of the brambles, he picked a bunch and gathering up some of the moss from the stone he encased the stems in it, wrapped his pocket handkerchief loosely round and placed them carefully in his saddle-bag. Then he mounted Jed and rode as fast as he could back to Newcastle where the same guard remembered him and let him through.

He would not pause for refreshment in the town although he looked about in search of his Spring maiden as he called her in his heart, but of course she would be within doors weeping for her father. He had to leave by the bridge before the gates were closed and he feared his reception there. Fortunately the guard had been changed since the morning and knowing his College pass would be useless he was ready to produce the Squire's letter.

As it happened the guard was willing to let him through for a shilling. "Every mouth outside the town is one less to feed if we're besieged," he chuckled. "And with hair that long I reckon you're no Parliament spy." Nat had not stopped to hide his hair but he would do so before he went much further.

As he rode he was yearning with all his heart to see his mother, the first time in his life that he had had such a longing on returning home. This surely marked a new beginning and happier times, if she could only survive till he came. But he was almost superstitiously afraid. It seemed to him a sinister omen that Bel Horden's father had died while he was speaking with her. Again his thoughts settled on his Spring maiden and as he rode further south in the evening light he could not shake her out of his mind. He dreamt about her in the seedy inn where he finally stopped to spend that night, scarcely noticing the bed bugs and the snoring of a travelling medicine man who shared his bed.

It was very late evening the next night when having safely delivered a tired Jed to Sir Bertram, he walked the last two miles to Darrowswick. As he breasted the hill he discerned something white at the bedroom window. Someone had spied him and was waving a kerchief. Could it be his mother? Pray God she was still alive.

His father opened the door before he reached it. It must be his mother above. Clasped in his father's arms he choked out, "She lives still. She waved to me."

"Not merely lives but is much better. I don't know how it is but it seemed that as some of the poison seeped from her mind so did the suppurating matter from her leg. As you know, much came away the night before you left and the doctor came and is greatly pleased with her condition. When you have had some refreshment you must come up to her."

"I shall come at once. I will eat and drink freely when I have seen her." Carefully he took out the windflowers and carried them upstairs. They were still recognisable.

His mother turned from the window and held out her arms to him. He laid the flowers on the bed and ran to her and knelt down and she embraced him. This was more than he had ever dreamt of and he had not even told her the outcome of his mission.

"I thank God you are back, son."

"Oh Mother, Sir John and Robert Horden are dead, but I did not have to slay them. The Lord has taken them in His own way."

She leant back on the window seat and gave a strange cackling laugh and clapped her hands. "Well, praise be to Him."

Nat shrank a little from her but said nothing. He got to his feet and fetched the flowers. "I couldn't bring Daniel but I picked these on his grave."

She took them delicately onto her palm. "Ah wood anemone, the windflower. They are beautiful. We will press them in the family Bible, Joseph."

Nat saw that his father too was gazing at them wonderingly. It was a joy to hear her speak of an activity jointly with her husband. She had always seemed so separate, so deliberately cut off.

Now he told them all he had learnt but left out any mention of the Horden daughter. He would tell his father alone, but not till he had written her a letter. He had no wish to be told it was unwise or worse, improper to do so. He was sure she was no slave to convention herself but she might well have an elderly relative who would warn her from corresponding with an unknown young man. I will be open with her and tell her who I am and how I found out her identity and I will offer her my heartfelt sympathy. Of course she may know nothing of one case among many that her father tried, but I must explain what my inquiries were about. If she never replies I will be very sad. She is a girl in a thousand. Then he laughed at himself because he had known so few.

For the rest of the vacation he was thankful to bask in a family life that had a harmony he had never known. Though his mother was very fragile she was, by the end of his vacation, able to limp about the house or sit outside in the spring sunshine and though she was quiet she seemed at peace and above all she showed Nat the affection that she had never done before.

"You are at last filling the gap that Daniel left," his father said, "which I could never do. This is all I have prayed for. I only trust she will endure your going back to Cambridge without sinking into that former apathy. Before I have feared the effect of your return because you were not Daniel. Now I fear your going, because you are yourself and she has found she loves you. A sweet irony."

"I will write often. And Father, if there should come any letter for me from Northumberland, pray forward it." Then he told his father of the chance meeting but not all that was said at it. "She has not replied," he added. "Of course she may not have received my letter. Did I do wrong to write?"

His father looked at him with a humorous raising of his eyebrows. "She has captivated you in that brief encounter, has she not? I can see it in your blushes. No, it was not wrong to express your sympathy, but it would have been forward to ask her to enter into a correspondence with you."

"Oh, I did not do that, sir."

"Then she may not see that a reply is called for or she may send a few words of formal acknowledgment, but remember that letters are not easily sent. Messengers must be found willing to take them and they demand extra payment in these troubled times. But do not fret for her, my boy. God will send you the right woman in due course. Not a baronet's daughter and not a Horden. That would be a torment to your poor mother."

Nat nodded and said nothing more. It wasn't possible that he was in love with Bel Horden. He scarcely knew her. He was only curious and if he heard nothing from her he resolved to write to her again from Cambridge.

Bel received her letter while she was hanging out the best Holland sheets. She and Ursula had washed them in the hope of selling them in the town. After her father's funeral they had been going carefully through the whole house to assemble goods which could be sold. They were piled up on the table behind the screens in the great hall, a new use for this grim space.

Bel looked at the directions on the letter and didn't recognise the hand. There had been various letters from creditors since her father's death so she finished pegging out the sheets and took the basket inside. "I'll read my letter on the bench, Urs," she called. "Can you put the stew-pan on the fire so it'll be ready for dinner?"

"Yes, my precious."

The late April sun glinted on the seal as she broke it and unfolded the letter. The first thing that leapt out at her was her name BEL printed in capital letters. What was this!

'May I presume to address you as BEL,' she read, *'not having been vouchsafed any other name? I do however now know who you are and will therefore reveal that my identity is also more than NAT.'*

She sat back against the wall of the house with a huge smile of delighted surprise. She had thought often of that young student with his well-worn dark doublet and breeches, his hat comically pulled down over his mild, pleasing features, neither handsome nor plain but utterly open and transparent. He had been both devout and humorous which was a wonderfully refreshing mixture. So how had he found her out and why had he written? She returned avidly to the letter.

'My name is Nathaniel Wilson of Darrowswick Parsonage, near Easingwold in Yorkshire and my business in Newcastle was to make inquiries about the Horden family.'

Easingwold! Cranmore House was near there. Could he have been sent by the Parliament people who closed it down? Surely he was no spy?

She read on. *'I learnt later that day of the death of your father and this is the principle reason that I am writing to you, to express my great sympathy for you in your sorrow. I believe he might already have died when we were praying for him in the church.'*

We? thought Bel, *you* were praying.

'I trust you have been able to find comfort among your friends and family.'

Only from Ursula. But what business could he have had with us?

'I will be open with you about my purpose in seeking news of your family. It was your father who had occasion to put on trial my brother, Daniel, in September 1640.'

Bel clapped her hand over her mouth. Daniel Wilson, the hanging one-eyed body. No, oh, no. The black cloud fell about her in a storm of ice. That sweet youth an avenging angel! It must not be. She forced her eyes to return to the page.

'All I sought was some information about his death and burial which we were not able to obtain by written representation through the since-disbanded Court of the North. Learning that your brother Robert had died some time ago and that Sir John too had just succumbed to a long illness, I went to look at the village where my brother died and discovered his burial place which gave me comfort.'

The body is somewhere there! I may have passed by it. But who spoke to him? Who knew where the body was? Mary told me there had been a stranger in the village the day Father died but everyone was fearful of him since the last strangers proved to be murderers. It was a mystery. She turned back to the letter.

'As I believe I mentioned to you, my mother was ill and I was able to take her some wild flowers from his grave. She has since recovered although she is very frail. It was in Nether Horden that I learnt of you and realised I had had the great privilege of conversing with you that morning, unaware of your family connection.'

Mary didn't say he spoke to anyone!

'May I reassure you that though I have always been certain of my brother's innocence I do not hold it against your father that he felt he had to convict him. My brother was simple and unable to give a clear account of himself. I am also aware that there was great anger and fear among the people at the time and that they took upon themselves to carry out the

sentence against your father's wishes. At the time I was given an account of the circumstances of Daniel's death by a witness who urged me to flee lest I also be suspected. The one piece of evidence that might have saved Daniel remains mysterious to this day. That was the existence of a fat boy ...'

Oh no!

'... whom Daniel himself told me he saw, who may have been the culprit in the rick-burning for which he was charged. I will never uncover that puzzle and I know you are unlikely to have any knowledge of the incident at all. I am not disclosing the name of the person in the village who helped me in my recent visit, because he might not want to be identified. As far as I am concerned the affair is past history. I rejoice that my visit has brought comfort to my mother and healed the rift that formerly lay between her and me. I regret that I told you she had not loved me as a child. You also spoke of your own unloved childhood. That still saddens me greatly but I believe you had found a new closeness with your father just before his death. That he should have been taken away so soon grieves me more than I can say. Let me repeat my condolences and also my gratitude for your kindness to me that morning when you helped me so readily in the recovery of my horse and guided me to the inn for his stabling. The memory of our time together is very precious to me and I beg to remain a little more than a passing friend and also your humble servant,

NAT

Nathaniel Wilson.'

Bel let the letter lie in her lap and clasped her head in her hands. The mystery of the fat boy! That will haunt me to my grave. And that he of all people should want the answer – the only man I have ever met that I believe I could have liked. My cloud will hang for ever between us. I can't answer his letter, because I could never tell him my guilt, just as I can never tell Ursula. How could I tell a devout young man that I was his brother's murderer, that I have a devil in me and am for ever damned?

She had a faint recollection of saying wild things at the house of Alderman Johnson, implying that it was unsafe to be near her for death stalked her everywhere. Certainly guilt clung about the deaths of her father and brother, even of Patrick Dawson for if he had not been drawn to her he would not have come. It was at least a blessing that Nat's mother had recovered. No evil curse had been passed to her, but she still felt that if she had not spent time with Nat her father might have lived.

She sat long, rereading the letter and wondering about the sender. He was nothing to do with Cranmore House so his motives for writing were just what he had expressed – true sympathy and a genuine interest in herself. His honesty shone like a light. Can I not reply? But honesty must be met with honesty.

Ursula called her to dinner. They ate together in the kitchen now and Bel had usually no hesitation in showing Ursula every letter that had come. But this one was different. She hid it away in her closet and Ursula was too sensitive to ask about it. There had been nothing yet from France. How could she tell if hers reporting her father's death had even reached them? She had described the funeral which the village had not allowed to pass quietly. The procession to the churchyard contained every inhabitant, only excepting Nurse, though this Bel did not write to her mother.

Nurse had come to her the night before the funeral in a passion of tears and begged her to take a handful of silver she brought in her apron.

"Oh, Bella, forgive me," she had said. "I took their money – those murderers. I haven't spent a penny. It's blood money."

"And what am I to do with it?" Bel cried, horrified at the confession.

"Give it in at The Crossed Swords for the tenants after the funeral."

There would be some irony in them getting drunk on Puritan money but Bel couldn't bring herself to take it. Nevertheless there was money there for the wake and she supposed Nurse must have handed it in herself as coming from the Hall. She had since taken to her bed with a cold and not been seen about. I have to forgive her, Bel thought. She didn't know their ill-intents and the temptation was too much for a poor old woman.

Life fell back into the pattern she had established since the funeral but she thought every day about Nat's letter and took it out often to read again, studying his handwriting which was very fine and flowing, pondering on his choice of words, wondering what he was doing, what his home, his father and his mother were like and how much he still grieved for his brother and in his heart loathed the name of Horden.

In the mornings after the basic duties which Mary and Tom helped with, the fires, the chopping wood, the hens, Bel and Ursula would turn out the next chest or closet on their list and select items which would not be useful to them and could be sold and they added them to the collection behind the screen. Bel would write to the provision merchants whose bills had not been paid and invite them to come and take goods in payment.

"We are going back to a barter system because we have no money," she said openly. "Our tenants cannot pay their rents because their farms have been raided by the army, but I am determined to free Horden of debt."

In May she received a letter from the Parliamentary Commission for Sequestrations, addressed to her father, and telling him that officers would come to seize the assets and arrange for all income to be paid to Parliament funds for the army. A clause said that a fifth might be permitted to be retained for his wife and children. It was the standard letter sent to all on the lists and she was about to throw it on the fire when she remembered Alderman Johnson and decided to walk to Newcastle and show it to him. He had been keen for her to leave and her father's body to be removed as soon as possible but she thought he might be willing to help if it was his influence that was sought rather than his domestic convenience hazarded.

She took Tom as escort. Tom with no horses to care for had all the jobs about the Hall that a man might be expected to do.

"What we need," Bel told the Alderman, "is a troop of soldiers to guard us night and day from Parliamentary forces."

He was a florid gentleman and he turned a brighter shade of red at her words. "We are not even sure of the loyalty of our Trained Bands and with a siege of the town constantly threatened we have no one to spare for homes beyond the walls."

Bel flashed back, "I said what we *need*. I never thought you could produce it."

"What then, my young lady? I am a busy man."

"My father believed in justice and the power of the law. This paper from Parliament is unjust. I have never been a Papist, nor was my father. We never willingly harboured a Catholic Priest except when my mother lived at home. Why should our land be sequestered as they call it? And now that my father is dead and *my* name is not on the list and the Hall is my only home, how can Parliament have the power to take it from me?"

Alderman Johnson scratched his head. "Many things are being done all over the country that are unjust because Parliament needs money for its forces. But as to their power, until they have forces enough in the north, I do not believe they could send men to seize the Hall. I advise you to sit quietly and do nothing. Surely your mother will return from France now you are alone."

"I have had no reply yet to my letters. But she and my sister are staunchly Catholic and fear imprisonment or worse if they come to England."

"And could you not go to join them?"

"Abandon our property? No. I will fight this, whoever wins this mad war."

"You are a young lady of great spirit. Reply to them that your father is dead and hence the sequestration order must lapse. I wager if the King wins the next battle all laws made without his signature will be null and void. Now, my wife will insist on your taking dinner with us before you return."

Bel did write the letter and heard no more from the Committee of Sequestration. In June the Earl of Newcastle took most of Yorkshire for the King and Bel, knowing Darrowswick lay near Easingwold, wondered how Nat's family were faring. The news also reported that the Queen with three thousand infantry, thirty companies of horse and six cannon was heading from York to join the King at Oxford. Perhaps the war *was* turning against Parliament. Bel was thankful that Nat was at Cambridge. She knew because he had written to her again from there, delicately suggesting that his first letter or her reply might have gone astray. Knowing how she would have loved to be a student, he trusted it would not make her too envious if he described College life which went on despite the war. He was to be allowed to sit for the Bachelor examination and his tutor wanted him to stay and study for a Masters' Degree, but he felt he should be earning his living soon to help his parents. How was she faring since the sad loss of her father?

Bel ached to write back. He would find her silence so churlish and at last she asked the vicar to pen a brief note saying Arabella Horden thanked him for his letters but was unable to reply. She didn't divulge to the vicar who her correspondent was.

At last she heard from her mother who said she was heart-broken at the news but she knew how brave and resourceful dear Bel was and with Nurse and all the servants she would not lack company. Bel smiled at this. Henrietta was again with child, so of course there was no possibility of them travelling and England was still in turmoil. Could Bel not come to them? On the way she could stay with the London Hordens who, although they had behaved badly over the betrothal, would not refuse her hospitality. Once in France they could find her a French husband and the revenues from Horden could be sent there.

Bel showed Ursula this letter.

"Do you want to go to them?" she asked. "They are your family."

"You are my family," was all Bel said to that.

And so the summer rolled away and crops were harvested. Somehow the population survived and the tenants paid some of the arrears of rent.

Nat wrote again to Bel, delighted that his letters pleased her and to say that he had taken his degree and returned to Darrowswick to seek preferment to a parish not too far away, but that this was doubtful since the Scottish Covenant was proposed for England too. In the autumn he wrote that he was glad he had left Cambridge, because many of the Fellows had resigned or been dismissed because they would not sign the Covenant. He trusted that the sad disputes over matters of religion would not drive her further from a faith in God.

Bel was overjoyed that he persisted in so one-sided a correspondence, but each letter renewed her conviction that she must remain cut off from him.

His love for his brother shines out when he writes of his childhood and yet I can tell he is holding back with delicacy because he knows the guilt of my family. He is a good man. I could love him but if I write he will fall from his horse, or his frail mother or the noble father he speaks of with such love will die. If I can get through another year without my curse touching anyone around me, I will feel easier. Ursula's goodness keeps her safe and me with her. And now that I no longer hate Henrietta, her new baby girl may live and flourish. I have found a yearning love for my father but too late. And I am learning to love Nat Wilson, which can never be. My own cloud will stay with me, but if I am at last capable of love and if our tiny household remains untouched by this evil war, then that is as much as I can hope for day by day.

CHAPTER 19

January 1644

Bᴇʟ woke late and felt there was something different about the morning. She ran to her window and looked out. Although the sun was not yet up it was light enough to see that the sky was clear. Why had Ursula not wakened her to tell her the snow had stopped? Day after day there had been heavy falls from unremitting cloud. The ugly old baronet was still blessedly shrouded and the early morning light bounced off the unbroken white of the land, but the bitter chill of the air was gone.

Bel ran down and found only a small fire in the kitchen hearth to conserve fuel and Ursula already pounding the washing.

"You should have woken me."

"Young bones need sleep," Ursula replied.

"But the snow's stopped and it feels warmer."

"And we've just had Tom in saying a thaw will bring the Scots army down. They've been held up in Berwick by the snow."

"Oh, Tom is a merchant of gloom. But I know why the Scots are coming. They want us to abolish Bishops and become Presbyterians. The last war it was because *we* wanted to impose Bishops on *them*. Is the world mad? Ursula, you care about your religion but you have never tried to turn me Catholic and you have meekly attended our services because the law says you must."

Ursula smiled up at her. "That proves *I'm* not mad even if I look it"

"It proves you are a saint."

Ursula dabbed Bel's nose with some soap suds.

Perhaps it was because they had grown used to the last Scots occupation that they treated the news lightly, but three days later when the thaw was well underway news reached the village that the Scots army was marching through Northumberland, heading for Newcastle.

There were frantic moves to hide valuables, but what could one do with the stores of grain and the sheep and cows?

"*We* have so little left to take," Bel said, looking into the larder. "Our stocks went down during the long snow. I suppose the soldiers will kill and eat the last of our hens. I am afraid I am going to be very angry with them. If we hadn't sold Robert's good French pistol he was so fond of, I might have shot a few of them."

"No, no, my Bel, you are not a killer."

Ah, but I am, Bel moaned inwardly.

"Come," Ursula urged her, "we will take the flour sack to the attic and hide it under my bed and that sack of carrots and turnips."

They were half way across the great hall lugging these to the foot of the stairs when Mary came running in, red-faced, from the stables. "They are here. At the back door. One of them asked me where our horses were. When I said we had none he seemed pleased there would be stabling for theirs. The way he spoke, I think they mean to stay."

She had hardly got the words out when an officer walked boldly in through the kitchen passage and seeing the sacks said courteously, "Och, that is heavy work for women. Pray leave them where they are. Where are your menfolk? We have seen an ancient groom outside. Where are the rest?"

Bel marched up and stuck out her chin at him. "There are no rest and who are you that you walk into people's houses without their leave?"

"Ay, well, I am sorry, lassie." He was looking about him at the size of the hall and gazing up the stairs as if estimating what rooms there were up there. "But this place is now requisitioned by the army. It will make excellent officers' billets so close to Newcastle. Collect what you need and make your way to whatever friends and family you have there. I will give you a safe-conduct pass, though you will not find many of our men on the roads there yet. We are an advance party. Of course I should warn you that if the town does not yield it may well be bombarded. It will be given fair terms if it surrenders without delay and you may tell them that when you get there." He finished with a light laugh.

Bel clenched her jaw. They could take the Hall – just like that! Of course she had heard of other places seized by Parliament's forces but this sudden onslaught from the north; how complacent she had been that they would escape!

She glared up at the smiling officer. "How dare you presume to take our home from us? I know not where *you* live but would you like an English army to walk in and throw out your wife and children?"

"English armies have been doing worse than that to Scotland throughout the centuries. This is war, young madam. I will give you half an hour to leave while I give my orders." He strode out again and Bel could see through the open doors that the stable yard was full of soldiers.

She stared open-mouthed at Ursula and Mary. "What are we to do?"

"I'd like to run home." Mary was almost panting to be off. "They may be in the village turning my mother out of our cottage."

"Of course, go, Mary. I suppose refugees will be pouring into Newcastle."

Tom came in with a sack over his shoulder. "Mistress Bella, they're putting men in my quarters already. I've brought what I could."

"Oh Tom, Mary is going to the village. You must go with her to take care of your sister."

"Nay I cannot leave you. My sister has her man and though he's older than I am, he's not helpless. They'll surely not harm two old crocks like them. Where are you heading?"

"Newcastle I suppose, if we must." Bel's anger was still at boiling point but Ursula had already run up the stairs and was soon down again with a bag of bedding wrapped around her few possessions.

"Run up, Bel," she said. "I'll provision us before the soldiers get to the larder." And off she ran to the kitchen.

Bel was ashamed. Ursula has done this before, she reminded herself, pushed from pillar to post all her life. It truly is going to happen. Half an hour, he said!

She picked up her skirts and dashing to her room, threw off her slippers and slid her feet into a pair of leather-covered clogs suitable for the slushy snow. Then she ripped the covers off her bed, laid them out and threw into them shoes, some changes of clothes, shawls, a few books, writing materials, hair-brush and precious soap. Then she fastened the ends together and found the whole thing was almost too cumbersome to carry. Perhaps they would find carts going into the town. At least the table behind the screen in the great hall was empty. They had sold all they had stored there.

But now she must see what money there was in the house. She picked some ribbons from among her remaining clothes and extracted a key from under her pillow. Bouncing her giant bag down the stairs she ran into her father's office and unlocked the drawer in his desk. She took his pocket book which contained Clifford's letter and other important papers and his leather pouch of money. This had a brass ring for a belt and she tied some of the ribbons together and slotted them through it. There was no time to undress and insert it beneath her corset. She could hear men already trampling about the hall. She lifted her skirts and sat down on the upright chair and pushed the ribbon and pouch up her front, wedged the pouch over her left hip and wiggled one ribbon end round her back so she could tie the ends securely at her waist. Pulling down her skirts she looked aghast at the shelves of ledgers containing the estate's yearly records. How could she leave them but how could she carry them?

She opened the door and looked into the hall. Knapsacks were already standing about the walls with groups of officers keeping an eye on them. Their captain, as she presumed he was, came up to her.

"You are ready to go? Here is your pass. We are about to allocate quarters."

"And you, I suppose, will operate from here." She didn't try to keep the fury out of her voice. "Look at this room. There are centuries of history here. Do you propose to destroy it? My family have lived here for countless generations. Everything here is precious to me ..."

"My dear young lady," he broke in, "save your breath. The war will not last for ever. Your surviving men-folk will return and carry on their good work."

"There are no men left," she shouted at him. "This place is mine. I will come back and if you have touched anything here I will have your head." She stamped her foot and marched past him.

"By the Lord, Ma'am, I wish you were in my army," he chuckled.

Finding Tom and Ursula at the open great doors she dragged her bundle across the wooden floor and joined them.

"Nay, that's too big," Tom said.

The Captain came up and shouted to two infantrymen outside, "Escort these people. When you see enemy patrols ahead hand them over and return with all speed."

And so two brawny Scots shouldered the women's bundles and plunged out into deep melting snow. The little party followed, feet soon soaked despite their clogs. Bel turned at the iron gates and looked back. The snow had slid off the old baronet as he flourished his sword towards the Hall in defiance of the invaders now swarming about it. When would she see it again? She was walking into a blank future.

Ursula turned her comical grin towards her. "Wayfarers again," she said, "but the Lord is with us."

"Never mind the Lord," said Bel, struggling to smile back. "I've got you."

They soon joined the track from the village and followed it to the high road into Newcastle. Here there were people on foot and in carts heading for the town.

Where are we all to go, Bel wondered. If the town is to be under siege there will be too many mouths to feed. I don't want to be in an overcrowded place enclosed with walls and an army surrounding it. They will take command of the river and close the bridge. What will I do there? I mustn't be beholden to the Johnsons again.

"Ursula," she said, "we will be suffocated in Newcastle. Let us try to get right through and head south. If the Scots are held up besieging Newcastle, they will not be in Durham County. I'd rather take my chance in the open country."

"Whatever you say, my pretty."

There was the sound of hooves and wheels behind them and a familiar cart drew up alongside. Sam Turner in his civilian clothes was driving and in the cart among a pile of possessions were Mary and her mother.

"Get up and be quick," he shouted, reaching down to Bel. "What are you doing with an enemy escort?"

"They have kindly carried our bundles."

Bel scrambled up, then Ursula and Tom.

The Scotsmen threw the bundles in after them, saluted and turned and ran. They were in no danger. If Sam had a pistol under his doublet it was not visible.

He clicked up his horse at once and drove on.

"I hoped we'd overtake you," Mary said. "Sam wouldn't hear of mother and me staying in the village. We have a cousin in town we can stay with and Sam got leave to fetch us if he didn't wear his uniform. He's part of the garrison there now."

"I have no one in Newcastle," Bel said. "I don't want to stay there." She wriggled among the luggage to Sam's side. "Will we be able to cross the bridge and get out of the town?"

"I couldn't take you that far. I must sell the horse and cart in town. My father said if I brought it back the Scots would seize it. He'd rather have the money for it."

Bel made a lightning decision. "*I* will buy it. Tom can drive and we'll travel in comfort if they'll let us through."

"Why should they not? Fewer mouths to feed in the town. What will you give me?"

Bel beckoned to Ursula who came crawling towards her. "Urs, you must creep up my skirts and untie the ribbon and give me my pouch."

Ursula never hesitated. They were not overlooked by other travellers as the baggage was all round them and they were in a valley between. Bel didn't mind Mary and her mother seeing what they were doing. In fact she grinned back at them as Ursula wriggled inside and her skirt billowed up and down. Out came Ursula with the pouch and Bel counted four gold sovereigns.

"Will that do?"

"It's more than I'd get in the town, I reckon."

"Take it. And Mary," she turned round and held out to her a few silver pieces. "You haven't had your wages and that should cover three weeks or more."

What was in the pouch was all the money she had in the world and she had no idea how long it would last if they had to put up at inns or find an empty cottage to rent. The future was an unwritten page, but it pleased her to be generous. Mary could find work in the town or she might even decide to marry Sam now and share his soldier's pay. Either way she would be glad of a little extra. Bel saw Mary's mother hiding the silver away and nodding her thanks at her.

And then they were at the gate in the town wall and had questions to answer about the friends or families they hoped to stay with.

"We are going on," Bel said. And then to her astonishment she found herself adding, "I have friends in Yorkshire who will accommodate us."

They were waved through and Ursula looked at her in surprise and Tom said, "That's a mighty long way away."

Sam Turner said, "Oh, ay, you were sent to school in Yorkshire, were you not? Well, I wish you good fortune and I shall hand the reins to you, Tom, when I have delivered Mary and her mother to their cousin."

This was accomplished in a narrow back street just wide enough for the horse and cart. When all their possessions were unloaded, Bel placed the remaining bundles so that she and Ursula could rest their backs against them and be quite comfortable.

Sam was to walk back to his quarters within the town. Bel watched as he kissed Mary goodbye at the cousin's door. I fancied him once, she thought. He's a decent ordinary, shallow sort of lad but I know one that has a Cambridge degree. Everything that was racing through her mind now had taken her completely by surprise. She needed to close her eyes and slow her thoughts and see where they were leading her. This she would do as soon as they were heading south out of Newcastle.

First, Sam directed Tom how to get back to the road that would lead him to the bridge. He stroked the horse's mane. "He's called Juniper, God knows why, and he's not as old as you, Tom, but he's not young, so don't overwork him." Then he waved them off and disappeared in the other direction.

Tom was mumbling to himself that he'd never thought to go so far from home and Bel suspected he was hoping to be forbidden to leave the town, but when they reached the bridge they were questioned briefly and then hurried across as there were horsemen approaching from the other side to get into the town before the Scots came. Foot soldiers and townspeople were everywhere working on reinforcing the walls with earthworks and Bel was delighted to leave the place behind. Maybe it would hold out. Maybe it would be relieved by Royalist forces from the south, but either way she wanted to be moving. As soon as they were clear of Gateshead she leant back on her bedding bundle and closed her eyes.

"I am going to take a nap, Ursula."

It was evil to lie to Ursula but absolutely necessary because the mad, galloping idea in her mind was that they would go to Darrowswick and she had to understand how she had dared to think of such a thing.

What struck me, she told herself, was that everyone had someone to go to who loves them and I hadn't. But I have. Nathaniel Wilson loves me. I know he does. I know he would be glad to see me. And I to see him. Only I can't because I can never see him unless I tell him the truth. Do I tell him? Tell him that I am the fat boy who burned the rick for which his Daniel died. Has the moment come? Is that the place to which I am being driven?

Then, she thought, *this* calamity is not of my doing. Many evil things have happened where I am the source but this is not one of them. Unless it's a punishment. But who is punishing me if there is no God? Is it something within me? My cloud? Maybe I can never be free of it but perhaps this calamity has come to make me try. And then there is the overriding thought that Nat cannot write to me if he knows not where I am. So *I* must go to *him*. From our first stopping place I will write to him that I am coming. She was tense now with excitement.

"Look here, young mistress," cried Tom.

Her eyes flew open and she realised their cart was coming to a halt on the brow of a hill because ahead was not a small troop of soldiers but a whole army moving north, horsemen, gun-carriages, ammunition wagons, and lines of infantry winding through the valley below.

Tom turned round to say, "That's his carriage. I see the coat of arms. And that must be his lordship himself on his horse. Eh, that I should live to see this!"

"Who?" said Bel, shading her eyes from the low sun.

"Why, the Marquis of Newcastle. He's taking his forces to relieve the town. Will I not turn back when they've passed and follow them?"

"No, we are going on. If he is going north there cannot be any fighting with Parliament troops to keep him here. We are heading for Yorkshire."

Tom shook his head from side to side. Taking orders from a chit of a lass, he seemed to be thinking, was an unwise proceeding.

"You've been planning, Bel," Ursula said, "not sleeping. What are we going to do in Yorkshire? Were you thinking any of your old teachers would take us in? The Mistress went home to Lincolnshire, Madame Bouchon went back to France ..."

Bel shook her head. "No, but I do wonder what became of Cranmore House? It might be a roof to shelter us if we have nowhere to sleep. It was near Easingwold."

Ursula nodded. "That was where we walked to the Parish Church, about three miles. It took the girls all but an hour. I couldn't stay to see what happened to the old nunnery. I had to get to my Bel, but I know they left the chapel ablaze, said it must be purified by fire. I expect the dormitories are billets for the Parliament men now."

"We have to eat, Urs. If we found an abandoned house I could take pupils. Would anyone still want their children taught or have the means to pay for it?"

"Eh, Bel, I think you dream. There will still be rich folk but they would want an elegant school all fitted out and many teachers."

"You could teach cookery and needlework."

Ursula laughed then, her cackle drawing stares from the passing infantry. "No fine folk would let me near their children. Besides I do plain stitching not lacework and embroidery. No, my Bel, I will get the lowest tasks and you may find a school that would take you in to teach the youngest ones, but we don't have to go a great long way to Yorkshire to do it."

"That's where we are going." Having made up her mind Bel wanted to be there – now. The intervening miles at the slow pace of Tom's driving or Juniper's walking made her want to jump down and run. I am going to answer to Nat Wilson, to him and no one else. Oh to have him sitting beside me now so I could pour out the whole tale to him. "Will Juniper go no faster, Tom?" she called out.

They were three nights on the way, the last spent in a stable loft with Juniper snuffling below. Many inns were full with homeless people. There were tales of houses seized or burnt to the ground, farms where not a beast was left as unpaid soldiers foraged for the next meal. Bel was almost ashamed that they were still alive and that her home might be there for her to return to one day.

On the third morning they all rose with straw in their hair and stuck about their clothes. Tom moaned that his old bones ached and he never wanted to wake up again.

"I will drive," Bel said. "You must rest." She gave the innkeeper a brooch. "It is worth more than we owe you for our food and stabling for the horse but I have no money to spare."

"No one will buy this trinket off me."

"They will after the war."

"Ay, and when will that be? Folks expect food and drink today."

Ursula turned back her bonnet and gave him a quizzical look.

"Aw, get ye out o' here wi yon hag," he shouted, grabbing the brooch.

Once more they were on the way. This time Bel reckoned they were not more than ten miles from Easingwold. The discomforts of the journey, the horrid nights in unchanged clothes, the anxiety when they were stopped and questioned, had all served to lower her initial excitement at her great decision, but now it was back. It worried her that she had not after all been able to write and say they were coming. Her writing materials were all bound up in her bundle and there had been no space at night to open it up. The second night she and Ursula shared a bed with two orphaned children and she was afraid their nimble fingers would delve into her treasures before she could stop them. A carrier had called briefly for a pint of ale but would not wait for her to unpack and write a note. Now it was not worth writing as they could be there soon.

There! She tried to picture Darrowswick. Nat had written that it straggled along a lane, no duck-pond or village green, the lane ending in a short climb to the church. The parsonage was just over the crest, down to the right of the church but with country views from all the upper windows. Would he be there? How could she possibly explain herself to his parents?

She didn't regret her impetuous decision but its madness grew with every step of the reluctant Juniper.

They reached Easingwold at dinner time and Bel said they must stop and refresh themselves and if possible change their clothes.

"We are refugees from the Scots," she explained at the small inn.

The innkeeper's wife, hearing Bel speak in an educated voice, though looking and smelling like a tramp, said she could put a room at her disposal for a few hours. Ursula's cap was limp and grubby but she kept her face hidden and the woman accepted her as Bel's lady's maid with hardly a glance.Tom was allowed to go to the inn kitchen for a bite when Juniper had been fed and watered. So when Bel was alone with Ursula in a small, fairly clean back room with their bundles from the cart carried in by a serving-man and a bowl of water brought in she heaved a sigh of relief.

"Oh Urs, quick now, let us get as clean and respectable as we can."

"But, my Bel, who are we to impress? We passed the turning that would have taken us to Cranmore House. I thought you wanted to take a look at it."

"The people we are going to visit may know who has it now."

"Come now, what people are these?"

"Oh Urs, I know I have been hasty and I can't think where this will lead but I had to come here. They are not expecting us. They may not be at home, but it is a parsonage two miles away. Someone, I hope, is there who knows of my existence." As she spoke she was undoing her bundle and shaking out a clean gown and petticoat, corset, chemise and stockings.

"A someone who has been writing you letters?"

Bel looked up to see Ursula's eyes very bright and the fan of smiling lines at the corners deeply etched. She could only gaze back at them and nod her head.

"Then I think, my pretty one, that if it is only two miles on a quiet country lane, you might wish to go alone. I can stay and wash our clothes if the wife makes no objection. If she does, I will offer to wash anything in the inn she wants doing."

"Oh, Urs, you might get stained sheets and ..."

Ursula held up her hand. "Do you wish to go alone?"

Bel paused in her undressing. She had met Nat alone once. If she did manage to speak of her great sin, perhaps she would be able to tell Ursula too, but the speaking with Nat Wilson must be face to face alone first. The thought of a two mile solitary walk was suddenly bliss after the cramped days and suffocating nights. She could try somehow to control her wild emotions, prepare herself for a fearful ordeal.

"Yes, Ursula. I'll go alone. You and Tom stay here."

"Tell me the name of the place, so we may seek you if you don't return."

"Darrowswick."

Ursula tried to repeat it but it was more than she could manage coherently. Bel wrote it down.

"I will be praying, my Bel, till I see you again."

Bel nodded. She was now so intent on her mission that she could not speak. She brushed the dust of the road from her hair, washed and dressed and silently handed her pouch to Ursula. Five minutes later she was walking out of Easingwold market square on the road which the innkeeper's wife had pointed out to her.

CHAPTER 20

THE day was cold and there were the remains of the great snow on the fields for most of England had suffered from it. Bel was wearing her clogs and picking her way round puddles so she kept her clean stockings dry. Concentrating on this and the pleasure of motion held at bay her dread of the moment of arrival. She noted the colour of the dead grass emerging from the snow by the side of the lane. She saw an old nest in the hedgerow. She saw that the sky was a pure winter blue and that the shadow of a tree on the snow was another blue, so different. And then she saw some low cottages up ahead and the lane straggling between them and winding up a hill to a squat church with a tower and just to the right behind it she could see the chimney pots of a house. It was all real.

She stood still and stared. What am I doing? Why have I come here? How can I possibly do this thing? But it had to be. There was no going back. If it wrecks my life what is my life? There has to be a climax or a turning point or a great earthquake. I set myself to face it and the moment has come.

She broke into a run, almost scampering through the village. A man mending a field gate, shouted after her, "There's no one after thee." She didn't even look at him.

The start of the hill slowed her and she thought, I mustn't come panting and dishevelled. Now it was not dread she felt but a bursting longing to look on that young man again, just to see his eyes light up as they had when he found her waiting for him in the church. I can savour that but not for long. I have to tell him quickly, for I'll be a living lie until it's told.

She stopped and looked at the church. The door was shut but the two steps to it had been swept and also the path she now saw diverging to the right down to the house. Her heart was thumping as she started down it and then she saw that sitting in the front window was a woman with flowing grey hair streaked with red and an eagle face, all points, devouring her with fearsome eyes. It must be his mother.

She smiled at the face but there was no change in expression. The house had bow windows so the eyes followed her as she approached and when she stood at the front door. Not knowing whether the woman could move or whether the servant Jenny was in the house Bel lifted the knocker. Before she could let it fall the woman got up with a brusque gesture and presently the door was opened.

She was tall and as angular in body as she was in face. "What do you want? Who are you?" The voice was harsh.

"I have come to see Nathaniel Wilson." Bel said it with little hope now. Nat was not here, that seemed plain enough.

"He knows no young women," his mother snapped and seemed about to shut the door.

"He will know *me*."

"Why? What's your name?"

"Bel Horden."

"Horden!" The eyes became flames. "Horden!" A skinny arm shot out and pulled Bel inside. "Are they not all dead, the Hordens?"

"Not this one." She was being hustled into the room where the woman had been sitting. It was a shabby but comfortable parlour.

She was dragged towards the lowest window pane at the far right corner. "He thinks I have forgiven them but see. I cursed them and they are dead."

Bel read, roughly scratched, "Death to the Hordens." She felt a strange trembling deep inside at seeing the name here so far from home. Is this woman a witch? Did *she* kill Robert and Father? Had I nothing to do with their deaths? Oh why have I come and where is Nat?

"Where is Nat?" she said aloud.

"Nat? You call him Nat? And you say you are a Horden. Why have you come here? Did you know Robert Horden and Sir John?"

"My brother and father."

"Ah! You have come for vengeance because I cursed them."

"No, oh, no." Bel pulled her arm from her grasp. "Pray, Mistress Wilson, believe me, it is just the opposite." She had no idea if it was possible to get through to this woman. Nat had said his mother was better in her mind than she had been but the visit of a stranger who claimed knowledge of her son and then revealed she was part of a hated family seemed to have deranged her again. "I came to make confession. I was the most to blame for Daniel's death." There! She had blurted it out. It was to have been revealed secretly to Nat alone, but the words were spoken.

"You? How is that possible?"

"Look, may we not sit down quietly and talk of this. I hoped to tell Nat ..." For the first time she saw a fierce-looking meat knife lying on a small table next to the chair the old lady had been sitting in. Her eyes too followed Bel's.

"Ah yes, when the men are out and I am alone I keep a weapon by me. These days there are bands of robbers roaming the country. But maybe I was meant to have it handy." She picked it up. "The Lord knew vengeance was stalking me in the guise of a young woman."

"No, truly." Hope and joy were restored. Nat was only out, presumably with his father. I can keep her talking perhaps till they come back. She has forgotten already that I said I came to confess. I don't want to tell the tale now and have her tell Nat but if I can just make her understand ... Bel gestured to the chair and moved towards the sofa herself. "We can talk. I meant no harm in coming here."

The woman leapt towards her brandishing the knife. "No Horden sits down in my house. You named my Daniel. What did you say of his death?"

Bel felt a tremor of real physical fear. *How young I was and brazen when I was faced with an axe! This woman is mad and could use the knife.* A torrent of thoughts rushed through her mind. *Is she an instrument of God's justice? Have I not always wanted to be punished? I should let her do it but I want to see Nat first. Oh. how I long to see him!*

"I am so sorry," she began, spreading out her arms to show she would offer no resistance. "I am the Horden who is the most guilty of Daniel's death."

The woman lifted the knife and Bel dropped to her knees. As she did so she saw under the raised arm two figures descending the path outside. *Oh joy, it is Nat and his father.* The mother sensed what she had seen. She swung round, the knife still waving aloft. The men burst into a run and were through the still open front door and into the room before either woman moved.

"Bel!" shouted Nat. "Mother! What are you doing?"

She was still holding the knife. "She says she killed Daniel."

"No, no, no. Give me that." The father grabbed her arms from behind and the knife fell to the floor.

Bel, crouched at their feet, broke into sobs. "It's true. I could have saved him. I fired the stack. I was the fat boy. Oh Nat, let her kill me and then it's done with."

They lifted her up. She was shaking. It was all wrong. The quiet talk to him alone, the heartfelt sorrow, the purging of guilt was now impossible. As always she had spoilt everything by her impetuosity. Nat had kicked the knife under the sofa and was holding her. His father was soothing his wife and sitting her back in her chair, speaking calm words. But Bel was in Nat's arms and nothing had ever been more wonderful.

He drew her to the sofa and sat down with her. "Thank God we were in time. Oh, if she had killed you ...! But how did you come here?" He was gazing with those wondering light blue eyes, astonishment and bewilderment there but love too.

"I came because I had to tell you. I couldn't go on receiving your letters. It was hypocrisy. I couldn't bear you not to know, even though you would hate me. Those wonderful letters would stop."

"But what are you trying to tell me? You fired the stack?"

"Not deliberately, but it was my doing. I took a stick from the glowing ashes of the bonfire. But I was frightened and threw it away. It must have caught some straw."

"But the fat boy?"

"I was wearing breeches over my dress. He saw me slide down the tree. Your Daniel. He was right about everything. He was innocent. When I heard they had hanged him for it –"

She began to choke with sobs again, the picture of the body before her eyes.

"You were a child."

Now the Reverend Wilson came over to them.

"Nat, there is much here that we would all like to know, but first let us be a little formal. I wish to be introduced to the young lady and bid her welcome."

Bel saw an older version of Nat, rounder of face, broader of nose, with unruly grey hair round a bald patch and the same benign eyes, open and full of love. He held out his hand to her and she rose at once and clasped his.

"I am truly distressed that I upset your wife so," she said.

"And I likewise that she greeted you as she did. I do not believe she would have harmed you but it was a shock for her to hear your name. What may we call you?"

"Oh Bel, just B-E-L."

"You have not travelled alone? How did you come?"

"I walked from Easingwold where I have left a horse and cart, a dear friend and an old groom who has been with our family ever since I can remember."

"Did you invite Bel in one of your letters, Nat?"

"Letters!" cried the mother, rearing up. "You have been writing to a Horden?"

Bel said quickly, "I came quite uninvited. Something within me urged me to come and confess my guilt. I do not hope to be forgiven, but you all have a right to know the truth."

"I think we will all go into the kitchen and have some refreshment. Our Jenny is visiting her sister who is ill, but we have bread, cheese, apples, a jug of ale. And perhaps our young visitor can unburden herself of what she wishes us to know."

It wasn't how she had hoped to tell the tale. She was too conscious of the mother's face across the table, the eyes sometimes sharp and focussed, sometimes frowning in bewilderment and interrupting frequently to ask questions. "What did Daniel do next? What did he say to that?" And Nat and his father had to explain that Bel had been locked in her room and knew nothing of the details of the trial.

Bel stopped short of describing how she had gone to look at the gallows and found the body still hanging. She could not inflict that on them even if she had felt able to speak of the sight that had tormented her ever since. But she did tell them of her father and Robert and of the manner and timing of their deaths.

When she was silent, Nat's mother clenched her fists in the air and shook them at her. "Why did you say you killed Daniel? Why did you make me angry? Why bring it back? If I have understood it all, you never had a chance to own up to being the fat boy. You were a child playing games, a hayrick caught fire and my Daniel was blamed. I know these mobs. They act on rumour. You say your father never recovered from it because he loved justice. Your brother *was* guilty of inciting the mob and you have told us how you yourself were instrumental in his death. It is as I thought. The Hordens have paid the price. And even you, the innocent child, have suffered for it. Joseph, we must be satisfied."

Bel, looking up in wonder at the words 'innocent child', could read the expression passing over the parson's face. *His* bitterness had been over long ago but it was not the moment to dispute that point with his wife. He just took hold of her hand and lifted it to his lips.

"Anne, my love, I *am* satisfied."

Bel sat, drained and exhausted. She had eaten little but she picked up the pewter mug of ale and took a refreshing drink. She set it down and looked from one face to the other. Nat was sharing the bench with her so she had to turn and meet his eyes. They were beaming love and admiration at her but she said anyway, "I have disrupted your day. I must go. I have done what I came for."

She rose. He rose too, pushing back the bench, and took her arm to steady her.

"We are not going to let Bel go, Mother, are we? Father? She has had a long journey."

"A Horden sleep under our roof?" His mother had risen too.

"No, I will not," Bel said. "I must go back to the inn or they will be anxious."

"Then I will walk with you," Nat said at once.

That would be heaven. She couldn't refuse that. She met his eyes again. "Oh yes, please."

"We'll see you again," the parson said. "You are staying a while?"

"She's done what she came for," the mother said. "I'm glad she did but there's an end of the matter. She walked here alone. She can walk away alone. It's finished."

Bel inclined her head at her. So you say, she was thinking.

His father said, "Will you not stay and rest a little?"

"I need to get back or they will come and look for me. I love walking."

At the door, out of his wife's hearing, he said, "We will see you again, my dear, I am sure of that." He clasped both her hands. "May God bless you for your courage in coming to us. I thank you with all my heart. Nay, don't cry." He kissed her on both cheeks and then hugged her close. When they separated he too had tears running down his cheeks. He waved a hand and hurried back into the house.

Nat tucked her arm through his and walked her briskly up the path, past the church and down the other side of the hill. As soon as they were out of sight he drew her towards him. "My father and I are two of a kind. I want to weep too but it is with utter joy. You can have no idea how I have longed to see you again. Writing to you was the only way I could keep that longing satisfied. Nay, it wasn't satisfied at all but endlessly frustrated. Why could you not reply, I wondered, but I began to understand when you were speaking just now. This thing has hung about you like a cloud ..."

"My cloud! Oh, indeed, my cloud." She threw back her head and laughed a joyous laugh. It was so spontaneous, that he began to laugh too.

"How I remember your laugh when we were together in Newcastle! I think you are at heart a happy soul."

"I am now. Oh, how happy I am. My cloud has gone." She withdrew her hands from his and did a wild dance on the lane, skipping and swirling her skirts.

He watched her in delight. Then, still laughing, he exclaimed, "The village has eyes in all its windows."

"Let them look. I can't believe there is such happiness in the world.

This horrid world of war and theft and – oh, I must tell you, Nat Wilson – they have taken away Horden Hall. I am a homeless waif." She took his hand and pranced on, half-dancing still, hand in hand, till they were through the village. "I already told you I have a horse and cart, a bundle of other possessions, a very little money, a very good friend, an old groom, and absolutely nothing else, except that now," she looked up at him all smiles, "now I have you."

"Me, you have me, indeed. I also will be a lifelong friend if you let me."

She stopped and her eyes challenged his. "Friend! I hope you will be more than that." Doesn't he realise I am in love? It only needed the cloud between us to vanish for my love to rush out and engulf him. Surely he loves me too. She burst out, "What did your letters mean if it was not love? All those miles of travelling I was longing, longing to be here with you, dreading it of course, oh, how I dreaded being spurned and hated, but what does your father do, kiss me and thank me with all his heart, what does your terrifying mother do – after brandishing a great knife over me – but call me an innocent child, and now, what do you do? Oh Nat Wilson, now I am laid bare, my horrible sin, my deception in letting you write to your brother's killer, now I have fallen at your feet and been forgiven, oh wonderful, wonderful forgiveness, are you still only my friend?"

He was speechless for a moment but his eyes were speaking love and yearning. Then he began hesitantly, "How can I say more, so soon? This is only the second time I have set eyes on you, though I have *thought* of you often, but you are the daughter of a baronet."

"Fiddle to that; I am a homeless waif."

"The war will not go on for ever. You have other family. Horden Hall will be restored to you."

"That's what the Scots officer said, but if Parliament win the war the estate is sequestered, though I can fight that. As to other family, my mother and sister are in France and unlikely ever to leave. But I see what it is. I know you from your letters but *you* don't know *me* at all. I was in a strange state of mind in Newcastle that day, my father ill and yet I must have seemed full of levity. I told you I had almost no experience of men and what I had had not endeared me to the species. But you I took an instant liking to. Then you told me your scant experience of women had also been unhappy. We seemed to have a natural bond. And since then, I have been so blest in hearing of your childhood, your upbringing, your dear brother, your life at Cambridge and you know almost nothing of me. I am a closed book. Of course you hold back."

He was smiling at her torrent of speech. But she liked and respected his smile. There was no condescension in it and no false modesty either.

They were walking on now, not holding hands but companionably.

He said, "Bel Horden, I do believe I know you quite well now and if all things were equal I would declare that I love you. I don't want you ever to go away again, but I have no more to offer you than you say you have for me. I have no paid work at present and the way the church is I don't know whether I ever will have. I could be a schoolmaster if anyone would have me but that is a pittance ..."

"I could teach too. My darling Ursula would do all the work and Tom could be the man about the house. We could keep Juniper – that's the horse – and the cart too, so there would be no extras for carrying desks and books and such things."

"Bel, we have no premises. You speak as if we were a married couple ..."

"Well, why not? I *was* never going to marry but now I am never going to marry anyone else. Easingwold is a pleasant little place. We could rent a few rooms. Or there is my old school, Cranmore House. Do you know if it is still empty?"

"You will take my breath away. No, I know nothing of it since it was closed down. I didn't know you had ever been there. But now are you perhaps forgetting that marriages are usually arranged between families."

She stood still again. Had she misjudged him? Her tongue had been running away with her. "I'm sorry. I always think fast." Dear heaven, it was not three hours since she had set off from Ursula. "I'm sorry," she said again. "I must sound out of my mind. We can't be far from Easingwold now and you had better turn back and go home and forget this whole foolish encounter."

"That I will never do. Perhaps because I am older and more cautious I have hesitated to travel at your pace. But Bel, I do love you, more and more all the time. The idea of marrying you fills me with joy. Only, I see all the difficulties, the pitfalls. I am nobody and you are Arabella Horden. Your mother would certainly not consent."

"Oh she would be delighted to find that anybody would marry me at all. And you are not nobody. You are a Cambridge graduate. One day you will be a Bishop."

"They intend to abolish Bishops."

"Now you are teasing. Look, there is the little town ahead. You can come as my betrothed and meet my lovely friend or you can turn back now. I was betrothed once at a little ceremony but it was meaningless. I don't want ceremony. I want our minds and hearts to meet and say this is for life."

He took her hands then. "I Nat, N-A-T, would like to marry you, Bel, B-E-L, sometime when the good Lord shows us it is right. There, will that do."

"That will do very well as long as the good Lord is quick about it. Now come and meet Ursula. She is the ugliest and most beautiful person that ever lived."

Ursula had strung a cord across their small back room and standing on a stool was draping over it Bel's gown which she had brushed and sponged and her underwear which she had washed.

Hearing footsteps she looked round and Nat had to jump and catch her or she would have overbalanced. Bel looked up at him and saw him make no grimace at the poor twisted face.

"Ursula, my betrothed, Nat Wilson. He is very good at catching falling people. Nat, this is Saint Ursula."

"Saint!" cried Ursula. "Never." She too looked up at Nat and then back at Bel, who thought she detected just a flicker of hurt pass across her friend's bright eyes. Jealous? No, she was not capable of jealousy. But to have been left out of Bel's confidence ...

She flung her arms round her. "Oh my Urs, you are the first to know. I saw him once before and he has written to me the most marvellous letters."

"Ah yes, the letters."

"But I couldn't tell you then. I didn't know. I had to tell him things first. You shall hear everything. Oh, absolutely everything."

Nat held out his hand to Ursula. "Bel tells me you are her very, very special friend. I hope you will be mine too."

"Of course I will." Ursula's twinkling eyes were alive with joy now. "And I can tell you something, my Bel. Your cloud has gone."

"Oh, it has, it has. There will always be a sad thing, but it will not overshadow me as it did."

"Well, what are we to tell the wife here? Do we keep this room tonight? It has no beds but we can sleep on the bedding we brought. She has already asked Tom if he can work here. The young men enlisted. There is a room above her stables for him."

"But you should all come to the vicarage," Nat said.

"A Horden sleep there?" Bel cried. "Not yet. Think of your poor mother.

Will you tell them we are betrothed?"

He smiled. "I think that too is a not yet. If Ursula will also make it her secret I think it would be wise." He was trying hard not to look at the clothes line and Bel wanted to laugh aloud. "I had better go," he said. "But I hate to think of your discomfort ..."

"Nay, we were worse on the journey," Ursula laughed

Bel saw him off at the inn door and coming back inside, drew Ursula to her and they curled up on the bedcovers and talked the rest of the evening.

The winter day had closed in as Nat walked back and the chill darkness checked the exuberance of the last few hours. Without Bel's bubbling warmth and excitement he dropped into a pit of doubt and gloom. What had he done? He had committed himself to a penniless girl whose wildness reminded him chillingly of the marriage of his father and mother. I am like my father, quiet, cautious, not very adventurous and Bel is swift, impulsive, passionate. Their love was strong at first but mother tired of father's preference for a peaceful life. Can I ever match Bel's vitality? I do love her, I want her body as I have never wanted a woman before and I am overwhelmed by her rich, wonderful personality. But is this the dutiful, steadfast clergy wife my father always urged me to seek?

The question brought sharply back to him the disappointment he had felt earlier that day. They had been to see Sir Bertram Lauder about a living which was in his patronage and been told that everything had changed. A Presbyterian minister had been sent who had signed the Covenant for the abolition of Bishops and the changes to the Book of Common Prayer which Nat himself felt quite unable to do. His vision of a quiet country parish was fading. Was there any chance of a teaching position in a school or would that too be hedged about with requirements and conditions? Bel would certainly support him in that, but her enthusiasm would either bring success or provoke opposition.

As he walked, guided a little by the streaks of snow under the hedgerows and his long familiarity with the way, he marvelled at the speed with which events had overtaken him and emotions overridden his judgement. I cannot go back now, he thought, and my heart won't let me. I told Bel I would not tell my parents ... but, Father? I have never kept things from him. He knew of my letter-writing and the yearning I felt to see my Spring-maiden again. He is so full of love himself. He will accept her joyfully, though he will wonder at the speed of developments. But Mother? Her son marrying a Horden! Bel called herself my brother's killer, though I think her sense of guilt is now dissipated – her cloud – but I fear it will be more than my mother could ever stomach.

He was about halfway home when he heard a shout behind him and looking round saw a woman carrying a lantern hurrying after him. It was their servant Jenny returning from her visit to her sister at one of the neighbouring farms.

"I thought it was you," she cried. "I had not meant to stay till after dark but she kept begging me not to leave her. She has had three orphans thrust upon her by the parish today and I was to tell them a story or they would not go to bed."

"She has menfolk there. She is not alone. Mother will scold you for staying late."

"I know she will, but the men were all out checking every gate and barn door. There are that many thieves and looters about."

"And why does she have to take three orphans when she is ill herself?"

"There are so many now within the parish that they have nowhere to house them and they are being put about anywhere that has room. They are to work, however young, and the parish allows a few pence each a week out of the poor rate for their feeding."

"I will tell my father. I don't think he has heard of this." Nat was already thinking; the care of orphans! Is that not a good work to which I could devote myself? I would need premises. Would the Parish pay me for the work? Would Sir Bertram lend me money, to make a start?

This, when he reached home with Jenny, was the first subject of conversation. His father was weary of his mother's questions about Nat and Bel. Why had he written letters to a Horden? How long had they known each other? What did it all mean? She had now fallen asleep in her chair and his father was happy to discuss Nat's idea. Cranmore House was mentioned and Nat resolved to go there next day and find out its condition and how it was being used.

Of course he called first at the inn in Easingwold. Bel and Ursula had been up early after a draughty night on the floor of the small back room. When he told them where he was going they were eager to accompany him and if Tom could not be spared from the inn they would take the horse and cart themselves.

Bel had been writing a letter to her mother by the light of the one candle the inn wife had supplied her and she arranged to send it by the carrier before they set off. "I have not told her about you yet but she has to know where I am and what has happened to our home. I have warned her not to plead for us to Parliament. As a Catholic she would do more harm than good. She can write back to this inn while we are in the neighbourhood."

Nat was impressed with her grasp of affairs. In the cheerful brightness of the newly risen sun he was full of eager hope. For all her bad night Bel looked radiant and Ursula, evidently fully appraised of the situation, was a bubbly fountain of joy.

Less than an hour later they were standing in the kitchen of Cranmore House where Ursula had spent many years tending the ovens and helping to cook for a school full of children. "Why, nothing has changed in three years," she cried, "except for the dirt."

Showing them round was the landowner, Edward Manners, a short, stout man who had bought the place after its closure as a school. He had rented it to a farmer who had brought his family to live in a small part of it and use some of the rest for storage and livestock but he couldn't keep up the payment when his cattle had been taken by the King's forces. He had returned to his poor farmhouse to eke out a living as best he could and the place was now empty. This told Nat that Edward Manners was a hard man. He had heard of him as having made a fortune through the wool trade and he whispered this to Bel as they walked about.

"A place for orphans?" Manners said. "I never heard of such a thing. There's no money in that. If the parish pay for the children's keep, where is the profit?"

"Profit, sir?" cried Bel. "You are too noble to seek such a thing. The place will be called The Edward Manners School and your goodness will go down in history. I am a baronet's daughter, robbed of my inheritance, but I am prepared to roll up my sleeves and sweep the straw and dung from the dormitories for the sake of orphans who like me have had homes and families taken from them by war. I think no shame in that, and I know you too will be proud to have your buildings put to worthy use."

Mr Manners' plump cheeks reddened and he threw out his stubby arms in an expansive gesture. "Indeed I am happy to see a good work here at – shall we say – a kindly rent but who is to pay for the furnishings, a warden and all the servants to run such a place, the upkeep, the coals, the laundry. The expense is endless."

Nat intervened. "I have a good friend in Sir Bertram Lauder who has offered to invest money in any enterprise I undertake." He looked at Bel. "Perhaps it should be the Bertram Lauder School." He was learning fast.

"I wager my bank balance is bigger than Sir Bertram's, for all he claims a baronetcy. I could have bought one if they were still offering them for money, but I am a modest man. What would you need to make a start? Of course I want a sober married couple to take charge."

"We will be married soon and we are certainly sober," said Bel. "What is more we are young and energetic and possess as you see a horse and cart which will be most useful in removing the good manure for you to spread on your fields round about. How much then can you let us have? Five hundred pounds?"

He gasped, then drew a breath and said quickly, "At eight per cent."

"Six," said Bel.

Nat stared at her in amazement. With her strong square jaw she looked twenty-seven not seventeen. He had indeed found himself an amazing woman. With a work like this to do, he told himself, Bel will never weary. Such a work would have absorbed my poor mother's soaring spirit too and I believe Mother will accept her when she knows her well. She may even learn to love her. What a joy that would be if love could bury vengeance for ever!

"Six!" said Mr Manners. "You will pauper me. We will go to my lawyer and get it drawn up. The Edward Manners School. I will have a signboard made."

CHAPTER 21

January 1644 – October 1647

Aɴɴᴇ Wilson put Bel through a long inquisition before she could endure the idea of her son's marriage to a Horden. She wanted not only all her history but finally whether she was a faithful member of the Church of England. Nat who was present feared Bel's honesty would jeopardise the outcome but she said simply, "I have attended our parish church since infancy, but I tell you, Mistress Wilson, that when you said I was an innocent child a cloud vanished and for the first time in my life I knew for sure God was up there."

There was a tense silence. "With that word," said Ann Wilson, "you have given me a reason to go on living. You may marry them, Joseph. I am satisfied."

After the wedding, attended by the villagers who had witnessed their very public courtship, Bel and Ursula moved into the parsonage. Much work was needed on the old nunnery buildings but as the Parish approved of the project, vagrants and the unemployed were sent to clean the place and whitewash the walls. Nat and Bel visited the homes of the wealthy and begged old furniture which the motley crew repaired and restored. Help was also enlisted from any orphan over ten years of age who hoped to come to The Edward Manners School.

The expensively wrought signboard was the first complete item to appear and Mr Manners himself came frequently to see how his five hundred pounds was being spent. The years of thrift that Bel had practised at Horden Hall made her wary of buying anything new. She kept accounts of every penny and against his inclination he had to be impressed.

"We will open in April," he declared, "and I will invite all the local dignitaries and send the children among them with begging bowls."

Despite the fighting raging up and down the country, the school opened and Ursula crowed happily that it was just like old times cooking for ravenous young appetites.

In July the war came the closest it had been when a battle was fought at Marston Moor. As news filtered in that the King's army had been defeated, Bel could only moan to Nat, "How many more orphans on both sides?" By this time she knew she would be adding one more infant to their numbers but she refused to rest.

In October shortly before the birth of Daniel John Wilson, Newcastle was assaulted and taken by the Scots army.

"Are you not glad," Bel said to Ursula "that I wouldn't stay there?"

It seemed miraculous that the conflict was passing them by until they heard that Parliament, having expelled all members who refused to sign the Covenant, was widening the requirement to lawyers, doctors, parsons, schoolmasters, anyone in fact of note and influence in the community.

"I cannot vote for the extirpation of prelacy in the Church of England," cried Joseph Wilson. "Let those who wish for change have it but why should we be trampled on and kept from our established ways? Anne, we will be turned out of our home. Can you bear that?"

"We have borne worse, Joseph. Bel can bring her cart and we will take our marriage bed to Cranmore House. There are still spare rooms there. We will work for our bread and board. Bel needs our help."

"Anne, you are a marvel. You are the strong pillar in our old age."

"I always wanted change and adventure and when I was young there was none to be had. Now it is to be thrust upon us."

The removal took place and Bel found her mother-in-law had a wonderful way with the younger children. This was a great joy.

"But will not Nat be barred?" Parson Wilson asked her.

"He has not received the demand yet and we are hoping they will pass us by. Our dear landlord has signed. He will always follow the power in the land. If the King wins he will become a staunch Royalist again."

But that summer the King was defeated at Naseby and his cause was lost. It was still a year before he gave himself into the hands of the Scots and baby Daniel was toddling about the corridors of Cranmore House.

Mary Turner wrote to tell Mistress Arabella Wilson that she and Sam had stood and seen the King brought into Newcastle and they had learnt that he was being proudly entertained in the town. But she added that Horden Hall was still held by the Scots and they had also billeted two officers in Nurse's cottage when she died.

"What, poor old Nurse!" cried Bel. "Well, there is one death I didn't cause. Thank the Lord for that."

Bel was still corresponding with France though the letters were erratic and often showed signs of having been opened. In December 1646 news flew round that the Scots were negotiating the sale of the King to the English since he would not sign the Covenant and it was expected they would leave England as soon as he was handed over and their arrears of pay settled.

So Bel's mother wrote, *'You must return to Horden with your precious heir the moment it is released to you'.* She added with a hint of disappointment that '*Henrietta has had another girl.*'

'At present our work is here,' Bel wrote back, *'but I will appoint Sam Turner as Bailiff to oversee the Hall when the Scots leave. Parliament shall not have it. They may still try to impose the sequestration order but I will fight it. Since Father's death I cannot see that even in their notions of lawfulness they can make it stand. One day Daniel and his dear little girl cousins will get together there and we will all rejoice. I know that England has closed its doors to you and now we too are under threat. We have had to accept a preacher to harangue our little community every Sunday or*

*be closed down ourselves. My Nat and his father go humbly to hear him,
though my mother-in-law and I always manage to have a sick child or two
to care for. England is a sort of prison but these walls which I once found
cold and prison-like enclose a place of abundant love, not least because my
beloved Ursula is here.*

*Good souls from both sides of our divided country help us with gifts
and if we are short of rent or interest payments, I ask my mother-in-law to
go out and talk to people and she shames them into filling her basket with
coins and sweetmeats for the children. She looks so gaunt I believe they are
sorry for her but truly she is as tough as old leather now and I love her.
Please, dear Mother and Sister, pray for our enterprise as I do for you,*

Your loving daughter and sister,

Arabella.'

It was the only time she ever called herself that. Everyone in The
Edward Manners School called her Mistress Bel to distinguish her from
old Mistress Wilson.

"Are you happy, Mistress Bel?" Nat asked on a day in January 1647.
"Do you know today is the third anniversary of our wedding?"

"I didn't know. I am too busy to know what day it is." She and Ursula
were making tarts for the children's tea.

He put his arms round her from behind and turned her to him and kissed
her. "One day, my dearest, you may be a great lady and our baby will be
Sir Daniel of Horden. I may at last be ordained and fulfil what I think God
has in store for me, but here and now I am very happy in what we are doing.
Are you?"

She gave him a floury hug. "I am very happy."

"There is not a cloud on her horizon," Ursula said, lifting her eyes to a
spot above their heads. "Ay, not a cloud," she chuckled.

It was at that moment that an ominous hammering came on the front door and four men were revealed lined up in their Puritan black, with their big white collars and their tall black hats making them look even more threatening. Bel was swiftly transported back to the visitation of the men who had come for Patrick Dawson but times had changed and so had she. They carried no axe only a paper. She invited them in and offered them refreshment.

They declined and unfolded their paper. She knew at once what it was; a copy of the Covenant. They had all heard that school teachers of every rank from the Master of Westminster School downwards had been ordered to sign. He, the most august, had refused and no one had dared to remove him, but as Nathaniel Wilson, was the son of a rebellious priest, it was a wonder it had taken them so long to track him down! It was the end of their joyous enterprise.

"What will you do," Nat asked them, "because I cannot sign this? Will you shut this haven of light and joy and turn out twenty young souls to beg their bread?"

"Edward Manners has signed and is willing for us to appoint our own people. You are young and fit, Master Wilson, and can surely earn your bread where you will not have the corrupting of young minds. Your father too has been giving Bible lessons to the children. He must go."

"And my mother, my wife, my son? They are entitled to support under the new law I believe."

"Your wife is of the Horden family. A Committee has been looking into the case and it is recognised that the sequestration order on Horden Hall can be lifted. I have brought the necessary documents. In those circumstances no help will be given to your family. You have a substantial property, but there will be levies payable on it, so we advise you to return to deal with those. None have been paid for some years."

"The Scots seized it," cried Bel.

She was furious at their sham legality but excited at the thought of home. To leave their work here would be an agonising wrench but to be in charge at Horden again and with Nat at her side ... his parents would have to come! More mouths to feed and how could Anne Wilson settle at Horden Hall? She could see her Daniel's grave. Give him a Christian burial in Nether Horden churchyard. Bel's mind raced on into the next phase of their lives even while the men were telling her that what the Scots had done was no matter for Parliament. They handed over their documents and prepared to leave.

When she escorted them to the door she couldn't refrain from speaking her mind. "You have been fighting the King for freedom from oppression. What do you call this? You turn an old couple and a young couple and their baby away from the charitable school they founded to be a blessing to the orphans which this mad war has produced. Do you think God is pleased with you?"

"The school will go on in safer hands than yours," and they mounted their horses and were gone.

"But will there be as much love in it?" Bel asked the empty air. "Ursula will be coming away with us."

CHAPTER 22

October 1647

LITTLE Daniel understood that on this October day he was someone special. Ma, Da, Gramma and Granda kept asking him "How old are you now?" and he had learnt to answer "Three," which sent them into ecstasies of delight. But much more strange and wonderful things had been happening; riding in a big box with two horses in front and sleeping in strange beds between Ma and Da. As long as he had Nana Sula as well the strangeness was not at all frightening. She told stories to pass the time in the big box and he loved to stroke her face while she talked. It was a source of endless wonder and interest as her laughing eyes were a source of endless fun.

But now the long hours of being cooped up seemed to be coming to an end. Ma was very excited and kept pointing things out to Da and the others. Then she lifted Daniel from her lap and stood him looking out of the window. "See, the gates of home, Daniel, shabby and rusted but we'll soon put that right. Now look out for the man on the horse. Wave to him. It's your great-great-grandfather, Sir Ralph Horden."

Daniel waved vigorously at the strange man who appeared to be waving a sword and yet was unmoving. Not understanding it he lost interest, and was only too happy to be released from confinement a moment later. He jumped down into the arms of a curly-haired man, but he was a stranger and so was the pretty woman smiling at the open door. So he pushed past them both and found a huge space to rush around in and then the excitement of stairs which he had never seen before.

Reaching the top and finding more space in front of him he looked back the way he had come and saw all the grown-up people kissing or shaking hands and looking about them

"I've done my best to clean up but it's terrible shabby," the pretty woman was saying.

Then he saw Da kissing Ma and exclaiming, "It's so grand! Thank the good Lord I didn't meet you here or I would never have dared to marry you."

Then Gramma looked up and saw him at the top of the stairs and screeched out, "There's Sir Daniel claiming his birthright. Mind he doesn't fall down."

And Nana Sula scuttled up and grabbed him.

"And what's special about today?" she asked, as she carried him down again.

"Three!" he squealed out with glee.

"Three and you've come home," Ma corrected him, but that was more than he could understand. Home had long stone passages and children who loved to play with him. This place was vast and empty. He began to whimper.

"He's tired," said Granda.

Gramma picked him up and carried him out of earshot of the others.

"That's right. Have a weep for me too, little one. They say you are to have a new name – Horden after Wilson because this is your inheritance. And my Nat will take the name of those who killed his brother. *My* Daniel, your uncle. Life is full of things hard to bear. You'll find out."

This had a threatening sound so he wriggled down and ran to Nana Sula where there was never anything but love and laughter.

"Are you hungry? I am," she chuckled. "Come. Mary has some supper ready."

And they all went into a kitchen where there were normal things; a big table and benches and pots and pans and food. Life was comfortable again and all the faces round the table were smiling.

ABOUT THE AUTHOR

Prue was born and reared in Newcastle upon Tyne in northern England. Prue enjoyed writing historical novels from an early age. She trained as a teacher, taught full time for four years and was a freelance writer during this time. She took a correspondence course in creative writing and honed her craft.

She is married and has reared five children. Her current occupation is writing articles, short stories and novels.

If you would like to contact Prue, feel free to do so at *pru.phillipson@btopenworld.com*.

THE HOUSE OF WOMEN

ANNE WHITFIELD

It lies not in our power to love or hate,
For will in us is over-ruled by Fate.
- Marlowe, Hero and Leander.

KNOX ROBINSON
PUBLISHING
London • New York

CHAPTER ONE

Leeds, England 1870

MONTGOMERY Woodruff scowled at the low, dirty clouds as though they had appeared just to torment him. He tugged at his lapels, jerking his greatcoat close as the wind tried its best to wrestle a way into his inner garments. The end of January had been unrelenting with blizzards, storms and freezing temperatures. Woodruff entered his carriage and yanked at the folded blanket on the seat, his impatience sending it sliding to the floor. With a muttered oath, he arranged the blanket to better suit his needs, ignoring his clerk who stood dithering in the elements waiting for last minute instructions. Woodruff sent him a withering glare before a curt command from his driver, Sykes, sent the showy black horses away from the three-storey Georgian building to merge with the traffic in the bustling streets of the great Yorkshire town.

Sighing heavily, Woodruff stretched his neck from the starched collar, trying to relax as they traversed around pedestrians and vehicles. Winter gloom and the cold sent most people hurrying home, shop keepers were packing up, women scolded children towards their own hearths while business men headed for the warmth and smoky atmosphere of expensive clubs.

Woodruff grunted. He also should be ensconced in his club, cradling a brandy and discussing world issues, but too many men wanted him for more than his views on politics and such like, no, they wanted much more — money!

He rocked sideways as Sykes guided his ebony beauties out into the surrounding snow-topped countryside and towards home. Home. His precious gem, and the only thing he cared about. A cold sweat broke out on his forehead. He wouldn't lose it, couldn't lose it. He'd sell his soul to keep it.

Drifts of snow driven by the wind and the gray evening light reduced visibility. Sykes slowed the pair, not wanting to damage their legs in the snow-filled ruts. When a figure, robed from head to foot in a dark brown cape, lunged desperately for the nearest horse's bridle, the horses skidded in fright, dragging the person a few yards.

"What in Christ's name?" Sykes cursed, in a mixture of fear and surprise. He reined in hard and applied the brake, halting his horses to an uneasy standstill.

The wild jolting of the normally smooth ride sent Woodruff careening onto his side. He swore violently. "What in hell are you doing, Sykes?"

"You, there!" Sykes threatened the staggering, shadowy figure. "Leave go, before I wrap my whip around yer ear holes!"

For a fleeting moment, Woodruff wondered if he was being held up. His heart hammered, then blood pounded in his temples as his rage took over. How dare someone rob me!

"I must speak to Mr Woodruff!" A woman's voice beseeched from within the capacious hood.

He reached for the door, but it was wrenched opened. "What the …?"

"Mr Woodruff, you must hear me!"

The hooded figure's desperate and needy manner instantly revolted him. "Leave at once! Can a person not travel the roads without assault?"

"Please, I must speak with you!"

"I know you not, Madam."

With a sudden flash of a slim white hand, the hood was thrown back revealing a pale, pinched, face with dark and imploring eyes.

"Olive?"

"Yes."

Woodruff peered at his former mistress and sighed deep within his chest. It had been a while since he'd sampled her wares. Lately, he'd simply not had the time or energy. "What possesses you, woman, to come out here in the depths of winter and throw yourself in front of horses?"

"You've not been near for months and I'm desperate." Olive shivered as she spoke, but Woodruff refused to offer the warmth of the carriage. To do so would be to accept her as one of his own class and that would never do.

"If you need money, then I'm afraid I only give if I receive in turn," Woodruff sneered at the frail figure. "I assume you have gathered another customer or two by now, to keep you in comfort?"

"I wish I could, but I'm unable." She snorted in contempt. "It's not money, though of that I'm in need too. No, it's something more serious."

"Are you sick? Good Lord, you haven't contracted a disease have you?" Woodruff's skin prickled at the thought.

"No, of course not!" Olive glared. "It's worse than a disease!"

"For God's sake woman! Spit it out. I have no time for riddles!"

"I'm with child! Your child!"

Woodruff fell back in his seat. Ice trickled beneath his skin. "You think it's mine?"

"I've been with no one else."

"And I'm to believe that, am I? Do you take me for a fool?"

"You know there's been no one else since you came calling. At one stage, you visited every night and during the day at times! How do you think I managed to entertain other men?"

Woodruff grunted. "Go home, Olive. I shall call and discuss this matter with you tomorrow."

She gripped his arm. "You promise?"

He wrenched out of her grasp. "Yes. Now go. I'm late for my dinner." He reached over and slammed the carriage door, forcing her to hurriedly step back into the snowdrift on the roadside.

The carriage lumbered away and he leaned back against the plush upholstery. If she spoke the truth, Olive's news meant another burden he must bear. His fingers in many pies of business brought their troubles. Workers at his mill and factories had gone on strike against the low wages he paid. He refused to be held to ransom, to pay the dregs of society more money and give them better conditions! Oh, no, not he, Montgomery Clifton Woodruff. The thought of the unscrupulous working class bringing his small empire crashing to its knees nearly gave him a stroke. It wouldn't come to that of course! No, he was working himself through some very long days trying to right the situation.

With luck, in a week he would have sold his mill in Halifax and paid off one loan. It made better sense to shift the mill and dabble in other ventures. Roads and railways held his interest, and the navvies, mainly the Irish, working on those particular schemes were glad to have the work, never mind low wages. They possessed no grand ideas to better themselves and that's how Woodruff liked it.

He rubbed his forehead, his mind whirling. His bank manager

sent him warning letters each week. He didn't know how he could delay meeting the man much longer, but if he went to him with a plan, then perhaps he had a chance. He could reduce his expenditure some more in some areas...

The carriage slowed to turn and pass through the wrought iron gates of Woodruff House. As always, the manor and surroundings filled him with a surge of pride. He doubted there was a finer home in all of England. He felt nothing for draughty castles and cold palaces, or large impersonal mausoleums pretending to be homes. No, Woodruff House was his ideal place in the whole world. Satisfaction filled him as the carriage drove down the impressive white granite-pebbled drive, bordered by tall graceful silver birch trees.

Movement at one of the windows caught his eye and Woodruff paused before descending from the carriage. Yes, I am home, you lot of lazy good for nothing wasters!

He heaved his considerable bulk out of the carriage and climbed the wide sandstone steps to admire the impressive bronze knocker in the shape of Woodruff's coat of arms decorated on the door. He checked it for smears but found none.

His old butler, Fernly, who'd served Woodruff's father opened the door, his face impassive. "Welcome home, sir."

The heat of the hall swept over him and again he nodded in approval. Divested of his outer clothes, Woodruff marched into the drawing room, hoping to catch his wife and children indulging in careless pastimes. He rubbed his hands together in glee at the thought of catching them out. It was a joy to harangue them for an hour or more on the benefits of their privileged life which he could squash at anytime he chose.

He detested his wife with a passion second to none, and regretted the day he married her. He conveniently disregarded it was her money that drew him to her in the first place. Nevertheless, their marriage could have been a contented one, if she had delivered him the son he longed for. The dreams of filling this house with a dozen, handsome, intelligent sons, and being the envy of all who knew him, slowly eroded with each birth of a girl child. Seven daughters had supplanted the longed for sons. They were the very curse of his life.

No one occupied the drawing room, which nonplussed him at first. Quickly, he turned on his heel and strode into the parlour opposite. It too was empty. Annoyed, he stormed along the polished parquetry floor of the hall to the library. Here at last, he found one member of his family.

Curled up on the sofa, her slippered feet tucked demurely under the long skirts of her lemon organza dress and across from a roaring fire reclined Faith, the fifth and quietest daughter.

"Father, you are home," she said, instantly putting her feet down.

"Have you nothing better to do girl than be idle all day?" He sneered.

Faith rose, slipping her book behind her back. "I've done all I was asked, Father. I've visited the soup kitchens in town with Grace..."

"As if I care about that! Where are those other layabout sisters of yours?"

Faith blinked rapidly. "I believe Heather took Letitia, Phoebe and Emma Kate to the milliners, while Gabriella is out visiting and Grace is in the study."

Woodruff glared at her. "Don't let me catch you reading again. If you can't find something useful to do, then stay out of my sight!"

He crossed the hall and entered the study, eager for a drink. "What the hell are you doing in my study?"

Grace slowly rose from behind the desk, her direct amber eyes meeting his furious scowl. "I'm writing up the house accounts."

"This is my room! The one room in this whole blasted house where I can achieve peace away from tittering females!"

'Very well. I shall continue my work in the library."

At five foot seven, Grace was as tall as he. Both she and Heather were the tallest of the girls and could eye him without having to look up. This annoyed him no end. "I want those accounts reduced, do you hear?"

"I don't think anyone can accuse me of being frivolous."

He stomped to the drink trolley. "When is dinner to be announced?"

"At seven o"clock, as always, Father."

"Well it better be edible tonight. Last night's meal was appalling!"

Grace paused by the door, one slender hand resting upon the brass doorknob. "Every meal in this house is edible, Father." She left the room before his tirade began.

With an unhappy sigh, Grace went into the library opposite. She felt nothing for the man who sired her, except perhaps distaste. The library was her favourite room, with bookcases lining each wall from the gold embossed ceiling to the plush dark green carpeted floor. A large fireplace stood at one end and occasional tables of oak and beech were dotted between comfortable sofas and armchairs. By the large bay window, stood an impressive desk of walnut inlaid with burgundy leather. She ran her fingers over it as she gazed through the window, absent-mindedly watching a red robin skip from the branches of a rhododendron bush in the fading light.

Hearing noise coming from the hall, she closed her eyes momentarily. Her sisters" voices reached her even through the thickness of the library's walls. Grace rushed to quieten them before their father roared like an enraged bull.

She was too late. Her father entered the hall at the same time, freezing the smiles on the faces of the four young women.

"Why can you not do anything silently?" He said scornfully. "Wasn't the money I spent on your governess enough to instil some sense of decency in you? Your mother has failed yet again, I see."

Grace stepped forward. "Take yourselves upstairs and change for dinner. You are late," she ordered, though her eyes softened a little, taking the sting out of her words.

"Heather, my study," Woodruff commanded.

Hesitantly she followed, giving Grace a surprised look.

"You might as well join us, Grace, for you will need to know what is happening and arrange things accordingly," he added.

They followed him into the study and stood waiting while he sat behind his desk. He placed his hands over his extended stomach and rocked back in the chair. "I have news regarding the dinner party we attended at the Ellsworths'. Amazingly, your mother performed her duty for once and made you all a social success."

Grace raised an eyebrow. "In all honesty, Father, your wife and daughters have been socially acceptable for many years."

He snorted. "With the local farmers? Do you think them to be acquaintances worthy of me?"

"I do believe our circle of friends are more than just farmers. I am sure we can count the odd alderman, a doctor or two, a solicitor, a Captain..."

"Don't be insolent, Miss!"

"Well, Father, you make the opinion that we do not venture into the correct society." Grace tilted her head. "Do you wish us to dine with nobility? Shall I send them our card?"

"Be quiet, you impertinent chit!" Woodruff flared. "I will rise to dine in their exalted ranks eventually, and if I can't do it by marrying you lot into their lines, then I'll find some other way."

"How ridiculous." She crossed her arms. "We are only second generation trade. Do you really expect a lord or an earl will come here and choose one of us?"

Their father's small round eyes narrowed as he grinned. "No, not yet, although many nobles have little money. They will marry beneath them from time to time to gain wealth once more."

"We have no fear on that account, sir. We've little compared to most."

Woodruff bristled. "Do you suggest I wish to remain so?"

Surprised, Grace frowned. "Are you not content, sir, with all you have? We're very fortunate..."

"What do you know of finance?" He flung his short, fleshy arms wide to incorporate the whole house. "All this requires a great deal of money. Position and status requires even more! The Woodruff name might not be linked to royalty yet, but I intend to have power and eminence one day, even if I have to buy it!"

"Surely, you are content..."

Heather stepped forward bringing the argument to a halt. "What did you wish to speak to me about, Father?"

Woodruff settled back into his chair. "I had a meeting today with Reginald Ellsworth. He has some business interests equalling mine. In fact, I own a profitable venture he wishes to take off my hands."

He waved in a dismissive gesture. "I am giving him a good price and in return he affords me the opportunity to marry one of you into his pedigree. Of course your marriage settlement from your mother's money has greased the way a little."

"No …" A cold shiver ran up Grace's back.

He held Heather's gaze. "Ellsworth has granted a union between you, Heather, and his eldest son Andrew. I believe you may expect a call from Andrew tomorrow."

Heather and Grace stood unblinking, trying to absorb their father's announcement.

"Come, come! No thanks? No gratitude, Heather?" Woodruff puffed himself up importantly.

"You … you cannot be serious, Father?" Grace hoped he was joking. He'd played evil tricks on them many times before.

He frowned. "And why wouldn't I be?"

"Well, Heather and Andrew have only begun a friendship. To speak of marriage to cement a business deal is unjust."

"Nonsense! It is commonplace."

"I had hoped our family would be different. We have seen the evidence of a marriage made solely for business reasons."

"Still your tongue, girl."

"But there has been no romantic involvement yet, Father. Has there, Heather?" Grace appealed to her sister before spinning back to glare at him. "Can you not let them grow to love…?"

"This has nothing to do with romantic notions you silly fool!" He roared, rising to lean over his desk towards her. "This is two mighty families coming together. This is Heather's duty to me, and her family. She is the age of two and twenty and will be soon beyond her use if she doesn't find a husband willing enough to look past this error."

Hatred filled Grace. She stepped closer to the desk. "Her age has nothing to do with this. You simply want to use her as a pawn to infiltrate a society that sneers at you behind your back! They'll never accept you..." His stinging slap jerked her head back. Sharp pain bit at her cheek and she put her hand to her burning face. "Heather," she begged, "say something please!"

Heather looked apologetically at her before glancing at their father. "M ... May I go now, Father?"

He spun away. "Yes, of course, but make sure you look your best tomorrow."

In the hall once more, Grace grabbed Heather's wrist. "What's the matter with you? Why didn't you make any comment or simply refuse?"

"I'm sorry, Grace." Heather lightly touched her cheek. "Does it hurt very much?"

"Forget about it." She shrugged. "I'm more worried about this situation."

"Please, don't be anxious. It's all right."

"All right? He's married you off without even asking your preference!"

"Thankfully, I like Andrew enough."

"Like?" Amazed, Grace stared into her sister's gray eyes. "Oh, Heather, you must more than like!"

"Leave it, Grace, please. I know you mean well, but it's my choice ..."

"No, it's not! It's Father's, obviously!"

"Andrew Ellsworth is a good man, and comes from a good respectable family. On past social occasions over the years I believe we got along well enough. I found we had much in common at the dinner party and although we have not met much since he came home from his tour in Europe, I'm pleased he's offered to marry me."

"He might have been bullied into it too!"

Heather stepped to the plush red-carpeted staircase. "Mr Ellsworth isn't father."

"No, thank goodness!"

"Don't worry, Grace, please. I want to be married, I long for it actually." She sighed. "So, I am content. I'm not as choosy as you when it comes to acquiring a husband." Heather smiled, her kind, generous temperament coming to the fore again, making Grace feel selfish.

Grace sighed, defeated. Of all her sisters, Heather was the one who felt the need to be married most, and realizing this, Grace knew any more argument would be fruitless. 'Very well, let us inform Mama."

Together, they entered Diana Woodruff's suite of rooms. The rich, opulent decor of paintings, vibrant wall colours, numerous plants, abundant furniture, and plentiful ornaments were not to everyone's taste, but then not everyone had to live within these three rooms all the time. Diana Woodruff had turned away her husband's demanding attentions for the final time two years ago, when she suffered her last miscarriage at the age of forty-one. Afterwards, Woodruff had gone abroad for six weeks and Diana recovered enough to move out of their bedroom and into another. A doorway was knocked through to the adjoining room and it became her sitting room to entertain visitors. She went downstairs only for dinner, and should they host a party. Other than that, her whole world centred in her three rooms, and she decorated them accordingly.

"Mama?" Heather smiled, entering the sitting room. A little colour tinted her cheeks and a sudden light entered her eyes, bringing a new beauty to her pretty face. Heather positioned herself closest to Diana. The importance of the statement made the middle sister, Letitia give her room.

Grace sighed at the transformation. She felt dejected at the thought of Heather marrying a man she didn't love just to escape their father.

"What did your father want, poppet?" Diana's cool blue eyes sparkled in anticipation. Her still youthful face, bearing few wrinkles, broke into a small nervous smile. Diana lifted her hand to silence her other daughters seated around her. She glanced up at Grace looking for clues.

Heather looked quickly around, seemingly for once wanting all her sisters" attention. She waited, taking a deep breath. "I'm to marry Andrew Ellsworth!"

The sudden gasps broke the silence of the room.

Grace watched her mother. She knew her mother forced to keep the smile on her face, but it was difficult. She also knew her mother's thoughts as though she had spoken them aloud. So, the mean scoundrel has kept to his word. He will marry them all off, one by one, leaving me alone in this enormous house. Leaving me alone with him!

Within seconds, the Woodruff girls were hugging Heather. Their voices all joined as one, pelting Heather with questions she couldn't answer at once.

"Shh, shh!" Grace calmed them. "We can talk after dinner, but it's late and Father will be displeased if we aren't at the table waiting for him as usual." She ushered them out and towards their own bedrooms.

"Grace?" Diana halted her departure.

"Yes, Mama?"

"What do you think of this business?"

Grace raised her eyebrows and adjusted the lace cuffs at her wrists. "It is exactly that, isn't it? Business."

"Your father will do the same to all of you, you understand don't you? I want to see you all happily married, but only to the men you yourselves choose, not men who will further benefit your father's ambitions."

"I know, Mama."

Downstairs, the bell rang for dinner, causing Grace to groan. She hadn't changed her dress. "If he complains I will say it was he who held me up!" Grace remarked, accompanying her mother downstairs.

"I doubt he will, my dear, for he has much to celebrate this night!"

The House of Women is now available for purchase in paperback and eBook direct from our website.

Visit our website to download free historical fiction,
historical romance and fantasy short stories by your
favourite authors. While there, purchase our titles direct and
earn loyalty points. Sign up for our newsletter and our free titles
giveaway. Join our community to discuss history, romance and
fantasy with fans of each genre. We also encourage you to submit
your stories anonymously and let your peers review your writing.

www.knoxrobinsonpublishing.com